Lincoln's Agent:

The Hunt for a Killer

DAVID SPITZ

HISTORIUM PRESS

Follow the Author

www.davidspitz54.com

Historium Press

Macon Georgia 2022

www.historiumpress.com

Paperback ISBN: 9780578294155

Ebook ISBN: 9780578294162

For
Thomas
A LIFETIME OF SERVICE
&
Special thanks to
Shannon Tripp

Chapter 1

1858
St. Joseph, Missouri

Arnett gazed up at the sun, his eyes burning from sweat as he wiped his face with a red bandanna. Already his skin reddened from the time he stood beside Martha's grave talking to her. *Minutes? Perhaps, hours,* he thought.

"I know what you are thinking, Martha, that I've visited you a lot lately. God, I miss you so. I never understood how a person could miss someone this bad, but I find myself in deep thought often, and it always brings me here. Seventeen years. Has it really been that long? I wish you could see our Annie, she is turning into such a fine young lady. Prettier than you, if you can believe that, and smart as a whip.

"I am so proud of her, as I'm sure you are. Doc says she will make a fine doctor. I'm taking her to the train station so she can head back east, to one of them higher schools of learning. A college, Doc Jansen called it; some medical school. Our daughter is growing so fast, Martha, you'd hardly believe it.

"But, you know why I'm here today. Just cannot put my finger on what is nagging at me, Martha, but it might be the war coming. I think this just might destroy the Union. I know that's why we left Harrisburg to get away."

Arnett lowered to one knee, brushing the dust and the dead leaves from the oak tree off the headstone. The etched letters still read clear and tore at his heart - Martha McCann, beloved wife of Arnett McCann, born on this day April 15, 1824, died on May 30, 1858. Arnett ran his gloved hand over the inscription as tears welled up in his eyes. *Damn, we were just kids back then.*

He soaked up his tears with his bandanna and sighed. "Things are changing, Martha; too fast for my liking. A storm is brewing, and I'm afraid its the likes of which this nation has never seen. The papers say there is no way around it. I have this bad feeling in my gut now for some time, and I feel like I am about to be thrust right into the eye of this storm and no one can stop it or avoid it. A lot of people could lose their lives. I'm really scared for Annie."

He put his hand on his bent knee and lifted himself up, looking across at the new beehives he had just finished white washing. With her fondness for honey, the bees had been Martha's idea, and now the humming hives were another constant reminder of his wife's absence.

"Father, dinner's on; father!"

Arnett gazed over his shoulder up to the farmhouse. Annie stood leaning out the screen door and he waved to her, acknowledging that he had heard and went ahead to the windmill to wash up. As he pumped the water pump, washing his hands beneath the cool mountain water, his mind reeled back to that early horrific day... a day which would forever haunt him and make him question his actions on a day when Martha needed him.

In July of 1851, with a short winter past, and with spring and early summer as dry as a bone, the low mountain springs and rivers eked out a meager supply of water. Which meant the bear population came down from the hills scavenging for food and water, scarce in the high country because of the drought.

Arnett left early that morning to attend a meeting with the district Judge, Richard Stanley, leaving a neighbor, Ben, to help Martha while he was away. The judge had a special job for Arnett, one the judge would not elaborate on, except in person. It was Doc Jansen's wife, Pearl, the town busybody and nursing assistant, who stormed through the judge's door and proffered the horrible news. When Arnett sped to meet up with Doc Jansen, the news was more than he could bear as the man described the scene. Even now, seventeen years later, the conversation glued in the back of Arnett's mind.

"From the looks of the carnage the bear must have attacked Big Ben from behind while he was tending to the bees," the Doc said. "He bore deep abrasions across his back, his face, and over most of his body."

"What of my Martha?"

Doc sat in silence for a moment, staring down at the tiny baby sleeping in her wooden rocking cradle. "I found her under the hay wagon. I thought all the blood on her was Ben's. The trauma put her into labor, and she held on long enough to give birth to this little one."

Doc sat next to the fire, his elbows on his knees and covered his face with both hands, sobbing. Arnett rose and reached for a bottle on the mantle, stoked the fire with an iron poker and watched the flames flicker across the ceiling. He took a long drink of the whiskey, then offered some to Doc.

"You did all you could my friend," he said, touching Ben's shoulder.

"I could have been here sooner," "Doc replied.

"I'm the one that should have been here, dammit," Arnett cursed, throwing the bottle into the hearth, the glass shattering and the liquor exploding the flames. Doc reared back as Arnett crumpled to his knees and pounded the floorboards with his fists.

In all his years, Doc never remembered a time he ever saw Arnett cry and curse, except maybe when Dan'l, Arnett's father, died.

Arnett walked to the back door, picking up his Sharp rifle standing in the corner and checked to see if it was still loaded. Doc watched Arnett replace the gun at its resting place.

"From the looks of the area she put up one hell of a fight," Doc said, trying to soothe Arnett's pain.

Arnett huffed and continued staring at the gun. "You know, I bought this for her shortly after we got hitched. I never thought she would get the hang of using one."

"You taught her well, I'm sure," the Doc answered. "Don't second guess yourself."

The baby whimpered, aroused by all the commotion, and Doc Jansen leaned over to the cradle and rocked her back to sleep with the toe of his boot. "You know, Arnett, you now have a fine-looking daughter and you need to figure out who is going to look after her while you're working, not to mention she's going to be needing a name I might add to mark in my registry."

"Annie, after my mother," he whispered. "We had already discussed it before... before all this."

Arnett laid his badge on the table and stared down at Annie. "Annie McCann has a good ring to it," he stated to himself.

"Annie is all you need to mark in the registry and in your family Bible. You know what else has a nice ring to it? Deputy Marshal Arnett McCann."

Arnett shrugged, unable to wrap his mind around all the changes in just one morning – his appointment and his loss. He knelt beside her cradle and brushed his fingers over her downy soft cheek. "And yet, this child is going to have a rough go of it with no mother and an absent father."

Arnett's mindfulness returned as he sat at the table watching Annie prepare the plates for the evening meal.

"What?" she asked, feeling her father's eyes watching her.

"I was thinking about the day I returned home. You were so small, Doc told me how he brought you in to this world.

Now look at you such a pretty lady. What's that look for Annie?"

Annie's eyes filled with sadness.

"Well, I often wondered if I was the reason mother died in childbirth."

"Oh no, please don't ever think that," Arnett replied, holding her hand in his. "It was the bear... she tried to save Big Ben's life. She was trying to keep him warm, from going into shock, I suppose."

They both sat in silent while they ate, consumed by their own individual thoughts of grief, until Arnett changed the subject.

"Are you all packed for your trip to Pennsylvania tomorrow?"

Annie shrugged, still fiddling with her food and shoving it around the plate just like her mother used to do when worried about something. "I have most of it done I think. I was going to finish it after we ate."

"Don't worry about the mess I will take care of it," Arnett replied with a feigned smile. "The sooner I learn to do it the better."

Annie smirked. "Somehow, I don't think you will be concerned about that, father."

"What do you mean?" Arnett answered.

"Being a lawman, I just think you won't be home much. I can't imagine what this place will look like in a few months after I've gone."

"Hmm, getting quite sassy these days, just like your mother."

Her right eyebrow arched in surprise. "Really? You know, you hardly ever talk about her. I'd love to know more about what she was like. Don't think I haven't noticed the time you spend at her grave lately."

Arnett pushed back from the table and sauntered over to the fireplace, staring at the flames instead of into his daughter's imploring stare.

"Oh," he started slowly, trying to recall images he had tried to forget. "Just look at yourself in the mirror. There is a lot of your mother in you, Annie."

"No, I mean when you first met her, while you were courting her."

Arnett chuckled, recalling the first time he met her. "Well, if you must know... she was fiery, independent, and not afraid to let me know when I upset her about something. I had never seen such a beautiful woman. She was tender-hearted, and so intelligent; you're a lot like your mother in that respect."

"What did she like about you?"

Arnett paused, thinking to avoid Annie's question and then decided to go ahead.

"Well now, you are getting personal, chuckling. Let me put it this way. Your mother was... how shall I say this... well, forceful. She knew what she wanted and she went after it. Sometimes how she went about it didn't always turn out the way she planned it."

"Was mother forceful with you, father?"

Arnett leaned against the mantel and laughed. Annie joined in, not quite sure why she was laughing along with her father but at least the tension broke. Without warning, Arnett stopped and seriousness shadowed his face.

"God, I miss her, terribly."

"I shouldn't have reminded you, Father. I'm so sorry."

"You have every right to know these things, sweetheart. She's your mother and you never had the chance to know her, to be held by her, but I can tell you one thing, she'd be very proud of you becoming a doctor, and how you've turned out. Annie, I need to tell you, as well, that I am as equally impressed with how you just took everything in that Doc taught you."

"Thank you, father, it warms my heart knowing you are proud of me. Which reminds me, I need to finish packing the books Doc Jansen gave me."

Arnett watched his daughter ascend the stairs and recalled how much she reminded him of his graceful and bold Martha. A chill sped up his spine as the late evening Missouri winter permeated the walls of the cabin and he stoked the fire, bringing the flames to a roaring glow as he sat down in his favorite rocking chair and took up one of Martha's books which remained on the same side table she left it on all those years ago. Brushing his fingers over the spine, the title gleamed in muted gold letters – *Sophie's Misfortunes.* He had read the book so many times over the years, nearly all the ones in Martha's small library of books in the bookcase on each side of the hearth, and the reading helped him keep her memory close. Between the conversation with Annie, and holding the book close to his heart, dreams of her filled his mind as the river's mist floated across the wildflower field, up the front porch, and seeped into the crevices of the cabin and his mind. Back to those days of long ago, when all was right with the world...

*****

"You sure are a funny looking kid."

Arnie turned as he walked along the main dirt road on a wooden sidewalk in the front of the mercantile in the heart of St. Joseph, Missouri.

"Your kind of funny looking yourself in those piggy tails," Arnie retorted.

"Got a name?" the funny looking girl asked.

"Why? You don't need to know my name," he said, wrinkling up his freckled nose and squinting from the bright sun above.

"Cause, I'll just have to call you that funny red headed kid."

"It's Arnie, if you think you need to know."

"My name's Martha."

"I know the kids at school call you Mattie."

"I like Martha better."

"Hmm," Arnie scoffed.

"Where ya going?" Martha asked.

"I have to go to work."

"You're too young to work," she retorted as she tagged along.

Arnie tried to pick up the pace, not wanting this little whippet of a girl to follow him and tired of all of her questions. "I'm almost sixteen."

"You never finished answering me."

"Answering what?"

"My question, silly.'

"If you must know I'm going down to the livery."

"You're a stable boy?"

"No, I'm not, my pa owns the livery. I help out; it's a family business." The girl's invasive manner annoyed Arnett and he stopped in his tracks, hands on hips, and glared at her.

"Why do girls always have to be this way?"

She didn't answer, instead just bit her lip coyly and widened her blue eyes to act innocent to his question. She twirled one of her braided pigtails in her hand and cocked her head.

"Can I see the horses?" She persisted, purposely knowing how much she was annoying him as his cheeks flushed with anger.

"They're mule horses," he replied, balling his fists.

"What good is a mule horse anyway?"

Her question brought an unexpected smile to his face and his cheeks reddened as she smiled back in victory. The dust from a passing buckboard clouded the street, and Arnie rushed across to the mercantile on the corner in tactical retreat from this girl who stirred confusing emotions in his gut. She rushed behind him, weaving through the wagons and people on the streets and sidewalk, then followed him into the store.

Arnie palmed a dull red apple in his hand and called out to the grocer, Mr. Woomer.

"Are these the only apples you have today?"

"I know you like the best for your animals, Arnie," the man replied, "but yes, those are it for today, I'm afraid. Where's your buddy Tommy today?" he asked as he kept his eye on Martha as she walked around the store. "She with you?" he asked Arnie, nodding his head in Martha's direction.

Arnie's lips tightened in a line as he followed the direction of Mr Woomer's pointing finger.

Is she with me?

*****

Arnett stirred in his rocking chair, pulling at blanket that Annie managed to cover him without disturbance, Not so distant memories continued to fade in and out as he settled, once again, and drifted backwards in his dreams. This time, they stood in the woods behind the house, Arnett lifting Martha's elbow with his fingers as she squeezed one eye shut and sighted a line down the barrel of the shot gun at a bottle on the top of a rail fence.

"Lift your arm just a tad, and keep your eyes looking straight down the barrel. Focus on the bottle," he said as he stood behind her and let his jaw rest on her shoulder. His breath tickled across her neck and behind her ear.

"If you don't stop, Mr. McCann, I'm never going to learn to shoot."

"Hmm, you might just be right, Mrs. McCann," he chuckled, pecking at her ear. Sliding his right hand down her arm to her hand, he slowly put his finger on her shooting finger.

"Just let me squeeze the trigger so you can feel how light the pull should be on the trigger, okay?"

She nodded yes, her shoulders tensing.

"Relax and take a deep breath... hold it... now, breath out."

A loud boom ensued as Arnett squeezed the trigger. The bottle exploded in a thousand tiny shards.

"Oh my, oh my, I hit it, I hit it!" she squealed, jumping up and down, and dropping the gun, Arnett caught it in midair before the stock hit the ground.

"Ouch," he hollered after grabbing the Sharp's hot barrel.

"Are you okay?" Martha asked.

"It's nothing, just a slight burn."

"Let me see," she said, holding his hand. She never saw the burn, for Arnett pulled her close into a deep kiss which led to a hurried rush to back to the cabin, clothes thrown every which way – a wild passionate encounter worthy of a scene from Shakespeare as the fireplace flames and the moonbeams from the window danced across their entwined bodies.

*****

"What's the matter father?" Annie asked with a mischievous grin as Arnett massaged his neck the next morning at the table.

"Slept wrong last night, I guess; by the way, thanks for the blanket and for not scolding me for falling asleep in my chair again."

"Well, I thought I might, but seeing as it was our last evening together, I thought I'd keep the image in my mind."

Arnett smiled at her as they loaded up the wagon with her trunk and headed to the station. For the ten mile trek, they chatted over trivial things, neither looking forward to the goodbye nor the unknown future lying in wait for both of them. Arriving at the train platform, Arnett clicked the mules forward and pulled the buckboard close enough to pull the trunk down and waited for Annie to call a porter and check in her luggage.

They walked together, arm in arm, to the car, their steps slow and deliberate.

"All aboard." the conductor commanded.

"It's time, father," she said, holding back her tears as she put her arms around him. "Please, keep yourself well. I have to go now, and you shan't see no more tears in my eyes."

Arnett stood motionless, his emotions surreal as he waved goodbye to her and watched the train disappear into the distant woods around the bend.

Chapter 2

Doc Jansen
1841
St. Joseph, Missouri

"You just keep ice on that leg and tell him to keep that leg up so the swell will recede, Sadie."

"Yes, siree, Doc Jansen; I will tell him. Don't mean he'll take heed none."

Doc turned toward the young boy standing holding the horse's reins. "Thanks for making sure Fannie was fed this morning, Tommy. Here's a penny for you."

"No need, Doc. I like horses."

"Looks like the rain has stopped, sun's coming up yonder. Maybe you can get some fishing done after chores, Tommy."

Tommy glanced at Sadie who had a big smile on her face. "Why you call your horse Fannie, Doc?"

"After my first love while I was in college," he paused before saying something he would have to explain. "You can do that someday... with any luck... college and first loves."

Tommy scratched his head. "What in tarnation is college?" he asked, laughing.

"What so funny?"

"Well, cause I'm going to Kentucky and raise horses."

Doc chuckled. "You and your brother been hanging with that McCann fella too much."

"How is Mrs McCann and that baby, doc?" asked Sadie.

"Well, Sadie, I am heading there now. She has about three weeks left, I reckon."

"Well, she told me to send my boy over there and she'd send me some of her honey. Here, Tommy, you take this basket over to Mrs McCann with the Doc; and then, Doc, you send that boy of mine home. He has chores to do. I got enough damn things to do around here with all the dang cleaning, cooking, and what not." Sadie started one of her rattling and raving spells and turned to waddle back in the house, raising her hand up with her back turned and waving to Jansen. "I have to git this black ass back to work."

Tommy and doc looked at each other, laughing as Doc grabbed the reins.

"Come on up here, Tommy."

"Sure thing, Doc."

Tommy loaded up the basket and scooted next to Doc Jansen as he turned the buckboard away from the morning sun, still shaking his head and chuckling to himself over Sadie's ranting.

"Dang, I'm hungry. You hungry, Tommy?" The boy nodded with a smile. "Well, our luck, maybe Martha will have breakfast ready by the time we arrive."

Doc pulled a Cuban out of his suit, struck a match and started puffing. *Good thing Sadie sent Tommy to town in the middle of the night. Her dang fool of a husband would have walked two days on that broken leg.*

Jansen grabbed the reins and with a slight snap of the whip stirred Fannie forward. "Giddup thar, Fannie, Martha be having that baby by herself."

Fannie started a slow trot and Doc's covered buckboard gave a jerk and rolled on down the dirt road toward the McCann place. The early morning's sun peeked through the black locust and maple trees that bordered the narrow trail, and the dew kept the dust to a minimum.

"Now we can see, Fannie; come on, giddup," he said with a click of his tongue. Doc reached in his white suit's breast pocket and pulled out a whiskey flask, and drained the last of the liquor from flask. Smacking his lips, he wet them with his tongue, wiped his mouth with his sleeve and pocketed the flask, all while holding the reins and smoking his cigar.

"Mother Mary. Make hay, Fannie. Martha's been up about an hour. Approaching the last curve toward the McCann spread coming out of the tree shade, Doc noted the beehives in the distance. Half the beehive boxes strewn haphazardly across the landscape with fresh whitewashed splintered wood scattered over the area; the bees in a frenzied buzzing panic in search for their queen.

Tommy's eyes widened and he stood up as Doc eased his horse to a stop.

"Woah, Fannie. I need to take a closer look." Fannie nickered and pawed the ground. "Easy there, girl, I know I smell it too."

The marsh hawks and buzzards circled overhead as Doc approached the gruesome scene.

"Martha, Martha McCann? Martha?"

The night's home visit to Sadie's lagged on him, and his tired eyes strained in the bright morning sunlight, not to mention the hazy yellow dusting of pollen floating in the air. Taking his spectacles off, he rubbed the moisture from his eyes and readjusted the round frames on his nose.

Once his eyes regained their focus, he searched the area. From his perch, Tommy pointed over to the forest edge on the other side of the house.

"Doc, look over there!"

"No; oh, no."

Looking to his left, the massive body of one of the largest grizzly's he had ever seen in this neck of the woods lay on its stomach with an outstretched paw, its massive head laying in a pool of blood. A bullet had left a nickel sized hole just above the right corner of the grizzly's eye. Fannie turned her head, pulling away from the scene as the smell of bear perked her ears and flared her nostrils.

"Don't you be fretting, Fannie. He's good and dead."

Doc looked at his pocket watch. *Eight a.m. Martha shot him dead in his tracks. She must be tired out in bed after this ruckus. Hope she's alright.*

"I'll say one thing. Arnett sure did a damn good job training her to shoot."

Then, out of the corner of his eye, he noticed the McCann's buckboard off kilter with two bodies lying beneath.

"Oh no, so that is why you were nickering, Fannie?"

His gaze caught on the gingham dress Martha always wore when working around the farm, tattered and stained with blood.

"Oh my God!" both he and Tommy echoed as they ran near.

As the doctor reached the side of the buckboard, he squatted near, touching Martha on the shoulder. She did not budge. He put his fingers to the side of her neck and lowered his ear to her mouth.

Still breathing, he said to himself.

After checking the other body and seeing it was Big Ben and not Arnett, he felt the man's neck and closed his eyes. Dead.

He looked up into Tommy's wide frightened eyes, then stood up and grabbed him by the shoulders.

"Tommy... Tommy" he shouted. "Listen to me. I know what your mama said about coming straight home, but you've got to get to my office in town and send for my wife... do you hear? She is taking care of some of my patient's there as my nursing assistant, and she needs to come right away to help me save Mrs McCann's life. Do you understand?"

Tommy nodded, tears filling his eyes.

"Go, now... and don't dawdle!"

Tommy turned and bolted down the road heading to the town as Doc turned back to the horrific carnage before him.

The blood soaked mud from the previous night's rain and from mostly from Big Ben's body squished underneath Doc's boots, staining his white pants while he checked again for a pulse at Martha's neck.

Still beating.. Faint, but she's alive. Looks like she put up one hell of a fight.

He picked her up and carried her into the house, placing her on her bed, then rushed out to retrieve his doctor's bag still on the wagon. Once back inside, Martha moaned and he listened to her heart with his stethoscope, her heartbeat growing fainter by the second, and then on her swollen stomach for any signs that her unborn baby was still alive. A steady pulse throbbed in the doctor's ear and he sighed relief.

Thank God, the baby is still alive.

"Martha, Martha, can you hear me? I have to take the baby now; if I don't, neither of you may survive."

Martha moaned, again, and the Doc recognized the last throes of death shadowing her face.

"I have to do this now, Martha. I'm sorry."

He took his scalpel and cut Martha's gown down the middle and exposed her belly and legs. He tore part of the gown to use as a rag to wipe the blood off his scalpel as started cutting into her flesh.

Martha gasped out and flinched, easing to a gurgle as Doc's sharp scalpel sliced through the layers. Even when he first learned surgery, the smell of human entrails never bothered him, but in this life and death moment, his gut heaved as he watched his friend's wife slip from this world before his eyes. He knew he had only moments left to save the baby. Slicing her stomach muscles from the bottom of her navel downward to her lower abdomen, he pulled back the skin and exposed her uterus.

"Too bad this had to happen, dear; the baby's as ready as it will ever be."

Pulling the taut tissue away and exposing the baby, he eased the baby girl from its safe haven home for the last eight and a half months and cut the umbilical cord. Holding the baby up by its tiny legs, he gave he a couple light smacks.

The baby jerked and released a wail, then he took the cleanest part of Martha's dress and cleaned the baby the best he could. Taking a nearby quilted blanket, he wrapped it around the baby and placed her inside the nearby awaiting wooden cradle. Her cries quieted as the warmth and gentle rocking lulled her back to sleep.

"Arnett, you wanted a son, but you have an incredibly beautiful baby girl."

He turned his attention to Martha, but her knew from the grayish tone of her lips, she was gone. He sighed, closed her eyes, pulled the sheet over her, and closed the door behind him.

After giving Martha's ghost time with her child alone, he moved the baby and the crib into the main room of the cabin to await his wife and Arnett's return. He knew for certain that Tommy would tell all when he saw the Doc's wife, who would, in turn, search for Arnett before heading back out here to the farm.

Now, all he could do was wait for them to show up. He checked on the baby once more, moving the cradle close to the fire, and grabbed another quilt draped over a chair in the main room.

"Don't fret, child; I'll just be a minute."

Sauntering back outside, he laid the quilt over Big Ben's body and bowed his head in a silent prayer.

Guess I have some graves to dig. I need to send word to the coroner.

Doc knew the couple kept an ice cupboard to keep the goat's milk fresh. A pail of goat's milk sat on the churning table and he gave it a taste.

Still good. At least one problem solved, he thought.

Two glass baby bottles sat next to the cook stove just waiting for the baby's arrival. Inside the cook stove the breakfast fire still burned, so he went outside and fetched water from the well to start a boil for the bottles.

Doc stood over the water on the stove mesmerized by the bubbles of air churning up from the bottom of the iron pot and sanitizing the bottles. He sat his glasses down and rubbed the tiredness and sadness from his eyes.

"I was supposed to have been here last night. Maybe I could have kept this tragedy from happening. You fool, you would have gotten yourself killed, thinking to himself."

Sighing, he looked down at the water imagining Arnett's shocked face and paused.

"God, I could use a drink"

His hands trembled as he grabbed up a kitchen towel and took the bottles from their bath and set them to the side to cool. While waiting, his mind wandered back to his school days in Pennsylvania's medical school as a young adult. John, his roommate at the school, stood in the doorway of his dorm room.

"Ben, headmaster wants to see you in his office."

"Dang, this can't be good," he scowled, rubbing his hands through his thick hair. The night before he caused quite the scene in a fight over a girl at the local saloon.

It was not that big of a 'to do', as far as Ben was concerned. He really liked Sally, but had violated the headmaster's strictest rule for residents about to graduate. Headmaster Stencil stood, giving the students a serious stare over the top of his rimmed glasses, pondering over the perfect chosen words for the lecture he was about to give.

"You one-hundred would-be doctors attending Pennsylvania's best university for medical doctors, welcome!"

He towered over the pulpit with his thumbs stuck through the top lapel's buttonholes.

"This year's graduating class knows what kind of work I expect from the graduates. They may think they know everything; they do not."

The upper class-men chuckled.

"Book and lab work will be more intense than you are used to. Since 1765, the brightest, most skilled physicians this country has ever seen graduated from this school. For you new arrivals, you will work with cadavers, as well as patients, over at the infirmary with practicing licensed physician."

"And I must say, someone did a good job bringing that stiff back to life," Ben wise cracked to John under his breath, not realizing the joke carried loud enough to make the others around him snicker.

The headmaster's face turned red and he cleared his throat, directing a snarling glare across the room indicating his intolerance for silliness. Slamming his bible, which he always carried, on the pulpit, the interns silenced while the headmaster looked for the source of the laughter.

"This behavior is unacceptable and will find you disbanded from this school and unable to ever obtain a physician's license. Understood?"

"Yes sir!" the group answered in unison. The headmaster directed his stare at Ben and John. Ben glared back with a slight smile, while John just kept his head down.

"Class dismissed," the headmaster seethed.

"We had best be careful from now on, Ben, else we might jeopardize our license."

"Hhmph," Ben answered back, without giving the headmaster's glare another thought.

Famous last words, he thought, as he touched his fingers to the side of the glass while keeping a sharp eye on the baby.

"Doing fine; keep a restin', girl; the bottles are nearly finished."

He filled up the bottles with the milk and set them inside the warm water to take the chill out the cold milk. So many things he'd learned through the years, more so from experience than anything that school ever taught him.

"Wonder, what the good folks would think if they found out I was practicing medicine without a license," he said to the baby who cooed a soft gurgle.

"Damn, I could use a drink myself."

Doc fumbled around the cupboard for shine or a bottle. None. While waiting for the milk to warm, his thoughts wandered again back to what brought him to St. Joseph in the first place. Ben broke strict rules of going into town to see Sally the night before finals. Of course, Sally's old beau showed up and tried to get between them. Ben would have no part of it and a fight ensued. The next day, as sure as the headmaster's warnings, finals started without Ben.

Professor Stencil suspended him with no assurance of any kind of reparations on his account. Just dismissed, and that was that. John later told him that while the headmaster oversaw the finals, he kept peeking at his watch with a smile. Ben just knew the man was counting the seconds before he would be rid of him for good.

Ben knew nothing would matter to the wrinkly old man even though he excelled ahead of the class as well as lab work. Still, Stencil wielded power over his future. It wasn't the first time. The past four years contained a long list of clashes and accusations from the headmaster as to whether

Ben could handle the everyday pressures of practicing medicine.

Ben accused the headmaster of using his father's alcoholism against him, for his father's reputation as a lush was well known throughout the community. Deep inside he knew Stencil would make sure he'd not make it through med school intact. When John came that morning and said that the man wanted to see him in his office... well, he knew the outcome before he even heard the words.

After much self-doubt, Ben rose from his bunk, looked in the small mirror with disgust and headed for the office.

"Enter."

Ben walked and cleared his throat "You, wanted to see me, sir?"

"Sit down Jansen."

"Prefer standing sir."

"Suit yourself son." Stencil, who stood a head taller than Doc, took advantage of that and glared down at him. "'I have been trying to figure out for the life of me, why someone with your intelligence insists on defying authority and carrying on with your shenanigans, since the first day you have been here."

Stencil walked behind Ben and stared out the glass window in the door, watching the new residents scurry to their next class.

Ben huffed and clasped his hands behind his back. "The problem is, sir, you had me pegged to be like my father since day one. Everyone in town knew he had an alcohol problem and you just assumed I was like him. You never gave me a chance to prove to you otherwise. Why do you think I busted my ass? I'm the smartest intern here and you know it."

"That I do know, Jansen, but that doesn't take away from the facts. The fact is you break rules to suit your fancy. You also have an over inflated ego. Two traits that cannot be tolerated in medicine."

Ben chuckled in his gut. *This guy has got to be kidding. Overinflated egos not tolerated in medicine? Every doctor he met let the 'God-complex' take over on a regular basis.*

"Therefore," Stancil continued. "I have no recourse except to expel you for good."

Ben turned and stared Stencil in the eyes, "Unbelievable." was all he could muster and all the man deserved, in truth.

Doc's eyes teared as he palmed one of the bottles and popped a rubber nipple over the rim.

"Hmmm, a lot of water sure has crossed under *that* bridge." Doc willed himself into better thoughts such as the day he road into Missouri.

St. Joseph was a small pioneer town at the headwaters of the Missouri flowing into the Mississippi. He crossed the Mississippi by ferry into St. Louis, a major transport hub for goods coming across Illinois from Chicago and the East plus goods such as cotton and slaves which came up the Tennessee and Columbia Rivers through the Ohio and Mississippi Valley.

Doc rode through St. Joseph with his medical bag hanging from the horn of his saddle. His intent was to travel along the Missouri and find his way west using his profession to help people along the way in order to pay for his keep.

He was much younger, them days. And Arnett was just a boy, learning from his father how to make horse tack for mule bridles out of leather sinew. The night before, gushing rain made a muddy river of the main street and Doc needed to lay his head down somewhere dry.

Chapter 3

St Joseph, Missouri

1835

The winter snows turned to early spring downpours as the moisture supplied cool misty air from the Dakotas. A damp foggy night spring rain sprinkled restless pioneers who spent the harsh winter holed up in the ever-growing city of St. Joseph, Missouri. The citizens of the township consisted of ambitious men who saw opportunities, Eastern city folk heading West through Kansas and beyond to the Colorado mines in search of fortune.

The Osage and Missouria native tribes no longer warred between themselves nor with anyone else. Smallpox, and the onslaught of pioneers pushed them further west into Oklahoma and Kansas. However, it was not uncommon to see a tepee set up along the Missouri since many French trappers took Indian wives and some even adopted the way of life.

Trades of all kinds could be found within the city – a blacksmith, the general supply store, and the livery stable. And it was not unusual to see Conestoga's camped out along the outskirts of the city waiting for the harsh winter to subside. St. Joseph, however, was just the beginning of their treacherous journey along the Oregon Trail, even though they had already traveled far from the eastern coast.

Many pioneers ended up not making the trip west. Instead, some found spouses, opportunities and eventually became local citizens, melding into a normal life instead of moving on. Steamboats brought German, French, and Irish immigrants from St. Louis up the Mississippi seeking a new life, many choosing to stay. St. Joseph became a tight knit family, a melting pot of nationalities.

When Doc Jansen arrived in St. Joseph, after riding in a downpour most of the day, and looking for a less soggy spot to spend the night, he stopped the first drunk stumbling out of the saloon the location of the city stable.

"Down thar a piece," the man belched and pointed. "You cannot miss it, less your drunk as I am."

"Thanks, fella; you best be off to bed before the law gets wind of you."

"What young man you talking to," the man replied with a laugh and slap on his knee.

"You," Doc answered, chuckling. "Be seeing ya," he said to the man as he directed his horse in the direction the man pointed.

"Which reminds me," he whispered to his horse. "I need a drink. Now, which dang pocket did I put that flask in? Ah, there it is," he said, after fumbling in both jacket pockets and taking a drink as he made his way to the livery stable.

He pulled back on the reins and looked up, the misty rain dripping from the brim of his hat and he squinted his eyes to read the sign above the doro.

"McCann Livery Stable."

He hopped down and led his horse into the a fresh clean stall, then sat in the corner and hung his dingy white jacket on a hook to dry. In two shakes of a lamb's tail, Doc finished off his whiskey and fell over asleep in the fresh hay.

Early the next morning, two voices roused him and Doc eased up to a sitting position, rubbing his pounding head.

"You check a horse in last night, Arnie?" asked an older-sounding man.

"No sir, I was up in loft reading. I didn't even know when you came home last night."

"The word is 'got', son, when I 'got home', you understand? Don't they teach you anything in that dang school? You sound like them settlers coming through. I think you been hanging at Blacksnake too much again."

The man came up behind Doc's horse, still not seeing him in the corner. "Dang fool left a saddle on a wet horse. Arnie, run over to Blacksnake and ask Woomer for horse blankets. Ours are all used up. Go on now, times a'wasting. Make sure they're soft."

The man took the saddle off Doc's horse, still cursing under his breath about the owner's stupidity when Doc cleared his voice to announce his presence.

"Ahh, what's all the ruckus so early in the mornin'?"

The man looked over the fence into the next stall, noticing Doc standing there dressed in his white trousers, waistcoat, and necktie.

"You the dang bum that almost kilt this animal? What ya doing here anyways, this isn't a dang hotel?"

"First off, sir, I'm a doctor, not a bum. I was cold, it was late, and I was soaked when I got in last night. So, I had a couple of swigs out of my flask. Guess I was more tired than I thought and fell asleep. Animals are just like people. They can be doctored the same way."

"Yea right, a doctor. Rub him down with a currycomb if there aren't any cloths."

"Currycomb?"

"This is a currycomb," he said, tossing the brush to Jensen. "This would have helped dry him and kept him from sweating. Every livery stable has them."

"Like I told you, I was tired out. I apologize."

"Don't apologize to me. Apologize to him, he's the one you almost kilt. You got a name?"

"Jansen, Ben Jansen, from Pennsylvania."

"Well Mr. Ben Jansen from Pennsylvania, I'm Dan'l McCann. People learn by their mistakes. Where are you going? West?"

"Yes, that is the plan. Need to make some money first."

"Shit, you mean you can't even pay me?"

"Well, depends on how much is it?"

"Two bits should do it."

Doc stood up and reached into his jacket's pocket. "Here this ought to cover it."

"Last night's, maybe. If you want work, you can roll up them white sleeves and clean out those empty stalls, unless Arnie has something to say about it."

"Arnie?"

"My son, that's one of his jobs. Say... are you running from the law?"

Doc arched his eyebrow. "Not that I'm aware of."

Dan'l handed him a pitchfork. "Well, that's good, then. Wheel barrel is out back. Just dump the shit on the big mound. Locals will come by and get it for their gardens." He scrubbed his course hand over his burly beard. "I have to go see where that dang boy of mine got off to. Just keep working till I get back"

Doc looked that the empty stalls and sighed. "Dang, this will take all morning."

Dan'l strode out into the dusty street, hands on hips. "I could have sworn it rained last night," he muttered, as he tipped his hat to a couple of ladies walking by. Then, he scurried out of the way as three buckboards raced down the street, bringing more dust flying up in the wind. Dan'l took off his Stetson and banged the brim against his leg, adding a cloud of brown to the already thick air. "This town is getting so a man can't even cross the street without getting ran over between all the horses and buckboards. Dang covered wagon's oxen tearing the road up," he scowled as Tom, the grocer, stepped outside his shop after hearing Dan'l's tirade.

"What's the matter with you, Dan'l?"

Dan'l adjusted his hat back on his head and pointed to the street. "You've been here awhile, Tom, almost as long as I have. You recollect this many people around these parts?"

"Dan'l, people are just trying to get where a man can breathe. With all the migrant boats coming, the coastal cities are getting too crowded. Guessing they like that new feeling of coming out here, till the Injuns get them. Half of them won't see the light of day."

"Maybe so, but a man's going to try, anyhow. Never know these days. Tom, nice talking, I have to get a move on before we both get ran over. Say, you haven't seen that dang boy of mine, have you?"

"Go easy on him, Dan'l, He's still a lad, you know."

Dan'l scowled again after leaving Tom and walking down to the edge of town into Blacksnake trading post. While looking at various items throughout the store and still unable to find his boy, Woomer came out of the back room.

"I assume you're looking for Arnie, Mr. McCann? He's with the negro boy, Ben. They ran back to the livery with the blankets. They were going to ask you about going fishing... must have just missed them."

"Yea, must have been on other side of street when I was talking to Tom Watkins. What do I owe you?:

"Depends on whether you use all of them I sent with the boy. Don't need to concern yourself, Dan'l, your account is in good standing"

"I'll get with you later about them blankets, might have more supplies to get."

"That'll be fine, good day to you."

Dan'l never noticed the man standing in the corner, the man dressed like a southern gentleman lawyer ready for trial rather than a frontiersman ready to head west. After Dan'l left the post, the man called Woomer over to him.

"Who was that?" the man demanded.

Woomer shrugged. "You mean McCann? He owns the livery stable; never mind him. He's harmless despite his gruff appearance."

"Have you ordered those rifles we talked about?"

"Not yet; why, is something wrong?" Woomer asked.

"No, but the organization says were moving too slow. We want everything moving on an even keel. Don't forget you stand to make a lot of money and we have an army to arm."

"You look here, Bickley, this kind of thing takes time. You seem to forget Maximillian is taking a great risk shipping rifles across the border. Too many at one time is just dangerously stupid. The Feds find out and were done before we get started."

"Yeah, well, if the Northerner's keep pushing our way out of Missouri, we will lose Kansas. And this Yankee lawyer, Lincoln, if he becomes the next President, then you can forget about Illinois joining us. Or have you forgotten who bank-rolled your son's plantation in Mississippi? You think he could run that himself without them darkies? We also know about your trouble and your darkie lover with your child."

"You mention that again Bickley and I'll kill you with my own hands."

"Take your hands off me, Woomer, or you won't see the sun set."

Woomer stepped back, appalled by the hatred seething in Bickley's eyes. He had seen that hate before, years earlier for the red man, and all because another human possessed a different color skin.

After Bickley turned and walked away, Woomer sat on his stool behind the cash bar and buried his head in his hands rubbing his eyes, a tear welling up as he ran his hands across his balding head.

"God, I wish I had never got talked into running with these fools. Bunch of damn hot heads."

Most of those haters, that prejudicial culture, almost wiped out the Indians, pushing them so far west other tribes slaughtered them, as well as the settlers gobbling up the land for their own means. Boats from across the Atlantic brought immigrants by the thousands seeking new lives and fortune. And Bickley was one of those greedy, prejudicial fortune-hunters.

Disgusted with Woomer, Bickley walked out of the trading post, mounted his horse and headed out of town, almost barreling over Arnie in his haste.

"Hey you!" Dan'l hollered at the stranger, to no avail. "You alright boy?"

"Yea pa."

"Come on, let's see how much that fella has finished."

Doc sat on a log stump, leaning on the pitchfork, behind the stable after just finishing the last wheel barrel load.

"Doc Jansen."

"Out here"

Dan'l surveyed the stalls and nodded his head.

"Woooo, almost cleaner than what Arnie does. Nice work Jansen. Think you can handle a drink?"

Doc wiped his brow with the back of his manure-smudged arm and nodded with a smile.

"Good. Arnie, head to the house and tell mamma we have a guest."

"Yes, sir, pa" he replied, giving Jansen a wink; thankful someone else scooped the poop instead of him for at least one day.

"A bottle will do just fine, kind sir," Doc added as the boy raced out of the stable.

"A bottle might just give mamma a reason not to like you or me." Dan'l reached his hand out and helped Doc stand.

"Then, a drink it is," he replied, and he followed him over to the saloon while brushing off as much of the dirt as he could from his former white attire.

When the saloon doors swung open, Dan'l eyed the men leaning against the bar and lounging at the tables.

"That's a somber look there, Mr. McCann," Doc noted. "Anything wrong?"

"Well, if you're going work for me you have to get one thing straight."

"And what would that be sir?"

"Don't call me sir or mister. People call me Dan'l or McCann."

Doc's eyes widened. "First, I did not know I was working for you; second, I'm a licensed physician and I'm headed to Oregon just like all these other poor souls who, after pirooting with these painted ladies when they've had too much popskull, will need a doctor in their midst. Third, I would work for myself doctoring if I had the desire to stay here."

Dan'l held up his hands in protest. "Now, now, pill man, you're beginning to puker me."

"What can I get you fellas?" the bartender asked.

"A couple of popskulls if you would, Alvin. This here's Ben Jansen from Pennsylvania. Says he is a pill man."

"Hey," Alvin replied. "we could use another doctor. Sam's so old he can hardly see. Things could really pan out here for you if you a mind to stay. Nice to meet you, pill man. You be a friend of mine if you a friend of Danl's."

"Appreciate that Alvin, but you'll have to ask Dan'l about that."

"Still deciding on this one," Dan'l said, giving Jansen an odd look as a young woman dressed in little more than a corset and bloomers stared down at them from the stairway railing and waved. Doc smiled back, taking a swig of his liquor, then Dan'l hurried him out of the saloon after finishing off his jigger of shine.

"Who's that?" Doc asked, curiosity swelling along with other things.

"Come on," he said, rustling him out as the woman sauntered down the stairs. "Annie will be perturbed I'm drinking with a stranger when I need to be home."

Chatting about nothing special, the weather and the population growth, they walked back to the livery stable, passing a couple of ladies and tipping their hats to them.

"Oh, by the way, nobody told me who that young lady was; you kind of changed the subject on me."

"No, it was intentional; you have enough troubles."

"Troubles? I have no troubles, my life's an open book."

"Exactly my point, greenhorn, Lilly's a peck of trouble. She has ruined more men than a porcupine has needles. You will figure it out. A little old for you anyway."

"Just curious, that's all; never said I had intentions." They both chuckled.

"Sure, you didn't, pill man."

"Yea right."

Bickley, who lurked around the store earlier sat on his horse across from the livery, talking to someone McCann had never seen.

"Get the door Jansen," he said, keeping a keen eye on the pair.

"Sure," Doc replied, opening the creaky barn door while eyeing Dan'l as he glared at the two men.

Bickley returned an equally suspicious glare back, whispering to the man standing next to him. "See you when we get together at Kansas, Anderson."

"He going to be a problem, sir?" said the man, pointing towards McCann.

"Doubtful, just a local that's curious, that's all; business as planned."

"Right, have a nice ride."

"See you in Kansas City."

Bickley touched the brim of his hat, gave the reigns a snap, dug his spurs in the horse thighs and started off. McCann turned his attention back to Jansen, who was already on his horse.

"Make sure that animal is warm to the touch all over before you saddle her, greenhorn," he said as he saddled up his own horse and rode up next to him.

"Greenhorn this, greenhorn that," Jansen muttered.

"Alright, pill man, settle yourself. Nothing worse than an uppity medicine man. We did not exactly meet on the best of terms, pill man."

"Pill man," Jansen muttered, shaking his head."

"Okay, Doc Jansen, if that's the way you want it."

"Doc will be fine, Mr. McCann."

"Not mister, remember? Dan'l or McCann is good enough."

After a few minutes of riding out to Dan'l's ranch, Doc broke the silence.

"How did you get yourself into the livery business, McCann?"

"Well, my father came up from Harrisburg in Illinois. Started selling horses to the Army; this ranch is the result."

"What about you, Doc? Time to spill your guts. What are you running from?"

"Myself I reckon. I like alcohol and women too much. When you come out of doc school, they want you to work under an established physician before you hang your shingle, but I'm too much of a loner, I guess. I wanted to see more of the West before it disappeared like everything else."

Dan'l nodded and the two men tied their horses to the gate and Doc followed him into the modest two-storied farmhouse. After a nice meet and greet with Dan'l's wife, and a hearty meal of beef stew, they retired outside, put up the horses and Dan'l threw a couple of logs on the firepit. The two men sat silent watching the embers crumble as the gentle spring air wafted across the grassy plain stretching to the horizon. Annie, Dan'ls wife, came out and asked the two men if they wanted coffee. Both said yes.

"Smoke?" asked Doc.

"Believe I have a cigar in my jacket; want one?"

"No, I twist my own." Dan'l replied, pulling out his tobacco pouch.

"Here's your coffee, gentleman."

"Thank you, Mrs. McCann," replied Doc with a nod and a smile as she hurried back inside.

"Quite a charmer, your wife, Dan'l."

"Well, we agree on one thing, Jansen."

"Say, who were those two back at the stable. They looked a bit on the shady. One standing looked pretty young."

"No idea, never saw 'em before."

"Looked like a peck of trouble to me," replied Doc, his brow furrowing.

"Lots of shady looking fellas in town for me these days. Comes with the territory, I suppose, being the last outpost before Omaha. People escaping what's coming due to the issues with the slaves, I reckon," reassured McCann.

"What's going on with this slavery thing out East anyways?"

"Depends on which side you fall on. Never know talking with strangers. You need to be careful before you tip your hand. Could get yourself shot or hung depending on which side you are on."

"You've got no quarrel with me; we've settled. But is it getting that bad?"

"Pretty much. Both parties are split into different factions Only thing that might settle it is war. That's why all this migration is headed west."

"That, and probably the same reason you came out, Dan'l."

McCann nodded and narrowed his eyes at Doc as Annie came back out and refilled their coffee tins.

"You know, Jansen, I am serious about you a staying. Doc Brackett is getting too old. People are getting where there is not much trust to his doctoring or his eyes. Might a pan out well for you."

"I wish you would stay Mr. Jansen," added Annie. "There are already ten women in town who need more than a midwife. Brackett's not able to visit all of them, too much for him."

"Annie is right. You should stay," prodded McCann.

"What do you mean, midwife, Ma?" interrupted Arnie.

"Don't you, worry Arnie, you will learn soon enough. Off to bed now," his mother said with her hands on her hips.

"Go on Arnie, Doc and I have business to talk."

"I could show you around and introduce you to the locals and such," Arnie shouted from the porch.

"You should be in bed, young man!" Annie shouted back.

"Aww, c'mon, Ma. I am not a kid no more. I am almost as old as Doc here. I should be on my own,"

"He's right, Annie, There's only about five years between them. But you, Doc, best not get my young'un in trouble. There will be trouble on you if'n yo do." he said, pointing a finger in Doc's face.

"Understood," Doc chuckled, holding his arms up like he was under arrest.

"You two can get started in morning after breakfast. Now, off to bed for all three of you gentlemen," Annie announced, crossing her arms.

"You heard the lady," McCann said, shoveling dirt over the fire with the side of his boot. "You can sleep with the horses, Doc. That's what you seem to like."

"Dan'l McCann, he'll do no such thing! No guest of ours will sleep in the barn except maybe you if you insist on treating our guests like paupers. He can sleep in with Arnie."

"Come on, you heard the lady," McCann laughed.

"Come on Doc, this way," she replied, directing him back into the house. "Arnie show him where the bedding is and make a pallet for him."

"Yes ma'am."

As they both laid down on their beds, the candlelight flickered shadows across the ceiling, and Doc chatted with Arnie about his time at medical school, leaving out a few details, like the fact that he really didn't have a license. The boy didn't need to know everything about him anyway.

"You see, Arnie, things aren't always cut and dry."

"What do you mean Doc?"

"You'll figure it out, in due time."

Arnie shrugged and yawned. "Why'd you come here, Doc?"

"Well, like all these others lost souls, I suppose. New life, new opportunities, running from a war that might or might not happen."

"You really think there will be war?"

"Only a matter of time."

"I guess it depends on who gets elected in Washington."

Doc chuckled. "How do you know so much about politics anyway?"

"Pa loves it. He knows the mayor, the sheriff, and the judge. They all play cards together."

"Interesting. Who else plays cards with your dad?"

"Strangers traveling west, once in a while. A couple of free Negro's that they won't let in the saloon. I 'spect some people are afraid of them."

"Afraid of them?" Jansen asked. "Why on earth would they be scared of them?"

"Many reasons I guess, they're different, their color, where they come from, the unknown about them is probably the biggest thing. Ben and I go fishing together all the time. Why Doc, he is no different than you or I. He's smart about animals too."

"In what way, Arnie?"

"He can get horses, mules, and dogs to do things most people don't have no inkling how to? I saw a mule pulling a buckboard one time being stubborn as heck. Mule would not budge an inch. Ben walked right up to that mule, rubbed his face, stroked his head, and whispered in his ear, then gave him a pull and that ole mule just started following him. Darndest thing I ever did see. Ben, told that driver not to whip that mule no more. I thought that driver was going to whip Ben till Pa stepped in. Driver asked Pa what he cared what happen to a darkie. Pa told him 'because that child works for me and don't you be beating on no dark-skinned people, or you'll have me to answer to."

"Interesting, I knew your Pa was a good man."

"He doesn't like no one beating on anyone, animal or man."

Arnie sat up, the candlelight lighting up Arnie's curious glare.

"What's that look for, Arnie?"

"So, are you staying, Doc?"

"Thinking on it, but I think we need to sleep. Curious to see more of this town. All the locals here like your Pa?"

"Most, but there are a lot of bad men."

"Well, can't let a few bad apple spoil a barrel."

"Yep, Ma says that too."

"Good night, Arnie."

"Night, Doc."

Think it just might pan out for me here Doc thought as he yawned and turned on his side. I am beginning to like these here McCann's.

Darkness fell across the river town of St. Joseph as the rain that fell the night before morphed into a damp fog blanketing the whole area.

Like all the other foggy nights, small fires all along the river bank glowed in the eerie gray from the settler's campsites who paused to rest before heading West, and the few Indian teepees of the Missourian and Osages Indian, who were learning to live in peace and silent fear of these migrating white man.

Doc rose at the crack of dawn and he eased the door shut, trying not to wake Arnie while still in his skivvies and carrying his clothes tucked beneath his arm. He crept by the kitchen, peering through sleepy eyes and watched Annie pour water into a coffee pot while a soft song crossed her perfect pink lips.

Dan'l is one lucky fella, he thought.

"Thank you for the thought, Mr. Jansen."

Startled Doc quickly shoved his legs into his trousers and coughed. "What? Sorry, I never realized I said it aloud. I apologize, Mrs. McCann."

Rubbing his still sleepy eyes, trying to not make a fool of himself, at which he was sorely failing. Beautiful women always had this effect on him.

"No need to apologize, Mr. Jansen You did not speak aloud," she answered while pouring a cup of coffee with her back to him. "I can always tell when someone has a thought pointed in my direction; coffee?"

"Thank you, Mrs. McCann," Doc said, eyeing her with curiosity.

"The natives call it the gift of Omens."

"And how long have you had this gift, Mrs. McCann?"

"Since she was a little girl and the Ossage found her alone after a Missouria raiding party killed off her family," Dan'l replied, walking through the doorway and pulling up his suspenders. He slouched down at the table next to Jansen.

Annie brought two cups and the coffee pot over on a silver tray with buttermilk cream and a crystal bowl of sugar cubes.

"Annie's premonitions saved our lives many times. We had a Missouria brave show up at our doorstep one afternoon shortly after we built this place. We thought he was up to no good. I reached for my Sharps, but Annie had already sensed he needed help and meant no harm to us. She told me to stop. It was a good thing; I would have kilt him right off the get go."

"He was trying to make me understand he wasn't there to hurt us. He was wanting Doc. Brackett. Half the tribe had come down with the pox. Army came by on their way to Leavenworth and herded most of them like animals to there and treated them terribly till they could figure out what to do with them. Kept them a half mile from the fort. Over half of them died, and the rest were taken to Oklahoma territory. The ones that lived were constantly fighting with the Choctaw and were almost wiped out."

Annie finished preparing breakfast and pointed to the stairs. "Dan'l, get that boy of ours up, please. Breakfast is on."

"Yes ma'am."

Dan'l rose from his chair and walked to the bottom tread and yelled.

"Arnie, get yourself down here; breakfast is ready."

Annie scurried about the kitchen, setting the food on the table, a delicacy of ham, potatoes, eggs, biscuits, and more coffee. Doc reached for the ham when he looked up and saw Annie glaring at him, then thought better of it.

"Your husband's a man of many talents, Mrs. McCann."

"Please, use Annie. Yes, he is. It's one of many reasons I said yes when he proposed. Is there someone in your life Mr. Jansen?"

"Please, use Doc or Ben."

"Ben, is there anyone in your life?"

"I guess you could say the headmaster's daughter at my former school, but the headmaster had other ideas concerning me," he replied, clearing his throat. "As well as a few others I shouldn't mention."

"A lady's man?"

"Them more than me. It seems to be a curse that gets me into more trouble than not. Although I do have an eye for beautiful ladies, such as yourself."

"I think we need to change the subject, Doc," Annie said, her eyes widening.

"Change the subject from what?" Dan'l asked, coming back in the kitchen, noting her wide eyes. "You talking 'bout something you ought not, Doc? I know my wife pretty well, and I know that look in her eyes. What are you talking about with this stranger, Annie?"

"Please, can't we all just change the subject," Doc pleaded.

"It's nothing, darling; we were just talking about Doc's problem with the ladies," Annie said in a hurry as McCann's face flushed red. "Besides, Doc's not a stranger, he is our guest."

"Wait a minute, I don't have a problem with the ladies," Doc answered.

"What's all the fuss; what's going on?" Arnie asked as he scooted his chair up to the table and grabbed a biscuit, stuffing it into his mouth.

"Nothing, Arnie, and stop snatching the food. We are just talking 'bout grownup stuff," she added.

"I like grown up stuff," he replied, biscuit bits tumbling out of his mouth.

"Don't talk with your mouth full," Annie and Dan'l both siad at the same time.

"Alright, alright, I didn't do anything."

"I'm having a second thought about you, pill man, if that's really who or what you are." Dan'l retorted.

"Hey! I take offense to that." Doc replied.

"It's not Doc's fault, I was just asking him whether he was attached to someone, and he didn't want to talk about it much," Annie answered.

"Arnie, what in tarnation are you digging at?" said Dan'l, turning to his boy and scowling.

"I don't know my ankle just started itching this morning. It woke me up."

"Let mom give a look see."

She pulled up his britches leg and leaned down for a look. "Looks like some kind of rash."

"Probably just from scratching," said Doc. "Let me take a look, Mrs. McCann."

"Sure, Doc," she replied, backing away as he knelt down beside Arnie for a glance at his leg.

"Looks like the rash is irritated from scratching. Possibly a small bite from an insect." He walked over and retrieved his doctor's bag from the rocking chair where he left it the night before, and took out a small squat brown glass jar with a tin lid. "Here, let me put this ointment on it. It will help with the itching and keep it from getting infected. Should be alright, might check his bed later today for any mites or such."

"Finish up, we need get going," said Dan'l, pushing away from the table and setting his hat on his head. "Arnie, saddle up the horses."

"Yes sir."

"And saddle Doc's horse. too."

Doc buckled up his medical bag and attempted to ease the scowl and concern still wrinkling Dan'l's face.

"You know, that there is one smart lad you have."

Dan'l gruffed in his throat. "Sometimes he's too damn smart for his own good."

"Well, I suspect its because he's at that age of trying to figure out how to be an adult and still keep that part of his boy life around awhile."

"That what's wrong with you, Doc?"

"Nothing wrong with me, Dan'l, except I like beautiful women too much."

"That and the alcohol, right? Never mind, don't answer. I see Arnie bringing round the horses."

The sauntered outside and Doc smiled in Arnie's direction.

"Here you go, Doc." passing him the reins.

"Thank you. Say, Arnie, you never told me your given name. What is it?"

"Arnett." Dan'l interrupted.

"Call me Ben; okay?"

"Okay, sir."

Dan'l looked across at Doc as they all mounted their horses. "Doc, most call him "Bull" for his head head."

All three of them laughed and spurred the horses to a trot Doc rode up next to Arnie, still chuckling.

"Get them arms wrestling with mules, Bull?"

'Nah, mostly putting hay up in the loft. and wrestling with the neighborhood boys."

"The lad I saw you with in town?"

"No, his older brother, who's a lot bigger than me. What's with the lad bit, Doc?"

"That would be Scottish heritage from my father's side, mother was Irish. They met on the boat on the way to America. My daddy was killed brawling in the slums. My mom and I drifted awhile and ended up in Philly, she met a rich doctor, married, and I ended up in a medical school."

"Hmm, Ma says we are Scots, too."

Doc nodded and turned to Dan'l as the three of them headed to town.

"So, Doc, you never told me," Dan'l prodded. "Why were you going west; a woman?"

"Something like that, had to do with the head-masters daughter. I do apologize about the little incident at breakfast this morning... just, well, you know..."

"I don't fault anyone Doc. Straighten yourself up and you should do well."

"Thanks for the confidence, Dan'l."

Doc stopped his horse a minute and stood in the stirrups, holding onto the saddles horn and scanned around the area.

"What's the matter, Doc?" Arnie said, spinning his horse around to come up next to him.

"Well, Bull, I'm just a trying to figure the layout of these here parts."

"We have some more riding to do," replied Dan'l. "At least another twenty minutes I figure?"

"If I am to doctor here, I reckon I need to know the layout."

"You'll have time. Doc Brackett's not exactly ready to cash in yet. Now, come on, I 'spect you'll figure things out just fine."

The three rode at a slow pace enjoying the beautiful bright blue sky. Rain from the night before left behind a spring calm and crisp morning. The prairie grass with new sprouting bowed in the slight breeze as their horses made a path, pounding down the tender shoots with their hooves. As they approached the edges of the woods on the outskirts of the town, whirlybirds seeds spiraled down from the Samara trees over them.

Far off in the distance, across the newly green hills, the top of the solitary church's steeple rose above the horizon like a coastal lighthouse beckoning travelers to come spend an afternoon in the fair city of St Joseph.

The flat high ground surrendered to the hills leading down to the headwaters of the mighty Mississippi and Missouri rivers. Back toward the higher ground, patches of snow still clung to winter in the higher elevations., not ready to give up their frosty attachment to the mountains.

St. Joseph's growth mimicked St. Louis, booming from the onslaught of Eastern Immigrants and the streets filled with all sorts of people walking up and down the lanes, visiting the stores, riding their buckboards, and chatting along the way.

Before coming into town, Doc considered their horses... or rather, their mules, and curiosity rose in his mind.

"Tell me something, what's the deal with your family using mules instead of horses, Dan'l?"

"Well, Doc, you'd have to ask the expert back there. He seems to know more than I do. Didn't take him long to understand them."

Dan'l looked over his shoulder at Arnie.

"Bull, you still back there or are you sleeping in that saddle?"

"Just enjoying the ride, Pa,"

"Come up here and explain mules to this here greenhorn."

Arnie huffed. "I don't think he's going to be around long enough to tell him everything I know. Besides, I'm still learning myself."

"We all are, son." Doc said.

"Well, if'n you really want to know, Doc, a donkey is actually a mule's father, They're called Jacks. And you know the mother is a mare. You know you're riding one; a horse and not a mule?"

"Yes, I know a female horse. I used to ride one of my father's stallions. Nice horse, fast. He got to where every time he was around a mare, he'd get quite... well, you know..."

Dan'l laughed. "No need to get all sensitive around Bull, Doc. Arnie's worked around four legged and two legged animals all his life."

Doc's face turned red, bringing a laugh from the three.

Arnie grinned from ear to ear. "Anyways females are called Jennies, and I know what you mean about the stallions. The excitement is because a stallion is ready to mount a female horse or donkey, if you get my meaning."'

Doc chuckled. "Yes, I think I get your meaning. So, how long have you been working mules, Arnie?"

"Oh, long before Pa started. He's too old to bother with learnin' new stuff about mules."

"Hey, I'm not that damn old. Old Scanlon taught me all he knows and he's been gone a while now."

"Well, I'm better than you at it, anyway."

"Wow, who's being conceited?"

Dan'l gave Doc one of his patent glares and Doc held up his hands and smiled. "Like the pot callin' the kettle black," Dan'l said.

"Come on; I was just joking, Dan'l."

"How do ya know I wasn't just joking?"

"Geez." Arnie retorted. "Good thing, ma is not riding along. She'd have both your hides."

"Well, he's right about that."

"Leak time." Arnie said, pulling up alongside some bushes, dismounting and tying his horse to a branch.

"I said it before and I'll say it again, Dan'l. You've got a pretty smart boy."

"Yep, I do; going to be the best mule breeders in these here parts. Turning out to be an fine young man."

"Pa, we got riders approaching." Arnie said, hurrying out of the bushes and adjusting his britches. "May be nothing, but they sure look shady to me," he added, mounting his horse.

The three men waited while the two men on horseback approached them. Dan'l recognized them as the two across from the livery stable from the night before. The older one appeared to be the leader.

"Just stay calm, boys, but we might want to unstrap our holster though, just in case," Dan'l instructed, then directed his words to the two strangers. "You boys look like Fed sympathizers."

Bickley, the leader, a rough looking character sporting a long scraggly dark beard and full dark mustache, wearing an equally shabby, dark suit and hat, retorted back.

"Only someone who is a John Brown followers would think something like that," Bickley said.

Dan'l opened his jacket, revealing his double pistol gun belt.

"Don't follow politics of the day. My only business is just owning the livery stable. I have not the time nor desire for such nonsense; but I do think that the two of you are about to trespass on my land."

"Don't see no sign no where's," Bickley replied, spitting a wad of tobacco juice into the brambles.

"The sign is right over there," Dan'l replied, pointing with his rifle,

"Kind of hidden, isn't it?" Anderson said, sarcasm flavoring his tone.

"Not hidden, but I don't 'spect you can even read it, stranger," popped off Doc.

"Who the heck are you anyway?" Anderson scowled.

"Don't mind him," answered Dan'l. "I want to know who the hell you are trespassing on my land?"

"Don't see no deed in your hand," Bickley replied.

"This is the only deed I need," said Dan'l, holding up his rifle. "Arnie, you have a bead on them?"

"Yes sir," Arnie answered from the bushes. "Looks like we got the jump on you, mister."

"Bull, show this varmint, how good a shot you are."

The intruders heard Arnie cock his Sharp, and Bickley held up his hand.

"Hold on there, mister; seems your bluff worked. Put up your gun, Anderson," Bickley ordered.

But Anderson kept his aim at Dan'l's head, his horse pawing the ground as he chuckled.

"Dang, I was ready, almost pulled the trigger too," Arnie retorted." "You best settle that one down a bit. He's going to end up with a bullet in his gut."

"Settle down, Anderson; there will be another time. We got more important business to attend to than these people."

"Your time's a coming," shouted Anderson. pointing at Arnett.

"Don't be threatening my son, fool, or you will find yourself with a gullet full of lead."

Bickley motioned to Anderson to lower his weapon. "Okay mister, no need to be all riled up. We don't cotton to unneeded trouble. We'll take the North side trail if the gentleman has no objections. We have business to attend to."

Dan'l nodded and the two men headed off to a different trail, far away from them and Dan'ls property. Doc wiped the sweat from his brow with the back of his hand and Dan'l slapped Arnie on the back.

"Good job, Arnie. Guess, it is time to start calling you Arnett. Handled yourself just how I would've."

"Thanks, Pa."

"Told you he was turning into a fine young man. Unlike you, greenhorn. You just sat their as yellow as a corncob."

"He's alright, Pa, I liked his comment about that fella not being able to read. His face turned red as an apple peal."

"Shit, Doc 'bout got us killed making comments like that."

"Really don't think he was wanting to scuffle, Dan'l," said Doc. "He seemed like he was in an awful hurry to get somewhere. He backed down way too easy."

"You might be right, Doc. Remind me to stop by Woomer's before we head to Brockett's."

"For a muleskinner you sure know people." Jansen retorted.

"A lot like animals. Let's go, we're burning daylight." replied Dan'l, as all three of them laughed and spurred their horses towards town.

Arnett remained quiet the rest of the way, processing how close they were to a shootout.

Cannot seem to get him out of my head, hard telling when he will pop up again, he thought. *Going to have to start working on my shooting without Ma finding out.*

Chapter 4

The Knights Golden Circle
Washington D.C.
U.S. Senate
1858

"Order, order I will have order in this chamber," Senator Cass of Michigan demanded, banging his gavel. "The U.S. Senate is now in session. The proposal's debate is brought forth from Texas U.S. Senator Sam Houston, with the topic to protect the interests of our southern states. Senator Houston, you may have the floor."

"Thank you, honorable Cass. I come here today not to just do business for the fine people of the great state of Texas. I come here to bring forth this bill that will not just protect Texas's economic well- being and southern values, but to protect our way of life that we hold dear to our hearts."

Members of the Senate's Northern states grumbled as the Senate Majority Leader banged his gavel hard on the desk top. "Again, I will have order in this Chamber. Let the man speak."

"Thank you, Sir. But without the ability to protect our interests in our own states, as well as those southern countries of Cuba, Mexico, and the Caribbean, and Central America, nor the interference of the Buchanan administration, is vital not to just the South, but the rest of the country, which provides us a much-needed labor force. Without this labor, our economy will collapse along with the rest of the nation. How can we continue here in the South to feed and clothe a growing nation and protect our livelihood if Lincoln becomes President? He will destroy our sovereignty and the values we hold so dear. I reserve my time."

Doctor George W. Bickley sat in an observation booth high above the Senate floor with two gentlemen from the Fire-Eaters group. The vote moved forward. The southern constituency was losing.

"Mr. Rhett," said Bickley, "if this bill does not pass, I plan to approach Jefferson Davis at once. We must plan for serious secession. It is looking like the abolitionist movement means to destroy us. If we are destroyed economically, it might as well be by war."

"You're a hothead, Bickley; we are nowhere ready to fight the Union Army."

"I have over ten thousand men right now," Bickley retorted. "You are worse, than any of them damn Copperheads. Either join us or stay the hell out of the way. Breckinridge, at this very moment, is redirecting funds to the South, while Buchanan sits on his hands, while the Republic falls apart right under his nose."

Mr. Rhett was about to reply to Bickley's comment, but Bickley stormed from the chamber, his face red as a beet.

Four years earlier
July 4th, 1854
Lexington, Kentucky

George Bickley left Washington along with a member of the Knights of the Golden Circle, a secret society of pro slavery advocates. His meeting went well with Buchanan's Secretary of War, John Floyd. Floyd, however, was not the only cabinet member serving as a knight of the secret order. Secretary of Treasure, Howell Cobb, and even Vice-President Breckenridge were loyal members of the order.

Cobb, Floyd, and Breckinridge managed to secure large amounts of funds and armaments, as well as vital seaports, for the Confederate cause, storing stockpiles of rifles, ammunition, and material for uniforms and other supplies, such as cannons, transferring them to different southern arsenals, right under the Union's nose.

Within five years of their first organized meeting, the Confederacy adopted its own constitution and secured an army. Four hundred-seventeen thousand arms were then bought by six cotton states.

They also discussed the importance of bringing Texas into the fold to increase the armament to over one million. Getting the border states to join the Confederacy was also high on their list.

They launched an espionage network of not only males, but also female agents, and their arm reached far into Texas as well as the Kansas territory along the Missouri border.

The suggestion of war sprouted near the Missouri Kansas border whose southern supporters tried desperately to keep abolitionists like John Brown, from gaining a foothold along the border. This would give the Knights control of the western movement coming out of St. Joseph, Missouri that led the pioneer movement push west along the Oregon trail that ran along the mighty Missouri River.

Fights broke out among Southern sympathizers against loyal unionists not only in Missouri and Kansas, but also Southern Illinois. If Southern Illinois joined the secession, it would give the Confederacy not only control of the Ohio River but ultimate total control of the Mississippi River.

"The key here, gentlemen, is to get State Legislature Logan to bring the Greenville militia into the fold of the new Confederate of States. That is at least another two thousand men and gives us control of the Ohio River, in Southern Illinois, and do not forget, access to St. Louis. The Yankees would have no access to the West without going up into Iowa and then, only in the warmth of summer," Jefferson Davis, the Confederacy's new President, said, pointing to the map on the wall.

"I hear tell he's not the Copperhead everyone seems to think he is. If he were so damn sure, he wouldn't be head of a militia."

"Good point, Doctor Bickley. We need somebody on the inside of his militia to see if we can find out where his loyalties are. Your group is handling the rivers areas to Kansas territory. are you not?"

"We're stretched thin. but there's a lot along both rivers who don't cotton the Union's way of thinking."

"His Excellency desires a Mexico takeover, with South Texas and the Southwest along with safe passage through South America once you leave the Caribbean. If we can get the Knights to handle the rivers to St. Louis, there will be no boundaries to the Circle expansion; bigger than the world has ever seen before."

"I like the way his Excellency thinks."

"Thank you, Doctor. I have a man who has been recruiting secretly within the Illinois militia as we speak. He is just awaiting orders. I plan to head to Cairo at once. We, also, have a very skilled woman agent, and here she is..."

Maddie Cronin sashayed into the room, decked in her finest burgundy brocade jacket and flounced skirt with matching satin hat with peacock feathers. She tossed her golden hair over her shoulder and glared at Bickley.

"We never agreed to have a woman present in this conversation," Bickley unexpectedly declared.

"Maddie is our in-house agent," Mr. Davis said.

"In-house agent?" Bickley asked.

"Meaning she strategically placed herself within the White House, with Vice-President Breckenridge's help."

"My brother and I are already working on a developing communication plan of infiltration and deliverance of top-secret Union information. Once our plan is in place, it should help us considerably," Maddie answered.

"You think a woman can effectively run an espionage ring?" Bickley scowled.

Maddie faced him, her face beet red.

"Careful Doctor," President Davis warned. "She is not only a beautiful southern lady, she's also a very capable one."

Bickley crossed his arms and lifted his chin to show off his superiority complex, and what he truly thought about women. Maddie despised those sorts of men, those who thought women were nothing more than objects to use for their pleasure. Maddie produced a derringer from the back of her dress and fired a shot over the doctor's ear. The bullet lodged in the wall near the window.

Bickley's face turned a ghostly white. "That was uncalled for Maddie," Davis said angrily.

Maddie pocketed the derringer while Bickley wiped the smirk and the sweat away with his linen handkerchief.

"You could have killed me," he barked.

"Why, my dear Doctor, rest assured, if I wanted to kill you, you would be lying on the floor bleeding out," Maddie mocked, using her most fluent Southern Belle accent. She strolled around the table while running her white gloved forefinger along the men's collars.

"Please Senorita, save the acting for the theater you Americana's are so fond of. We have serious work here. It has been ongoing for five years and his Excellency is getting impatient."

"We can't hardly do anything, with all respect to His Excellency, until the Union gives us just cause to start the secession. Senator Houston's bill did not pass, and I can tell you there is an election coming up. If the right person is voted in office, we just might avert all-out war. Vice President Breckenridge is doing all he can to divert Union monies and is placing known military attributes in command over southern military posts," added Davis.

"As a military commander, his Excellency should be well-aware these things take well placed planning and time," she added, batting her eyelashes.

"Maddie, please, enough," the President commanded.

"Why, Mr. Davis, I do declare. As a Savannah lady, we must always defend our honor where gentlemen like Mr. Bickley are concerned."

"Believe me, I am well versed concerning the protocols of the Southern *femmes du monde*."

"Mr. Davis, I do remember you did not waste your dear mother and father's monies on the time you spent as a child in France."

"Yes, my instructor was, shall we say, quite bourgeoisie da femme."

"That must have been an exquisite experience for such a young lad."

"Yes, Madam. Grace quite."

Maddie and Jefferson Davis laughed and admired the beauty of the conversation, as well as each other's mocking of French etiquette.

"Shall we, Madam?" President Davis held out his elbow for Maddie, signaling the end of the meeting.

Little Dixie Area
Kearney, Missouri
1854

"Jesse! Jesse! Dang burnet, Zerelda, where the hell has that boy gone off to?"

"I don't rightly know, Reuben. Seems he was going off with Perry down to catch some fish this morning."

Zerelda sat next to the fireplace working on a quilt, the morning breakfast plates still piled up in the dry sink for an hour.

"They're supposed to be working in that hayfield."

"Now, Reuben, don't you be fretting none. I told them they could go. I do declare, Reuben, sometimes you forget that lad is just a boy. You forget what it's like to be a young boy, honey?"

Doctor Reuben Samuel smiled and put his arm around Zerelda.

"No, I haven't forgotten dear; and I can tell you, I also haven't forgotten Frank running off to Illinois and joining up with that dang militia that lawyer fella started up. All this dang talk of war has made everyone skittish."

"Frank's a grown man, Reuben, I suspect he knows what he wants out of life by now."

"That part does not concern me, Zerelda. We have no idea which side this lawyer is cottonin' to. Frank hasn't written you one letter since he's left."

"Come on, Reuben, you got no cause to be talking like that about Frank."

"I don't? What happens when war breaks out and Frank finds himself on the wrong side?"

"You really think there will be war, Reuben?"

"The framework is already taking place, as we speak."

"Oh my, what's going to happen to my boys?" Zerelda clutched the quilt so hard her knuckles turned white. She looked up at Reuben with tears in her eyes.

"There now, wife, don't you fret none. Whatever happens is the Lord's will. We can't change that."

"Tell me you're not involved in this, Reuben."

"Come on, I'm a doctor. I don't have time for this nonsense."

Reuben knew it was a lie, but he said it anyway as he walked out to stand on the porch, smoking his pipe, and overlooking the one-hundred-acre farm to search for their sixteen-year-old Jessie. He leaned on the porch railing and looked over toward the wooden shack where his slave, Perry, stayed. Staring at the shack, warm thoughts of Sally, Perry's mother, filled his mind, and of her smooth dark skin. *Like rich coffee in the morning*, his mind whispered... then adding, *if Zerelda or Jesse ever finds out Perry is my son, Jesse will kill him, his mom... and maybe, even me. And Zerelda must never know of my involvement in this fight.*

He sat down on the step and rubbed his eyes, remembering the day Sally told him she was with child. *Oh my! If these crazy fed bastards in Washington ever find out some of the things going on on these southern farms and plantations, they will kill all of us.*

He looked up to the sounds of horses nickering and hooves pounding across the field. Seeing the flash of blue coats on the men riding in, he rushed inside to get his rifle off the fireplace mantle.

"What's wrong? Sally asked as she started on the dishes in the sink. Zerelda looked up, her brow wrinkling.

"Never you mind; I'll get rid of them."

But as he turned to walk back outside with his gun raised, a voice stopped him in his tracks.

"Stop right there, doctor. Turn around slowly and raise your hands."

Zerelda rushed up behind him and screamed.

A Union soldier stood in the doorway, pointing a pistol in Reuben's direction.

"Hush up." the soldier said to Zerelda. "Where is that son of yours... where is Frank? Tie the horses down, Lieutenant, and let's have a look around," the man shouted over his shoulder.

"Yes, sir. You heard the captain; everyone dismount."

Reuben set his rifle to the side and stroked his bushy long gray sideburns.

"What business they want with Frank?" Zerelda asked, her fingers balling up the quilt in her hands.

A private, standing in the doorway, approached Zerelda, pointing his rifle toward her. Reuben lunged at the soldier, shouting at him to leave her alone. Captain Longstreet pulled his revolver out and smacked Reuben behind his head, and he dropped to the floor. Sally backed up against the back wall as Zerelda bent over to help her husband, her tears dripping from her chin.

"Get outside and attend to the horses," Longstreet said to the soldier, shaking his head.

The Lieutenant walked past the private and stood next to Captain Longstreet. "Don't you mind him, lady. Get up; you leave him where he lays until you tell us where that boy of yours is. Where the hell is he?"

"I don't know, he left last month and hasn't been back," Zerelda cried, streaks of tears flooding down her wrinkled cheeks.

"She is a lying, Captain. There are tracks heading down to the river. Two sets of 'em."

"Them be tracks made by the slaves who go down to the river to fish," Sally added, her voice quivering.

"Private Smith, get up here on the double."

"Yes, sir."

The captain met him at the door and spit a mouth full of tobacco juice in a glob on the ground. "You, go check out that slave cabin. If no one's in there, burn it down."

"No, don't burn down Perry's cabin," Reuben pleaded.

"Shut up, old man. I might spare a few things if you tell me where the hell is that boy of yours?"

"No idea, he doesn't like me much," Reuben answered, lying.

The captain glanced to the Lieutenant and nodded. The lieutenant tightened his leather glove and hit Reuben squarely on the jaw. Blood splattered across the floor.

"Hit him again."

Zerelda screamed and fell to her knees, pleading for them to stop.

"Ma'am, were going to keep doing this till you tell me where Frank is."

The captain's anger grew by the minute, his face reddening. Zerelda knew in her heart she could not betray her son. *What should I do? What can I do? God, please keep Jessie and Perry out of this*, she kept praying.

"Hit him again," the captain scowled. More blood sprayed, this time from a gash above the eye. Zerelda sobbed and rocked back and forth as Reuben's long gray sideburns filled with blood.

"No, no more," she replied, clasping her hands in front of her chest. "I know not where he is. Frank's a good boy. He hasn't done anything."

The captain paced a bit, scratching his stubbly beard. "Bring him outside; we don't have all day for this.

He walked on the porch and watched the men burn the slave's cabin, all of them whooping and a hollering like it was the Fourth of July. He gazed up at a huge oak tree that stood in the front yard.

"Anderson, bring the rope. Let's hang the traitors. Get him up. You two," he barked, pointing to two of the soldiers, "help the Lieutenant."

"No, you can't do this," Zerelda shouted from the porch.

"Get back, ma'am; we can do any damn thing we want."

The two picked Reuben up by his arms and dragged him across the floor. A trail of blood followed him out the door. Zerelda followed them outside, horrified, her heart ripping apart. *Thank God Jessie's not here to see this.*

"Get that rope ready." Anderson threw the rope across a limb. "One more chance, you two. Where in the hell is that boy of yours?"

Sally's mouth twitched, almost revealing the answer when her eyes fixed on Reuben's face.

"Sally, don't tell these bastards anything," he cried out.

"Shut the hell up." Anderson took his rifle to Reuben's stomach as hard as he could. "Can we do it now, Captain? Can we string him up?" Anderson's eyes bulged at the excitement of getting to enact a hanging.

The captain looked at Zerelda, then back toward Anderson. "Well?" he said, taunting her. She remained silent. "Pull him up," the captain ordered, keeping his eyes on her face.

The lieutenant helped Anderson pull on the rope and Reuben spat and coughed up blood, his fingers gripping the tightening cord around his neck.

"Now, lower him. It's only going to get worse ma'am," he said back to her. "A man can only take so much of this."

She still said nothing, so he raised his hand up in the air. "Back up," he shouted. Reuben's eyes rolled back as they raised him again, his feet kicking and his cheeks turning blue.

"Lower," the captain commanded. He narrowed his eyes at Zerelda and grinned. "Just keep going, fellers, till this bitch breaks."

Perry glanced over at his fishing partner. Jessie's eyes fluttered in the morning sun as the boy leaned against a tree and dozed. They had a good morning fishing, but the catfish stopped biting hours ago. He reached over into the wooden bucket and pulled the string of fish out, admiring the morning's work.

"Jess. Jess?" he said, shaking him awake.

"Wha... what? What the hell's got into you, Perry?'

"Let's go back; we got plenty fish for supper."

"Alright, don't be shaking me like that; I could a hit you."

Perry stood up and sniffed the air, then looked up toward the cabin. "Oh, shit, fire!" he yelled.

"Wha... what?" Jesse stammered. Perry dropped the fish line and started running.

"Somethings on fire, Jesse!"

The two ran up the hill towards the farm. When they reached the top, they both shielded their eyes from the black smoke billowing from Perry's cabin. The barn was blazing, as well, in a hellish ball of fire, and then Jesse saw them.

"No, you damn Yankees! What the hell have you done?"

Jesse reached for the pistol Frank gave him before he left, then scowled as he realized he left it on the side table in his room.

"Dang blasted!" he shouted.

At sixteen, Jesse James had no fear of anyone. He could outrun, outride, and outshoot, better than most adults. Ten to fifteen yards across the front of the house, he saw his mother standing with some soldiers. *Is she crying?* he thought. Then he caught sight of his stepfather, Reuben, dangling from the tree, covered in blood.

"You bastards!" he yelled. Reuben had been the only person who took interest in him and his brother. He taught them how fish, hunt, ride and shoot; more importantly, he tried to instill in them an ideology to grab hold of whatever filled their inner souls and minds; thus, the main reason Reuben never stopped Frank from leaving to seek out whatever it was he needed to be a part of.

Anderson grabbed his rifle when he saw Jessie running toward them, but the captain raised his hand.

"No, we don't murder children. But we can teach 'em a lesson." He reached for a whip attached to one of the saddlebags, and when he turned around, Jesse was almost on top of him.

He lashed out at Jesse with his whip, slashing Jesse's face. Jesse tumbled to the ground as two more slashes sizzled across his back. Zerelda rushed over and stood between Jesse and the Captain.

"No! He's just a child, you bastard; leave us be!"

The captain grinned, again, and looked around at his men watching the scene.

"Burn 'em out," he growled. "Burn 'em out! And cut that piece of rebel shit down." He mounted his horse, looked around, admiring the handiwork of the day. "Mount up, men. Lets ride!"

Zerelda linked her arm with Jesse's as Sally rushed over to Perry.

"Boys, help Reuben," Sally said, "the buggy is behind the house. Bring it around, Perry."

"Yes, ma'am."

The house was just about burned out as the three helped Reuben into the buggy. Zerelda gazed at the destruction, her fingers across her opened shocked mouth.

"Dang bastard Yankees," she blasted. Both boys gasped, surprised at her outburst. It was the first time they ever heart the meek Southern woman curse.

"Where are we going, Mrs. Samuel?" Perry asked as they loaded up and headed down the road.

"Yea, mama; what are we going to do?" asked Jesse.

"Not rightly sure, boys. First thing we're doing is to get Reuben to a doctor; giddup," she said with a pop of the reins.

Zerelda tried to go as fast as she could without causing more harm bouncing Reuben around. Sally wrapped him in a blanket and held him tight against her bosom, humming a soft tune in her throat to try and calm all of their fears. The boys, slumping against the buckboard walls and silent in their own thoughts, tried to dissect what just happened along with the uncertain future ahead of them.

Jesse already knew what was coming from Frank's letters, an he was already planning on how he was going to get his hands on a gun and a horse. The seed of revenge had been planted long ago when his father left the family for California Gold. They never heard from him again. He needed to find Frank, and the persistent thought needled him as the wagon ambled down the country road. For as long as he was old enough to remember anything, his older brother Frank knew what to do... and what to say. He was always there for Jesse... until now.

Chapter 5

Frank James
Missouri Frontier
1852

The brown gelding nickered and neighed, shifting from foot to foot.

"Easy there, fella; quiet now."

The rider reached for his canteen and took a drink. He pulled back into the bushes after hearing what he thought was someone humming.

"Shh, sounds like a man to me," he whispered in his horse's ear.

Logan eased his rifle out of his saddlebag, and caught a bead through the eyepiece on a shadow coming through the bushes.

"State your business mister. I've got a bead on you," Logan called out. The rider looked up, surprised, and flipped his poncho to reveal a side arm tucked in his waistband.

"Not looking for trouble, mister. Not out to harm no one. That thing could go off and then we'd both be in a pickle barrel."

"Might just go off on purpose. I said, state your purpose."

"Easy there, mister."

"You have a name?"

"Frank."

"Got a last name?"

"James."

"Now we have that settled, answer my damn question. I'll give you two seconds."

"I'm looking for someone. Cole Younger."

"What business you have with this Younger fella?"

"Heard he might be out this way."

"What's your business with Younger?"

"He's a cousin. Come on, mister, what is with all the questions? I am just a teacher. Who the hell are you anyway, the law?"

"Why you so worried; you in trouble, boy?"

"Not that I've heard."

Logan watched this young man's gun hand closely, then lowered his rifle. "Teacher, hmm. Name's Logan, Captain Logan."

"Last I heard, Captains don't wear civvies."

"I'm a militia captain. We're out of Greenville, Illinois."

"Kind of out of your area a bit, aren't you?"

"No, I've been up to St. Joseph. On my way back. Now your one to be asking a lot of questions, son. If you're going my way, you're welcome to ride along if you want."

"Depends, on where you're headed."

"Well, you said you were looking for Younger. He's in my militia."

"Well, I'll be dog gone."

The two of them shook hands and turned their horses into the forest, heading out.

"Where are you from, Mr. James?"

"From Clay County, Missouri; Cole is also from Clay."

"What's with Clay County boys crossing over to Illinois for?"

"What do you mean?"

"Most from along the Mississippi joining up every day."

"I'd say we all have heard of you. I never heard your name, but we all understand you don't like all this secession talk."

Logan nodded. "Can you shoot?"

Frank chuckled and stopped his horse, then pointed up to a tall pine near them. "See that cone hanging off that piney? The one way up yonder?"

"Yep, I see it."

Frank drew his pistol and fired toward the cone, blowing it apart, then he laughed as the captain's eyes widened.

"Pretty good shooting for such a young man," Logan said.

The two continued riding, and Logan offered some of his thoughts on his position with the Union.

"The militia I happen to command is for one purpose - protecting the citizens under my authority."

"So, you are a lawman after all?"

"Yes and no; I'm a state legislature in Vandalia. My father started this militia when I was young in Murphysboro, Illinois."

The two men rode in silence for a while enjoying the beauty of Eastern Missouri's Mississippi River trail. Logan glanced at his pocket watch, looked up at the sun, and took a swig from his canteen.

"We should be in St. Louis within a couple of hours. If you are interested in joining up, we can keep traveling together. Otherwise, I'm crossing the river into Illinois. I'd like to have an answer by the time we get to St. Louis."

Frank rubbed his bearded jaw, considering. "Who else is from my neck of the woods?"

Logan hesitated, pondering Frank's question. "Well, there's an Anderson and a Quantrill."

Frank slapped his knee. "Well, heck fire, they're all cousins! Tell you what, I'll ride along to where-ever it is you are going, and if I get a good word from Cole, I will sign up; fair?"

"You're not a very trusting fella, are you?"

Frank turned and looked Logan in the eyes. "No, I'm not; my stepfather taught me that, besides would you trust a fella pointing a rifle at him when you first meet him?'

"Guess not." Logan said, chuckling

St. Louis, Missouri
1852

St. Louis, Missouri was a booming river town. Settlers settled here, seeking a better life out west, as well as immigrants, who recognized opportunity. The streets that were once just dusty wagon trails had become hardened clay from heavy wagons transporting freight from the many paddlewheel boats traveling up and down the Missouri and Mississippi Rivers.

The dock hands down on the riverbanks kept busy unloading unrefined cotton and tobacco. Some days, the trade was so busy, paddlewheel steamers had to wait for hours for their turn to dock. From all corners of the earth, travelers came up the Mississippi from New Orleans and down from Chicago's ports.

Native Indians from the boot hill of Missouri mingled alongside Europeans and Louisiana French fur trappers around the docks. Slaves were also brought in by the Knights of the Golden Circle, looking to add Missouri and Kansas on their list as slave states.

The Mississippi's long curve into the South had become the conduit for residents who decided to stay and settle the city. St. Louis started as a small French trading post started in 1763 by Pierre Laclede, and became the center of trade before the settler's trek towards the unknown Western frontier. The city remained unrecognized by the United States until 1822, but by the time just thirty years rolled by, the city swarmed with 160,000 people called it home. German, French, and Irish immigrants laid their claim and started building a life in this up and coming haven.

Logan pointed up a hill in front of them. "We're here. Right up that hill and beyond those trees. Ever been to St. Louis?"

"No, I've heard a lot about it from Mr. Samuel."

The name invited an inquisitive stare from Logan,

"My stepfather," replied Frank.

Logan spurred his horse forward. "Well, we're not getting there by sitting here."

The trail turned into a street crowded with houses on each side and people walking and in carts up and down the thoroughfare. Frank gazed at the faces, bewildered.

"Too damn many people for my liking."

"Wait till we get further down by the river."

The street widened the further they rode. Frank noted the hard clay streets, and listened to his horse's hooves clack down the ones made of red brick. A woman from a high window of a house overlooking the street, dumped a pail of water, barely missing them. Frank looked up and gave her a scowl, but she paid him no mind.

"The port is just down the street," Logan said. "We need to ferry across the river into Illinois there."

"Is it as bad as here?"

Logan laughed. "You really don't like this many people, do you?"

Frank slowed as a peddler stopped him.

"What do you need, my friend? I have leather boots, and blankets, and tin cups..." the peddler asked.

"I need for you to get the hell away from my horse before I send you into next week."

"I declare, such rude manners!" the peddler replied back, scurrying away.

Frank reached over and picked an apple from a costermonger.

"Hey you! Those aren't free!"

Frank reached into his vest pocket and threw a coin at him. The man missed the coin and it rolled down the street, with him scampering after it.

"I've never seen such a colorful crowd of people. I may have to rethink this."

"We won't be much longer," Logan replied, as they approached the ferry. "How much, mister?"

"Lessee, two bits for the horses and two bits for you; it's four bits."

"I can count," Logan answered, handing the ferryman eight bits to cover him and Frank.

The flatboat ferry, large enough to carry three freight wagons or three sets of riders, rocked in the shallows as Frank and Logan dismounted and eased their horses onboard. Two husky slaves, with arms and shins as big as small trees, pushed the ferry with long cane poles and pumped the foot-controlled paddle. The ferry rocked along with the current, making its way to the other side without much effort from the slave boys despite the strong current underneath.

"Shouldn't take long now," Logan said.

The river was calm, unlike the Missouri that Frank had seen while making trips to St. Joseph with Dr. Samuel when he was about Jesse's age.

"You never said anything about pay," Frank said, suddenly.

"No, I didn't. We will discuss business after we get off this river." Logan replied.

As they approached the East bank, the two slaves grabbed the tie down ropes and jumped in the water to pull the ferry up to the bank. Frank and Logan mounted and started off the ferry. Two riders waiting to go back across sat on their horses in their way.

"How you want to handle this?' Frank asked, whispering.

"Take my lead; don't give them an inch. They'll move, and if not, we'll ride through them."

The horses nickered down the plank and onto the bank as Logan started off in a trot right towards the two riders. Logan pulled his whip out. Seeing a whip, the two men stepped aside as Logan and Frank rode in between them, staring them down as they passed.

"They didn't give much of a fight." Frank said.

"Didn't count on them doing anything. Pretty sure they figured we were from the militia." Logan pointed to the mark on his saddle. "Greenville Militia. Not many want to mess with us. We're law here." He punched his spur into his horse's side, lurching him forward and shouted over his shoulder to Frank. "Just another fifteen minutes, and we will be at the camp."

Hill's Fort was home to Logan's Militia, on the outskirts of a small village named Greenville in Western Illinois.

"Two men approaching, Lieutenant!" came the cry from a militiaman standing guard.

The lieutenant walked up the stairs on the inside wall of the fort, took his eyeglass and peered through the narrow eyepiece.

"Stans, open the gate; it's Captain Logan!" commanded Burgess.

"This fort's been here a while," Frank said, gazing up at the garrison walls.

"Since the Revolution against Britain," Logan replied.

"Well, I'll be danged."

Hills Fort was built along the rolling farmland outskirts of Greenville, Illinois, a good morning's ride by horseback or covered wagon from the Mississippi river; and for the purpose, after the Revolution, to protect Greenville from Indian attacks and other unforeseen threats coming from the Mississippi River.

Built like most forts at the time with two-story square block buildings on each corner of the high stone walls surrounding the fort. During times of peace, the men used one of the blocked corner buildings for resting, or eating during inclimate weather, and bunk space in the upstairs; but, for the most part, most of them spent their days outside around firepits, waiting for something to happen in between their daily drills.

A few of the men sat around a fire irritated, grumbling, and bored. There had not been an escaped convict, slave, or bandit to chase after for some time, and the men grew restless. Even the local Illiniwek, the Indian mound builders, weren't any more trouble after most were shipped off to Oklahoma territory reservations.

"I gather you know the other fella, Younger?"

Bob Younger, Cole's brother looked toward Cole. "Is that Frank James? My God, it is."

Both stood at the same time and walked toward the two riders.

"Kinfolk," Frank acknowledged to Logan.

Frank dismounted as the two brothers shook hands with Frank, and they hugged each other.

"I never thought I would see you on this side of the Mississippi."

"Question is, Cousin Cole, why are you here?" The three men laughed.

"Don't forget protocol, privates."

"Yes, sir, Captain Logan."

"Request my brother and I take care of your horses and show Frank the lodging facilities, sir."

"There will be time for that. You know the rules for new recruits. Follow me Mr. James."

Cole followed Frank as they pulled the horses behind them and headed toward a two-story building with a wood-shingled slanted roof and a huge stone chimney stacked alongside the outside wall. They entered the ground floor entrance, crossing the small porch supported by hewn pine posts.

A tall black man, dressed in Union blues, approached and took the horses' reins. Logan introduced him.

"Frank, this is Henry. He tends to the officer's quarters, keeping things tidy, cooking meals, and takes care of the livery stable across from the officer's quarters."

Frank shook Henry's hand.

"Nice to meet you, Henry," Frank replied.

Henry nodded, but did not smile. "If you get special orders from the Captain, I will be the one delivering them."

Frank arched his eyebrow and nodded as Logan searched his desk for a saddle insignia for Frank. Henry retrieved a Bible from the mantle, and the three stood waiting for Logan.

"Sure, you still want to do this?" Logan asked.

"Yes," Frank replied.

"What?"

"I mean, yes, sir."

"Put your hand on the bible. Repeat after me: I do solemnly swear without reservation or forced upon to uphold the laws of the State of Illinois and the governing laws of this Greenville, Illinois State Militia I do solemnly swear."

Frank repeated and Henry handed Logan a piece of paper. "Sign here, if you can write, Logan stated, pointing to a space below a lot of words.

Frank scanned over the passages.

"Just states you will follow orders and regulations. Every man gets a manual. I expect you to read it," Logan said.

"Yes, sir," Frank answered, signing the bottom.

"Welcome aboard. Reveille is at six a.m. sharp. Cole can show you around."

Henry walked out the door with Frank. "Welcome, Mr. James. Remember, officer's, most of the time, will call you Private. So, if you hear it, pay attention, even if there are more than just you. Come on over to the livery stable."

"Yes, sir."

The two men walked over, leading the horses.

"How long have you been here Henry?"

"Since the War of 1812."

Frank whistled. "What was that like?"

"Don't remember; I was too young. My father was hanged by the British, accused of being a French spy. Story goes, my mother fled New Orleans, and I ended up here. She was afraid owners would take me away from her, being a son of a marked man. She snuck aboard a paddlewheel. The captain caught her, raped, and killed her. They never knew I was there until a maid found me in a storage room, and I sort of just made my way here to the Fort... probably on account of my Louisiana cooking. I help Schmitty, our cook, sometimes."

"Heck of a story, Henry," Frank said, whistling again as Cole removed the saddle from Frank's horse and ushered him into a stall. "Thanks for taking care of my horse, Cole."

"Just following orders. You get all squared away?"

"Gentlemen, I'll leave you two cousins to get reacquainted," Henry said.

"Thanks, Henry. I look forward to some gumbo soon."

Henry finally smiled, his white teeth gleaming proud as he sauntered away.

"Guess there is no need to instruct you on putting your patch on your saddle. Seeing how you won't be getting it till Black-Jack sees you in action."

Frank chuckled. "Black-Jack sounds like a pirate name. Are you talking about Logan?"

"Yea, I mean Logan?"

"What?"

"Yea, I mean Captain. Never call him that to his face unless you want k-duty. Come on, let's see what cousins Bob and Jim are doing."

"They're here too?"

"Yep, we all joined up same hour. You know how hot it was getting for us Youngers in Clay. Chasing down runaways in North Missouri is not too healthy for us southern boys."

The two finished grooming and storing Frank's tack. "Don't worry about feeding him. Henry's boy will do it once he figures out where the hell he went to."

"For an old fort it sure is laid out nice."

They continued walking pass the campfire rings toward the enlisted quarters.

"Hey Schmitty, this here is my cousin Frank James, just joined up."

Schmitty looked from his cook kettle and wiped his hands on his apron, extending it to Frank.

"Happy to meet ya, Frank."

Frank shook his hand and widened his eyes, noting the man's accent. Shmitty quickly picked up on it.

"Ahh, it's the accent. I am a Cajun French from Louisiana, and my mother was Indian."

Cole laughed at Frank. "Frank's, led a pretty much sheltered life Schmitty, A schoolteacher was all he ever wanted to be. Seen my brothers, yet? Come on, let's get you set up. They're inside."

"Jim, looked what Cole just dragged in."

Jim slapped down his sorry hand of cards as another round finished and Bob shoveled the mound of cigarettes and sugar cubes towards him. "Dang blasted cards... Well, I'll be; I never expected you here, Frank. Thought you would be teaching in some high-falutin' school."

Frank pulled up a stool and joined in the game as Bob shuffled the deck and handed out the cards.

"I did, too, Bob, but work is getting slim in Clay. Too young to be stuck taking care of a farm, with just Jesse's help. Just luck I ran into Captain on the trail."

"What happened to your stepfather?"

"Nothing that I know of... he's probably still there ordering Jesse around."

"Dang, Cole, break that jug out," Bob shouted.

"Get it yourself; you're the one wanting it."

"Same old Cole," Jim retorted, chuckling.

"You remember that time we were racing horses and Cole passed us and jumped that cliff? Damn near kilt me trying to keep from going over that ravine," Frank said, laughing. "You know I dislike losing at anything."

"That be true, cousin."

"Yeah, horse racing, women, or poker." Bob said.

"Especially women." Jim retorted.

"If'n, I didn't know better; I'd think you're jealous."

"Frank couldn't be jealous; he's afraid of women."

"Like hell, Bob. I've had my share of fun. Say, on another subject, how did the Captain get that name you were calling him?"

"You mean Black-Jack? Think that would be obvious." Cole said, laughing and taking his hat off as he ran his fingers through his long greasy hair. Still, no one answered Frank.

"How old is little brother now, Frank?" Cole asked.

"Jesse is sixteen now, sprouting up like a cornstalk."

"And your mom, how is she getting along with husband number three?"

"Doc? Fine, and Samuel has been good for Jesse, really."

"Sounds like you're not too sure about that."

"Just some of his ways of teaching, a lot of naysaying..."

"Naysaying, now that is a new one, Teacher," Cole said, laughing.

"Last hand, and I'm turning in."

"That's alright, Teach; you have to pass the manual test tomorrow night."

Bob huffed and laid out his hand. "Don't reckon it will bother Frank much, brother. Two Kings and three sixes."

"Dammit, Bob," Jim growled.

Bob stood and bowed. "I thank you, gentlemen."

"Bob, you've been winning all month," interrupted Cole. "I have nothing left."

"It's all good, Cole. Now that Frank's here, we have a new one to beat." He slapped Frank on the back as each of them headed to their own tent.

"It's been a long time since I laughed this hard, cousins," Frank shouted to them.

"Here, here, Frank; have a good sleep."

For the next month, another thirty men joined the militia. Frank was amazed at how easy Logan was able to recruit young men into the fold. Logan had a way of connecting young men who were downtrodden, family outcasts, or plain troubled youth that had no direction in life. Frank was no longer the rookie.

And Logan recognized Frank as the thinker of the whole militia. Leader potential. Now and then, someone would bring a St. Louis paper with them. Politics of the day in various articles put the men on edge. The Kansas territory soon applied for statehood, and the question of whether Kansas would be a free state or a slave state was a hot topic. Missouri was split North and South, respectively.

In the summer of 1853, the militia moved from Greenville South to Marion, Illinois, a day's ride on a fast horse. Logan grew up in the neighboring county of Jackson in the town of Murphysboro, Illinois and attended law school in Shiloh, Illinois. One of Logan's first assignments was district attorney for the city of Shawneetown, on the Ohio River where he had met his wife Mary, while visiting her father, while she attended a Catholic school for girls in Uniontown, Kentucky.

Her father was Logan's boss and he asked for her hand even though she was still in school. Eventually he agreed, but only if Logan promised to wait tell she graduated.

Talk of an impending secession of states over the slavery issue consumed the editorial pages of Kentucky, Tennessee, Virginia, Southern Illinois, Southern Missouri and Kansas. Especially in Kansas, which had yet to decide whether to enter the Union.

Sergeant Thomas Akins woke from a night of drinking at the local tavern in Greenville. He had left Hills Fort the afternoon before on a sortie for Captain Logan, to load up a supply wagon.

Sergeant Akins had built up a powerful thirst loading fifty-pound bags of flour and salt pork. Corporal Adams always went with the sergeant on supply forays. After a few drinks at the saloon, they finally bought a bottle.

"Corporal, break out that bottle."

"Sarge, you know Logan will have our heads if we show up soused."

"You let me worry about the Captain. That's an order, Corporal."

The Corporal weaved, trying to reach behind his back, fumbling around underneath the bags looking for one of the bottles he always tried to sneak inside the fort. Akins took his hat off and wiped the sweat from his forehead.

"Come on, hurry it up. It will be dark before we get back. What the heck are you doing back there?"

Adams turned to look back at the sergeant. Weaving, he lost his balance on the bench and fell off the wagon on his back. He looked at Akins and let go a inebriated guffaw.

"Dang you, Corporal. You're soused."

"Well gee, Sarge. I'm sorry. Now, where's that bottle? Right here, Sarge," he replied, after stumbling back to the buckboard and reaching under the bench seat.

"If you're going to drink with me, Corporal, you're going to have to hold your liquor better than that. Give me that."

Sergeant Akins stood over Corporal Adams and took a long drink from the bottle.

"Man, that's good." wiping his mouth with his sleeve."

The corporal looked over his shoulder and burped. "Rider coming, sir."

"I can hear a dang horse when it approaches."

The rider reined in the cantering horse, kicking up dust which covered the sergeant and Corporal Adams.

"Dangit, what's you're damn hurry, private?"

"Captain sent me looking for you two, sir."

"What's he worrying himself for?"

"We're leaving Fort Hill for a new location in the morning. He was concerned you weren't going to make it back tonight."

"Damn blasted him. I know how to follow orders." Akins slid the bottle underneath one of bags discreetly. 'Get off your backside, corporal. Time is wasting."

Sergeant Akins bent down to lace up his boots and burped so loud it echoed through the night air.

Captain Logan was already dressed in full uniform even though the militia had not yet been acknowledged by the state. He watched Akins come out enlisted officer's barracks, noting his red eyes and how he rubbed his temples with his fingers. *Hangover.*

"Reveille in ten minutes, sergeant."

"Aye, sir," replied Akins, saluting, as he headed over toward the first barrack. Private Younger woke to the sound of Akins banging his hand hard on the door.

"Wake up you low life landlubbers, on the double!"

Frank rolled out of his bunk. "Why the hell is he using Navy talk?"

"Don't rightly know, but I wouldn't ask him," Cole answered. He's a testy one."

"You don't want to find out either," one of the other men answered.

Gathering up their gear, their horses already saddled and ready to go as they lined up in front of their horses at attention as the bugler blasted reveille as they saluted the flag. Frank twitched when the small cannon went off, as Henry brought Logan's horse around.

Once Logan mounted, the order was given for the troop to mount by twos. The flag and fife crew stayed at the fort playing while Logan trotted passed them and saluted with the rest of the troop followed. Three mules with supply packs and a covered cook wagon traveled behind.

"What's this Logan fella like?" Frank asked Cole as the men rode alongside each other.

"A militarily booker."

"One of the men told me he was just a politician."

"He is, but he's not a copperhead, I can tell you that."

"Quiet in the ranks you two. Keep on yapping your jaws, you can bring up the rear with the skinners."

Cole looked at Frank and grinned. *Going to be fun*, Frank thought.

The next couple of years passed quick as the men built a camp in Williamson County in Illinois. Boredom set in for Frank until one day, two years since joining up with the militia, his brother, Jesse, stumbled into camp, starved and ragged from searching for his brother.

"Rider approaching!" One of the camp's gate guards hollered.

"Can you make him out?" Sergeant Akins asked.

"No Sir, looks to be a bit ragged sir."

By then, Akins had already reached the top of the wall's guard area and took out an eyepiece.

"We'll keep a close eye on him till he reaches far enough to hear us."

"Not moving very fast, Sarge."

"I have eyes, private; whoever he is, he looks kind of sickly. State's your business, young'un! I said state your business young'un before I order my guard to put a ball in ya."

"That dang horse is moving like he doesn't have a rider, sir."

"Go down there and see what he's up to, private; while I keep a bead on him."

"Open the gate!" With his rifle at the ready, Private Edwards reached the young man cautiously.

"He doesn't look too well, Sarge."

"Grab him, Private; he's falling."

The boy collapsed into Edward's arms. "Easy there, young'un; where you hurt?"

Edwards took the riders canteen off its perch on the saddle. "Canteen's empty, sir."

A crowd of men gathered at the gate. "James, fetch that man water."

"Yes, sir."

Frank hurried and ladled a scoop of water into a cup from a nearby water barrel and ran over to the boy laying on the ground. When Edwards stepped back, Frank gasped.

"My God, it's my little brother, Jesse! Jesse... Jesse, wake up!"

Frank poured some water on his brother's forehead and wiped Jesse's face with his wet hand.

"Here, take a drink."

Putting the canteen to the boy's mouth, Jesse coughed and opened his eyes.

"I... I... am looking... for Frank. For... Frank James."

"I'm right here, Jesse. Help me get him inside on a cot. It's alright, Sarge; he's my little brother."

"Help Frank get his brother to the infirmary."

Being family, Cole was the first to help. "What do you suppose he's here for Frank?"

"No idea, Cole, but sure we'll find out in due time."

After a few weeks of Jesse coming in and out of consciousness, thrashing beneath the covers, and Frank ladling more water down his throat, Frank paced back and forth as the doctor checked on his condition.

"Not going to do ya any good pacing around like that, Frank," said Bob.

"He knows, Bob. I'd be doing the same thing," replied Cole.

Chapter 6

Spring 1861
Williamson County
Southern Illinois

In the early spring of 1860, the militia had been training as hard as any army.

"You think Captain Logan is going to side with the Yankees?" Bob Younger asked.

"Could go either way, I reckon. Fairly sure of one thing though, Akins sure as hell won't follow Anderson," replied Cole.

"Whose side you on, Frank?"

"You know me, Bob, I always side with family, Quantrill's family. It's how Jesse and I've always played it."

"Jesse seems to be getting a little deeper into it."

"Yea, I know; he's my brother, remember?"

"Quiet, someone's approaching," Bob stated.

"Frank. Bob," whispered Jesse as he squatted down next to them.

"Hey, Jesse, just talked to Quantrill. Seems we are not waiting for Logan to return with a decision; the lieutenant just received a telegraph from Washington. The Confederate Army just attacked Ft. Sumter in Virginia; so, we're all heading back to Missouri."

"What do you suppose that means for us?" Jesse asked.

"Don't know about you guys," replied Bob, "but Quantrill said he received a message from Anderson, and we've been ordered to quietly leave in the dead of night. Three a.m.

sharp without allowing suspicion. Pass the word and take whatever you can carry - food, water, and ammo."

"Hey, we should steal the ammo supply wagon. Dix, the ammo guard, is with us."

"Good idea, Bob, I'll pass the word to Quantrill, Is Cole in the barracks?"

"Yea, they're all hitting the sack."

"Well, see if you can rouse them without arousing suspicion."

"What do we do with Akins? He sure not let us leave without a fight."

"Tie his ass up and gag him. Knock him out if you have to."

"Why don't we just put a knife in him and be done with it? Be one less damn blue belly to worry about."

"Not a good idea," Frank stated, thinking about what the Yanks did to his stepfather. "Cold-blooded killing, that's the Yankee way, and I am not cotton to what a damn Yankee does, even if it is war."

"Frank's right, Bob. He's taken good care of us."

Jesse looked at his pocketwatch. "It's two now," Jesse said, gazing up at the moonless sky full of clouds – a perfect night for a getaway.

"I'll alert Dix and help him with the team."

"Alright Frank, Every-one meet at the corral."

And so, after the firing at Fort Sumter, dominoes fell and every southern state across the land fell away from the Union and the clashes began - Fort Adams-Louisville, Kentucky, Ft. Anderson-North Carolina, the Arsenal Academy-South Carolina, Fort Bliss, Texas; along with forts and arsenals in Florida, Georgia, Tennessee, Mississippi, Arkansas, Alabama, North and South Carolina, and Louisiana.

The arms and men stolen that night helped form the Confederate States of America's Army and Navy. Millions of rifles confiscated and used against their American brothers and cousins.

Cole Younger stood at the water basin preparing for a night's sleep. In a tiny mirror on the wall, he noticed a shadow approaching him, cast against the wall from the fireplace's flickering flame. Just about the time Bob reached him, Cole pulled his knife.

"Damn you, Bob. I just about stuck you."

Bob held his forefinger up to his lips for him to be silent.

"What's going on?"

"It's tonight," Bob whispered as he pointed to Akins snoring away in his bunk. "Tie him up and gag him."

Cole nodded, moving to the head of the cot. Cole reached around Akins under his jaw with his arm and stifled Akin's cry with a hand over his mouth and the Bowie knife at his nose.

Akins struggled, but in a flash, Bob grabbed a rope and sat on top of him. With arms flailing, Cole took his leg and pinned Akins left arm under the crook of his knee, threatening to snap the bone if he moved one more time.

One of the bunkmates rose up from a drowsy sleep. "Hey what you guys doing over there?"

"Shut the hell up and get over here and help us."

Johnson got up from his cot and stumbled over, still half-drunk from the night before.

"Grab his arms so I can put this knife up before he cuts himself," Cole ordered. Akins gave up, realizing he might be able to fight two men off from a dead sleep, but not three.

They sat him up and finished tying him. "Get him a drink before we gag him," Bob ordered Johnson. Johnson grabbed a metal cup from the table that still had whiskey in it from the night before.

"Damn you!" exclaimed Cole, right after Akins spit the whiskey back in Cole's face.

"You're going to pay for this, you treasonous bastards."

Last thing Akins remembered was staring at Cole's fist before it connected between the bridge of his nose and eyes. They finished binding him up and pushed him back on his bunk.

"Always wanted to do that," said Cole.

The rest of the men in the barracks where Akins lay tied up were southern sympathizers from the same area where the Youngers and James families grew up.

They joined Logan's militia because they felt Logan would be the best choice for continuing their fight against Union tyranny thrust upon the poor farmers along the Western border between Kansas and Missouri.

Quantrill smiled at the men who chose to meetup in the woods at 2 a.m.

"Last chance," he stated. No one budged or thought to turn back. Quantrill glared over his shoulder, back to the fort. "Go to hell, then, blue belly. We will see them on the battlefield. Sergeant, expose the colors."

The sergeant trotted up to the soldier beside Quantrill, reached up and yanked the cover off a black flag that read in white letters: "Quantrill's Raiders".

The troop started out at a slow trot until the last two trailing the ammunition wagon left the fort. After that, they broke into a fast gallop, leaving the Union behind.

The first year of the war saw some of the bloodiest guerrilla-style revenge fighting along the Missouri and Kansas borders. Most of Quantrill's men farmed and had families along the Dixie area, including the James and Younger's family.

Guerrilla tactics often resulted in pillage of Unionist farms. If a farmer was found to be a sympathizer, he was hung in his front yard as a warning to other would-be Union sympathizers. *Like for like*, Jesse thought.

Chapter 7

Late July 1861
Washington, D.C.

President Lincoln turned away from a small lit fireplace and eyed his newest chief of staff wiping his forehead with a handkerchief.

"General Halleck, I saw your report on the Western Theater along the Kansas/Missouri border. These guerrilla outfits must be squashed if we are to keep the rebels out of Missouri. We must control the Mississippi above all else."

General Halleck stood and unraveled a map of the Missouri and Kansas border. He reached over and sat an oil lamp on the edge of the map, spreading it out on a table, and taking a pointer, he ran the brass tip from St. Joseph, Missouri down along the border to an area known as Dixie.

"Intelligence suggests there are two different groups. operating at proximity. We have Quantrill's Raiders operating from Dixie here in the South up to Lawrence, Kansas. The other group runs from Lawrence up to St. Joseph. This one is led by a man they call bloody Bill Anderson. Believe me, his name says it all. Anderson is the main reason the press is calling Kansas, "Bleeding Kansas".

"They're on the move constantly, both groups have been known to band together."

"How do you intend to stop these guerrillas?"

"I have put a lot of thought regarding this problem, Mr. President. We need a man that can trail this group without attracting attention, so we can set a trap for these fellas."

"Have anyone in mind?" Lincoln asked.

"Yes, sir. Marshal McCann. He's quite capable, sir."

"Then let's get him started forthwith."

"It'll be put in motion as soon as I get back to the office, Mr. President."

"Make sure he gets what he needs."

"Yes, Mr. President."

Lincoln turned back to the fireplace and rubbed his forehead. *If I can regain control of the western Missouri border and shut these guerrillas down once and for all, I can concentrate on the heart of the Confederacy. Atlanta,* he thought.

"Madge, Madge? Now where did she get off to?" General Halleck murmured to himself. As he turned to go back into his office, his secretary rustled papers behind him.

"You need something, sir?"

"Yes, I do. Bring your pad and come into the office. We need to get a dispatch sent off at once."

"Right away, sir."

Madge worked for General Halleck ever since he made Major General and followed him to Washington when he joined Lincoln's administration as General Chief of the Armies. He looked up from his desk as Madge entered the office, watching her as she settled in the leather chair and awaited his instruction.

"Ready?"

"Yes, sir."

"Take this down. Attention: McCann, stop. Beekeeper, Repeat, Beekeeper. Proceed step two. No connections as usual. Stop. Communication will be after mentioned in earlier communication. Stop. Beekeeper, top priority. Follow protocol. Kansas/Missouri border. Stop. From G. H.

"As for you, Madge, follow protocol for scripted messages as soon as this telegraph is sent. Destroy this before you come back."

"Yes sir, General."

Since the war an everyday discussion in the White House, Maddie Cronin manipulated her way into the hierarchy of the Administration by whatever means, with the help of her brother and Vice-President Breckenridge.

As she walked back to her desk, the memory of the night President Buchanan, being the only single President, invited her to a ball at Josiah's recommendation. Her brother had his own agenda, courting the President's friendship like a devoted knight. Both laughed at how Breckinridge manipulated Halleck into keeping Maddie on after Buchanan's defeat. The one access to Lincoln's General Chief of Armies that the "Cause" coveted.

Breckinridge was a main participant of the *Knights of The Golden Circle* and managed to divert millions of the Union's funds, as well as hand over the keys to all the Southern forts, armaments, and whatever else he could do under Buchanan's nose.

Nowadays, with all the chaos of the war, a constant crowd scurried back and forth down the hallways in the White House from office to office.

I hope Daniel is in his office, she thought.

Daniel Cronin sat at his desk as Maddie, his sister, tapped the glass window to get his attention. She could make out the hazy outline through the frosted glass of her brother behind his desk and another man seated in a chair in front of him.

"Hold that thought a minute, Willington, sis is knocking."

Daniel put his suit coat on and opened the door, stepping into the hallway. "What is it?"

"You need to see this."

"Important?"

"Important? Yes, and in code," Maddie answered.

He took her note pad and read over the message. "Interesting; you know anything about Bee- Keeper?"

"Not really, but whatever it is, is already in motion."

"See if you can find out who is on the receiving end, but be careful. Don't prod the General too much. Don't want to arouse suspicion."

"He doesn't have much arousal left in him I would think," she said with a sly look.

"You're terrible."

"Yes, I know. I'll let you know when I find out anything more," she said, giving him a wink as he closed the door.

Down in the communications room she tried her best to steal a glance of who the message was being sent to, but the operator slid the paper away from her gaze.

"I can destroy this. You don't have to watch me send it."

"Why, darling, that's alright; I have orders from General Halleck. I must return it to him post haste per his explicit orders."

The man grimaced and narrowed his eyes. "Highly unusual for Top Secret messages."

She shrugged. "All I know the orders came from the Vice-President himself."

"Suit yourself, you can have a seat there."

She sashayed over to the settee near the telegraph stations. "Why thank you, kind sir. I've been with Halleck ever since he made General, and I declare I don't recall ever being down here," Maddie said, batting her eyelashes and watching the operator's cheeks turn a deep pink.

The tap, tap, tap of the transmitter keys filled the room as ten operators sent messages across the telegraph lines. Out of the corner of his eye, the operator watched Maddie still glancing to the paper on his desk.

I need to let Halleck know his secretary has prying eyes, he thought to himself.

He slid the top secret papers beneath the machine, then finished sending off the message.

"Here you go, ma'am; all finished."

"Thank you so kindly."

"Someone need to help you find your way back?"

"No, I'll manage. Thanks again."

"Pleasure is all mine."

After Maddie sped her way back up the stairs, and he saw her shadow disappear, he leaned back in his chair and hollered towards the back office door.

"Jones!"

"Yea, what do you need?" poking his head out the communications office. The operator wrote down a note in a rush and handed it to Jones.

"Don't take the time to read it. Get it over to Secret Service at once. Run; don't walk."

"Yes sir!" he replied, heading out the door.

"Didn't expect you so soon, dear brother," Maddie said, looking up at her brother who leaned over her desk. Daniel held his forefinger to his lips showing silence and handed Maddie a note.

She unfolded the paper and read.

They are on to us or are suspecting we are the White House leaks. We must go now. No time to wait. If you know where the escape tunnel secret door is, nod, and meet me there in five minutes. Nod if you understand.

Maddie's usual sunny disposition shadowed over with fear and she nodded.

Daniel turned and headed down the hall as he always did, acting completely normal so as to not attract attention. Maddie at once grabbed her things, pausing long enough to pull her small derringer from her garter at the top of her stockings, checking to make sure it was loaded, and headed out the door, praying she would not run into Halleck along the way. Another fleeting memory flashed in her mind, the day Breckenridge gave the derringer to her while they were still wrapped together in the satin sheets after a fierce passionate encounter.

"It's not just for your protection dear," he had said. "I expect you to use it on yourself if you should be found out. They torture and hang spies, especially those of us working directly in the White House."

She glanced in a mirror above the mantel, put on her hat and gloves, and took a breath, trying her best to keep calm. She closed her eyes to say a little pray without arousing suspicion as two of the other secretaries passed by in the hallway, the message ringing loud and clear as one of them peeked in the doorway.

"Maddie, have you heard the news?"

She took another breath and acted like nothing unusual was happening. "No, what's going on?"

"Stanton's on his way over and he has Secret Service Agents with him. Everyone's in a frenzy."

"Oh, my. Thanks for letting me know. Do you know why?"

The woman shrugged and continued on down the hall, while Maddie's insides roiled with fear.

Oh, God help me.

Easing into the hall, she made her way along the corridors, downwards to the tunnel entrance, then froze as a few of the staffers stopped in front of her. And then she saw why.

"The men are ready, Mr. Secretary Stanton."

The Secretary gathered the guard detail after reading Jones' note.

"Thank you, show them in."

"Captain Derrickson, are the men ready?"

"Yes, waiting outside, sir."

"Very well, time to arrest these traitors."

The two men walked side by side, followed by four of the Secret Service armed guards.

"Is the President secure?"

"Yes, first thing we did."

"Excellent."

As they entered a side door one of the guards approached Derrickson. "We have a male cornered at the tunnel entrance, sir. The female has not been located yet."

"Very well lead on."

Maddie, unable to unfreeze her legs, looked for a place to disappear. The Secret Service had Daniel cornered. He was kneeling with his hands claps together behind his neck, and an agent pressed a rifle stock to Daniel's chest as he coughed, trying to catch his breath.

Her heart raced, not because of what was happening to Daniel, but what was about to happen to her if she stayed watching the events unfold in front of her like a nickelodeon picture show. Suddenly, she heard a whispering voice.

My God, she thought, *Am I losing it? I am hearing things in my mind.*

Then, she heard it again. A staffer she'd seen a few times talking with Daniel stood in a side doorway in the hall. She had her forefinger to her mouth and motioned for Maddie to follow her. Maddie recognized her as one of the many maids who worked throughout the offices and the President's residence.

"We must hurry!" the young girl whispered. "Half the ring has been found out."

Maddie followed her to a private room, where the woman tilted one of the candle scones at the fireplace mantel. The whole fireplace shifted, revealing a secret stairway down to the lower depths of the White House.

Maddie's mind raced as she watched her rescuer light a candle as they spiraled down the stairway, reaching the bottom tunnel.

"Come on; this way," the woman said, holding the candle up before them and illuminating the dark hallway.

Maddie chuckled nervously. "Are you for real, or are you leading me into the spider's web?"

"Shhhh, I don't know if the Secret Service has agents at the other end. President Jackson had this tunnel built after the War of 1812 in case he ever needed to leave quickly."

Two concrete stairs led deeper and to a slatted wooden door. She grabbed the handle and pushed open, the outside sunshine blinding her. She turned to say something to the maid, but the woman was already gone.

Breckinridge's carriage sat nearby and the driver waved to her as she raced across and dove into the opened door.

"Hurry, driver, at once," Breckinridge commanded. He leaned in the door and whispered to Maddie, who gasped for breath. "You've been compromised. We must get you out of here now."

She nodded and cowered near the floor of the carriage, patting down her skirts and hiding her head below the windows after Breckinridge closed the door. The carriage lurched forward as the horses whinnied and charged at the sound of the driver's whip. Maddie lost her balance, stumbling and grabbing the opposite door's handle causing it to crack open. She sat back against the bottom of the leather seat, slamming the door shut after regaining her composure.

Only then did her mind drift back to her brother, who now awaited his fate at the end of a rope.

One question loomed in her mind. *Who betrayed them and why?* Good thing Breckinridge was on board, or she'd be suffering the same fate as Daniel. Tears welled up in her eyes at the thought of her brother's situation.

She waited a bit before moving back up to the seat for fear of being recognized, riding in Breckenridge's carriage as it maneuvered its way through D.C.'s streets in the noon crowds.

After a little while, when she recognized the tops of the buildings through the window, she knew they were close to the train station and she sat up and straightened her voluminous skirt. The carriage slowed to a stop. Maddie took out her brass compact mirror from her silk purse and brushed back the stray hairs which escaped from her bun as the driver opened the door for her.

"Where am I to go?"

"There's a horse tied up on the other side of the station, all ready for you. Hole up in Manassas and keep a low profile. When this blows over, contact Jefferson and let him know your new alias. Find someplace where there are plenty of soldiers about so you can gain trust and information. Good Luck. It's been a pleasure knowing such patriots."

Maddie smiled, wondering again about her brother. "Shall I ever see Daniel again?"

"War is strange ma'am; who knows our fate but God?"

He helped her down from the carriage and she watched as he climbed back up to the driver's seat, popped the reins and disappeared down the lane. Maddie lowered his head and the veil from her hat across her face, yet all the crowd of people at the station paid no attention to the Vice-President's carriage arriving at the platform... or its passenger.

Instead of going straight through the depot, she walked around the side, glancing back to assure herself there were no followers. And just as the driver said, a lovely brown gelding stood waiting, nickering and stomping his feet as she approached. Attached to the back was a tapestry bag and she unlatched the clasp to peer inside. Breckinridge thought of everything – clothes and food for the journey to Manassas.

"Hi there, fella." She calmed him and herself with a soft stroke across his nose. "Ready for a ride?"

She mounted and straddled the saddle, her skirts cascading over her feet in the stirrups. She kicked and leaned into a quick canter, getting as far away as possible as she wove the horse through the streets and out of Washington.

After an hour or so at that speed, and noting the sweaty lather on the horse's neck, she slowed him down to an easy walk and breathed deep the soft afternoon breeze rustling through the trees.

"Well, now," she said to the horse. "Who should I be now, fella? Mmm, haven't used the name Kathleen for a while. Yes, I do believe I like that for now. And we have to name you since I have no idea who you are. How about Buddy since you are my buddy in this escape?"

The horse nodded his head and nickered, appearing to approve the choice.

After following Bull Run on her way to Manassas for a while, a group of Union soldiers came upon her while Buddy stepped carefully along the trail bordering the creek. She gripped the reins with one hand and clutched her derringer with the other, knowing her position precarious as a woman alone in the woods. Yet, she knew how to take care of herself.

"I wouldn't hang around here, ma'am," one of the officers said as they walked near. "Rebels are gathering around Manassas. You realize you are heading right smack into the middle of a battle, Miss?"

"Can you tell me sir if there is a farm close by? I've traveled down to help at the hospital near here."

He pointed southward. "If you keep following this turnpike you will run into it and right smack into the war."

"Oh, my!"

"The medics are setting up a field hospital at the farmhouse. We can use all the help we can get."

"Thank you, sir, and good luck to you all."

She trotted down the road to the farmhouse and tied her horse behind the barn, hoping it was far enough and out of harm's way. Soldiers scurried about like army ants preparing for battle. Someone barked an order to a not-so-young Lieutenant in a dingy battle-soiled uniform and scruffy beard.

"Lieutenant McCann, set up the battery facing this of side of the creek."

"Yes sir!" McCann answered.

Her contacts within the "Cause" insisted on concentrating on agents within Lincoln's inner circle.

"The big fish, first, always."

Two days before, during the transmission of the telegram, she received the name of her next mark, a Lieutenant McCann, a suspected Union Intelligence Officer, the directive coming directly from the commanding officer at West Point. One thing she never expected was for him to be so handsome or to find him here in Manassas.

"Are you looking for someone Miss?"

"I'm a volunteer, here to help."

"Excellent," the doctor said as he washed the blood from his hands in an already red-drenched water basin. "We need all the help we can get. I hope you're not squeamish around lots of blood, body parts, and the dead."

"No, I am not, I'm Kathleen, by the way," extending her hand, but the doctor held up his hand, not wanting to soak her silk gloves. He pointed at a nearby nurse who fluffled a pillow beneath a soldier's head.

"Andrea, right there, can get you squared away."

Maddie walked up near to her as the woman set her hands on her ample hips and eyed her up and down. Maddie extended her hand, to which Andrea shook with a limp paw and disapproving scowl.

"Well, I hope you brought something more fittin' to wear. Those fancy things of yours won't last with as much blood as we see here. I welcome you, and it won't be long you'll get your first taste of what its like here. We should have another group arriving from the field soon. You can start tearing those petticoats of yours into long strips for bandages at that table over by the window."

Maddie's stomach heaved as the smell of death and festering gangrene smoldered in the summer heat. She hurried over to the table and stuck her head out the window. *Why would anyone want to do this for a living? But I'm here for a purpose, and now that fate has brought the mark in such easy reach... well, all should go as planned.*

She saw him from the window. Something about the way his dark hair curled on his neck and those piercing blue eyes made her stomach flip-flop. *This isn't going to be as easy as I thought, and besides... why is Jefferson worried about a lowly Lieutenant? Shouldn't we be concentrating on a Major or someone higher?*

She drew a breath, sucking in the fresh air, and steadied her heart and mind. The years she spent honing her manipulative powers over men of power and wealth were legendary, according to the very men who she brought under her spell. The easy part with this mark, however, was that she found McCann extremely sensual, with an animal-like magnetism she had never felt, except once in her life before... for Josiah, her half-brother and former husband.

Haunting memories flooded her mind and she gripped the edge of the window frame. Her powers of seduction and manipulation she learned well from the age of thirteen as a way to deal with the uninvited attention from her own father. Of course, she didn't understand at first, because no one, especially not her timid mother, discussed such intimacies, so she assumed her father's assurance that all the young girls her age spent the evenings with their fathers.

For years he was an absent father to her as a child, but things changed as she grew taller and her breasts rounded.

"Turn over," he'd say to her as he crawled in the bed beside her. Sometimes he only sat beside the bed, watching her sleep. Only, she wasn't sleeping. Other times, he'd stroke her hair and whisper his made-up excuse of 'it's a father's privilege to be his daughters first.' The same excuse he used to control her like he did her mother, all saturated in the rank smell of liquor.

And then, the one evening which changed everything, and freed her from his abuse. The door handle to her room twisted and over his heaving shoulder she watched the moonlight cast a glow down the hallway as the door swung open. Her father, too busy satisfying his lust remained oblivious to the light, until the sound of the hammer on the pistol cocking back, and he rolled off to the side as her mother pulled the trigger.

That scandal brought her mother in front of the Mexican Tribunal in lower California for attempted murder. Her father, powerful enough to avert consequences of his actions, escaped a bullet and fled to the Americas with his daughter. Her mother, however, was not so fortunate.

Goosebumps sped up her arm as the breeze whispered across her neck. *Why the memory now?* She wondered. *Why now should I remember the ghostly footsteps echoing down the hallway deep in the night and her mother's accusing glare?*

After all, in the end, she escaped his control, and became the one who controlled, instead. Her father no longer held power over her as he sank further and further into his alcoholic fog. She often thought of her mother as being timid, yet she saw a flash of courage that night when she fired the gun and when the Tribunal Guards hauled her away.

Perhaps the memories swarmed her mind due to the sudden and unexpected attraction to this man... Arnett McCann. Meeting him here, her targeted mark, was by design; the intense desire rousing in her heart was not. Arnett was suppose to be the enemy, but for some reason, he didn't feel like an enemy although they hadn't even shared two words to each other since her arrival. Yet, she had and would do anything for the "Cause", tucking the secret of the real reasoning behind their cause deep in her heart.

Mexico's involvement in helping the Confederacy meant to not allow emancipation of the slaves, but the politician's involvement was not the only reasoning. Helping Mexico however, to regain what it had lost with their war with America was a key factor in supporting the Confederate cause.

Josiah's expansive cotton plantation amassed massive influence with Maximillian, Mexico's new revolutionary leader, clothing and feeding his army, bankrolled by Josiah's family fortune on his mother's side. Only a few knew exactly, the reasoning behind the Cause.

Constance's marriage to Josiah, her own half-brother, contracted by her father, was her first introduction to how to handle powerful men. She learned her father's lessons well, seeing his manipulative control over her mother.

Maddie shook the memories from her head as one of the other nurses touched her on the sleeve and handed her a stack of linens with a knowing smile and wink. Maddie winked back, understanding the signal between two fellows for the "Cause" and set the linens down on the table. Rifling through the layers, she found a small note, read the inscription, then stuffed the paper in her mouth, chewed, and swallowed; coughing as the rough paper caught in her throat. She glanced over her shoulder at Andrea, the head nurse, who stood there with her hands on her hips pointing at the barrel of water in the corner.

"Water is over there. Now, stop standing there daydreaming. We have work to do."

Chapter 8

Arnett McCann
1861 - Battle of Bull Run

"Lieutenant."

"Yes Colonel." replied Arnett.

"Some Congressmen are going to follow us over to my tent for a briefing. Keep them occupied, while I prepare. Make them feel at ease, they well be accompanying us to Manassas tomorrow."

"Yes sir."

Arnett watched Logan enter the Secretary of War building, studying him intently. As a Lieutenant, who had never met Logan, many had talked of his reputation as a leader, and one could obviously see why they called him Black-Jack.

The whole Union Army was heading to Manassas, Virginia near a small river named Bull Run. Lincoln ordered all thirty-five thousand Union troops to march the twenty some miles from Washington D.C. to Bull Run River, where General Stonewall Jackson and 20,000 Confederate troops awaited word from Lee to advance toward America's capital.

Arnett with the rest of the officers, stood outside newly appointed Brigadier General, Irving McDowell's office, while giving the usual motivation speech to his commanders in the field.

"Gentlemen, the confederacy revolt must be put to an end now! The President wants these rebel law breakers to feel the wrath of the Union Army," he shouted, banging his fist hard on the mahogany desk.

Arnett was one of the first junior officers to notice

something in the works while seeing all the activity in and out of the General's office. He had been lucky enough when he graduated from West Point in the class of 1861, to bivouac outside of Washington, the Nation's capital.

From outside his tent, General McDowell's office lay straight across from him near the horse enclosure, which was his ideal location to spend his days and nights. He had always preferred to be around animals than most humans, with the exception of his wife Martha, his parents, and Doc Jansen.

Doc was a great friend who helped him through the loss of Martha. His parents died of the pox helping all they could to save what was left of Missourian tribe.

Then, Doc convinced a Kansas district judge to hire Arnett as a Deputy U.S. Marshal. Doc also helped Arnett with his application draft to enter West Point on encouragement from the judge, which neither knew the judge's real intent.

Arnett started as a Deputy U. S. Marshal's office out of Kansas City. The Department of Justice decided he was a perfect fit for the job they had in mind, grooming the Deputy during his days at West Point as a cadet, even though he was a bit older than most.

Once the Confederates fired upon Ft. Sumter in North Carolina, well laid plans from the Justice Department set in motion and outlined Arnett's future. His skillful studies during school had basically been turned into battle strategies and rules for engaging the enemy.

The Cadet's studies, like mathematics, came to a quick conclusion. The professors focused on one thing, to prepare them for the fundamentals of commanding troops in the field. Most were battle hardened from the Mexican War, a few of the instructors former senior officers from the War of 1812, of which one was the stable master, Davey.

Command field experience consisted of instructing the younger cadets, shoring up the bunkers, and guarding the outlying areas around Washington. Arnett and most of his

West Point classmates were assigned to the Army's third corps. Their job was the last defense of the Nation's Capital.

McDowell stood with his back to his desk rubbing his hand across his receding hairline and feeling a headache coming on. He walked over and gazed longingly at the drink decanter and empty shot glasses sitting there beckoning him.

"I'm not a field officer," he whispered, pacing back behind his desk and noticing a young lady through his window trying to wind her way across the dusty street with her skirt lifted with her hands. He rubbed his forehead again.

"This is insane, a disaster in the making," he whispered again, reaching for a drink this time. He continued to watch her weave through the maze of horses, buggies, and pedestrians as he sipped his whiskey.

"Captain," he hollered over his shoulder.

"Yes, sir?" Captain Anderson replied from the General's library, marking his place in one of the many law books the captain had access to thanks to the General. General McDowell fixated on the pretty lass crossing the street, realizing he saw her cross at almost the exact same time every day since he had been in Washington.

His fingers fumbled in his uniform breast pocket for his pocket watch. *Ten a.m., like clockwork. Too bad Congress' work is not as reliable*, he thought.

"Captain?"

"Yes sir?" Captain Anderson replied, still standing at attention in the doorway. McDowell drained the glass and turned around, frowning at this mousy thin fellow before him. He smirked at Anderson who waited for instructions. *How in the world did this fella ever make it through West Point? God we are in deep trouble.*

"Anderson, have Lieutenant McCann bring my buggy around. The other one, not the field one."

"Yes sir!" he replied, saluting.

"Now."

"Yes sir; right away sir. Thought you had something more to add."

"Don't think, Anderson, just do; clear?"

"Yes sir."

McDowell watched Anderson leave and looked down at the order on his desk. Time to go see what McClellan wants.

Lieutenant McCann sat with an arm in one of his boots and a polishing rag in the other one focusing on the job at hand. The General meticulously demanded clean boots when preparing for a march, and although he had no such orders for a mirror polish, his gut told him he best look his best.

The "gut-feeling" an acquired characteristic from his mother Annie. He remembered the day the Missourian showed up at their door beckoning for help. Times of concern and anguish , and memories of his mother always helped him stay calm. He looked up as Captain Anderson approached him.

Standing with the boot still on his arm, he waited on Anderson to reach him.

"McCann!"

"Yes Captain."

"Major General wants you to bring the buggy around; the parade buggy, not the field one."

"A parade sir?"

"No idea; just do it."

"Everything okay Wayne? General, giving you a hard time again?"

"You know how it is, Arnett, brass always has their hand up someone's ass. He just happens to like mine."

"Okay Wayne, on my way soon as I can get these damn boots situated."

Arnett walked to the stable, grabbed a harness and walked over to Daryl's stall. Patting his forehead, he led the fox trotter out of his stall and over to the General's parade buggy and hooked the harness up.

"Thought I heard someone in here," said a small man emerging from the shadows of the barn.

"Just me Davy."

"No one told me we were having a parade today."

"That's exactly what I told Wayne earlier," Arnett replied, chuckling. He put his white gloves on after getting on the buckboard. "Big brass meeting I suspect."

"Be easy with that old trotter. Bring him back in one piece."

"Will do. See you in a bit, Davy."

The old man watched Arnett roll the buggy out, scratching his gray beard as he took a puff off his pipe. *Now that is ironic,* he noted. *The captain should be changing places with McCann. Crazy ass Army.*

"Woah, Daryl. Morning, General, sir."

"At ease McCann," the General said, grabbing the roof rails and climbing aboard. "Brass quarters."

McCann clicked with his tongue, spurring the horse forward and slapped the harness straps soft against the horse's back. Daryl jerked forward and Arnett maneuvered the buggy around, making a U-turn and heading toward Washington. As the buggy sped down Pennsylvania Avenue, passing the Treasury building and up to the War Department, the July sun blazed hot and both men poured sweat.

Heavy cannon traffic and supply wagons heading out to the bivouac area toward the south packed down the dry dirt, leaving ruts in the road and dust clouding the hot air. Arnett wiped the back of his neck with his kerchief and pointed.

"Looks like something's up."

"Yes, I suppose so," the General replied. "Wait here for me."

"Yes sir."

Arnett helped the General down from the seat, catching him as the General's heel caught the buggy's foot pedal. Arnett grabbed his arm avoiding a terrible tumble.

The General chuckled. "Too damn tall for these things."

More like he is as nervous as a goat around a mountain lion, Arnett thought.

After the General went inside, Arnett watched a civilian walk up to the two guards, present his papers and entered the door. Arnett shook his head, amazed by the expensive duds the man wore, not to mention he'd never seen such jet black hair and mustache before in his life. *Most likely a politician,* he thought.

Inside the room, tensions rose.

"But Secretary Cameron, I'm not trying to be disrespectful or anything of such a great importance. I am just an administrator. I know nothing of battlefield strategies. I can get you the men and supplies you need for this war, but I am not someone you would want to command troops in the field."

"Sit, General. Look, I understand and appreciate where you are coming from; however, this is not going to be a good situation for anyone, me included. Look, our whole damn army officers, me included, are all green or too old from the 1812 war to do much good. You think the Confederacy is as well off or any better? The President has no choice. The Nation has no choice. Look, sometimes we are asked to do things we are not sure we are able to do."

The Pennsylvanian secretary sat back down at his desk and continued. "I am nothing more than a businessman sir. I know how to get things done. I am neither a soldier, nor a politician. You believe the Nation should stay together, General? Lincoln's message?"

The Secretary paused for a moment studying McDowell's face. His cheeks flushed a light reddish pink. He never meant for his own serious doubts to come out in such a fashion. They should have never gotten to this point in the first place.

"Sir, I apologize," replied the General, looking straight into the Secretary's eyes. "I've been unprofessional, unbecoming of a United States Officer."

"Accepted, Irving. I understand your concern for the well-being of your troops under your command. Nobody wants this war any less than you. However, Lincoln needs every able-bodied officer that can motivate this greenhorn army into a fighting machine. That is why the day after tomorrow you are going to take the Michigan First and head to Manassas in Prince William County here. The Confederates have around fifteen thousand on the other side of the river and more coming every day. What intelligence we have suggests they plan to attack D.C. We cannot let that happen, not again."

Another man entered the conversation.

"Colonel Wilcox, glad your Michigan bunch have joined this theater. This is General McDowell, the Commander."

"Commander Wilcox," McDowell said, extending his hand.

They shook hands. "Colonel."

"Now that the formalities are over, time to get to work," Cameron said, spreading the map of Virginia Commonwealth over his desk. The three men perused over the day's strategies.

"Gentlemen, this is where most of the rebels have been massing their troops along Manassas, just North of Richmond. If we can get your men to this creek."

"How many rebels, Mr. Secretary?"

"Balloon reports say around fifteen thousand and more coming every day. We have raw recruits overseeing the defense of D.C. New bunkers are being built, as we speak. We cannot, however, depend on them alone. It is imperative the first battle squash any uprising and not allow it to fester like a bad infection."

McCann stood at attention beside the general's buggy when two expensive buckboards adorned with American flags pulled up to the War Department. *Must be more politicians.* He scrutinized the five men as they exited the buggies.

One, in particular, stood out over the others as he stepped down off the buggy. At first Arnett thought it to be Lincoln, the new President, but quickly dismissed the thought.

Nah, can't be, no security to speak of, he whispered to himself. The two men gazed at each other a minute, both pondering whether they knew each other.

The man looked to be in his early thirties, unlike the other gentlemen who looked older and more refined, both wearing top hats and expensive suits. One of the gentlemen walked up the short stairs toward one of the guards and spoke a few words with him.

Arnett turned his attention back toward the only younger gentleman, the only one not wearing a hat. His hair was thick and coal black, and he had broad shoulders and muscular arms outlined beneath his simple black homespun suit. He stared back at Arnett with black as night eyes beneath bushy eyebrows. Arnett never saw so much black on one man in his life, except for an undertaker.

"Secretary's aide will be here in a second, sir, he's briefing a couple of his generals at the minute."

"The aide?"

"No Sir, the Secretary."

The Congressman chuckled pointing his cigar at the young guard with a grin showing off perfectly straight white teeth, unsure whether to join in the laughter.

"No need, private, nobody else pays much mind to my jokes." The guard stood straight as an arrow, his eyes straight ahead and showing no emotion.

After a few minutes, the aide escorted the two new gentlemen into the parlor.

"Good morning gentlemen, I am Captain Anderson, General McDowell's aide. Yes, I am doing double duty these days. I am sure this meeting will not last much longer. The Secretary will see you now."

"Thank you, Captain."

The Secretary shook one of the men's hands. "Governor Sprague, nice to see you again and I thank you for your state's response."

"Your welcome, Secretary Cameron."

"Senator Wade, likewise; Congressmen Wilson, Lane Washburn, welcome."

"Mr. Secretary, this is the young Congressman from Illinois' ninth district. Congressman John a. Logan. He's the gentleman who wrote the letter requesting to be allowed to watch an early end to this nonsense of secession."

"Thank you, General Wilcox. Glad to meet you, Congressman Logan," he said, extending his hand and shaking Logan's. "I want you gentleman to know the President and I, as well as the rest of the country want to squash this rebellion as quickly as possible; however, we realize this may turn out to be more difficult the longer we wait. Therefore, General Scott under General McDowell's command, will take the First Michigan to Bull Run at early morning's light.

"Observers can watch from the hill at Spindle's farm. I ask, for your safety, that you try not to get too close to the fighting. Stray artillery and bullets kill; battle is not a pretty sight."

"How many soldiers do the rebels have, sir?"

"Well, Governor, not enough to whip us," he replied, chuckling. "The recent balloon reports suggest about ten thousand, however the weather has not been cooperating.

"That is why we are sending two armies. Your carriage drivers can follow the First at a safe distant down to Centerview Hills. Be aware, it is an eight-hour march. It will be hot, dusty, and a bumpy ride."

"Do you know who is commanding the Confederates, Mr. Secretary?"

"That's a good question. What's your name, again, sir?"

"Representative Logan, John Logan, sir. Most in my neck of the woods call me Captain."

"Captain? I thought you were a Representative?"

"I am Sir, from the Illinois Ninth District. I run the Southern Illinois state militia.

"Well, Captain, a good officer knows who his opponent is and studies his tactics thoroughly."

"I agree, Mr. Secretary. I was a Lieutenant in the Mexican War."

"We may have to have a talk later, Mr. Logan."

"Part of the reason I am here, sir".

The men chortled and slapped each other on the back.

"Gentlemen, I suggest you rest well. Tomorrow will be a long day. Take care of your own needs, gentlemen. Army has enough problems. Good day to you all."

Wilcox motioned for Logan to follow him outside.

"General Wilcox, I appreciate the use of your carriage and driver. I have neither the time nor the knowledge of the D. C. protocol for such matters. I am one the only freshman

Congressmen making this observation trip to Manassas," said Logan.

The two gentlemen walked down the stone spiral staircase. General Wilcox, dressed in his full blue Army uniform, scrubbed his scabbard against the stone wall as they made their way to the front entrance of the War Department building conversing in whispers.

"You say you've seen some action before in Mexico?"

"Yes General; I was a Lieutenant. However, I was not on the front lines, but I have seen the not so pretty results of war. I would like to get as close as safely possible tomorrow. My constituents in Illinois have not fully grasped the meaning of secession from the Union, and I would like to see for myself as to how serious the Confederacy is, when they stare face to face the consequences of their actions."

"Well, Congressman, I assure you we aim to squash them like ants. We have sent Patterson's army to block Johnson from joining Beauregard by going around their left flank, while we get our men into position at Centerville. Twenty-five miles between here and Centerville, Tomorrow will be a long day but a quick resolution to this rebellion. You can observe from the battery. Lieutenant McCann will know where to place you out of harm's way."

Logan saluted. "See you in the morning, General."

Logan paused and pondered a minute, watching as Lieutenant McCann held the door while the General entered the carriage. He had no idea where the path he was about to take would lead him, or the thirty-five thousand men he would be going with.

July 21st, 1861
Four a.m.

Arnett looked up from his cot at a fly in his tent which interrupted his early morning ritual of entering his thoughts, hopes, and prayers of the day in his journal. Deep in thought, the fly buzzed into his brain as he scrawled out a letter to his daughter, Annie.

"Dear daughter, I cannot help but think of only you in the earliest of the morning. If, whether I shall be able to make my final entry at the end of this fretful day. For on this day, we shall at last engage the treasonous classmates who resigned a week ago to fight against the Union.

Be assured, my lovely girl, that I will not be on the front lines, but instead have received orders to field the mules pulling the artillery, and to go with a group of politicians who are here to watch today's impending battle.

I miss you terribly and know not of when or if I will see you again. And so, I leave you to return to making honey and raising mules for the army.

- Father."

"Lieutenant McCann," called out Anderson as he stuck his head in McCann's tent.

"Yes sir, Captain Anderson. Be out in a minute."

Arnett looked at the pad's unfinished notes, shook his head and rubbed his hands through his brown hair. After pulling his boots, he sat the note pad on the small table next to his cot, then hurried outside to meet the Captain.

"Looking sharp, just like you graduated, a sure-fire West Point Officer."

"Thank you, sir."

Captain Anderson tugged on his goatee and spit out a chump of tobacco. "I was being sarcastic, soldier," Anderson said.

"Sorry, sir; I don't have an ear for sarcasm."

Anderson huffed. "Orders have changed, McCann. Rebels amassed earlier than expected on the other side of Bull Run. You are commanding the battery."

"Captain? I am just a Lieutenant."

"I know your rank, Lieutenant. Haven't you heard? We are at war. If you're lucky enough to survive you just might make Captain."

"Yes, sir; who do I go see?"

"Sergeant Jordan is getting the horses ready for transport, Report to him and make sure everyone knows their job. Keep them from getting those mules all worked up. I understand you know a little about horses and mules?"

"Born and raised around them my whole life, sir."

"Take half the battery over to Mathew's Hill and the other one over to Dogan Ridge. Sergeant Jordan will oversee them. Use flag signaling just like in the manual. If the smoke gets too thick, use couriers. Good luck. Get going already, soldier!"

"Yes, sir," Arnett replied with a snappy salute. He saddled his gray mare and headed for the makeshift corral at the rear of the encampment.

The infantry of the Michigan First had just rose from their tents. Major Bidwell commanded four hundred and seventy-five enlisted men. Twenty-five officers barked out orders as Arnett rode slowly through the mayhem of men scrambling before battle, while the officers continued screaming, red-faced and urgent.

An ocean of white tents stretched before him, fires glistening in the early morning light before sunrise as blue uniformed men scurried about, following orders. Arnett wondered how many before him would see the light of the following sunrise... *or would he?*

Chapter 9

Confederate Encampment
Bull Run

"Sir."

"Yes, Corporal."

"General Johnston's men have arrived."

"Thank you, Corporal; send him in."

"Yes, sir."

General Beauregard unrolled a map of Manassas and pointed to the tiny river on the map named Bull Run.

"Assuming the Union troops will not advance across the river after a six-hour march, we can out flank them here. Now that Johnston is here, that brings our numbers up considerably. We can implement Lee's plan to the letter. How are your troops morale this morning?"

"Itching for a fight," replied General Jackson. 'After entering the tents, up and down the lines, I passed through the ranks about nine last night. The men are in good spirits."

"That's excellent news. We will draw them into Sedley Springs and place the guns up on the hills, here, at a downgrade. This will allow us to maximize the range and accuracy. Questions?" No one replied. "Okay, you have your orders; make Lee proud. This is where we take the fight straight up Lincoln's backside right into the White House."

General McDowell
Union Forces

"Wilcox arrive yet?"

"Yes, sir; they're forming their lines now on the other side of Sedley Spring on both sides of your flank. But we might have a problem, sir. We have a battery commanded by a young Lieutenant, recently graduated from West Point, a lieutenant named McCann. No combat experience nor the battery under him."

"They've been trained have they not?"

"Yes, sir."

"Nothing to worry about then. If they survive today, they will have earned their place. We'll split our forces when we're ready to attack and outflank them on both sides. Once we push the rebels back across the railroad, we will be able to cut the supply route to Richmond. Their reinforcements will be in the Shenandoah, as we speak. That will leave them with only eighteen thousand men. Out flank them here at Henry's Hill; we will have them surrounded." The General paused, looked at his pocket watch and continued.

"Two a.m.; time to get going. Major, take your men down to the Stone Ridge. See if we can catch them by surprise. You have thirty minutes to get started."

"Yes, sir!" he said, saluting as he left the General's tent.

The air was as dry as scavenged bones picked clean in the hot sun as the men scurried about. Morning fires still burned so as not to arouse the other side as the men formed ranks. Arnett's men reached their goal just below Henry's Hill to the left of Centerville.

The makeshift hospital was ready to receive the wounded and dead, and the men prepared the cannons along the ridge. As the early morning fog burned away from the river's surface, a hot and humid day emerged, beading sweat along their brows along with the fear in their eyes as they marched along the turnpike since two-thirty in the morning. Arnett ordered the animals fed before the march and again when they reached their goal.

As overseer of livestock, Arnett made sure their supplies contained at least a thousands of pounds of grain and hay a day depending how many days they were in the field. He dispatched four of his men just to cut hay in surrounding fields, using two teamsters on each four battery supply wagons, just to take care of the animals alone.

Scouts rode along both sides of the flank keeping their eyes and ears focused for possible ambushing rebels. The horses, with large round full stomachs and strong shanks carried the heavy yokes needed for pulling the wagons laden with plenty of ammunition and cannons.

Arnett scanned over the landscape with his field glasses, pausing for a moment to reread his orders.

"Sergeant!"

"Yes, sir."

"Have a look see at these orders. Tell me if you are reading, the same thing I am? This has got to be a mistake. We should be up on Henry Hill where we can best utilize our guns, not down her below."

"Glasses, sir?" he asked, after looking at the orders. "I do declare, Lieutenant, if the rebels cross our flank here, we will all be exposed. I am not in a hurry to be a prisoner or die this early in the game."

"Orders come straight from Wilcox, that's the only recourse, unless we can explain it to the captain."

"Too damn late anyhow, Lieutenant. They're massing troops three deep."

"Get the guns ready Sarge, while I keep an eye out for our signal to start firing."

"Right away, sir."

Arnett watched the Sergeant scramble over to his men who scampered about like red ants swarming an injured scorpion. He watched in amazement as the men unhitched the horses, moving them out of harm's way, the positioned the big 'fifteen-hundreds' in a row along with cannon balls tacked in pyramids.

Pride swelled in his gut watching them work together as a team, but concern followed over the fact that their commanding officer had no business being a field technician. For a brief moment, his mind drifted back to thoughts of Martha and Annie, then he took a deep breath and turned back to the task at hand.

General McDowell's men formed their lines opposite of the Confederates. Then, as if General McDowell read his mind, Arnett saw the signal.

"Fire!!"

He whirled around hollering to his men already aiming their guns and cannons at the ready.

"Fire!" he shouted.

Sixteen-pounders assaulted the Confederate lines. Raining down booming thunder and fire across their heads and filling the valley with spraying dirt and smoke. Boom, Boom, Boom, one after another, up and down the line the cannons pounded.

The onslaught continued for hours, on and on until early afternoon and Arnett's stomach growled from lack of food, along with the nausea as he watched fellow men, and the animals, fall like dominoes in pain. Screams of fear, blood streaming into the river waters, and a field of strewn body parts filled his eyes, and his nerves tingled, wondering if he was going to be next.

Both sides fired first with the smaller Parrots aimed at the other sides field artillery, then the Confederate's infantry first line lowered to their knees, pointed their rifles and fired toward the Union. Men dropped like flies. The smell of death and gunpowder permeated the hot summer air.

"Sergeant, fire the fifteen-hundreds!" Arnett screamed at the top of his lungs.

Kaboom, Kaboom, Fifteen-hundreds shook the ground, the trembles vibrating inside the soldier's ears, some losing their hearing as their brains absorbed the shock and knocking down a few of the men standing too close.

Arnett scanned the battlefield with his glasses, keeping track of McDowell or Wilcox's signalmen since missing a command might cost his men their lives. The roar of the shouting and gunfire echoed across the once peaceful hayfield as the Confederates regrouped after an infantry from the Union side.

This just might be it, Arnett thought.

Confederate General Jackson rallied the troops, shouting encouragement and motivating his men along the lines as hand-to-hand combat with bayonets broke out. The Confederate lines held and pushed back the Union lines.

A young private charged up to Arnett on horseback and handed Arnett a note, to which he read the orders without delay.

"Move up to Henry Hill. Repeat. Move up to Henry Hill immediately. General McDowell."

Arnett watched the young courier ride back to the lines, back into the thick of the action, then his body blown backward to the ground, writhing in pain with a a hole in his belly gushing blood. The boy gasped out, and Arnett thought to run to pull him to safety, but before he took a step, the boy stopped moving. A group of six or more Confederates rushed upwards, stomping across the boy's fallen body, their eyes full of fight and focusing on Arnett and his men.

From the sidelines, the safety of the Sedley Spring churchyard, Congressman Logan and his aide watched in horror as a cluster of Confederates raced towards Arnett's position. Arnett fired his pistol, shouting 'retreat', but before he could scramble to the top of the ridge, a bayonet ran through his side. Without thinking, Logan sprinted over to the lines, grabbing a rifle from a fallen victim, and fired, killing the Confederate in one shot and kicking him off Arnett. With his heart racing, he hoisted the Lieutenant over his shoulders and struggled to the hospital just as the Confederates broke through the lines. Arnett faded in and out of consciousness as Logan's voice pounded in his ears.

"Evacuate... Retreat!"

Time slowed and the smoke-filled air tinted with splattering blood and screaming men as his eyes burned while lead shot zinged past him.

After setting Arnett down on an empty cot, he raced over to the doctor and ordered an immediate evacuation of the wounded as far away as possible towards Washington. The Union line broke to pieces. , and with great haste went inside the hospital and hollered out to evacuate the wounded as far away as possible toward Washington D.C. The Union line had collapsed. He returned to Arnett, and again, lifted him across his back and joined the retreating line trailing out the back of the make-shift hospital towards safety.

Maddie, in her new persona of Kathleen, helped escort the wounded out of the church, a slow ambling line of men on crutches and litters moving away from the chaos and towards Washington. She bit her lip to keep from smiling, watching the frightened eyes of the Union soldiers as they retreated. Today was a good day in her mind. That brash Union army who imagined today was all sewn up, now scurried away with their tails between their legs.

Still, General Jackson rallied his troops and pushed all the way through the Union lines causing widespread pandemonium. Logan had no idea how long the melee lasted, nor how much lead buzzed by his ears as he marched on with Arnett, but what must have only been minutes felt like eternity. His lungs and throat burned from the noxious small of gunpowder, smoke, and death.

The Union cannons stopped belching fire on their side of the battlefield, the leftover smoke hanging like a cloud over the dead bodies scattered like discarded rag dolls. The Confederate cannon, however, continued pounding without let up.

Logan reached the wooden pasture fence near the churchyard and slid Arnett over just as a Napoleon exploded near them, splintering the to rail in a spray of shards. The force toppled both of them into the tall grass, and Arnett moaned from the pain in his side and the force of the blast. Logan scurried across and touched his fingertips to Arnett's neck to feel a pulse.

"Faint, but still there, fortunately," he whispered.

From their position, Logan flagged down a volunteer helping the wounded, who rushed over to him and kneeled next to Arnett.

"Sir," the man said with a dazed expression, "we have to evacuate. We have orders to evacuate back to Washington."

"Yes, of course, we know that, Private. Go around back and get one of the wagons. What's your name, son?"

The man looked at him with blank eyes. "Silas."

Logan patted his back. "You are doing a great job, Silas. Now go around there and bring back a stretcher for Lieutenant McCann.. And some bandage wadding for his wound," he added as the boy hurried away and he compressed his palm into Arnett's side; the blood spilling through his fingers.

Logan scanned the inside of the church, amazed by the sheer number of bodies laying on the floor and across church pews, some moaning in agony, others in eternal silent stares to the ceiling.

After a few minutes, the soldier returned and they laid Arnett on the stretcher, carrying him outside to join in the retreat.

Congressman Shank pulled up in his carriage and he waved to Logan.

"Congressman Logan, put the Lieutenant in the back seat of my carriage," he offered.

Logan's hearing returned and the faint sound of someone calling his name startled him. He looked up into Shank's face and nodded as they loaded Arnett inside.

"Sorry Stephen. My ears weren't quite working."

"Are you alright, John?"

"Yes, I think so. I'm not sure about Lieutenant McCann, though."

"We have to hurry, then. Rebels are barreling across the river. We need to go now!"

Logan regained his bearings and climbed into the carriage. Everyone inside the carriage rode back in ruminating silence and shock, their gaze fixated on the smoke in the distance and the carts passing by loaded down with mangled bodies. Rows of soldiers in blue trudged past with battle-weary and defeated eyes; faces smudged with mud, blood, and shock.

Gunshots and moans in the distance saturated the slight breeze filtering in through the carriage windows, and both Logan and Shank rubbed their foreheads in disbelief.

Any other time, especially while in session in Congress, Logan and Shank sat on different sides and spouted their views across the aisle. This ride was quite different – no arguing, no judging, no opinionated banter, just a slow reflective ride absorbing the horrific images of what just unfolded before them as the sun hid her bright rays in the veil of dark sadness.

Logan was sure after today's mayhem that Congressman Shank would resign his position and return to his beloved South Carolina, aggressively pushing forward the views of the Confederacy.

Congress had yet to declare war, officially, as there were still many southern Congressmen who stayed to try and quell separation by legislation means, hoping for a bipartisan resolution.

With Lincoln on his adamant Emancipation Act quest, insisting the bill be brought to the floor for a vote, several states, sensing the winds of change, seceded from the Union, with key figures turning in their resignations and signing allegiance with the Confederacy.

Politicians seeking officer commissions within the Confederacy prompted Lincoln to put pressure on Secretary of War Cameron to send a strong and clear message to the rebels, as a debate whether to start an immediate draft to reinforce an army... all with no end in sight.

The thirty-some-miles trek back to Washington D.C. stretched long in a slow painful unorganized march while the rear guard watched for another attack.

In the opposite direction, the Confederates, high on a victory, proclaimed Richmond, Virginia the capital of the Confederacy. Logan shook his head, remembering McDowell's words that 'the rebellion will be squashed before the day is out." Unfortunately, as they all knew quite well now, the best laid plans do not always work.

Arnett sat up in his bed, wincing and clutching the wounded area in his side. A tall and skinny medical surgeon stood by his bed writing notes on his clipboard.

"You were lucky, Lieutenant."

Arnett rubbed his blurry eyes as the fog of the ether wore off.

"Huh?" was all he could muster as he raised up on his elbows.

"Easy, soldier; you have a concussion from cannon blasts. Be extremely cautious not to pull the stitches out of your ribs."

Arnett opened his mouth to speak, his words punctuated with coughs and gasps as his stitches pulled.

"Where... am I... anyway?"

"In a D.C. Hospital. And just who are you, anyway? You must be someone special."

"What... do you mean?"

"Well, you've had a congressman checking on you, twice now."

Arnett wrinkled his brow in confusion as the pain surged up his side. He collapsed backward onto the pillow, out cold.

The next day, after resigning his commission from Congress, Colonel Logan arrived at the hospital, standing over to the side with "Kathleen", the nurse attending Arnett.

"How's the Lieutenant?" he asked her.

"Doing much better, sir."

"Is he fit to move?"

"Possibly, but he's going to need additional care."

"As I suspected," Logan replied, gazing over at Arnett. "He's been assigned to me and I'm going to need a nurse for him; you interested?"

"Where are you going to take him, sir?" she asked, fearful the Congressman might say his residence on Pennsylvania Avenue. She surely didn't need to be anywhere near the White House any time soon. Even this field hospital on the outskirts of the city was too close for her comfort, but she kept her hair bundled up in a nurse's cap and dressed the part so no one might recognize her.

"Illinois."

"I'm not sure he's fit to travel as of yet."

"Well, as soon as he's able."

"I'll get the doctor."

Logan pulled up a chair next to Arnett.

"What did you do before war broke out, soldier?" Logan asked.

"I drove General Wilcox around Washington in his carriage till I was demoted to battery."

"I saw your records; a West Pointer?"

"Yes, sir."

"You have just been reassigned to me."

"As your driver?"

"No, as your commanding officer."

"How did I get here?"

"I brought you in."

"He saved your life, Lieutenant," Kathleen said, approaching his bed.

"And who are you?" McCann asked.

"Nurse Kathleen Hardin meet Lieutenant Arnett McCann," Logan replied.

Arnett attempted to sit up and shake her hand. "

"Lay back till the doctor gets here," she snapped with her hands on her hips as the Doctor walked up next to Arnett and examined his wound.

"A few more days till those ribs heal up a bit. You can report back for duty by the end of the week."

"Thank you, sir," Arnett replied.

"Who's next, nurse?" the doctor barked, directing Kathleen on to the next patient.

Arnett sighed and watched her walk away, his curiosity growing for the young lady with mesmerizing eyes.

"Oh, wait." The doctor paused and handed Arnett a letter in a sealed envelope. "This arrived for you today."

Arnett winced as he pried open the envelope and laid back to read the words.

"Former Congressman John A. Logan, now soon to be Colonel Logan, is privy to your other duties after being briefed by intelligence. Miss Kathleen Hardin, a.k.a. Madelyn Cronin, former employed at White House under General Halleck, is one of the main suspects of White House leaks. Her brother, Daniel Cronin was hanged yesterday for intelligence espionage against the United States after confessing, alerting us to Miss Cronin's alias and whereabouts. She is suspected to be a key player in the Knights of the Golden Circle, a major financier of the Confederacy. Logan does not know her; you know that he knows. Remember keep thy enemies close. Godspeed.

War Department."

Chapter 10

Early August 1861
Washington D.C.

Congressman Logan pulled up to the gate of the curved drive of the White House.

'Yes, sir?" said the uniformed soldier approaching the carriage.

"I am Representative John Logan of Illinois. The President is expecting me."

"It will be a few minutes, sir, as we confirm this."

"Yes," another guard replied, scanning over a list in his hand. "He is on the visitor's list for today. You have any weapons on you? Open your coat," he demanded as opened the door to the carriage, and patted Logan down as he exited. The guard turned to the porch guards and motioned for one of them.

"Tell Secretary Nicolay, Logan is here."

"I just need to see your Capitol passes before we can let you through," the guard said, his eyes narrowing at Logan. "Not use to seeing Congressmen pull up driving their own carriage these days. You, understand?"

"Quite alright, there is a war on after all."

Logan handed him his pass, and the man scanned over the document. "Looks like everything in order. Open the gate."

Logan mounted back up to the driver's seat, gave a slight snap with the reins and pulled up alongside the huge white columns of the White House.

"Woah, there, girl," said, as another soldier took the reins, and aided down Logan from the carriage.

"Be here long, sir?"

"Never know with Mr. Lincoln. He just might have a story to tell or two."

"No doubt about that," the man replied, and they both chuckled.

Walking through the foyer a butler took his coat and top hat, replying with a small bow. "Secretary Hay will be out shortly, Congressman Logan."

Just then, Secretary Hay came out of a set of double doors, and Logan's gaze glanced upward to the flickering shadows cast across the wall by the glass chandelier.

"The President will see you now in the Oval Office."

"Thank you, Secretary Hay."

He followed him inside, his eyes making a straight path to the tall thin man leaning over the fire in the fireplace, staking a few logs across the andirons and stoking the glowing coals.

Lincoln looked up, his head at a slight tilt, and extended his sooty hand to Logan. He hesitated, but gripped it in a firm handshake as the President stood up straight and shook his head.

"I must tell you we really hate to lose you in the House. You have been a good statesman. But, right now, Congressman Logan, I believe we need good leaders on the battlefield, after what I witnessed at Bull Run last week."

"Yes, an unfortunate circumstance. I hear you were a hero at the battle, saving that young Lieutenant's life, helping all the wounded, evacuating the hospital, which shows true leadership."

"Sincerely, I did what any man would do under the same conditions."

Despite the hot August weather, after Lincoln stoked the coals, a small fire ignited and the flames flickered shadows over them both. Logan recalled the several times the two had talked while Lincoln campaigned for State Senator of Illinois, in Little Egypt.

The country lawyer who ended up President, Logan thought, repressing an ironic chuckle in the back of his throat..

The two men sat across from each other on twin couches as Logan studied the President's face, the lean deep cheekbones and ruminating eyes which kept a fixed gaze out the window behind the burled walnut desk. He knew not to interrupt Lincoln's train of thought, and after what felt like an eternity in silence, Lincoln stroked his beard and spoke.

"May I call you John? I dislike having to use such formalities."

"Yes sir, you may, if I can call you Abe."

Lincoln slapped his knee and laughed. "Yes, of course... like the old days, right? Now... let us discuss the wither to why you are here."

Logan added his own chuckle to the conversation, more so due to Lincoln's slow mid-western drawl that most mistook as coming from an uneducated man from backwoods Illinois. One such man, Stephen Douglas, lived to regret his assumption about Lincoln's "frontier backwardness", as he called it. Logan took that as a lesson and quickly changed the conversation to a more serious tone.

"May I?" Logan asked as he pulled his letter of resignation out of his breast pocket. He slowly and deliberately handed the letter to Lincoln. Secretary Nicolay stood quietly by and reached over to retrieve the President's glasses.

"Thank you, John," Lincoln said, putting them on while unfolding the letter. "Does Speaker Grow know of your intent?"

"Yes, sir, he does," Logan replied. "You will see, Mr. President I have come to ask for an officer's commission. I have served the great state of Illinois as a prosecutor twice, served in the state and now the Legislation branch of our great Nation. I also command Illinois' largest southern state militia. With a great cause, the militia could become a full regiment with your blessings. I understand some may join the southern cause, but I believe I can convince them otherwise if given the opportunity. Sir, I know I was a Copperhead, but your opponent Mr. Douglas is wrong, no man should ever suffer oppression. It goes against the grain of human dignity."

Lincoln listened with quiet interest at Logan's pitch for a commission. "May I ask, John, is this also a party switch? Is your intent to leave the Democratic party?"

Logan looked directly into Lincoln's eyes. "If the Democrats keep leaning toward secession, then yes, I intend to leave the party."

"Make no mistake John, a party switch is not a requirement. I have known you to be a man of your word; however, John, I believe you would be better served as the great orator that you are in swaying your fellow Democrats toward the battlefield in supporting the war. Many call this my war, but we must hold the Constitution intact."

"Sir, would I not be doing the same work by keeping Little Egypt within the throes of the Union? The Confederate stronghold of Clarksville is merely a few hours boat ride before the Columbia meets the Ohio. If we can take Clarksville first than we can best the protection from Confederate gun boats on the Mississippi and keep St. Louis out of Confederate hands. This is my argument for the need of another regiment in the Western Theater."

Lincoln rested his chin in his palm and considered. "Let me discuss with Secretary Cameron and General Grant to see the plausibility of another regiment. Of course, we will also have to address Congress on this matter to obtain the funds to supply another regiment. I will make a promise on this day of an offer of a commission, but I cannot, yet offer you a new regiment."

"Thank you, Mr. President; it is all I can ask."

The two men shook hands. Lincoln watched Logan leave, and turned to Secretary Nicolay,

"Wish we had more men like Congressman Logan."

"Yes, sir; I agree Mr. President."

Logan stood on the White House porch admiring the view of which not many men had the privilege of seeing, especially in the summertime.

Logan took out his pocketwatch and squinted his eyes at the tiny ticking hands. The meeting took a scant twenty minutes.

With the new commission secured, Logan spent the next few weeks into August, finishing up the last of his legislative duties.

His last, inevitable task? That of telling his young wife that they were about to go back to Illinois. His mind conjured the look on her face, that of disappointment since she loved the social aspect of being a Congressman's wife – the political talk, the dinner parties, and her frequent visits with the First Lady.

Logan sighed as he finished up in his office and closed the door, setting off to face her.

All things change... and with this war, more change was coming. With his mind fixed about what he might say to her, he knew he had one more item to take care of before he left Washington.

Chapter 11

LOGAN
August 8th, 1861

"Of course, I'm hurt, John. How could I not be? People here in Washington are just beginning to know who we are and where we came from. You are one of the best speakers Washington has ever known. Look what you did for Mr. Lincoln. You made Mr. Douglas look like a fool. And now, you want us to return home? Like we're a disgrace or something."

Mary looked away from him, eyeing the city street outside their brownstone; through the slight rain the pavement glistened and carriages sloshed down the cobblestones. She'd miss every single thing about Washington.

"I'm sorry you feel this way, Mary. There will be more parties and such. I assure you my work here is not finished." He knelt beside her, taking her hands in his, and tried to urge her to look at him. "We have a chance to change the course of history. To put Little Egypt forever in the history books as a major player in the world's stage.

"This is not just Lincoln's war. This is the Nation's war. Not to make things light, but rather to put an end to this evil of slavery once and forever. This war must end, and the Nation must reunite together, and we all must do our part."

"We are going home and make those hotheads in Little Egypt, realize the Constitution is at stake. I have a chance to bring them back into the fold and under the Union flag once again. It has to be done, Mary; it's the only way, and I am the only one that can hold the state together, along with Springfield. As long, as I am alive, there will never be a separate Illinois."

Mary finally turned and stroked her husband's dark hair. She adored him, his fiery passion about worthwhile causes, and with his words he convinced her it was the right thing to do. . In his heart, he knew she loved Washington and did not want to leave so early in his career, but when she kissed him on the forehead and smiled, he knew she would support him no matter the cost.

"It's all right, darling; home we will go if we must, but you know, Mary Todd will not be happy with you or her husband. We have become awfully close. Let me be the one to break it to her tonight if Mr. Lincoln has already not done so."

"Of course, darling," he replied with a tender kiss.

Logan sat at his desk in his Congressional office thinking about the conversation with his wife the next morning, after he had received his orders from General Grant. The paper lay on the desk in front of him and his eyes scanned the words once again.

"Your resignation from your Congressional seat in the House has been granted. Also, you have obtained the commission as Regimental Colonel. The newly formed regiment will be named the Illinois Thirty-first. Your orders are to at once begin the process of recruiting troops and picking your officers at your discretion. Once completed, you will be under the Command of General John Alexander McClernand; signed General Ulysses S. Grant, Union Army, on this day August 7th, 1861."

The night before, the ball hosted by Mary Todd Lincoln at the White House was exquisite. Logan's wife stayed close to Mary, who wasted no time introducing her as Colonel Logan's wife. His wife beamed, telling him earlier that she decided she liked being a Colonel's wife as opposed to his former title.

One of his helpers, a Lieutenant, peeked in the door. "Sir, your bags are in the carriage. You have about an hour before the train leaves for St. Louis."

"Thank you, Lieutenant. Please, send Lieutenant McCann in if you would when he arrives."

"He's waiting just in the lobby, sir."

"Fine, send him in"

McCann rapped his fist on the door as the helper cracked open the door.

"Come on in," Colonel Logan said.

"McCann reporting, sir."

Logan smiled. "No need for such formalities around me Arnett. Rather I should say Major McCann," handing him his decorative leaves for his uniform.

"I don't understand, sir."

"I have been instructed to choose my officers and I choose you to be a Major. You're accompanying me to Illinois to help set up this new regiment. We leave in an hour, Major. I know you are surprised... what's wrong?" Logan asked, noting Arnett's wrinkled brow.

"Yes, sir... just that doesn't give me much time to say goodbye sir."

"No need to."

"Pardon sir?"

"Your, nurse, will be accompanying us. Don't worry, I am well aware of your 'other duties'." Arnett stood there, dumbfounded. "Don't you think you better get packing, Major?"

Arnett saluted and smiled. "Yes, sir; right away, sir. Thank you."

Arnett stepped back into the hallway and sighed, wondering how many more knew of his 'other duties'. *This could get sticky indeed*, he thought.

Marion, Illinois
August 1861

The streets bustled after the townfolk heard from the courthouse sheriff's office that Congressman Logan, Williamson's County's favorite son, was returning from Washington.

After being away so long, the burgeoning growth of the city astounded him with wide streets, enough for buggies and buckboards to pass each other, four deep, back and forth to the railway station and farms.

Three and four-story brick buildings lined the main thoroughfare, facing east across from the railroad, filled with shops, and restaurants, and the parallel road to the station merged into the town square where the red-bricked Courthouse sat judging over the booming city.

As they exited the train car, Mary linked her arm with her husband's and smiled.

"I forgot to tell you, John," Mary said. "Sheriff Hendrickson wants to talk with you before we head home."

"I'm assuming it must be about whether I'm giving a speech this afternoon." Logan said.

She nodded and Logan flagged down a hired carriage to take their trunks and Mary to the local hotel; then, he made his way to the Sheriff's office.

"Sheriff here?" John asked the Deputy sitting at his desk with his feet propped up on the top.

"Well, howdy, Congressman; good to see you," he replied, setting down his feet and offering his hand.

"Thanks, but I've resigned."

The man smirked. "So, it's true; you've joined Lincoln's craziness."

"Craziness? Well, I wouldn't say that; but come to my speech tomorrow and you will understand why."

The deputy crossed his arms and gazed out the front window. "That may be, but I have to say it; there's a lot of bad blood where Lincoln's concerned. A lot of it is right here in Marion. We just had a runaway the other night and we found him hung in East Marion. And that sort of things happening not just in Marion. It's all over."

John crossed his arms, as well, grimacing at the news. "I suppose there is a lot going on out here. Tell me, is the Sheriff in court?" he asked, changing the subject since he was determined not to talk politics with him.

"Sure is," he replied, but Logan already turned to make his way up the granite staircase to the State's Attorney's office, more so out of curiosity to take a gander at his former office he used a decade ago as a young prosecutor.

*****

"Okay Judge, I'll, fill these forms out and get them back to you, may be a couple of days. Mary tells me, Congressman Logan is due back today. Something about a speech being given in front of the courthouse? You know when that's supposed to take place?"

"No not as of this morning, Judge. Train should have already made its Carbondale stop, by now so I am assuming they're on their way. And I'll send one of the deputies to let you know."

"Thanks, sheriff, You get them forms filled out pronto, you hear? These financial issues in down at the sheriff's office are a sight to be seen. You only have thirty days before it goes to the courts."

"Yea, yea I understand. You understand a war has just started right?"

"Go on get out of my office and get them forms filled out. Maybe Logan can help you," the judge barked with a snort.

The sheriff turned and headed out of the office as Logan climbed the last stairs.

"Help you with what, Sheriff?"

"Congressman Logan. How much did you hear?"

"Enough to know you're still having finance issues within the your office."

The sheriff smirked and changed the subject. "So, the rumors are no longer rumors anymore? Are we splitting from Springfield?"

"No, I've accepted a Colonel's commission from Lincoln."

The two men had started down the stairs. Logan's gaze darted around to make sure no one eavesdropped. "Look, sheriff, Lincoln is right. The Union must be preserved. I met General Grant while I was in Washington, and he convinced me the Confederacy is wrong, as well as slavery."

Sheriff Hendrickson, a man with massive arms and a trunk to match, along with a inflated ego and delving mind, which made him a great sheriff, stopped a minute on the marble landing of the last descending stairs, and looked out the window in disbelief. John paused a moment, as well, letting the sheriff understand what he just said. He turned and looked John straight in the eyes.

"Those kind of words are going to upset people, John, maybe even Mary."

"Mary? What does Mary have to do with this conversation?"

"Her brother just left for Tennessee's Fort in Clarksville to join the Confederacy with some of the young boys in the Militia."

"Does she know this?"

"Maybe you should tell her, unless she already knows, instead of discussing this with me. By the way, another group just left with that hothead Quantrill last night. I heard it this morning when I arrived back at my office."

"How many?"

"You'll have to ask Akins that. They left him tied up at camp. That was right before Sumter. Mary's brother had just left for Tennessee's fort in Clarksville to join the Confederacy with some of the young boys in the militia. Half of the militia has already left for the other side. Quantrill convinced them you were staying with the Union. After Akins was found he came to the states Attorney's office and shared the news."

The judge peeked out of his chambers, noting the sheriff and Logan in deep conversation on the stairs.

"Sheriff," he shouted, his face red. "You need to fill those forms out now, or you could lose your job over this."

"Okay, okay," the sheriff replied, waving back at him with a dismissive glare in his eyes. He directed Logan down the stairs and lowered his voice to a whisper.

"Something else you need to know. Elizabeth wants to see you before your speech. She's heard the rumors."

John stood a moment stroking his mustache and sighed. "I suppose she's upset."

"To say the least, John. I would say she's livid, Anne is too."

"Not surprising, considering my mother is from North Carolina."

"When do you want to do your convincing?".

"At two, tomorrow afternoon."

"I'll spread the message to whoever is around the courthouse."

The sheriff strode into his office, tossing the papers the judge wanted filled out to the side, and eyed Logan as he nodded to him and walked to the courthouse doors to leave.

Logan looks tired, he thought.

A crowd had already formed at the courthouse as Logan walked across the street, focusing on his steps and his words as he descended the steps to the street.

"There he is now," a man said, pointing in his direction. The eager crowd hummed like honeybees, like the ones McCann said he raised at his home in St. Joseph years ago. As he looked up to meet the critical gazes of the ten to twelve people gathered before him, he wondered about where Arnett had gotten off to at the moment.

He raised his hands to quiet the crowd.

"I just wanted to say a few words to you, wonderful people of Marion. I will give a formal speech tomorrow afternoon concerning my return. Tell your families, your friends, and whoever else you see. It is most important for all to hear, so make sure as many Williamson County citizens as possible can attend."

"Are you leaving the Democratic Party?" another man growled, one John remembered as a new militia recruit who signed up before he left Washington.

John caught a glimpse of Mary waving to him from across the street and turned to the crowd. "I apologize, but I must be going; my wife is waiting on me. I will not say anything official till tomorrow. Tell everyone to come so we can put an end to these half-truths."

"Come on, Logan," replied the man he recognized as the local hot head intent on spreading discontent with his quick temper. "Quit talking like a politician, you can tell us now. Dang politicians, you can't trust any of them." the man continued, provoking a bevy of agreeing nods from the crowd.

"Why don't you shut the hell up." another recruit said, defending Logan.

About that time, Sheriff Hendrickson sauntered over toward the scene, watching the crowd and placing his hands on his hips to reveal the pistols at his side. He walked straight up to the hot head and narrowed his eyes.

"Why don't you just follow the young man's advice and move along before I run you in and you spend this war in jail."

The hot head looked around, embarrassed seeing the crowd averting their eyes away from him.

"Sure, Sheriff; whatever you want," he replied, jerking away.

"Alright, now, move along. Come on, that means everyone," the sheriff replied, fearing a fight between the hot head and raw recruit. Within moments, the clouds burst open with a gully-washer, and the townsfolk scrambled to get out of the rain. Logan rushed across to his wife, who opened up her parasol and they rushed beneath the awning of the mercantile.

The sheriff sprinted back up the steps to his office, slapping the rain off his Stetson as he entered the room.

"If I didn't know any better, I'd think Logan brought the rain with him."

"Just might have at that," replied the deputy sitting at his desk.

"Good thing I left the top on my wagon. I could feel that rain coming on... along with more storms on the horizon, I'm afraid."

Across the street, Logan and his wife waited under the safety of the awning as Mary linked her arm with his, noting his worried stare into the downpour.

"Mom's coming over in the morning."

"Yea, I know. Sheriff told me she wanted to see me. Isn't there something else you've been meaning to say to me, Mary?"

She squeezed his hand. "Yes, there is. I just wanted to wait for the right time, but obviously the sheriff beat me to it. Believe me, John, we tried to stop him. Your mother and sister just had too much pull on him."

"That dang sister of mine. That Carolina blood has a grip on them."

Mary took out her lace handkerchief and dabbed the tears at the corner of her eyes.

"Please, Mary, don't cry. The blame is not on you. I blame Annie on this one." Logan put his arm around Mary, pulling her close as the rain slowed to a mist.

"Let's get going, I have a speech to write."

"You'll do fine, John; I know you will."

Chapter 12

August 19th, 1861
Marion, Illinois

"John, John you need to wake up?"

'What...?"

"You need to get up. Your mother will be here soon."

The Colonel rose from their bed, rubbing his eyes. Mary hummed a hymn while she opened the draped curtains at the window, letting an already hot morning air into the bedroom.

The sun peeked on the horizon as another day and a light breeze eased through the window, waving through the lace curtains.

"What time is it?" her husband asked.

"Five, I reckon; the birds are chirping. Looks like another hot day. I'll bring you some coffee while you dress. Not good to face an unhappy mother first thing in the morning still half asleep."

"I suspect it wouldn't matter how I look, she's going to be unhappy. Everyone in town knows mother is not happy." John washed his face in the basin, still bent over with his mustache dripping.

"Here's a towel, Please, don't get this wood floor wet."

"Yes, dear."

I am about to command an entire regiment in the Union Army, and I am being ordered around like a schoolboy, John thought heaving a long sigh and chuckling to himself.

"You, okay?"

"Yes," he answered, putting his white cotton dress shirt

and pulling his suspenders up around his shoulders. "Considering I'm about to enter a war, with extraordinarily little training as an officer who didn't start at the bottom at West Point, and with only my militia training."

"John," Mary said, standing there holding an unfolded blanket. "The men joined that militia because of you, no one else. They think highly of you as a fair person and a leader. You've proved that every training day for the past five years. They will join in droves, I just know it. You will be okay. Just, please, don't go and get your damn fooled head blown off, not sure how I would survive that. Your breakfast is on the table. Now, go eat before your mother arrives; we have a big day ahead."

John smiled and pecked a small kiss on her forehead. "Yes dear, You, are a good woman, Mary; I could have done much worse."

Once downstairs, John sat down at the table and picked at his eggs and cornbread, thinking how to approach the crowd with his ideas about the war, these people who were his family, friends, and former constituents. In truth, he loved them all with a passion, wanting to serve them in the best way possible, but he never thought how difficult a task this would be until the day before at the courthouse.

"Where did McCann get off to?" Mary asked.

"Oh, I sent him to the encampment to prepare for this afternoon. Kathleen is at the boarding house."

"Those two are like lovebirds in a nest in the springtime."

"Hmm, they are?" John replied. *If she only knew.*

"Your new uniform is over by the hanging on the coat rack, already pressed."

John rose and walked to the coat rack and stopped, staring at the uniform – the blue felt hat, much like an ordinary Stetson, and the two gold blades surrounded by gold leaves. He grabbed the yellow sash on a peg, along with his saber.

Mary had sewn on the orange bar with an eagle's wing spread on the shoulders of his jacket. Admiring the new decoration, he ran his forefinger across the wings.

You have come a long way, John A. Logan. Father would have been proud, he thought, his memory drifting back to the day they pinned Lieutenant Bars on his shoulders during the Mexican War.

"Turn around, husband; let's have a look." Her smile stretched from ear to ear and eyes filled with pride. "Your mother should be proud instead of fretting so."

"It'll pass," John replied, trying to display an uncaring aloofness.

"You can't fool me, husband; it bothers me that she is so contrary towards her own son," she replied with a frown as she tied the sash just so. "There; have I told you how proud I am, not just the uniform but your decision?"

"Yes, wife; I believe on the way home yesterday from town. I never tire of your compliments for they drive me to do better."

"Do not fret, dear husband; your decisions are wise. You chose me for your wife, did you not?"

"I recall the decision was not mine entirely."

They both giggled and held each other tight, enjoying a moment's kiss until a knock at the door brought them back to reality.

"She's here. God help us."

He watched Mary head to the door. *Yes, you've done well John*, he said to himself and took a deep breath for what was about to come.

"Why, good morning, Miss Elizabeth," Mary effected to the gray frowning woman at her door.

"You can forget the pleasantries, Mary. I'm sure you know why I am here."

"Be rest assured, Mrs. Logan, you're not going to convince him to change his mind."

"Why look at you, Mary Logan, standing by your husband's side when your own brother was smart enough to join the Confederacy with his friends following him. That damn Lincoln will destroy us all, you mark my word."

Mary shut the door, watching John's vindictive mother walk to the parlor. John stood at the fireplace, gazing at the photos on the mantle rather than greeting his mother's disapproving glare.

"Son," she barked. "So, the rumors are true," she added, her eyes scouring his uniform. "You betrayed your party, and our sovereign way of life. You should have been a General, not a lowly Colonel. You're a leader, why are you doing the opposite?"

"Doing the opposite? Really, mother? You're not going to convince me, to the day that I die, that I made the wrong decision. The God Almighty Bible itself says slavery is wrong at Ephesians 2:11-22."

"Don't be quoting the bible to me, son; I know the verses very well... and I also know that damn Lincoln will get us all killed, you mark my word."

"I see there's no further discussing this matter with you mother. But you need to know my mind. The Union must be kept as one country for all people. It is in the Bill of Rights. All men are created equal in the eyes of God."

"I will not be preached to, John. History will not be kind to you for turning your back on yo.ur party and neither will I. As far as I am concern, from this day forward, your sister is my only child."

"Mother, you can't mean this. Am I hearing you correctly?"

"Nothing wrong with your ears," she said, abruptly turning to leave. "I can see my own way out. I've said my peace."

Mary made sure and slam the door as John's mother exited their home. "The gall of that woman, to chastise you like that in your own home."

John stood paralyzed like a statue.

"Are you okay, John? You're white as a ghost."

Within a few minutes, another rap at the door interrupted John's quiet musing.

"Now what? Surely, she isn't coming back?" Mary asked, exasperated.

Sergeant Thomas stood at the doorway with his hat in his fidgeting hands.

"Oh my, thank goodness it's you, Thomas," Mary replied. "Come on in; John is in the parlor."

Thomas strode in and cleared his throat, bringing Logan to attention. "Major McCann sent me to see what we needed to prepare for your speech today."

Logan grabbed pen and paper and wrote down instructions.

"It will be an ordinary drill; however, the timing has to be perfect. You must come down Main Street and stop at the courthouse steps, at attention, like the real soldiers you are. You know, by the book. You must be there by one forty-five. No sooner, no later. If you arrive early, stand at ease down the street until you hear the community band start to play, then continue forward. Timing needs to be perfect; we are only getting one shot at this. Where is McCann now?"

Thomas pointed towards the town square. "Talking to the sheriff in front of the courthouse."

"Thank you. That is all, Sergeant."

"Uh, sir."

"What is it?"

"We lost a large portion of the men when they heard you had stayed with Lincoln."

"Who? Come on; out with it."

"Cole Younger and his brothers, the James' boys, and Quantrill."

"You try to stop them?"

"No, sir, but they jumped me in my sleep."

"Well, we can't do anything about that now."

"Aye sir," he replied. Logan shook his head as the Sergeant left.

"If you're finished, I will put breakfast up and bring the carriage around," Mary replied, peeking in the dining room. John rose from his writing table and glanced at the pictures on the mantle again, sighing at those innocent days before this blasted war.

"God help us," he whispered.

Mary gathered up her husband's plate and placed it in the dish basin to be washed later after the evening's meal. She stopped a minute, looked to the ceiling and whispered a prayer.

"Please, God, watch over our country, my husband, and all the husbands and sons, cousins, brothers, and uncles. Most of all, I pray for my mother and sister-in-law. There will come a time they well regret the way they treated John in his own house and I pray you saw it all."

The streets of Marion crowded as citizens came far and wide to hear the one man they cared about the most. Never had such a large crowd assembled since Militia Day. New recruits queued outside the recruitment office across from the courthouse for most of the day, with boys admiring the uniforms and hats, then signing up on a impulsive moment.

"You have to sign up to get one of those." a burly sergeant told the young boys, chuckling. "All of you are still wet behind the ears. Go on; git before I spank your bottom and send ya back crying to your mommy."

The Sergeant came from behind the counter as one of the boys made a face and hurried out the door.

"What's going on, Sergeant?" McCann asked.

"Nothing, Major, just a couple unruly youngsters too young to sign up."

"Sergeant, I understand you're not used to this kind of duty, but those young lads have older brothers and cousins, as well as fathers who enlist. Keep the gruffness to minimum, shall we?"

"Yes, sir, Major, but I'm pretty sure they will only be the enemy anyhow." McCann turned with a quizzical look as the Sergeant pointed to the sleeve of one of the uniforms.

"Wrong color, you see, according to them."

McCann shrugged and gazed up as a young woman entered the door.

"Miss, can I help you?" the Sergeant asked as Kathleen entered the door.

"I'll handle this one, Sergeant," Arnett answered with a smile.

"Afternoon, Kathleen; what's going on with you?"

"Came to see if you ready to grab some lunch before the Colonel arrives for his speech."

"Yea, sure; especially since we haven't been able to get together much. Let's head to the diner. You want anything from the diner, Sarge?"

"No, I have provisions."

"You best be ready. There might be an onslaught heading our way."

"Let's hope so, Major; enjoy your lunch."

"Thanks."

"He's really drawing a crowd already," Kathleen said, looking across to the platform set up in the square adorned with red, white, and blue bunting. "You know, Logan is one of the best speakers I've ever heard."

"Hmm." Arnett scoffed.

The ride to the courthouse was short and silent. Mary understood that what happened earlier at her husband's expense would be hard enough on anyone. She knew it was going to be tough trying to recruit for the North when so many from the area thought they had already been set upon to join the Southern cause.

Some, like Mary's brother, had already left to join that cause, not waiting to hear what their militia leader had to say. The ones that did not follow Quantrill to Kansas left for the Tennessee mountains or headed to Nashville to join the Confederacy. Many would stop and talk with her along the streets while she shopped, always asking the same question.

"How is John doing now that he has left Washington? Did he resign his position for one in the Confederacy's Congress? Or is he seeking to volunteer our militia for a commission?"

She always provided the same answer, which quelled any more discussion.

"Now how on earth would I know what he is thinking when he is busy doing the country's business?"

A Marion citizen named Johnson pulled his carriage alongside the Logan's.

"So, it's true you've done joined that damn Lincoln bunch in Washington. Now you have the nerve to steal men for them damn Yankees?"

"Back away from my carriage, sir, or I shall whip you like a horse," Logan demanded.

"Johnson! Back away from the Congressman now or I'll run you in!" Sheriff Hendrickson hollered from the middle of the street.

"What's it going to be, Johnson?" Logan shouted, holding the carriage whip above his head. "This or the deputy?"

"Damn fool," Johnson muttered as he pulled the reins and turned away from the carriage.

By the time Logan pulled up to the courthouse, the streets looked like a Fourth of July celebration, so thick with people the deputy had to guide the horse with a hand at the bit to keep it from being skittish.

Downtown Marion had become a celebration second only to the Fourth of July, or even Marching day which had to be scrapped since this time the militia would be off to war. Now, a great civil upheaval arose among the county residents and throughout the country with no one trusting anyone, especially strangers and sometimes not even their neighbors. The tension among the crowd permeated the air.

"Glad you two are here," Logan said to Arnett and the Sheriff.

"The only thing that could keep me away would be orders, Colonel."

"Appreciate that, Major. Are the men in position?"

"Yes, sir; itching to go."

"Excellent. Where's Kathleen?"

"She had to take care of some female thing. You know how that is?"

"Yes, I do," Logan replied with a smile. He took a deep breath. "Well, I guess it's time. Is the booth set up?"

"Yes, Sergeant Akins is manning it, as we speak."

John put on his officer's Calvary Stetson, which sported a large golden feather for special occasions such as this.

When he reached the top of the courthouse stairs, his men arrived with Jones, the oldest fifer in all of Illinois, leading the troop now in full military Union uniform and marching to stand at attention with two lines of soldiers directly in front of the steps.

"Attention." commanded Arnett.

Arnett, stood beside Jones, his saber pointed straight to the sky and tight against his left shoulder, the shiny steel glistening in the sun.

"At ease," Logan commanded.

The crowd quieted. The only sounds floated from the treetops as a flock of birds scattered to the sky, singing for the Marion County hero who once, long ago, saved the esteemed Governor from impeachment due to an illness and ascended from this fair city to his elected post in Congress. Like the birds, the crowd arrived in droves to hear for themselves the rumors of Logan's betrayal by joining forces with Grant and Lincoln.

Logan cleared his voice and gazed out across the stern faces. "There comes a time in everyone's life when a man has to stand for something. For his convictions, for his country, for freedom. Now most of you all know me, my beliefs in the God Almighty, the rule of law, for I am a lawyer always first."

"Yes, yes!" the crowd chanted at the last two remarks.

"Traitor!" A man hollered. "You were one of us; and now, you come here and betray us!"

McCann's eyebrows raised at the word "traitor". He considered ordering the men about face so as to face the crowd. He looked up, directly into Logan's concerned eyes. Arnett took it as a sign to wait and nodded to the Colonel.

"Let the man speak," another in the crowd added.

"I know some of you are quite upset with my decision; however, some of you are in dire straits. Understandably, you are upset. But, dammit, slavery is plain wrong. Even evil. We are a diversely populated country. We can overcome this divide. We've bolstered our freedom by taking away another person's freedom, a belief entirely against the foundation blocks set forth in the Constitution. So, now I ask you, do not concern yourself with fighting for another unit in another State. This is our regiment, formed by men of Williamson County and the rest of Southern Illinois. Major McCann..."

"Yes, sir," Arnett replied.

"Read the President's proclamation to the good citizens of Williamson County."

Arnett reached into his breast pocket and unrolled President Lincoln's Executive Order:

"By the order of The President of these United States, I hereby so order on this day that Illinois U.S. Congressman John A. Logan is hereby distinguished with the Commission of Colonel in these United States Army, under the command of General John McClerand, Colonel Logan is to recruit as many men as possible forming ten companies from the Williamson County area and beyond. It is so ordered this new company shall be named the Illinois Thirty-first and upon completed training in Cairo, Illinois, and will be mustered into service. Signed, President Abraham Lincoln."

The crowd cheered, hats flying into the air, as the words moved the citizens to back Logan's cause... some, but not all. Being a lawyer and a statesman, Logan earned the respect of the citizens from the way he carried himself, whether on his horse commanding the militia, or giving an eloquent speech to constituents. The undeniable ability mesmerized his listeners. Logan was a man who commanded another person's attention and always came straight to the point. A natural leader. Within moments, men pushed their way into line to sign up, their patriotic duty and consuming desire to join the Union cause.

"Sergeant Akins, escort the recruits over to the booth, so they can get sworn in," McCann shouted over the frenzied group, directing the men towards the queue.

Their hero, Black-Jack Logan, was going to protect Southern Illinois.

"Right this way, gentlemen, if you will."

Major McCann sat at the booth and signed up five hundred men in the first three hours. Most just farmers, store owners, and such. Even those not old enough, or ones whose mothers would not let them join because of their father's ideologies, hovered close by, eyes full of fervor and anxiousness to join them.

"I wouldn't be too fired up over not getting to sign up, son. This isn't going to be no picnic," said the sheriff to one of the boys. The boy, who waited in line to see if he might pass the muster, frowned as his mother approached and grabbed him by the ear.

"If your father sees you signing with these bastards, he'd whip you silly."

"But mom I'm eighteen," the boy protested.

"Like hell you are," she said. "You may be eighteen, but you ain't got sense enough to choose the right side. You're still wet behind the ears."

Some of the older men chuckled at the youngsters,

"You men take heed, to what I just said. War is not a game. This is serious business. Our quarters are being built right now down in Little Egypt," replied the sheriff.

"That's right," McCann interrupted. "I expect full respect in the treatment of others, especially your commanding officers. Your life is going to depend on the men standing next to you. As soon as this foray is over you will be learning to march in formation at the training grounds in Cairo. You want to add anything, Colonel?"

John stroked his mustache. "I am still the same when it comes to issues within the ranks and will deal with them in the same way. I will not tolerate fighting among each other, nor insubordination toward my officers; understood?"

"Yes, sir," a couple of new signees answered.

After many hugs from the enlisted men's families, the men formed a double line stretching around the corner of the courthouse. Three loaded supply wagons pulled up behind the long line, ready to depart with the enlistees.

Families lined up along the main street, along with woman, children and old men too old to handle the vigorous physical demands of daily military life. One of the eight non-commissioned officers brought Logan's horse around, and he mounted up.

"Sammy, you know the drill," Logan commanded to the horse with a nudge in his side with his boot.

An older man at the head of the procession started the march with by tatting on his drum.

"Present colors!"

With that, the United States flag, along with a new blue flag emblazoned with "Illinois Thirty-first" in silver thread under a rampant American eagle, popped at the top of the flag poles raised by two soldiers behind the drummer.

A military parade took over the streets of Marion County, but this was no ordinary parade full of joy. Men marched towards a fight against their own brothers and families, especially in Illinois, Missouri, Kansas, where the complicated ideologies divided hearts and minds.

Several residents watched the event unfold from the upper floors of one of the buildings, scowling in disgust that a Union Army marched through Little Egypt. Two of the onlookers were Colonel Logan's own sisters.

"I hope they kill you before you reach Cairo, John Logan. Damn you," one sister cried from a second-floor window as he passed by on his horse. "You will regret this decision. mark my word!"

A local newspaper reporter, also looking down from the building windows, jotted down his notes to include in the next day's edition as the two women started a catfight between them over the rightness or wrongness of their brother's decision.

"Sergeant Akins, see that the Colonel's orders are carried out in an orderly manner," McCann said, directing the men in order along the parade route to the train station where a train awaited to take the men to the camp.

"Yes, sir, Major. You heard the Major; line up by fours."

Immediately, those who previously served in the militia fell into line and started marching while the raw recruits stood there, dumbfounded.

"Attention!" Sergeant Akins ordered, waiting on the captain's orders.

McCann looked at the Colonel. Colonel Logan nodded.

"Give the order, Sergeant," McCann commanded.

The men climbed, four at a time, into the train cars. Within twenty minutes, the men were all aboard, cramped for space, but their hearts full of excitement.

"Feels like I'm wearing my younger brother's pants," one soldier commented, bringing laughter and a few "off-the-cuff" comments.

"At least you're not wearing little sis's pants," one commented with another round of laughter.

"What's the holdup?" one asked.

"One of the mules from the supply wagons is being contrary," someone answered from the edge of the car. They watched out the window as two soldiers pulled on the stubborn animal.

"He must be a Confederate mule," another recruit said, which increased the laughter as the mule nearly sat down on its hindquarters.

"Colonel Logan! Colonel Logan!" a Marion citizen shouted, pulling up the reins on his horse as he approached McCann and Logan who watched the troops board the train.

"Yes?" Logan answered.

"Sheriff says you have a cable waiting on you at the office."

"Thanks," Logan replied. "Think the Captain can handle the trip to Cairo?" he asked McCann.

"No better time to find out than now," McCann replied. "Captain, take over, we'll catch up later."

Yes, sir, Major," the captain replied with a salute.

Arnett and Logan rode back over to the sheriff's office, both wiping their sweaty brows from the heat and sat down across from him at his desk.

"I never heard such a wonderful speech," the sheriff said.

"I say, Sheriff, summers keep getting hotter here every year," Logan replied, fanning his face with his hat and changing the subject.

"You are right about that, sir." He held out a piece of paper to the Colonel. "Here you go, sir; the telegraph office sent this cable over while you were giving your speech."

"Thanks, Sheriff." He paused his hat-fanning and read, his eyes lighting up at the news. "Seems Congress has approved the Illinois Thirty-first. We are now official, but seems I have to make a trip back to Washington."

"Congratulations, John; great news," replied the sheriff.

"Now the real work begins," Arnett added. Congratulations, Colonel."

"Very true; however, I would appreciate keeping this quiet until after we secure our force and I arrive back from Washington. One more thing, Arnett, would you mind keeping an eye on my Mary for me. Hopefully this will be a quick trip."

"Sure thing, Colonel."

Later that evening, Mary, John, Arnett, and Kathleen dined at the local diner on the square for supper, sharing an evening drink and conversation before John headed back to Washington the next morning.

"You might as well see this, Major," Logan said, handing Arnett the telegram after they finished dinner.

Arnett held the paper to the side, scanning the words in private.

"Something wrong, Arnett?" asked Mary.

"I have to return to Washington by train tomorrow," interrupted John.

"What? Back to Washington? Why didn't you tell me earlier... I have to get home and pack."

"No, you do not have to go, Mary. I'm sure you would like to catch up on some of our old friends but this will be a quick trip to finalize the details about the new regiment." Mary frowned and John took the cue that they needed to discuss this more at home. "If you two will excuse us, I have an early train to catch in Carbondale in the morning."

"Do you need me to take you to Carbondale tomorrow, sir?"

"No, Mary can take me in her carriage. Besides, I suspect you and Kathleen need a little time to get to know each other a little better before you have to leave with the men. Also, I need your ears and eyes in this neck of the woods."

"But what if Mary runs into trouble on the trail coming back from Carbondale?"

"Listen here, young man," replied Mary, "I am perfectly able to hold my own on the trail. I have traveled many a time by myself. Matter of fact, I traveled back and forth from Shawneetown while John was first appointed district attorney of Williamson County, and oversaw our move during our first year of marriage. Many a highwayman felt the wrath of my horse whip, believe me. Besides," she said, reaching for the pocket of her dress, "I have this little beauty," she added, pulling out a silver pearl-handle muff pistol.

"Believe me, she knows how to use it," Logan said. "Her dad taught her well."

"Thank you, darling, for the vote of confidence."

"You're welcome, dear."

As they walked out the door, Logan noticed Bickley and some other fellows, those opposing his decision, at a table against the wall, eyeing them as they walked out the door. Mary and Kathleen walked ahead of them, with Arnett and Logan following. Logan whispered to Arnett.

"You get a look at the two shady ones watching us as we left?"

"Yes, and I recognize one of them as a troublemaker I knew from a few years back in St. Joseph while I was still working with my dad."

"Keep an eye on them two while I am gone, but don't let on you're watching them."

"I'm already on it. I'll let you know if I find out anything later when you return."

"And make sure to start training the men," he said louder so as to not worry his wife, knowing Mary had a keen ear attuned to her husband's whispers.

"How far is it to Carbondale from here?" Kathleen asked Mary.

"About two maybe hours by carriage with a fast horse. We always leave at first light. John is an early riser, anyway. I should be back before sundown. I wouldn't worry unless I'm not back in a couple of days, and if I have trouble, I will be sure to cable Arnett. He really is such gentlemen."

"Yes, I've noticed," Kathleen added, her cheek flushing pink.

"You know, Kathleen, you could do a lot worse."

"I'm beginning to see that," she said, laughing, As they rounded a side street, two men came out of the shadows.

"You know them?" Logan asked Arnett after he noticed Arnett's fixed stare on the younger one.

"Not personally, but I've had the same distasteful introduction. One time we ran into him on the trail in Missouri and two of his buddies tried to block us on a trail my father owned. Had a bead on them with my Sharp's. They backed off, and the ugly one was not too happy."

"Something's going on with them, better keep a good eye out."

They reached the house and went in to settle for the night. Arnett and Logan sat by the fire talking strategic training points while Arnett took notes, adding his West Point training into the mix.

"It's getting late, let's call it a night," John said with a yawn.

Later as Arnett laid on his mat thinking about what the future was going to be like, juggling his double duty and relationship with Kathleen between business and personal. while attempting to not get too involved.

I will have to be careful, what I say around her; she is a crafty one, for sure.

Daylight came quick for Mary. She hated not being along her husband's side, especially when he was going so far away. She fiddled around in the kitchen, putting together a quick breakfast of hotcakes with maple syrup fresh from the neighboring woods.

The sun crept over the horizon, promising another dog day, and Mary bit at her fingernails, fearfully awaiting the lone trip back home, especially now with such divisiveness hanging in the air.

The war affected everyone in ways they never imagined. She respected her husband's choices when it came down to entrusting her protection and the loyalty that came with it. Mary was sure John made a sound decision, introducing this McCann fellow into their inner circle.

Mary's astuteness shined when it came to going about her business of everyday life, especially concerning new people introduced into her life. She watched their mannerisms and listened to their words, a habit learned from Mary Todd Lincoln, whether they were someone of good character.

To her, McCann fit the bill.

Cairo

The train carrying the new recruits rolled into Cairo during the early evening hours, the Union's newest regiment's home for the next six weeks. A few passengers, buckboards used to carry freight, and several two-wheel carts wheedled around the small one-building station as the doors to the cars opened and the soldiers exited on the platform.

"Sure isn't Missouri," Akins commented. "Dang blasted mosquitoes," he scowled, slapping the back of his neck, and then, again as several other men followed his lead.

"Form a double line Lieutenant," the captain ordered, and the men matched to Camp Smith, the bivouac next to the fort.

Not far upriver, another small community, Cave-In-Rock sat on the bank of the Ohio, which was of great concern since the actual cave in the rock, or mountain, which hid pirates back in the last century, was large enough to hide Confederate troops. With a bit of strategy, they could wait for nightfall to attack Fort Defiance by coming from Nashville via the Tennessee and Columbia rivers, and use the cave as a hideout.

Once the last of the soldiers gathered in line, Akins nodded to the drummer.

"Okay, Sam, start the drum roll."

Late Spring rains turned the Illinois peninsula into mucky swamp trails left by heavy cannon wheels, and heavy freight buckboards, which made the march difficult as the supply cart's wheels lurched into the half-dried trenches, while the soldiers marched around some of the left-behind carts still stuck in the mire.

Usually in a hot month, such as mid-August, the summer heat left the land dry and flat. overflowing with brown prairie grass, and trickling creeks draining from the low lying foothills from the Missouri Ozarks along the rock formations from Shawnee land, into the Ohio River.

The glue-like mix of mud and water caked on the soldier's boots and before an hour passed, the march slowed to almost a standstill.

"This dang place is nothing but a damn swamp from hell laden with flying insects," one man said.

"I suspect you'll see much worse than this place, Mister Hendricks, before this war is over," one of the Corporals replied.

Another half hour passed, and they reached Camp Smith on the west side of the fort, at once setting up their tents in organized rows.

"Camp Defiance," Sergeant Akins spat. "Should have been named Camp Swamp."

Fort Defiance, aptly named due the vital importance to the Union's cause as the first line of defense when it came to protecting Pittsburgh to the northeast, St. Louis to the northwest, and the war's western theater, before the Thirty-First arrived in August of 1861.

The Army's job, under Grant assigned to General McClernand, was to keep the rebel force away from Kansas and Missouri, and, of course, Illinois and the Ohio valley. Ten different regiments trained at the same time while protecting the two rivers.

When the fort first opened, Cairo was a small river town with a population around five hundred. Soon after the war of 1812, the army saw the importance of a needed fortification where the Ohio river drained into the Mississippi, an ideal spot for new regiments to train which drew men from the three surrounding states of Indiana, Kentucky, and Missouri.

In 1858, about twelve-hundred men, at any one time, trained and patrolled the waterways from piracy and outlaws who liked to use the cave upriver to hideout. When Grant became General, he took control of the Union Army at Fort Defiance.

Grant headquartered at a building on Sixth street and lived at the local hotel in Cairo, south of the hotel, with the field between the town and Camp Smith used as a parade field for Fort Defiance. Grant watched the troops progress using a field glass from his window as they drilled on the field.

At the outset of firing upon Ft. Sumter, and by the time Colonel Logan arrived at Fort Defiance, the number of troops swelled to ten thousand. Regiments as far away as Michigan and Pennsylvania also trained there.

Governor Richard Yates, upon receiving a notice from Washington that a new regiment was being formed from Logan's militia, requisitioned seven-thousand new Sharp rifles, six-thousands muskets, and fourteen artillery batteries.

Ten-foot-high levees were built to protect the fort not only from attack but, also, from flooding that happened every spring and winter. In the center of the arched levee, three twenty-four-pound cannons sat, draped by three twelve-pounders on both sides.

To the Northeast, six million pounds of cotton, along with millions of barrels of molasses, sugar, and the South's biggest commodity – slaves – housed up near Shawneetown.

While the soldiers at Fort Defiance prepared to back the Union's ideas of freeing them, many of the slaves either escaped via the underground railroad coming out of Georgia, hiding in the Illinois Central Railroad storage bins at night, or joining the Union Army ranks and fighting for their freedom against their former owners. The lack of manpower and funding for this incomplete rail-line left it wide open for the Underground's use, and also made the Mississippi and Columbia Rivers of vital importance to the Union and Confederacy's supply lines.

When the Confederates heard of this travesty of escaped Negros joining the Union army, their own army offered freedom to their own slaves to fight alongside their "masters", but most knew the promise would never be honored.

Chapter 13

Late August 1861
Washington D.C.

"Secretary will see you now, Colonel Logan."

"Thank you, Captain Anderson."

"Good to see you again, Colonel."

"Like wise, Secretary Stanton. Please, call me John."

"Well, John, I would like nothing better to do that, except in times such as these I prefer to call my officers by their rank, Colonel."

"My commission is finalized?"

"Yes, Congress, or what's left of them, approved it and the President signed it yesterday. I believe congratulations are in order. Congratulations on your commission, sir. Cigar?"

"Yes, please; thank you."

The two men sat together in silence for a moment, the haze of smoke filling the room. Finally, Stanton stood and poured two glasses of bourbon. Handing Colonel Logan his glass, he raised it in the air.

"Colonel," was all he said.

An uneasiness settled in Logan's gut as the minutes passed in more silence. Secretary Stanton sighed and, finally, turned from staring out the window.

"I was not for this, John. I usually do not like the idea of giving politicians such a high rank. It rarely works out; however, in times of war, one must do their duty. You have an impeccable record in your state legislature, and here in

Washington where you showed great leadership in turning a disaster into an orderly retreat at the field hospital. I respect you highly for that.

"The Union needs more like you than ever before. General Grant says you have quite a following in an area that is strategically important to the Union's success. It is imperative you get as many of these men to join this new regiment. Training is to start as soon as you return. A facility is being drawn up in Cairo as I speak. We chose Cairo; one, to protect the Mississippi and the Ohio from being overtaken by the rebels, and two, to incorporate as many as Illinois citizens, from going to the Confederate ranks. Depending on how this plays out, likely your regiment will not serve all their time in Illinois. Organization headquarters will be Jacksonville, Illinois. Any questions?"

"Who is my commanding officer, sir?"

"General McClernand."

"It makes sense to me, sir; most of my volunteers will be coming from my congressional district. With that in mind and, of course, with the training taking place in Cairo, that we organize in my district."

"I have no problem with that, Colonel. Since Jacksonville is your reporting headquarters, all your communications, your request orders, and meetings will be with your commanding officers."

"Very well, sir."

"You have two months to get this outfit up and running."

"Understand, sir."

"Good luck, Colonel."

"Thank you."

"By the way, your first meeting with General McClernand will be in three weeks in Jacksonville. He will expect a full report. You have a West Point officer that is an aide with you, correct?"

"Yes, I do."

"Yes, I thought so. He said good things about you. My advice is, listen to him. He excelled at West Point in intelligence."

"Yes, sir, I will."

Colonel Logan walked out onto the street, leaving the war building. The President declared martial law in Washington, so more uniformed soldiers than ordinary citizens swarmed the streets, much different from the days when he and Mary lived on Pennsylvania Avenue.

With so many soldiers walking about, Logan felt like he was being watched. *Maybe he was*, he thought as he scurried across the street.

He stopped by the commissary and instructed the supply sergeant where to send his new uniform, the hotel nearest the White House. He tried on the Colonel's hat, pushing his hair behind his ears while the Commissary attendant held out the jacket for him to try on.

"Say what did you do before you signed up for a commission, sir."

"I was a member of the House."

"And you joined the Army? Don't understand that one."

"You will someday, Sergeant. Every man has his convictions. Mine just happens to be righting wrongs, and the Confederacy is wrong."

"You want your Sharp's with you, sir?"

"No, I'm traveling by train as a civilian, so you can just sent the case to the station with the luggage. Now, no more questions; just do your duty."

"Yes, sir, Colonel; I'll have these at the train station immediately, all packed."

Colonel Logan walked out of the commissary, the uneasy feeling remaining with him, as if the man grilled him for information. *Maybe it was just the Sergeant's nosiness, or maybe it was just breakfast*, Logan thought. But then, again, walls sometimes had ears, and people within those walls, loose lips.

He thought of stopping in the saloon to have a quick drink to settle his queasy stomach, but instead continued on to the Secretary of War's office to send separate cables to Mary and Arnett via the military code service.

While he walked the few blocks to the War Department, he thought how serious his position was, and the security the new regiment was going to have to follow, if they were to be successful. Both sides started using their own techniques for spying.

Secretary Cameron stressed the importance of secrecy while his new regiment was assigned their duties. "The Confederacy must not know where your regiment will be assigned before we even get started. We want them to think you are staying put in Little Egypt."

"Very well, sir."

Back at his hotel room, he wrote out his cables. He was anxious to get back and missed Mary terribly. Romance was next to impossible in time of war, especially not knowing when or if he would see her again. After his decision of leaving Washington, they sold their house after convincing Mary that being an officer was more important in the country's time of need.

He lay on his bed, sleep eluding him, gazing up at the hotel ceiling, recalling the time he had to tell Mary they were not going to stay in Washington. Images whirled through his mind of Mary Todd Lincoln's ball and his attempt to convince Mary he was right.

"Mary, a man without convictions or of sound moral judgment cannot stand idly by while the country falls apart," he said, pacing back and forth in front of the fireplace.

"I am not one of your legislators, John. I am your wife and your life partner. I will not have you talk to me otherwise. Look at me, I want to see your face. You are not a military man that has the training needed to carry out such an endeavor. Sure, you commanded a bunch of young lads in the militia, but this is different."

"Tell that to Mr. Lincoln, Mary; he thinks otherwise."

Kneeling in front of her he took her hands in his. "Mary, you know since the day I asked your father for your hand more than two years before we started courting that I care more about you than anything. I know you do not want to leave Washington, but this Nation needs us to do our part. I have loved you since the day I met you when you were fifteen. You know I would never foolishly do something that would jeopardize our relationship without thinking it through thoroughly. We are needed back home to protect our home and the people that have supported us. They deserve that from us. If only we could have been there instead of Washington, I could have persuaded your brother not to join the Confederacy."

Mary pecked a small kiss on his cheek. "I know you, John. I know you are not trying to throw something back in my face that we disagree on. I understand what you are implying about my dear brother. It is not to shame me. I understand that about you. I agree with you; Hilbert would never have joined the Tennessee Army if it were not for classmates at the Academy who talked him into the decision. I also realize, he tried to get you to bring the militia into the Confederacy fold. I love you so much John, and you know I would follow you into Hades if needed."

"Mr. Lincoln said we might just have to do that to end this silliness."

"Okay, John, then back home we will go."

"The war won't last forever, Mary."

"We may not either, dear husband."

Later he sat down to write in his journal.

"My dearest Mary. It has only been two days, yet I miss you terribly. I hope you doing well. Forgive the military code cable. Military policy in time of war. I feel as if I cannot see the end of the terrible times facing us. I shall arrive in Carbondale around two a.m. I apologize for the shortness, so I await the hours before I hold you again. I miss you terribly. John."

A knock on the door awakened Logan and he bolted upright. "Sir, the sun has just sat."

"Can you send me a carriage for a ride to the train station?"

"Yes; any luggage, sir?"

"No, should be loading now by the commissary."

"Right, sir; I'll bring the carriage."

Logan poured water into the basin and washed his face, combed his jet-black hair and dabbed a bit of wax to his mustache as he gazed in the small mirror on the highboy dresser. He put on the black suit he always wore and checked the inside pocket to make sure the cables were still there. Looking about the room for one last check to make sure he left nothing behind, he closed the door and hurried down to the waiting carriage. As he sat against the leather seats, warmed through the window by the rising sun, he patted his coat jacket at the breast pocket, recalling the last letter he wrote in the room upstairs before he left. This one, dated August 1861, was to the Democratic Chairman, August Belmont, and outlined his every single thought about resigning from the DNC.

The carriage stopped at his old office before continuing on to the train station and he reread the letter while standing behind his old walnut desk, his fingers trembling with the resolute words.

"After much thought and consideration, I can no longer stand with the democratic party beliefs. If we as a people believe in this Republic Constitution's Bill of Rights and rule of law, then we must uphold that slavery is wrong.

I, as a God-fearing man, and a lawyer, cannot condone slavery, nor the path to which the Confederacy wishes upon our nation. In all sincerity I shall follow my heart and my President's acceptance of my resignation as a House Representative, return to my beloved home of Illinois to make sure Illinois remains a free state. I shall also await further orders from President Lincoln. Sincerely, John A. Logan.

Logan sat a minute and looked around his out the window as the town passed by. The nation was experiencing a new era thrust upon it by different ideologies, a divided nation intent on war, with lots of young men ready to die for those beliefs on both sides. He shook his head, frustrated.

John wondered how this was going to affect his own life as well as Mary's. However, John was also a realist; he knew that no one in this great country could know or even imagine where their future lay in the grand scheme of events unfolding before them all.

"Sir, is everything alright? Did you say something" Adam's voice startled John, who was engrossed in his thoughts unaware of Adam standing in the doorway.

"Adam, sorry, I didn't see you. I was just muttering to myself, is all. Yes, everything is fine; it is the future I am concerned about." He looked down at the paper, tri- folded it and stuffed it in an envelope, writing the chairman's name on it.

"While you're here, Adam, can you deliver this to the chairman's office?"

"Yes, sir, my pleasure Mr. Logan. I just happen to be headed there."

"So, are you joining this craziness, or are you going to stick it out here at the capitol?"

"I'm staying, sir. I would like to someday be sitting where you are."

"I thank God for that, Adam. That may very well happen. I am afraid, a lot of young men like you will be sacrificed to save the Republic. I wish you well."

"So, you're leaving?"

"Yes, I have important work to do to preserve my state from making a terrible mistake."

"I'm sorry to hear that, sir. I wish you well and Godspeed. By the way, I never got the chance to tell you, but that was a brave thing you did at Bull Run. Everyone is talking about it."

"Thank you, son." Logan stood and handed the envelop to Adam, and they shook hands. Logan walked back to his desk, turned to say something, but Adam had already left.

John walked down the long hallway and out the Congressman's exit away from the busy. He turned and looked back toward the hallway for one last time before walking out the door.

"Perhaps I shall be back someday, God willing," he whispered.

The carriage waited for him at the front drive and Logan hopped back inside.

"Where to, sir?"

"Train station. Time for me to get back home."

After a few days travel and several stops along the railway, Logan arrived back in Marion after giving numerous recruitment speeches; the first, to the young men who served under him in the militia. He words reached deep into their hearts.

"Do not let your party affiliation convince you to make a decision that will affect you and your family for the rest of your lives. People that plot against our government will suffer repercussions, and in some circumstances, death or loss of property. I, for one, intend on staying and honoring my patriotism for a better and more perfect Union. We must not let others, who are enslaving others, divert out mind and cause, which is for the common good."

The fanfare and celebration of the citizens and nonmilitary government observers transformed, doing an about face, and the question of whether this war would be over in days (if not weeks), dissipated as the days passed. The former eagerness of the new recruits fading to concern after realizing that most of them knew zero about the realities of surviving and dying on a battlefield.

Cairo, Illinois

Ft. Defiance

"Colonel Logan, good to see you again."

"Like wise, Major McCann.

"How was the trip, Colonel?"

"Eventful."

Arnett wondered about Logan's worried brow. The two men walked in unison the short distance to the bivouac.

"The secretary informed me of your assignment, that of our good nurse Kathleen."

"Yes, we have been keeping eyes on her since before the war broke out."

"I was under the impression that while you were at the infirmary, you two were romantically involved."

Arnett chuckled. "Well, mostly her; I assure you, my part is strictly business."

"Business?"

"Let me be blunt, Colonel."

"By all means," Logan replied.

"You see, I work under the Judicial System. My orders come strictly from Mr. Bates."

"The AG?"

"Yes, my West Point appointment was through the AG's office."

"Should we be discussing this?"

"Well, I consider you a friend first, John; we are both on the same side."

"Go on, then."

Discussion of the intended target lasted far into the night. Logan placed the official document on the table for Arnett. Lincoln's aide delivered it while he was writing his party resignation.

Arnett read over the directive.

"Colonel Logan, upon resignation of your congressional seat in the House of Representatives, you shall return to Illinois to muster a new regiment which shall be called the Illinois Thirty-first. Training will begin in Cairo, known as Little Egypt, Illinois. Upon the mustering of the Thirty-first, Congressman Logan's commission shall be that of Colonel with Lieutenant McCann's promotion to Major, forthwith. Recruitment shall begin at once, along with the immediate defense of the Ohio and Mississippi Rivers in the area assigned. Signed, Secretary of War, Simon Cameron."

After hours of strategic planning in Arnett's tent, Logan stood and stretched his arms.

"I think the plan is good. I'm just concerned whether you can pull it off. It would be best for all concerned if Mary doesn't know either. I know your convictions, John; and deception is not in your nature. And just so you are up to date on the lateste, you need to know that it was Kathleen's brother who was the spy that passed the information from the President's office to Breckenridge. He has since visited the gallows under Lincoln's orders."

Logan's eyebrow arched and he nodded. "Well, that is some news."

"Hey, you have anything to drink in this tent?" Arnett asked.

"You mean the bottle under my cot?"

Arnett chuckled and watched Logan reach under his cot, retrieving two tin cups and a bottle. Logan, also, produced a cigar from his coat pocket and tried to hand one to Arnett.

"No, thanks," Arnett said, pulling out a packet of tobacco and stuffed a wad in his jaw. "Picked this habit up from Grant," he said. "I figured it is good enough for that General, then its good enough for me."

Arnett sat back on his chair, watching Logan light his cigar and pace across the dirt floor while puffing out the smoky cloud like a steam engine.

"You know, Arnett, a lot in Williamson and the surrounding counties wish to throw their support to the Confederacy."

"Just one more cog in the wheel to break," Arnett replied, raising his glass. They both finished off their drinks, shook hands, their minds and hearts bonded in the plans ahead of them, then Arnett slipped out of the tent, back to his own beneath the hazy moon.

Arnett shook his head as he mounted his horse, knowing Logan, while not very good at deception, was even more terrible at keeping secrets. Everyone knew Logan's "tell", something Arnett learned after spending hours playing poker with his friend. *Now, with this new plan... how the hell am I supposed to juggle two top secret missions,* he pondered.

A nightwatchman named Thompson scratched his scraggly beard and watched Arnett ride off. His partner walked up, taking off his hat and wiping his sweaty forehead with the back of his dirty sleeve.

"Was that the lieutenant leaving?" he asked Thompson.

"Yeah, it was; but he was wearing Major leaves on his hat. Some strange things goings on around here."

"About to get stranger," the other guard said. Thompson turned around and was about to say ask what he meant, but the man disappeared into the dark forest, back to his post.

What the hell did that mean? Thompson thought as he sauntered back to his watch.

Later that night, after the sun went down, most of the remaining soldiers in camp huddled around their fires, eating and conversing about the last few days events.

Thompson walked up to one of the fires and pulled a leftover biscuit out of his pouch, chawing down on the stale bread.

"Surprised you're still here," one of the infantrymen stated.

"What the hell does that mean?" Thompson shot back.

"Your partner went over the fence earlier. Deserted his post."

"Not my damn partner," Thompson growled, standing up and nearly knocking over the coffee pot hanging over the fire. "You tell me right now, what the fuck does that mean?"

"Hey, hey, Thompson... easy; sit down and have a drink. It surely does not mean anything. He's an idiot anyways."

Almost everyone stood when Thompson bolted up, ready for a fight that never materialized, while one young officer remained where he was, his face aglow from the flickering flames.

"Sit down, boys," he said. "We don't need no fighting amongst ourselves. Be enough of that with Johnny Rebs a'comin'. Sit the hell down, take a drink and shake hands you two; that's an order."

"Didn't mean shit, Thompson," the infantryman replied, extending his hand.

"Fine," Thompson said, sitting down and taking a swig from a bottle of shine. "Anyways, if he did bolt, I reckon I could tell he was a Johnny Reb from the start. At least now we'll get the chance to shoot the bastard."

All the men laughed as the song of the cicadas and bullfrogs filled the night air. In the distance, a lone harmonica added its melody to the symphonic refrains. The young soldier stood up and stretched, tapping his fingers to the edge of his hat and saying, "Night, boys" as each retreated to their perspective bedrolls and tucked in for another quiet night, one of the last ones before war rose at the horizon.

"What's going on with McCann going from Lieutenant to Major?" One of the young men whispered, who had taken up his bedroll next to Thompson.

"Don't know and don't care to know; go to sleep. You're surely gonna need it before this week is up."

With that Thompson rolled over, adjusted his pack between his neck and shoulder, and closed his eyes.

Images of future battles ran through the young soldier's head – shells exploding, screams of pain, and rifle shots. He awoke swatting his ear, thinking a rifle ball grazed past, but it was just a mosquito.

"Damn mosquitoes," he muttered.

Adams waited till the cacophony of sounds eased to steady snoring, and he slipped past a guard with ease, walking his horse out of camp, and stopping to let his horse his drink out of a gully wash leading down to the river. He loosened the saddle and pulled the Union horse blanket out from under the saddle, replacing it with his civvy's jacket and making sure the buttons didn't aggravate his horse's skin. He knew his way, and the entail he received about a nearby Confederate camp holed up in the woods was sure to guide his way out of the stupidity wrought upon Missouri by former congressman Logan.

With stealthy steps, he clicked his tongue and guided his horse down to the river bank, to the location of the ferry crossing. In the muted moonlight, he made out the shape of the ferry, but no attendant waited to take it across to the other side.

"Halt; who goes there," a young guard blurted, stepping out from the bushes and pointing a rifle. "Get them hands up where I can see them."

"Easy, soldier; where be the ferry detail?"

"The Ferry's been shut down by that Logan group, It's none of your damn business anyways. I already know a few southern brothers that have crossed the river. Do you know where?"

"I wouldn't know, and I wouldn't tell you anyhow," he said, raising his gun.

"C'mon, son, my rear end is getting tired in this here saddle. I need to get across," Adams said, his hands up in the air and still holding the reins.

"Dismount and approach... slowly. Keep them reins up. Bivouac is a couple hundred feet away. Just keep moving slow with no sudden movements or I'll blow a ball right through that red-headed skull of yours."

"Let's not get nervous here, son," Adam said in a calm voice, as they climbed up the riverbank.

"Shut the hell up and put them hands behind your head."

Adams never thought much about how this would all play out. He just knew he had to get the information in his pouch to Johnston. He figured to just play along to calm the situation.

The kid relieved him of his rifle and pistols, and shoved him in the back to the bivouac camp.

I sure hope this kid has a leveled head or I'm a goner, Adam thought.

"Easy, kid, I would hate to get my head blown off before I can see the captain."

After a few yards through the privet and blackberries, both snagging relentlessly on his britches, another guard backed the eager soldier and held his gun alongside.

"I see you nabbed yourself a Blue Belly."

"I need to see Captain Johnston," Adams appealed to the two men.

"Shut the fuck up before the stock of this musket gets introduced to your skull," the other guard retorted with fire in his eyes.

After a few yards, they entered a clearing. A few tents, along with muskets stacked like pyramids, and men stretched out in rows, one after another, all prepared after a long day of training. A few of the men noticed the two soldiers wrangling Adams in front of them and gathered up, whistling at the catch.

"You're headed to Andersonville, damn Blue Belly," the men taunted and laughed.

"Not unless we hang him first," another said.

Captain Johnston looked up from the fire before his tent and set his hands on his hips.

"You, two, bring that prisoner here."

They pushed Adams to the ground on his knees, while an aide rifled through his pockets.

"I have..."

"Shut up," barked one of the guards. "Prisoners are not to speak unless ordered."

"Let him speak," replied the captain. "Who are you?"

"Dispatch, with important info for Captain Johnston."

"I'm Johnston. Now, come on, out with it."

The guard struck Adams in the back, and he lurched forward, coughing into the dirt. He reared up and blasted out his information.

"You're about to have a whole damn Yankee regiment right in your back yard."

Johnston narrowed his eyes. "There's only a militia we know of, and our spies sent us different information."

"Then, you tell me why a certain Southern female would send me to tell you, and why a wet-behind-the-ears Lieutenant who just made Major is headed this way with a full regiment of ten companies."

"So, she made it out. That's good news," said the man standing next to Johnston, a one Lieutenant Hilbert. "What else you got for us?"

Adams brushed off the front of his pants as he stood back up, glaring at the two guards who stood there gobsmacked that this man was actually Confederate. "Well, best be a good idea to vacate back across river and destroy the ferry," Adams added.

Lieutenant Hilbert extended his hand, which Adams shook. "Am I right that the commander of the Militia is my sister Mary's husband?"

"Yes, sir; and he's formidable, sir. If what he says about a regiment is true, we have no way to defeat those numbers. And there is nowhere to hide in a regiment's backyard, not even in Shawnee."

The captain pondered his situation. "Lieutenant, take ten men and destroy the ferry, the rest of you get ready to cross the river."

"Without the ferry?" one of the guards asked, a dumb frown gracing his face.

"Use the boats," ordered the captain.

"What about him?" the guard asked, pointing to Adams.

The captain pulled his pistol, turned around and shot Adam in the head.

"Fish bait." was all he said.

Chapter 14

Williamson County
Carbondale, Illinois
Train depot

Major Arnett McCann stood on the platform at the Carbondale train depot waiting for Logan's return from another one of the many trips to Washington. The train was delayed, which gave McCann time to work out strategies. He recalled the Secretary's advice before he left Washington with Logan the first time.

Cameron's words were: "You have to adapt to certain situations in the field as an agent. There are times when you will have to go against your commanding officer, and times when you will have to show your hand. Part of being an agent."

"You play poker, Marshal?"

"You better believe it. And a good poker player never tips his hand, McCann; that's why Grant and I picked you to go with Logan, plus your friendship with him helps. Not that we distrust Logan, but there are groups in Southern Illinois that just can't be trusted. The territory is just too close to the line for comfort, if you get my meaning."

Cameron assured Arnett that Logan was not their target. His assignment was to get as much information on Miss Hardin and this Bickley fellow as soon as possible, as well as the spy ring that had infiltrated the White House.

Washington D.C.
Four months earlier

Lincoln had no idea how long he stood gazing at the flicking flames in the fireplace with his elbow resting on the mantle, as was becoming his habit of late, as he thought back to the day of the revelation of the spy ring within the White House.

A knock at the door roused him from his rumination as one of the White House aides stuck his head in the doorway.

"Secretary Holt is here, Mr. President."

"Thank you, Thaddeus; please, send him in." To which Holt entered the room and shook Lincoln's hand. "Nice to see you on such little notice, Joseph."

"You're welcome, Mr. President. I have been mulling around in my mind about our discussions concerning the importance of counterintelligence, especially since Vice-President Breckenridge's defection."

"Have you had time to develop the list of possible candidates from the Point?"

"Yes sir, I have. As I'm sure you already know, several of the top staff resigned their commissions as soon as their home states seceded."

"I'm quite aware of that, Joseph. May I see the list?"

"And we received news from Arnett McCann via telegraph, sir."

"Excellent."

"The trap is set. Our agent has not been compromised, and everything is working accordingly," added Holt.

"We owe a great debt to those within our intelligence corps."

"They're special patriots, Mr. President."

"Yes of course they are. Tell me, you are left over from Buchanan's administration and a Southerner, are you not?"

"Yes sir, I am."

"Yet, you do not always side with the idea of slavery. Why is that if I may ask?"

"I am also a lawyer, and I believe in the Constitution. Slavery is the opposite of the Bill of Rights."

"The country needs more good men like you, Holt." Lincoln scanned over the list of names. "I only see three names here."

"Yes, sir. The other seven crossed out resigned, and are now rebels."

Williamson County

Back in Williamson County, Arnett tried resting as he waited for the Colonel's arrival by train, and mulled over his thoughts about the intended target, along with a barrage of images of his wife Martha, of Bull Run, and the day the Justice Department approached him about intelligence recon with the network of spies within the Pierce administration. His meeting with Secretary Holt burned into his memory as clear as a bell.

"Lieutenant McCann reporting, sir."

"At ease Lieutenant; I'm Secretary Holt."

"Glad to meet you sir," extending his hand to the Secretary. "I remember your speech at the Point, sir. It really resonated well with the young recruits, sir."

"Thank you, Lieutenant. We wanted to commend you on your actions during that spectacle of Bull Run. However, this is not why you are here. The President and I have agreed we need more agents in the field to gather intelligence as to what the Confederacy's next move will be. Because of your duties with the AG, you have been hand-picked by the President for this position. You have since developed a relationship with former Congressman Logan?"

"Yes, he saved my life, sir."

"Well, Logan is now a Captain and you will be officially using a U.S. Marshal badge under cover."

"I don't understand, sir. I'm not in the army anymore?"

"We are redirecting your official duties, that of U.S. Marshal, and Federal Agent. In other words, you are basically on your own, once and if, Logan can recruit enough men to form a regiment. You will report directly to Logan unless we have reasons not to."

It had been a long trip from that moment, and he was glad he was not commanding the raw recruits as they marched their way to Cairo. Especially since the mission was heating up. Yet, that meeting with Secretary Holt resurfaced along with some disturbing anxiety.

Arnett spent a great deal of time with Kathleen, acting like a doting beau should in their conversations and actions. Once, during a small excursion on a riverboat, a required outing according the "Nurse Kathleen" to aid in his recuperation, he even gave in to temptation. Arnett wondered what Kathleen's reaction might be when she realized the snare and deception.

A decade had come and gone since the day he stood at the train depot and watched Annie leave for the university. God how he missed her. She reminded him so much of his Martha – the same clever green eyes and auburn hair. With the passage of time, he realized he was no longer considered a young man, and the sudden acknowledgment created a sigh in his throat.

All his life, all he wanted to do was to be a lawman. The commander at West Point had said: "We don't get many, at

190 | David Spitz

your age, but times have changed. Above all else, do not, under any circumstance, compromise your DOG duties."

Logan's Arrival

"Everything okay?" Arnett asked Logan as they gathered his luggage.

"Yes, it is, my friend," he said.

"So, what led you to eventually being a congressman?" Arnett asked as the loaded up the wagon and headed back to the camp.

Logan took up the reins and spurred the horses forward. "Well, I'm surprised you never asked before, Arnett; but as a young child I was trained to race horses. Politics came later."

"Really?" Arnett asked surprised.

"Yes, my father dabbled in horse racing with his father as a child before he became a lawyer. My grandfather was a doctor and we lived in a small town on the Mississippi. We bred horses for racing, Which is why I was so intrigued by your passion for mules."

"But politics? How did that fit into your family upbringing?" Arnett inquired.

"Well, along with all of that, my father also dabbled in politics a bit. He served on a couple of boards, that kind of thing. Already had it in his mind when I was young that I was being groomed into a politician. It seems then and now I have a talent for giving speeches."

They both chuckled.

"Well," Arnett added. "I look forward to hearing more of your speeches."

Arnett said nothing about the mission, his real mission, or their own strategies concocted in Logan's tent that night, and

Arnett wondered how much Logan actually knew of his real mission at Camp Defiance or at West Point, for that matter.

A Spy Is Born

During the prewar days, President Buchanan often talked of the need of intelligence gathering to uncover Southern sympathizers loyal to the Constitution, in the government as well as the military. In eighteen fifty-eight, they found the perfect one and made him a U. S. Marshal – Arnett McCann.

Arnett was summoned to Governor's Wood's capitol mansion in Springfield, and ordered by the governor to continue to Washington where he was to meet with the Secretary of War Stanton on a top-secret mission.

The first thing Arnett asked the Illinois Governor was: "Am I no longer working for you?"

"Yes and no," the governor answered. "You are still working for the country, and as far as my office and your office is concerned, you are still a U.S. Marshal. That is all I can tell you, because that is all I know at this point. Godspeed and good luck," he said, shaking his hand.

The day he met the Secretary of War in his office at the War Department, he waited for the West Point Commander to arrive, making small talk.

Secretary Cameron talked about Arnett's political views, a moment of "information gathering" at the highest level, Arnett knew, but he made no bones about his feelings to the Secretary. After all, he had nothing to hide.

"Hello, Marshal McCann, glad to finally meet you. The President and I have been kicking around an idea. Since we know war is imminent, our discussions keep pointing to the same thing. The idea is, we need a set of eyes and ears inside West Point. We already understand there are certain cadets from the South that will resign their commissions in the

Confederacy, and we think you are a perfect candidate to keep an eye on who, what, and when this happens."

"Why me, sir, if I may ask? I'm just a state AG officer."

"Mainly, your records which Governor Wood readily supplied, along with his high regard of you concerning your patriotism. Look, this is a strictly on a volunteer basis. This job is dangerous, but the importance of this operation cannot be stressed enough.

"You come from Missouri, which right now, as we speak is a hot bed of divisional secession, especially along the western border of Kansas Territory. We understand... you are a little old to be joining the Point as a young cadet. So, to solve this problem, you are entering already as a Lieutenant, transferring to the Point on the recommendation of Governor Wood.

"Your status as U.S. Marshal under your State's laws, will remain intact, which will enable you to work on your own as needed. Orders will change, of course, and you will also have to follow all rules and orders from your superiors unless they are in direct violation of the Constitution. We want to know which of the top brass will be resigning, and what they are planning. In other words, we are asking you to be an agent for the Union. Infiltrate the Confederacy within the Point and gain their confidence."

"Mr. Secretary, do I have time to think on this before I give my answer?"

"Not much."

Arnett paused. "Are you concerned of my allegiance to the Union's preservation?"

"No, not at all. I have a meeting at the White House with the president in about twenty-four hours. I expect you to be there, with your answer." He held out his hand, to which Arnett shook. "Nice to meet you, McCann, and I look forward to working with you."

"Thank you, sir."

Marshal McCann walked out of Secretary Cameron's office that day proud and concerned about what the President and the Secretary wanted him to do. He had to wonder if this would end up costing him his life.

The possibility of facing torture... or worse, being strung up by his neck, or set in front of a firing squad, was a thought which whirled around inside his head. Yet, he also knew of the importance of what they were entrusting him with – and the nation's fate hung in the balance with any information he could gather.

The thought that the Confederacy could win was one Arnett could not fathom.

I need a drink, he said to himself as he headed back to his tent. Most of the various fires throughout the camp smoldered as Arnett wove through the rows of tents.

"Who goes there?" a young guard asked as he approached the Union's bivouac.

"Lieutenant McCann."

"Sorry, sir, didn't recognize you. "

"It's alright, soldier; just keep doing your job. And doing it well, I might add."

"Thank you, sir. Not often an officer compliments us or even talks to us for that matter."

"Stay alert and have a good night, private."

"Good night, sir."

Arnett walked over to his side table in his tent, looking underneath for a bottle and pouring himself a drink, then tossed his hat on the cot. He sat on the edge of the bed, taking a long guzzle from his tin, thinking about his conversation with Kathleen at the hospital while he recuperated from his injury.

He looked up, lifting his tin to the ceiling of his tent. "God help us," he said,

Draining his tin, he tossed the cup aside, pulled his boots off and lay on his bunk, eyes closed though sleep eluded him while memories haunted him... especially making him question his reasons behind accepting this commission.

The next day in the oval office, after meeting with the Secretary of War, he had the pleasure of finally meeting President Lincoln.

"Good morning, Secretary Cameron; is this Marshal McCann that I have heard so much about?" Lincoln asked, and Arnett's eyes rose up to meet the serious dark eyes of the President.

"Yes, sir," Cameron announced, presenting Arnett to him.

Arnett stepped up and saluted the Commander-In-Chief.

"No need for that, son." He shot a questioning glance to Cameron. "He's older than I expected, Mr. Cameron."

"Marshal McCann is highly regarded and more than qualified."

"So, you have accepted?" Lincoln asked, his eyes fixed on Arnett's face.

"Yes, Mr. President. I accept the orders and the consequences, whatever they are."

"Excellent; I cannot express my thanks enough. You do understand the importance of secrecy in this assignment?"

"Yes, sir; of course, sir," replied Arnett.

"Shall we?" Lincoln said, pointing to a chair, and he continued as they all sat. "Your earlier report on the Officers at West Point who resigned, enabled us to plan for their replacements as well as do thorough research on them. We also appreciate the information conveyed concerning Commander Beauregard's desertion of his post, as well as the others." Lincoln looked toward Secretary Cameron. "Let us begin the task at hand."

The secretary opened a file he had been carrying and went ahead. "We believe an organization is funding the Confederacy's secession and supplies. They call themselves "The Knights of The Golden Circle," and they have been instrumental in causing havoc on the Missouri Kansas territory border for years now. Information on the Knights has been sporadic at best. You play chess, Mr. McCann?"

"No, I prefer five-stud."

"Well, then you know how to bluff your way out of a situation?"

"I have many times, and I wasn't even playing cards at the time."

The three laughed as the Secretary continued.

Arnett looked over the paper. "I've seen this fella Bickley before. He's the leader?"

"We suspect him; however, we need to find out as much about this group as we can."

"Where have you seen him?" Lincoln asked.

"I grew up in St. Joseph, Missouri. When I was around sixteen, a new doctor came to town, and he stayed at our ranch awhile. We ran into Bickley and two others on the trail and they tried to cause trouble. I had a bead on them, so they backed off. But we saw them again across from our livery stable. Bickley rode out of town in a hurry, but we could tell he was up to no good."

Lincoln stroked his beard, in deep thought, as he listened to Arnett's story. "Are you married, Marshal McCann?"

"No, I'm a widower. I have a daughter that will soon be a doctor back in St. Joseph."

"Sorry to hear about your loss, but I'm sure you find many blessings with such an outstanding young daughter."

"Yes, sir, I do."

Stanton leaned forward and handed him a paper with his entry into West Point. "You will enter the Point as a transferring cadet, a Lieutenant in the Quartermaster Corp. Tell me, would you recognize Bickley if you saw him again?" Stanton asked.

"You never forget a face when you have a bead on them, especially the first one. I don't particularly like killing, but I have no qualms when it needs to be done."

"I promised Todd I would partake in lunch with him; you two remain here and go over details of the Lieutenant's orders," Lincoln said, rising from his chair.

"Thank you, sir," Arnett said, shaking the President's hand and realizing he had just been promoted by the President, himself. Arnett was about to ask if all this was a mistake when Cameron handed him his Lieutenant's bars.

After the President left, the two men sat down to the business at hand.

"I'm thinking, you should approach this Bickley with caution as soon as possible. Your wife kept bees, did she not?"

"How did you know about that?"

"Intelligence is nothing new, son."

"I'm beginning to see that. Yes, we raised mules and kept bees."

"Good; therefore, from this point on, your code name is Beekeeper. Sign all direct communications with Beekeeper only. Your contacts, and there will be several, will use the codes to name themselves. The number one order is to keep this information away from personal relationships. It may save your life and theirs. That about covers it. Oh, one more thing, your orders are to be followed for they will coincide with your assignment, understood?"

"Yes sir."

"Have a good trip."

After Arnett left the White House, he stopped at a local saloon. He needed a drink, and time to think. He wore civvies to the White House per Secretary Stanton's request, so as to not to bring attention to those working in the White House. Everyone was a suspect. It was now his job to find out which individuals were suspected Confederate sympathizers, who were the troublemakers, and who were not.

Chapter 15

September 1861
Ft. Defiance

"Come on you conscripts; you are never going to make private if you can't get these drills down."

General Grant reached for his whiskey glass, took a drink and continued reviewing the drills taking place within view from his window.

"Halt!" Akins roared. "We can stand here in this heat and mosquitoes, and eat rats tonight if the rebels have not eaten all of them by now. Your choice. We can stand here the rest of the day until you get this right. Understood?"

"Yes, sir," the men replied to Sergeant Akins.

"March; one, two, one, two, right face, one, two, one, two."

"They look pretty bad Major," Lieutenant Smith said to McCann.

"Don't need them to be a parade troop. All they have to do is survive and fight like hell, Lieutenant."

A young private approached and saluted. "Private Prentiss, sir."

"What is it, private?"

"General Grant is requesting a meeting at your convenience at headquarters, sir."

"Does Colonel Logan know of this?" McCann asked.

"Wouldn't know, sir."

"Take over, Lieutenant."

"Yes, sir, Major."

Grant's headquarters at the corner of Jefferson and Ohio, a former general store down the street from the St. Charles Hotel, sat in perfect proximity to Fort Defiance. Grant chose the white bricked two-story building as his office, partly because he could use his spy glass out the back window and watch the troops drilling.

McCann straightened his uniform while standing on the steps before he entered the building, not because he was nervous, since he was used to being around important VIP's, even military VIP'S. To him, Grant was just another down a long line of politicians and officers making up the grand Union. McCann always followed protocol, and he wanted to make sure his uniform looked suitable, even though, technically, he was not regular army.

He cleared his dry throat, wishing he had downed a tin of water before he left the parade grounds, then grabbed the wobbly brass door handle and entered a candlelit foyer serving as an office.

An oak-tread stairway led to the General's upstairs office, and an aide sat behind a desk and looked up as Arnett stood there, waiting.

"Major you can go head up the stairs; the General is waiting for you."

McCann thought it odd that there was no hustle and bustle of activity you would normally see in a general's command post. Still, shrugging aside the trepidation, he walked up the fifteen stairs, his footsteps echoing through the stairwell.

When he topped the stairs, another hallway with three doorways on both sides greeted him. Another aide sitting at a desk glanced up at him and pointed to the office next to him. Arnett rapped, lightly.

"Enter," a gruff voice commanded.

Arnett entered and saluted. General Grant stood at the window, his back to Arnett, peering toward the parade field through a spy glass in his hand, with a half cigar protruding from his lips. Captain McCann stood at attention, waiting for Grant to finish his spying. After about ten minutes of silence, the General turned and extended his hand.

"At ease, Major."

Arnett shook his hand and sat.

"President Lincoln informs me of your excellent work while at West Point, Marshal McCann." Grant studied McCann's unresponsive facial expression. "I gather you noticed my two most trusted aides on hand; I have a limited staff due to security reasons. With this war on, one can't be too careful, right? How about a drink, Major?"

Normally, Arnett would not have accepted, except his parched mouth begged for a drink. Arnett nodded and Grant grabbed a bottle, pouring two glasses, then toasting McCann.

"Shall we get started?" Grant continued without waiting for McCann to answer. "Two days ago, when McClernand and I posed for the press in front of the post office, I received this." He handed a telegram to McCann. "Read it aloud."

McCann cleared his voice. "Vice President Breckinridge. Confederate traitor. Stop. Two other Confederate spies. A brother and sister identified. Stop. Beekeeper."

Handing Arnett a manila envelope, Grant added, "Here are your orders. You not to discuss this with anyone; do you understand?"

"Yes, sir."

"Questions?"

"I'd like someone to accompany me, if it's possible?"

"Who might that be?"

"I would like to deputize Akins's, sir."

"Is he to be trusted?"

"With my life, sir; I've known him since childhood."

"Done. I do not have to tell you about the protocols for top secret information. That is all; you are dismissed."

"Thank you, sir,"

"I should be thanking you, son. Good luck and Godspeed."

The two men shook hands and saluted as U.S. Marshal McCann turned a military about face with the manila envelope tucked securely under his arm, leaving the building and his military life under Colonel Logan behind.

At thirty-eight he was one of the youngest U.S. Marshals in the service of the Federal Judiciary system and about to start his second tenure as a Marshal. First, however, he had two priorities he had to take care of – one, his withdrawal of his Major's leaves and to inform Colonel Logan of his new orders. The second, to figure out how not to tip off Kathleen.

He walked across the street to the post office where he had first been introduced to Grant by Colonel Logan.

"Afternoon, Major, what can I do for you this hot afternoon?" the post office clerk asked.

"I need ink, quill and paper, so I can send a telegram."

"You just tell me; it'd be quicker."

"Would rather write it out; sometimes I need to pause with my thoughts."

"Understood; here you go."

"Thank you," Arnett replied and went to the small writing desk in the corner placed by the only window for light. A slight breeze from the river drifted through the opened door, reminding him of early fall breezes off the Missouri so many days ago as a youth.

"My dearest Kathleen," he wrote. "I miss you so, even though we've known each other only a short while. There is good news - I shall return to Marion in a few days and leave this dreadful place of mud, humidity, and mosquitoes. My only regret is my orders have changed. I shall have to leave my dearest friend, John Logan to fight this war without my services."

Arnett paused a minute and looked out the window, feeling guilty for leaving his companion whose training was still in progress. After much contemplation, he decided what he wrote would suffice, for he had not even opened his orders and, therefore, was not exactly sure where they would lead him to next.

He picked up the items and walked to the counter, clearing his throat to get the clerk's attention.

"All done?" the clerk asked.

Arnett handed him back the items, waiting last to hand him the telegram.

"Envelop going?" the clerk asked, pointing to the manila.

"No," Arnett replied, turning his head upon hearing someone walk up behind him.

"Be with you in a minute," the clerk blurted, "after I send the Major's telegram."

"Quite alright," the man answered.

"Charge to the Fort?" The clerk asked Arnett.

"No, how much is it?"

"Two coppers," the clerk answered.

Arnett reached into his pocket and placed the two coins on the counter.

"Excuse me," Arnett said to the man behind him as he turned and walked out the door.

Arnett looked down the street to the livery stable, and considered buying a horse, for he was now no longer a Major in the U.S. Army. His mind redirected to the man's face behind him at the clerk's office... and a feeling of seeing him before fluttered through his mind. He dismissed the notion and walked back to the Fort to read his orders... before talking to Colonel Logan.

On such an afternoon as this, a humid day with a broiling sun, he was happy to chuck his uniform and put on civilian clothes, albeit with his Marshall's badge. The drilling on the parade ground finished as the men retired, taking care of their personal chores before the evening meal.

He looked up at the arched iron sign one more time and saluted. "Camp Smith," he said to himself, then continued on his way.

He sat at his small writing desk inside his tent, lit an oil lamp, and sat down to look over the contents inside the yellow envelope. Pulling out a stack of papers, a new U.S. Marshal's badge, a silver and polished star, fell into his lap. A formal letter from the Judicial Branch of the U.S. Government dated September 27, 1861, read:

> *To U.S. Marshal Arnett McCann Western District Marshal's Office.*
>
> *Your services are presently requested to resume as U.S. Marshal. Authority area includes, but not limited to Missouri, Central-Southern Illinois, and Eastern Kansas Court duties concerning courtrooms, jail housing, bailiffs, and jury have been waived by Federal District Judge Archibald Williams Kansas Federal District.*
>
> *The DOJ recognizes your knowledge of the Confederate Guerrillas known as "Quantrill's Raiders". We have knowledgeable information they are currently working as a group directly under an organization known as 'Knights of the Golden Circle'. The two Confederate spies working in the White House, a brother and sister, are tied directly to this organization. Your assignment is to locate the female spy, bring her in to be tried for treason. We have already apprehended her brother.*
>
> *The female spy, alias Maddie Cronin, as well as numerous other aliases, has been confirmed to be your female traveling companion, so this should be an easy target for you to apprehend. Your West Point mission is officially complete. Godspeed; you now have the authority*

in which your duties of a wartime U. S. Marshal dictates.
Your mission starts as soon as you inform Colonel Logan
of your orders.

Signed, the Honorable Archibald Williams."

Arnett put the contents back into the envelope and resealed it, breathing out a long sigh.

"Private?"

"Yes, Major."

"Have Sergeant Akins wait for me in front of Colonel Logan's tent."

"Yes, sir."

Arnett walked over to Colonel Logan's tent and approached the guard. "Can You tell the Colonel I'm here?"

"Yes, sir," he said, disappearing into the tent. He peeked out and held back the flap. "The Colonel will see you now, Major."

Logan looked up as McCann enter the tent.

"Major McCann." Logan said extending his hand. "What's going on, Arnett?"

"A long story, John."

"Well, sit. There is a war, but for you I will always make the time."

Logan stroked his handlebar mustache and produced cigars from his field jacket, handing one to Arnett. He studied Arnett's face, worried that something had changed his mind on which side to fight for. Arnett's face remained stoic.

Arnett took a long draw on the cigar and puffed out the air in a cloud. "You and I've been friends a while now, John, and I'm not sure how to proceed without offending you, unintentionally."

Logan's thick coal left eyebrow raised a bit. "I hope I haven't misjudged you, friend. Just get to the point, Arnett."

Arnett produced the manila envelope from inside his shirt. "You know from my records of my West Point tenure, that I was a bit old for acceptance. Was it not surprisingly that I was a raw recruit at thirty-eight?"

Logan chuckled. "Got to admit, it was puzzling they would accept one of your age; but then, again, most accepted are due to some sort of political wrangling."

"You're right about that. I was working undercover for the Federal courts to determine who was susceptible to their allegiance to Virginia; which, of course, and as we know now, most remained loyal on the North side of Dixie."

Arnett sat his Major's leaves on the table in front of Logan.

"I cannot accept these, Arnett. I just can't. We have a difficult job ahead of us. I don't have to tell you how important it is."

"I know all too well, John, but my orders have changed." He showed Logan his badge.

"So, you're telling me you're no longer a Major, but instead, a U.S. Marshal answering only to the Federal Courts in Kansas?" the Colonel's questioned, his voice raising.

Arnett placed his finger to his lips and pointing backward to the tent's flap.

Logan stood and paced inside the small tent, chewing the cigar and trying to quell anger roiling inside his gut.

"Those in Washington, the command, don't trust me, do they? Nor you, who is supposed to be my loyal friend."

"It has nothing at all to do about you personally, John. Being so close to Virginia, spies are everywhere in Washington. Really not supposed to tell you this, but it reaches as high up as the White House, of which I cannot disclose. You want that information, you will have to go to General Grant on that one. I just came from Grant's office, myself. I have a mission to do. I wish that it included you, but it is beyond my pay grade to choose. There is a letter of resignation you need to sign. You can present it yourself to Grant, maybe he can answer your questions."

Logan sat back down and faced the back wall of the tent, his mind racing whether he had put too much trust in McCann. He reached over to a small table and poured two drinks.

"I apologize, Arnett. I should not have displayed my injured ego in such a way." He handed Arnett a cup. "To your new orders, Marshal."

He threw back the drink, draining the cup with a cough, then signed the letter without reading any of the words.

"Oh, one more thing, if you'll read all the content of the letter, it states I have the right to deputize one of my own choosing from your command."

"And who might that be?" Logan asked, still perturbed.

"First Sergeant Akins, sir; he should be right outside by now."

"Guard!"

"Yes, sir." the guard answered, poking his head in the tent's flap.

"Send Akins in."

"You mind?" Akins asked, pushing the guard aside.

"You're going with the Marshal, Akins," announced Logan without giving a reason.

"Marshal?" Akins answered, confused. "Just what is going on here?"

"I have to swear him in with a witness, sir," replied McCann. "If you don't mind?"

"Swearing in? What in tarnation is going on?" Akins blurted, rubbing his forehead with his hand.

Logan reached over to the small table and produced a bible from underneath the table.

"Now wait a damn minute..." Akins added, holding up his hands.

"You want out of this damn army or not?" Logan asked.

"Put your hand on the bible, Thomas," Arnett requested after pinning on his Marshal's badge. "Do you swear to uphold the laws of the Federal Judiciary System in these United States of America and defend the Constitution of all enemies foreign and domestic. Say, I do, Thomas."

Akins hesitated and Logan added, "Do it, now, Sergeant."

"I do," Thomas repeated, but not quite sure of what just happened.

"Deputy U.S. Marshal," he whispered, looking at the badge on his chest.

"Job is going to be a hell a lot harder than this man's Army," said Logan. "You going to have to take orders from McCann."

The three men chuckled.

,"Now get the hell out of my tent, both of you."

Arnett paused and looked over his shoulder at Logan.

"Arnett, good luck."

Arnett saluted, and Logan reciprocated... without looking.

PART TWO

Chapter 1

1861
Shawnee Forest

The pair traveled through a thick forest, following the Ohio River toward a cave in search of evidence, on a tip they received from the local tavern owner in Cairo before leaving Ft. Defiance.

"Do you even know where this damn cave is?"

"Don't fret, Thomas. I know exactly where this cave is."

"What did you say this forest was called?"

"Land of the Shawnee. This trail runs down to the Cumberland gap. Injun's hunting grounds."

Akins stopped, drinking from canteen while his horse drank from the river.

"Well, I 'spect we'll have to go high around them cliffs."

"That's a good idea, Thomas."

"What's that you say?"

"It's a good idea; it will be harder to see us in all that foliage."

"You saying we have to hide from our own army?"

"I'm not saying that, but we have to keep low unless you want to be shot as a deserter or a Johnny Reb."

"Guess you're right about that, but we ain't likely to run into anybody in this rocky wilderness," Akins retorted.

"Never know what a Johnny Reb might do."

McCann pulled on his horse's reins and with a slight kick of his heels, the horse lifted its front legs and struggled for solid footing as it started up the steep incline into a thicket of trees. Exposed rock of different sizes dotted through the undergrowth, making it difficult as both men carefully navigated through the trees.

Arnett stopped, jumped off, and raised his horse's front leg with his back to the front, checking the shoe to make sure the graveled path didn't knock it loose.

"Good idea," Akins said, following McCann's lead.

They sat on a nearby rock, looking over the landscape while listening as the birds sang. McCann's ears peeled for the sound of rustling leaves, for any intruder sneaking up on them.

"Going to be a clear night, looks like. Let us get a fire going. I could use some coffee," Arnett said, gazing up as the sunlight muted to a hazy orange glow. The men settled in, roasting a rabbit they scared up for supper.

"Better than army food, anyway," Akins, said, chawing down on a rabbit's foot.

They stretched out on the ground, saying nothing, each opposite of the fire as the small flames danced shadows across the campsite.

"Best time of the day on the trail," Akins finally said. He took a slow pull on the bottle next to him, then handed it across the fire to Arnett. "You still see that gal you met in the hospital?"

Arnett took his handkerchief and wiped his forehead. He took a drink and then, another one, wiping his lips with his sleeve and swallowing hard. He put the cork back on and handed it back to Akins.

"She's the first order of business."

Akins's eyes widened. "Thought you were sweet on her?"

"At least I'm good at fooling people. There's more to this job than chasing bad guys."

Akins raised up on his elbow and scratched his head. "As long as I've known you, Arnett, you are worse than a puzzle with missing pieces. I can't for the life of me figure you out."

Arnett laid back on his pallet and sighed. "There's no one around now, Thomas; time I let you in on what we're up against."

Thomas sat dumbfounded as Arnett spelled out everything that had happened since Miss Cronin slipped out of the White House and assumed a different name, as well as her connection to the Knights of the Golden Circle. Akins whistled, astounded as the the sun slipped behind the cliffs of the Shawnee land.

"You know we may have to split up if the ones we're tracking get a notion we are following," Arnett said. "Being a lawman is tougher than the Army, on the trail; days at a time just by yourself. Someone wanting to send you to hell, just because you're a lawman."

"You're not going to get rid of me that easy friend. Just what is it we're doing here in this rocky deserted forest, Arnett?"

"There's a small village with a cave on the riverbank. We need to check out this cave, and then interrogate a witness. We have a long day ahead of us; reveille at two. Don't spend it in the bottle."

"Thought we was out of the army," replied Akins.

The next morning, both rose at first daylight, with a breakfast of biscuits, hardtack, and coffee; then, got their horses ready for a half-day ride back down the hill to the river.

"Let's try not to be seen before we get there," Arnett said. "Town may not be none too friendly to a couple of feds."

"Damn sure, we don't have to advertise it," Akins replied.

Arnett dismounted, allowing him to navigate the low-lying brush and thorn.

"What are we looking before we ride into this village?" Akins asked.

"Johnny Rebs and Confederate flags, plus anything else suspicious. Deputy Akins. Part of a job of a U.S. Marshal is interviewing witnesses, taking care of the courts, and bringing in fugitives. Which is what we are going to do."

"I know all that. What in Sam's hell am I here for?"

"You're the main witness," Arnett answered, chuckling.

Akins eyes widened. "You mean that dang blasted fiasco at the fort?"

"You got it," Arnett answered.

The men rose slow and easy across a grassy field. Arnett stopped, raising his hand for Akins to stop, then pointed two fingers to his eyes, motioning for Akins to keep his eyes peeled. Thomas nodded and the two men surveyed the area.

After a thorough look, they started across the brown field of once purple bee balm, and through toppled Ash and Black Maple trees. They crossed over two trees wounded by lightning during a thunderstorm, and the volcanic rock which slid from the hillside, gathering at the base of the trees, layers upon layers of high hard-stone cliffs.

"Careful of these rocks. They can pierce a man and horse's ankle to the bone. Stay with the horses, Thomas," Arnett commanded. "No use in both of us getting banged up."

McCann slid down the slippery cliff as if back in his childhood days, feet first, using his hands to slow himself down. When he reached a pine growing through the rocks, he stopped and carefully stood, leaning against the tree for support. He gazed down over the town below him with his spyglass, his eye fixing on a few people scattered along the main street.

"See anybody?" Akins asked.

"Just an old man sitting on a chair, and a few women, but no flags except a Union. The man is probably a town Constable."

Thomas was already one step ahead of Arnett, reaching for a rope on one of the horses. He tossed the end to Arnett; took two tries, but the rope finally reached him, and he walked the rope back up to the horses.

"Thanks, Thomas."

"No need, Arnett."

"Just the same."

"While I was down there, I saw a small trail leading down to the town."

The two maneuvered slowly into the prairie which led to the outskirts of town.

"Laura! I see men!" Janey hollered at one of the girls from an upper deck of the saloon hall. Akins gazed up at Janey, eyes squinting, and smiled as he turned to McCann. McCann scoured the streets, unaware of the beauty leaning over the railing.

"Kind of a ghost town," Arnett said.

"Hmm, I see more things than ghosts," replied Akins.

The old man rocking on his chair, paid little heed to them as they rode their horses up to him. The sign above the door squeaked in the slight breeze, reading 'Sheriff's Office'.

"Sheriff inside?" Arnett asked.

"I'm the sheriff," the old man said. "Whose asking?"

Arnett displayed his Marshal's badge behind his vest.

"Feds huh?" the old man snorted. "Why aren't you out defending the Capitol?"

"Because we're here," Akins retorted.

"What's your business here?"

"Where is everybody?" Arnett asked, ignoring the man's question.

"Well, if they're not in the whorehouse, they're back at Defiance."

"You're the only man here?" Arnett asked.

"That's not what I said, Marshal."

"Are the one that sent the telegram to Cairo? About the witness?" Akins asked, trying to act his part. He never liked being left out of anything when he was supposed to be a part of it.

"Not me. Ask the one at the whorehouse. Head whore is named Laura. Enjoy. Gentlemen," the Sheriff said, chuckling between his two yellow front teeth.

They headed to the whorehouse where Akins wasted no time ribbing Arnett over the look on his face when he saw Laura coming down the stairs, dressed in little more than what God gave her.

"If I didn't know any better, I'd think you know this Laura."

"Hold on there, Thomas."

"What," Akins answered, perturbed.

"Do I need to remind you again, this is strictly a business visit and that is all?"

"You really like to take the fun out of life, you know that, McCann?"

"I like fun a plenty, but not when I'm working. You think the boys we left at Defiance are going to be having much fun?"

"Dang you, McCann." The excitement leaving Akins' face.

McCann's thoughts confused his focus, and he wondered if it was that obvious.

"My, my look what we have here, girls. Two live ones," Laura said. Laura, a tall brunette with a flowing river of hair down her back, lifted the bottom of her dress and sauntered up to Arnett.

"Gentlemen, what can we do you for?" Laura asked, presenting her hand in a ladylike manner. Arnett took her hand in his palm and kissed the back of her fingers after removing his hat. He looked up into her green eyes.

"Hmm, a gentleman. Not many of them round these parts."

Trying not to tip off their former relationship, Arnett revealed his badge to her. "U.S. Marshal Arnett McCann, ma'am."

"And I'm assuming this other gentleman is your prisoner or your deputy?"

"That would be Deputy Marshal Akins, U.S. Army, retired."

"Didn't know the army was letting people retire these days. But we don't mind providing a little entertainment for retirees, do we, ladies? With the men all gone and such, well, you know how it is. A lady can get a little, uh, frustrated."

"I don't think frustrated be the word you're looking for, Laura dear," a blonde-haired buxom girl behind her added.

"Hush up, Jasmine, was I talking to you? Mind your manners."

"Not at all, I'm a minded, Miss Laura."

"Well, now, there you have it, gentlemen. Is there anything you can do to easy our frustration?"

"My, my," Akins said. "Like being in a candy store. Come on ladies, times a'wastin'."

"Shall we?" Laura asked, extending her hand to Arnett. "Janey, put the do not disturb sign out please. This way, Marshal."

"Lock the door, Laura."

"Sure, Arnett. We can talk in the back room."

He followed her through an upstairs bedroom, all adorned in faded burgundy velvet curtains and a four poster bed, to a back sitting room overlooking the street.

"What have you got for me, love?" Arnett asked, after enjoying a long hard kiss.

She whispered in his ear, kissing his neck, her breath hot on his skin. 'Well, there have been some late activities spotted going on down by the cave."

"How many times?"

"Hard to say. Some of our clientele off the keel boats have been talking. You know how it is? There are always rumors. Men on horses with torches and a small boat."

"Yea, more so in wartime."

"Can't be sure with whether it's ours or theirs."

Arnett sat back on the velvet settee. "Help me get my boots off. I'll check it out in the morning after breakfast."

"How come you acted like you just met me, Arnett?"

"You know, can't be too careful nowadays. Enough of the talk already," he said, easing her backwards to the bed.

"Where's my Deputy?" McCann asked, descending the stairs as he buttoned up his vest.

"He's already eating, Mr. Marshal sir," another of the girls answered with a strong southern accent.

"Marcie, you keep getting more beautiful every time I see you. Breakfast looks fine, Marcie. Thank you."

McCann sliced into a piece of ham with his knife and looked at the stack of food on his deputy's plate. "You have enough to eat there, Deputy?"

"What?"

"Might want leave some for the ladies."

"Shoot, they're too busy upstairs, fighting over whose gonna take a bath today."

"Hmmm," chuckled McCann."Laura tells me some men have been showing up at the cave during the night. Eat up so we can get back to Marion before dark."

"No way we can do that in a day. Especially taking the river road back to the wagon trail north, and that's if we don't run into trouble."

"Well, we have to try. Go get the horses, I need to talk to Laura before we leave."

"Hhmph," scoffed Thomas, mumbling as he headed to the horses. "Always having me doing everything, why I'll tell you."

Arnett watched Akins grab his hat as headed for the door.

"Scrappy little guy, isn't he? I have some biscuits and ham here in this bag for you," Marcie said.

"Why, thank you, Marcie. Can you be a dear and run those out to Thomas? I need to have a word with Laura before I head out."

"That's mighty fine, Arnett; mighty fine."

He watched her sway as she left, the saloon doors swinging back and forth as she went through.

Arnett walked back upstairs and rapped lightly on the door. "Laura," he said as he pushed open the door. She kept on tucking the blankets on the bed, ignoring McCann. "I get the impression you're upset about something," he said.

"Should I be, Arnett?" she asked, refusing to look at him.

"Dad burnet, Laura, I'm trying to say goodbye and pay you for last night." Arnett leaned against the door jam, stroking his thick spotty gray mustache. *Maybe I should have said it different*, he thought, studying her sad eyes as she finally looked up at him.

"Pay me for what, Arnett; services rendered?"

"Come on, Laura, you know how I feel about you." Arnett approached slowly. "But, I have to leave now. I have to finish the assignment."

"Damn you, Arnett, I know that. How long have you been coming here? You, men, think you can come in here and use us up, then break our hearts when you leave without anything. You think I want to live my life like this?"

She crumpled to the bed, head in hands, and sobbed. She had always been the strong one, comforting her girls when one of them fell hard for a customer. Now, it was her turn.

Arnett walked around the bed and knelt in front her, placing his hands on her legs. "You think it's easy for me always leaving like this?"

In the end, her clientele was, after all, customers; that is, until the first time Marshal Arnett McCann passed through this small town with the leader of the Clem Gang tied on a rope behind his horse.

That day, she sat on the upper deck of the saloon, enjoying coffee and a warm sunny day. When he looked up at her and tipped his hat as he rode down the street, butterflies swarmed her stomach... not to mention other parts. No man had ever made her feel that way. To her, they were just business to use for profit. *Sure, the sex was fun*, she used to tell her girls, *but never ever fall in love.*

"They're here to make us a living. Only a fool would fall in love with a saddle tramp. But, who knows, maybe we're all fools."

From the first time, ten years ago, she had been forced to heed her own advice. Yet, the moments in his arms were different; no one had ever moved her with such abandonment... and yet, with such gentleness.

"It's time I get back to work, Laura."

"We're never going to have a life together, are we?"

Arnett shook his head and left.

"Well, I see that went well, Arnett," Akins said, as the two mounted their horses and headed down to the river's edge to the cave.

"Shut up, Deputy."

"It's your life," replied Akins.

"Sometimes you talk too much, Thomas."

They rode in silence to the river, both ruminating over the evening's entertainment.

"Woo wee, this is one mighty river," Deputy Akins said, trying to break the silence. He wasn't quite sure what happened while he was tending the horses, but from McCann's sudden change of seriousness, he knew to leave well enough alone.

"But, I do believe it's not as big as the Missouri," continued Akin with the small talk. "See how the land lays out? Cave will be right where that upper rock is."

River foam bounced along the bank as the waves, small but still powerful, hit the small beach leading into the cave. A huge opening, carved from the river waters pounding against the rock for centuries, loomed before them.

The opening appeared larger at the top, the lower mouth flooded with standing flood waters rushing in and receding back into the Ohio. Large rock boulders leftover dotted the sides interwoven with river pines and black oak saplings growing through the cracks, along with underwater river plants clumping in small patches along the beach.

Arnett dismounted, keeping an eye on the river, not wanting to be surprised by would-be intruders.

"Days old campfire at the entrance, Arnett," Akins said, pointing to the burned out site. Arnett searched the beach for fresh footprints, then checked the charred wood for any indication of warmth.

"Cold as a cow's teat. Been here a few weeks... maybe a month."

Arnett went to his horse and grabbed a candle from his saddlebag, lit it and grabbed a stick, letting the hot wax drip on the tip, then walked up to the entrance and lit the torch.

"Stay here, and guard the entrance. I don't want to be surprised by intruders."

Akins nodded and perched his rifle on his arm as he watched the river.

Arnett followed a narrow path around a huge boulder. The torchlight flickered off the walls, shining on a group of bats hanging from the ceiling. A few of them took to flight, startling McCann as he entered the cave.

Akins stuck some chew in his mouth and leaned against his horse. McCann held the torch up along the first wall, illuminating old Indian pictures – men, women, children, buffalo – but nothing indicating anything sinister. He held the light to the backside of the boulder. Still, nothing.

The torchlight could only show so high, directing the light from the bottom first and then, the top. He thought he saw something, but disregarded it as a shadows trick to his eyes. Working his way back to the rear of the cave, the light flashed up, and there it was again, an unmistakable marking.

It was just as Laura had told him. He had to admit, he had his doubts, because clients that visit the whorehouse are generally high on alcohol and like to brag about anything.

"Thomas! Thomas! Bring another torch."

Thomas, half asleep beneath the Autumn sun, sauntered in slow, holding his torch up and adjusting his eyes to the darkness.

"Marshal, where you at?"

"Hold your torch up higher."

"Can't, the ceiling is too low here."

"Just follow my voice, then; eventually you'll see the shadows."

Picking away through the narrow trail around the boulder, Akins finally reached McCann. "What are we looking at?"

"Hold your torch higher across from me."

"This is what we're wasting daylight on?"

McCann struggled, pulling himself up on the boulder. "That," he said.

"Looks like a ship's anchor, or just a pirate's mark," Akins grumbled.

"That, or make it look like a pirate's mark. Whatever they used, it's no pirate mark. Look, it's too recent. Look how different, how much darker than the Indian markings. Besides, there hasn't been pirates on the Ohio since eighteen twelve."

"Hmmm," Akins said, rubbing the bottom of his nose. "How do you reckon they got up that high?" "

There," replied McCann. raising his torch to the ceiling, revealing a hole large enough for a horse. Another secret entrance.

"We'll I'll be. You already know this was here?" Akins asked.

"No, saw it when I was pushing my way up this boulder." he said, lying. Arnett was not ready to reveal his source of information, nor the whole mission... just yet.

After all, Arnett reasoned, the less his friend knew at this stage, the safer his friend would be. Arnett took a small pad out of his vest's pocket and drew two J's. A regular J and then one pointing the opposite direction with their backs to each other to form an anchor.

"That's all we need. Now, let's get the hell out of this bat infested cave.

"So, what now, Arnett?"

"We head back to Cairo along the river. We need to warn Grant, Quantrill, may be working in the area."

"You're going by that insignia that possibly could have been there for decades? Made by pirates, I say. Come on, now, Arnett; you can't really believe that this here symbol means anything?"

"I understand your feelings, Akins, but you haven't been a lawman long. Sometimes, you need to listen to your gut. I can tell you that insignia has not been there that long. That anchor is a message, and is someone's initials – J, J. We need to figure out just who that message is for. Come on, times a'wastin'."

"Or who JJ is," Aikins added.

Hidden among the trees above the cave, two men lay prone listening to Arnett's discussion with his deputy. Three nights earlier, two men climbed aboard a flatboat on the Cherokee River following it upriver to the Ohio, traveling at night with no lanterns and only the moon to guide them.

"Yantai, keep an eye on that bank for falling trees. If we get too close, use your pole, like I taught you. You hear now?"

"Yes, sir, Master Josiah," the black man said, gazing up at the millions of stars scattered across the sky. "The sky black as Anais himself," the Nigerian whispered.

Josiah looked back towards Yantai, the whites of his eyes glowing in the moonlight was the only thing Josiah could see. *A perfect night for staying hid*, he thought; *however it was a good way to get myself kilt in the process. Everything worth having is a risk,* his mind whispered as he tried to convince himself.

"Sammy, gets your pole moving faster or I'll whip the hell out of you when we get back," Josiah barked.

"Yessah, maussah."

"What did you say, nigga?"

'Yes, Master Josiah."

"He has a problem with that, doesn't he, boss?"

"Yes, Adams, he does. We might have to do something about that when we get back."

Sammy pushed faster upon hearing Josiah's comment to his keel man who was also the foreman over the Valencia Plantation.

Josiah Walker inherited Valencia from his father at a young age, learning from his example as he watched his father's foreman beat, chase down, rape, and execute runaway slaves.

He would leave them hanging in the trees for days at a time, close to the cotton fields in plain sight as a warning to other presumptuous niggers. Mommas would tell their children to look away, to just do their work, even though most knew who was hanging in the wind, being pecked by marsh hawks and buzzards.

When going to the fields from their one room cabins, all they had to do was look to the sky at the carnivorous birds circling above to know another had been caught. They always knew who was missing.

Sometimes, the foreman covered the heads with burlap, keeping the birds from pecking out the eyes, not to save the slaves from the ghoulish sight, but to keep the white folks from vomiting.

A guard sitting on a horse, retching in the bushes, was another chance for a desperate one to run from the hell of their life.

"Gittin' rough, boss; we're about to the big river."

"Keep that keel steady. I will let you know when it is time to turn. Get the paddles, boys; too deep here for poles."

"Yes, master."

"Glad it's a calm night," Adams said.

"All right, the cave is a couple of miles up ahead. Start crossing over to the other bank."

Josiah walked to the side of the flatboat with his spy glass, looking for barge traffic coming down from Pittsburg.

"Faster, Sammy, The quicker the better."

Finally, they reached the other side. The boat slowed to a crawl toward the bank, the same place every trip for the last year.

Josiah grabbed the lantern, along with a shovel and a canvas bag, then headed to the cave.

"Have them two watch the river, Adams. You know the routine." Josiah jumped the short distance, water seeping into his kneel-high boots from the top.

"Damn," he cursed, almost dropped the lantern. The moon peeked out from behind a passing cloud, enabling Josiah to delay lighting the lantern till he got into the cave. Taking two matches to light the lantern, he picked up the bag and carried a shovel on his shoulder and went inside.

A mixture of mud and wet sand made the digging difficult, causing him to pause several times to wipe the sweat beading on his forehead. Josiah was now thirty and he had been sole owner of Valencia Plantation for two and a half decades.

He had never married, even though Southern belles swooned over him as the most eligible and richest bachelor in all of Savannah. His known "pleasuring" abilities and physical six-foot frame was well documented by the many debutantes of Savannah's society, and upon occasion, his half-sister Maddie, the one destined to be his contractual wife.

He took the gunny sack and stuffed it as far back into the hole as he could, then started the work of covering. Afterwards, he packed the loose mixture with his boot, raised the lantern to guide his steps back out of the cave.

He looked around for something to brush away his tracks on his way out deciding there was no need. No one used the cave anymore, anyway. He flashed the lantern twice toward the flatboat and headed across to the river.

"Get ready to push off, Sammy."

"Yes sir, Mr. Adams."

Josiah handed the lantern to Yantai. and the three worked feverishly turning the flatboat back east toward the channel to Tennessee. Adams raised the keel to keep it from hitting rock and fallen trees.

They had almost completed turning the keel boat toward home, the current's waves pushing inland causing the boat's keel to rub against a sapling growing out of the river's sentiment almost cracking the side of the boat.

"Dammit, Yantai, hold this boat still." Adams shouted, looking at Josiah, waiting to see if it happened again. The boat steadied and they pushed off again, disappearing into the darkness.

A boat's Captain watched from his perch on a steam tug. "You see that, mate? Looked like a flat coming in from the cave. Then, I didn't see it again."

"No, Captain, I didn't see no lanterns burning."

"Yea, that's the problem; they weren't using lanterns. Guess I'll have to alert them at Defiance when we get back," muttered the captain.

"What's that, Captain?"

"Nothing; do your job."

"Asshole," the mate muttered under his breath.

Chapter 2

1862
Federal Judicial District Court
Kansas City, Kansas
Federal Judge Archibald William's Office

"We are both men of the law, Marshal, and we are duty bound as U.S. Citizens sworn upon the Bible to uphold the law of these United States, no matter how difficult it may be considering we are at war. Secretary Cameron and I both hold you in high regard as to your ability in bringing fugitives to justice."

Arnett had been summoned to the judge's office, after Union loyalists terrorized by several guerrilla entities working from the Ozark mountains along the Missouri and Kansas borders.

The guerrillas were not an official part of the Confederate Army, however, they were made up of Confederate sympathizers, most of who were men who had no qualms about who they killed in the defense of the Confederacy.

Arnett rubbed his forehead, waiting to see if the judge wanted him to reply. Judge Archibald Williams could sometime be hard to read, with his stoic face and unemotional words. He had a gift for setting traps with his speeches, ready to catch a person in lies or deception... an ideal thing to have for a man serving in his position.

Arnett also knew Archibald and Lincoln were good friends, yet he still had no idea why he had been summoned to his judge's office.

What the hell is this all about, he wondered. *What the hell have I done to be taken out of the field while chasing a supposedly notorious fugitive, leaving a deputy behind to track such a killer?*

Arnett's confidence was high where Deputy Akins was concerned; but still, he had never been called out of the field while on duty, without already having the answer in his own mind as to why.

Archie, as his friends called him, was a tall this man sporting a thick bushy mustache, and still wearing his robe from the morning's court sessions. He rose from his desk and peered out the window behind him.

"Pour us a drink, Arnett."

"No, thanks, I'm well. A little early for me, but I can pour you one, sir." Arnett fidgeted in his chair knowing full well that the reason for this meeting was about to be dropped in his lap.

He sat waiting for Archie's reply which never materialized. Arnett readjusted his hat resting on his crossed leg, waiting to rise and fix the judge a drink. Judge William's suddenly turned and looked Arnett directly in the eye.

"In war," the judge began slowly, "in war, men sometimes do things they normally wouldn't do."

"What?" Arnett started.

Judge Williams held his hand up. "Just hear me out Arnett. Do not say anything you might regret. Just listen. I received a disturbing letter from the President concerning an acquaintance of yours."

"And who might that be?"

"Do you know Madge Cronin from your days at the Point?"

"No, I do not," rubbing his forehead again.

"Apparently, she and her brother worked at the White House, Daniel Cronin was hanged for treason shortly after you left with Colonel Logan for Illinois. We came to find out they were working directly with a "Benedict Arnold" traitor, our former esteemed Vice-President Breckenridge. Now a General in Lee's army."

"What's this have to do with me?"

"Madge Cronin was able to escape with the help of our traitorous Vice. Seems you are presently quite close to her."

"Kathleen? Come on this is crazy. You think I'm involved in this conspiracy?"

"I'm not the only one. Lincoln and Grant, both think that is a possibility."

"So, the Administration, including you, think Miss Hardin is really this Cronin lady? Unbelievable."

Knowing the good Judge was lying about Lincoln and Grant, he decided to let the man reveal his true motive.

"She has used various aliases of which we are well aware of," the judge said, fiddling with something on the shelf behind him. Arnett prayed it wasn't a gun.

By now, Arnett tired of the direction of the Judge's questioning. "From your reaction, I can tell that Colonel Logan is right in his summation, that you have no idea or are not part of this spy ring."

"Colonel Logan... knows of this?"

The judge returned to his desk and retrieved a form. "Yes, he does. And you also have another problem, Arnett. Deputy Akins is also a suspect, and we suspect he is funneling Miss Kathleen Hardin's spy info to another agent, who is passing it onward via Clarksville, Tennessee's, Fort Defiance."

"How long have I worked for you, Judge? Four, five terms? Just what are you accusing me of?"

"I'm not accusing you of anything, Arnett, but there's other forces here that are needing hard facts. Someone get to you, Arnett? Did she get to you?"

"Come on, Judge. I never even met her till I woke up in that hospital and there she was."

"You sure about that now? Cause now is the time you should be telling me. If I turn around, you're not going to have a gun pointed at me, are you, Arnett?"

"I don't have a reason to, Archie."

At that moment Judge Archibald Williams knew Arnett was telling the truth. Not many called the Judge, Archie, except his small circle called the judge by his first name.

"So... there are no misunderstandings. They want you to sign this document."

"I'm not signing anything, Judge. You are obviously searching for information that I don't have. If you want to fire me, fire me."

"I know one thing, Arnett; it will settle this, once and for all.

He paused, then pushed the paper toward Arnett.

"What's this, Judge?"

"Only one way to convince them otherwise that you haven't been compromised."

"You mean convince you?" Arnett asked.

"You have to bring her in, yourself. That will convince them."

Arnett walked out of the judge's office, and put his hat on as his mind raced. *There is more to this, apparently. He was testing me. Maybe, the Judge is the one I should be concerned with. Well, I know one thing, it is not for me to decide whether he is one of them*, he thought.

The judge's line of thinking stuck to his mind like glue. He lost track of time, and he had no idea how long he had been walking.

I need a damn drink.

He tried focusing in on his surroundings, he really had no idea what section of town he was in.

Kansas City was becoming a sprawling city much like St. Louis. Settlers heading to Denver, or the southwest territories came through Kansas City. Even though, it had only been eight years since he pinned a Deputy Marshal's badge on his chest, the town sprawled forth like a tumbleweed fire since he returned to Kansas.

Arnett realized he had walked down by the stockyards and remembered a saloon up the street a short distance. He needed a drink bad. He had not had one since he and Thomas tied one on the last night before he was called back to his boss's office.

He walked through the swinging doors, sun rays splayed through two windows at the front, supplying the interior's light along with two small lanterns hanging from the ceiling behind the bar.

"Give me a double shot of whiskey."

"Yes, sir, Marshal."

"I know you?" Arnett asked the barkeep. The barkeep pointed to Arnett's badge. He leaned on his elbows against the bartop, exposing the badge in the sunlight.

"Keep it to yourself if you want to stay healthy," the barkeep replied.

"Whatever you say."

Arnett took a slow sip of his drink and looked in the large mirror behind the bar. A couple of soldiers walked past the saloon without so much of a look inside. *Must be on duty*, Arnett thought.

"A little early in the day, ain't it, buddy?" asked the barkeep.

"What's that?"

"You need another?"

"Huh, no, talking to myself; sorry."

He rubbed his head, again. *Apparently, the good judge has no idea what my real orders are, or maybe he does know and is fishing for more information, unless his loyalty should be questioned.*

This spy business is wearing on my nerves. Seems I even need to be wary of Thomas, despite being childhood friends and all. Women come and go, but a close friend... and now, he's probably already suspicious, seeing how he was called out of the field.

One thing to figure though, something eating at his craw - he was beginning to think the boys in Washington suspected the judge also. *I believe they are giving the judge just enough information to hang himself.*

"Want another one?" the barkeep asked.

"No," he said, throwing back the shot and tipping his hat as he left.

Arnett walked over to the livery stable to see his new horse.

"How's my babe doing?" he asked the stable hand.

"She's in her stall, gave her some oats earlier and brushed her all down, and put new shoes on yesterday."

"You took good care of her; I'll give you that. Here," he said, flipping the handler a silver dollar. The young man took the coin, shining it up on his shirt.

"Thanks, mister."

Arnett never heard him, for he had already entered Babe's stall.

"Hey girl, how are you doing?" he asked, stroking the mare's muzzle. The mare rubbed his nose at Arnett shirt.

"What's that, girl? Yea, I know what you want." He retrieved two sugar cubes out of his shirt pocket. "There you go," he said, softly, giving her a kiss on her nose. "Hey, boy, get her ready to ride be back in an hour."

"Yes, sir, Marshal."

The first night on the trail is about as lonesome as it gets for a lawman. Arnett got used to traveling with Akins, or a prisoner... for the most part. He had made it to St. Louis in record time and took a ferry across the river and spent the night in the little river town of Alton.

He bought a train ticket for him and his horse on the spur to Mt. Vernon. From Mt. Vernon, he decided to ride the rest of the way to Marion, although it was trip he wanted no part of, in truth.

He had brought women to justice before, but never a spy and especially not one he had fallen hard for in the line of duty. He did a lot of thinking on how to approach such a delicate situation. He told Akins this was just business, but his heart spoke different... the first time since losing Martha all those years ago.

Playing both sides during a war when your boss just happens to be a Federal Judge, and apparently on the wrong, is a tricky situation. And Arnett couldn't really talk to anyone about his feelings. The only other people that knew were Akins, Grant, Cameron, a former judge (now deceased), and the President, himself... and, of course, Logan. None of which would understand his infatuation with the woman. *Or would they?*

That night on the trail was the longest night Arnett could remember in his fifteen years as a lawman. *God damn women,* he thought, staring into the small fire as he sat up against a fallen tree, hoping the forest critters and any lurking humans, especially gray uniformed ones, would leave him alone. *That was all he needed, to be left alone,* he thought, pouring more Kentucky bourbon in his coffee.

Yet, he had gotten used to her lovely silky white skin, her luscious blonde hair and delving blue eyes. Something had to give, and it is not going to be me. He chuckled to himself. *Got to make a point to ask her, just how many damned names she has. I wonder if the Colonel knows about her. Bet you, Mary has figured out something is not quite right with this one.* Nodding off, he rested his head against the tree and closed his eyes.

The tin cup loosened from his worn-out fingers as images of Kathleen... Maddie... Kathleen... whatever her name, floated in an obscure clouded dream. His mind danced in circles, oblivious to everything around them.

Then, the images of Bull Run blasted his brain.

"Fire! Fire!" he shouted as he gave the orders to his artillery crew. One, two, three, four, exploding. The smell of gunpowder filled his lungs, causing him to cough. The pain in his side flared and his mind turned from cloudy to complete darkness. His body slumped from the tree to the ground while the explosions boomed, along with the screams of agony from his dying men.

His horse's nickering awoke him as the misty rain transformed into a thunderstorm. Arnett sat up, his hands and backside in mud as he shook his head, rousing him from the dull state and shooting pain of the bullet in his dream. The reality of the real bullet, the sharp pain in his side, burned, and he looked upward, the rain pelting down on his face.

He pulled out his pocket watch and wiped the water from the glass face. Seven a.m. He glanced over at his horse, the rivulet's of water running down her nose and neck.

"Looks like we got a bath this morning, Babe."

Lightning and thunder moved off to the east, the rain staying as Arnett put his hat on, grabbed the horse's blanket and saddled up.

"We'll be fine, Babe," he reassured her, stroking the horse's neck.

The ride was wet, slow, and lonely, as he pushed North passing several tiny villages, and then, he saw Marion a few thousand feet in front of him. The incessant pain shot through his side, again, and he held his hand to his side to ease the stitch.

Worn out from the emotional stress, from the mission at hand, his memories of Martha, and this obsession with Kathleen, he was barely able to keep his eyes opened, He grabbed his side, again, and Babe slowed as Arnett wavered in the saddle, threatening to topple off.

Arnett never noticed the sheriff's deputy standing in front of the office as he rode into town, watching him as his horse stopped in the middle of the street. Arnett slumped over Babe's mane. A young boy rushed over to him and took Babe's reins.

"That you, Marshal?"

Arnett looked up just as he fell off the horse into the murk muddy street.

"Yeah, it's me son," he answered with a raised eyebrow. "Son you want make a bit?"

"Sure, mister, what do I have to do?"

"Take Babe down to the livery stable and tell Charles I want the works for her. Another bit if you brush her down."

"Sure, thing, Marshall, Charlie's my grandfather."

Arnett picked himself up, and made the slow trek up the staircase at the local hotel. He was glad no one was in the lobby to see him in his muddy state, until a voice whispered over his shoulder.

"Oh my, what a surprise. Arnett!" Kathleen said.

He reached for her but she backed away, pointing to the mud on his clothes and boots. She smiled and arched her narrow eyebrow.

"How about a bath, first?"

And he yielded to her care, like the nurse she was suppose to be... instead of the spy she was... enjoying the relaxing warm bath in the clawfoot tub in her room, along with a fresh shave. She checked his side wound after he dried off, and gave him a clean bill of health.

Arnett sat on the bed, leaned back with his arm over his face, and was out like a candle.

"You poor thing, you're dog tired," she said, kissing him on the cheek as she sat beside him. "How about I order some food for us for later?"

Arnett groaned a 'yes' in his throat, and she left him there, closing the door behind her while he slept. When she reached the lobby, she hollered.

"Joshua! Joshua? Have you seen Joshua?" she asked the hotel clerk.

"He was out on the front stoop with the Deputy," the clerk answered.

"You have paper?" she asked the clerk."

"Yes, ma'am," he replied, reaching under the counter She grabbed the pad and the Register's pen and started writing, aware the clerk was paying a bit too close attention.

"Do you mind?" she scolded the clerk. He looked away as she finished; then, she went to the front door and tapped on the glass, motioning for Joshua to come inside.

"We don't allow their kind in here," the clerk stated, perturbed by Joshua's dark skin.

"Fine," Kathleen replied, opening the door and handing Joshua the note. "Run this over to the Deputy. The Deputy, mind you, not the sheriff. Here's a copper for you."

"Gee, thanks."

"Remember, the Deputy; now, scat."

She sauntered inside the adjacent diner to order some food. Upstairs, McCann took the derringer out of his inside vest pocket and laid it behind the wash basin. A few minutes later, Kathleen breezed through the doorway with a smile on her face.

"I hope your hungry, darling. Hop Si is bringing a fabulous meal up in a bit."

Her cheeks flushed when she saw McCann's pistol laying near the wash basin. She turned away from him and patted her cheeks with a handkerchief.

"You seem a bit nervous, Kathleen; you, okay?"

"Just wasn't expecting you back so soon, that's all."

"Hhmph," Arnett scoffed.

"I'll get the plates from hutch in the sitting room, so we can eat in bed," she said.

When she disappeared into the adjacent room, Arnett took the skeleton key for the main door and locked it, then tucked the key beneath the mattress.

Arnett stood blocking the doorway to the sitting room, watching as she rifled through her carpet bag, his elbow propped up against the door jamb, his hand resting on his neck. With his other hand, he held up her derringer he took from her purse earlier while she changed clothes behind the dressing screen.

"Looking for something, Kathleen, or whatever your name is these days, Maddie Cronin?"

Maddie froze, with her back to McCann she dropped the bag on the floor, the contents spilling out across the rug.

"How did you find out?" she asked in a calm voice.

"I knew from the beginning," Arnett answered. "Since the White House. The gig's up, your brother has been executed."

"Come on, Arnett," she said, facing him with tears in her eyes. "You and I are both made from the same cloth. There are thousands of dollars available for you and me. I know you love me... and our lovemaking last night proved it."

"It's sad, Maddie. You are a terrible spy if you don't even know when you've been played."

"Damn you, Arnett," she screamed, sobbing and fumbling through the contents on the floor.

"Looking for this?" Arnett asked, tossing the derringer on the settee next to her. "Go ahead, it's still loaded; you just might beat me."

She grabbed the derringer, pointing it at Arnett, her hand trembling.

"Such a fool I've been. I actually loved you," she sobbed, trying to get the courage to pull the trigger, even though she knew she couldn't.

"The sad thing is, I actually love Kathleen. It's just that, you aren't Kathleen at all, are you?" he replied, placing his hand over the gun and taking it from her.

Maddie jerked her head to a knock on the door.

"Everything okay, Arnett?"

"Yea, come on in Sheriff, were finished here." He unlocked the door and watched Maddie turn around slow, her head held high in defiance, as she waited to be cuffed.

"You're a fool, Arnett. I never loved you; my only love is for the Cause."

"Good thing," Arnett scowled back. "Get her the hell out of here, Sheriff. The charge is treason."

For the next week, Arnett stayed in his room going through several bottles of whiskey, attempting to dull the ache in his heart. The Sheriff sent for Colonel Logan's wife, Mary, knowing of Arnett's friendship with the couple.

"He's been this way now a couple of weeks, Mary," he said, walking up the stairs with her to the room.

He rapped soft, and opened the door. Arnett lay on a high back sofa snoring loudly in the main room, with an empty bottle on the floor, and his arm dangling from the side of the sofa still gripping the bottle neck.

The sheriff looked in the bedroom and shook his head; the floor was scattered with the remnants of Kathleen's belongings.

"I'll get the maid to start a bath and help with Arnett."

Mary walked over to the wash basin. "No water; have her bring up some fresh water."

"Right away, Mary," the sheriff said.

She slapped Arnett's face, but all she got was mumbling. She shook his shoulder and he rolled onto the floor, coughing and swinging his arms.

The maid, a small frail thing, handed Mary the pitcher of water.

"Sorry about the floor," she apologized as she poured the water over Arnett's head.

"What, what the heck?" Arnett mumbled from his drunken stupor.

"It's Mary Logan, Arnett; you're a drunken mess."

Arnett sat up, leaning back on his elbows with his legs stretched out on the floor. Mary reached over and handed him a towel.

"I had to arrest her, Mary; they'll probably hang her."

"My God, you really fell for her."

"You don't know the whole story, Mary."

He went ahead to tell her pieces of a conversation the two had before he had left for Cairo. About her abuse as a child. "She found out shortly after her marriage to Josiah, which was arranged by her father, that he was her half-brother. Of course, she told me all of this in her guise as Kathleen... not knowing that I actually knew the truth. What kind of a father makes his daughter marry a son, Mary, even if he was only a half-brother?"

"And you felt the need to protect her," Mary answered.

"Yea, I suppose I made excuses for her in my mind. I mean, what man wouldn't?"

"I hope I never have to find out," Mary answered.

"Find out what?" the sheriff asked, standing in the doorway.

Arnett looked up and wiped the water from his eyes. "Just talking about problems, sheriff."

"Well, we have bigger problems, now, it seems. She's gone, Arnett."

"What do you mean, she's gone?" Arnett said angrily as he started pulling on his boots. "My good deputy and Akins helped her escape."

"You're crazy, that's out of Akin's character."

"There was a witness. The only guard that was left alive... barely, I might add."

Arnett sat up on the sofa and buried his head in his hands.

Mary sighed. "Well, since you two have an escaped prisoner to worry over. I will take my leave."

"See you, Mary, and thank you," Arnett said. The sheriff waited till she was out of the room.

"One more problem."

"Let me guess... the good judge."

"He doesn't want you going off alone."

"She's, my problem."

"This came from Cairo yesterday," the Sheriff said, handing Arnett a telegram from Logan.

Chapter 3

Shawnee Forest
Deception

"Intelligence puts her in the Pounds area, somewhere along Hayes Creek in Shawnee land," the telegram read, with no other explanation.

Hallow's trail was one of oldest in the area, narrow with forest on both sides. Arnett went ahead, cautiously, letting his senses take over.

"Woah, girl," Arnett whispered, pulling his Sharps out of its leather saddle holster. "Whoever you are, I'd be showing yourself. If you don't want to find out what a fifty-two caliber can do to you, I would be showing yourself, with your hands up high. I'll come in after you in that gnarl you are hiding in, and it will be with gun a blazing. Now!"

He cocked the lever. Finally, a negro woman with a young girl came out of the gnarl. "Get those arms up high!" he ordered, raising his rifle to his cheek.

The woman trembled, raising both of their arms. "Don't shoot, mista; we free. We been emancipated by Mista Lincoln."

"You from the Hollar?"

"Yes sir." The woman wore homespun and sported a red kerchief over her head, tied like a scarf.

"Miller's Grove?"

"Yes, sir."

"What's your name."

"Miller."

"You Harrison's woman?"

"Yes, name's Lurinda, and this be Marcy."

"Never heard Harrison had any children."

"We found her wandering in the woods," she replied, stammering.

"Show me where Millers is."

"Please, mista, we not hurtin' nobody; we's free."

Finally, McCann lowered his rifle and holstered it. "You have papers?"

"Harrison has them."

"Come here, child."

"Please don't hurt her," she pleaded.

"No one's going to hurt her. You want to ride?" Marcy shook her head no. "Come on, child, not going to hurt you."

"Go on, Marcy."

"There you go," Arnett said, lifting the little girl in front of him. "Lead the way," he said, motioning to Lurinda.

The walk was slow, passing several blue beech trees and wildflowers as the trail gave way to high sandstone cliffs until they reached a flat area of yellow prairie grass. One area of flattened grass revealed a trail made by the Shawnee Indians, and now, Lincoln's emancipated slaves. Several children approached them as they entered the tiny village of Millers.

Harrison became the leader of the emancipated and escaped slaves, being the biggest and smartest who escaped Shawneetown's slave prison. Many wanted to go straight north through the underground railroad, but he convinced them to go Northeast into the Shawnee Forest.

"Well, I'll be. You're the second Marshal that's been through in a week."

"You're talking about my deputy, I assume."

"He said he was a U.S. Marshal," Harrison said, raising his voice.

"Little wry red headed fella, right?"

"That'd be him. Tried to play hell with one of the young lasses, till I chased him away with this." Harrison smiled, brandishing a Colt.

"You know slaves aren't allowed guns, unless you're in the Army."

"Well now, I reckon that dead deserter ain't in need it nary a more than we do. And we just happen to be free, thanks to Mr. Lincoln"

"Where did you find a dead deserter?" Arnett asked, thinking it might be Akins.

"Down by the Hollar trail."

"We notice fires at night, up by Ox-lot cave across Pounds Creek. That way," said the young black kid next to Harrison, pointing back east.

"You be talking about Crow Rim, son? Why you never told me about this?"

"Well, when I first saw him, Pa, I thought he was a ghost."

"A ghost? God Almighty! Next time you be sure and tell me these things and not listen to nonsense."

"Crow Rim? How far?" Arnett asked.

"Down through the holler, cross Hays Creek. You see, high sandstone rock stacked on top of each other. Shawnee used to shoot deer from it. Good shelter, plenty of water, you be a recognizing it. There's a water fall on the right side of the cave."

"Cave, huh?"

"Bring that paper, Lurinda."

"Paper?"

"You know the one with the lines drawn on it?"

"I get it mommy," said the boy.

"Thanks, son."

Harrison, a bear of a man with large hands, unrolled the small paper map on a makeshift table.

"We're here," pointing to a mark on the paper. "This trail will start dropping into the holler, till you come through a narrow passage with high rock on both sides. Right here," pointing again to it on the map. "You come right through some trees. At the bottom is Hays Creek. You miss the rim's waterfall, it won't matter."

"Won't matter?"

"Cause, you be blind as those bats in the cave!" he said, laughing. The others laughed, as well.

"You need food, Marshal?" Lurinda asked.

"No, but thanks," he said, pointing to his bag of food tied to his saddle's horn.

"Sun will be going down soon. Be hard to see between those cliffs."

"Yea, I thought about that. Just put my bedroll over by the cook fire, if' you don't mind?"

"No not at all. Gets kind of cold at night, especially when that devil's fog comes in the early morning."

The evening eased by quick as Arnett remained quiet, listening to the soft slave songs and stories told around the fire. Dreams of Maddie... Kathleen... whoever she was, and of Martha, and Bull Run returned with an odd twist of black smiling faces and Harrison's wild crazy laugh.

He was beginning to think they had put something in his drink. He had heard tales of African voodoo running rampant in New Orleans from soldiers at Fort Defiance who had been to the city.

The next morning, just as Harrison had said, the morning fog rolled in, thick and gloomy. McCann sat about the task at hand, saddling his horse when Lurinda's young daughter approached him.

"Where are you going? Don't you like us anymore?"

Arnett squatted down and took hold of the child's hand. "We grown-ups sometimes have jobs we have to do, even when would like to be doing something else. What's your doll's name, honey?"

"She doesn't have a name yet? Will you give my doll a name?"

Arnett turned toward his horse, lowering his hat between him and the child to hide the tears welling in his eyes. "You know, I have a daughter who was your age once upon a time. How about Annie?"

"Okay, child, let him finish his chore," Lurinda instructed, scurrying her daughter away. "You're a good man, Marshal."

"No, not really. Got a job to do like everyone else," he said, mounting his horse.

"Just the same, not many white folks like you in these parts would care a whip about any of us."

"Well, I guess I'm not like most white folk," he said, pausing and tipping his hat. "Just the same, take care of that young'un."

"We will, Marshal." Harrison's large black hand reaching out for Arnett's.

"Thanks for the hospitality," he replied, shaking his hand, then touching the brim of his hat. "Let's go, Babe."

Arnett hit the trail at a slow pace. toward Hayes Creek in search of the rim's waterfall and, hopefully, to bring Akins to justice alive.

He tried getting Akins's betrayal out of his mind and focus on the trail, but his mind rolled through all the scenarios that could happen.

Maybe the Judge knew this moment would come, pitting the two against each other, much like this damn war, Arnett thought.

Akins licked his wounds after his fight with the Yankee deserter while heading to the Rock for Josiah's regular scheduled drop for Knight's money, compliments of Quantrill's Raiders.

Getting Maddie to the Rock without them both getting hanged was priority one. The deserter surprised Maddie after she rode ahead, ignoring Akins's warning for her to wait. *Typical headstrong woman,* Akins snarled.

The deserter stepped out from behind a tree, demanding her horse, then he decided he wanted more. Akins knew something was up when she did not answer him. He left the horse, sped through the woods and snuck up behind the Yankee, telling Maddie to run. There was no need for him to say it twice... she was gone.

Blue Belly pulled a knife after the two traded several blows, neither getting the upper hand. Akins gave the deserter a wide berth. The deserter grabbed a tree limb, pushing it hard into Akins's gut, diving at him with his Bowie clinched in his teeth. Akins fell on his back with the man on top of him.

The deserter held the upper hand as Akins, out of desperation, shoved his right hand into the man's upper jaw. He fumbled with his other hand, scratching at the forest floor, gasping for breath.

Anything Lord, just anything, not done yet, he thought. After fumbling around in forest floor, he gripped a rock in his palm and with all his might, he hit the side of his man's skull. On the third try, blood spewed across his hand. The Yankee swiped his blade at Akins, weaving as the blows to his head dizzied him. Akins pulled a dagger from his boot, and shoved the knife between the deserter's rib cage, piercing the heart.

He pushed him off, the body rolling into the creek. Akins gasped for air and laid back for a moment.

"Shit," he sighed, realizing he had not escaped injury. He sat up, leaning up against a tree and reached down to his leg, the handle of the man's dagger between his fingers and the blade embedded in the fleshy part of his calf.

"Fucking coward. Fucking dead coward," he spat at the corpse bobbing in the bloody water.

His orders were to take Maddie to the cave to hook up with a small Confederate detail that had taken the over the ferry. Akins never knew the details about the cave, but he was sure it had to do with the Knight's money. He figured they used the hiding place to bury it... lots of it, and he aimed to have it for himself. Akins really did not like Maddie much, being looked down upon by a snooty antebellum bitch.

Akins' spied for the Cause while infiltrating the Justice department, relaying info from the White House, the Justice Department and back to Josiah, his main contact. Fooling the DOJ was easy; so easy that he found himself hired by McCann, himself. *Stupid fool. He thought the ruse at the Fort with the traitors tying him up and leaving him was real.*

Akins knew he had to move quickly into hiding, knowing full well that McCann was on his trail... somewhere. Akins pulled the dagger from his calf, wincing, then looked through the dead man's pockets, finding nothing. He found a small sapling and chopped it away to make a splint.

"Your worth something, I guess, you son of a bitch," he said to the man as he ripped the man's shirt into strips. He framed the two flat pieces for splints and tied his leg as tight as he could to slow the bleeding down.

The horses ran away during the melee, and Akins knew he could not walk out of the forest without help. He had no idea how far he hobbled trying to maneuver around boulders and trees, keeping as close as he could to the creek and hoping he might run into something or someone that would help him survive, then he saw it. Not realizing he had walked towards the waterfall near the cave. He stumbled across the other side of the creek, using his rifle like a crutch.

Through the sun's dancing rays across the forest trees, he noticed what appeared to be a cave opening.

Good thing I still have my rifle, he thought, *and I still have my pistol and knife, but how the heck am I going to get up there?*

Sloshing boots, wet clothes, and a leg still bleeding, although not as profusely as before, he sat on the cliff's edge, he adjusted the makeshift tourniquet.

A small fish near him tried to fight the current. Akins dove for it and threw it behind him to the ground. "You shall be my supper tonight. That is, if I can get to shelter up in that cave before dark. I could use some cleaning myself."

The more he put weight on the leg, the better it felt with the cold water from the creek rushing over the wound. He walked the trail till the rim's bluff sloped down to where he could start his upward climb toward the rim. After a couple of days of catching fish, and staying close to the cave, he finally started planning how he was going to walk out of this predicament and cash in on the hidden money.

He hoped the money was still there and that Maddie had not pilfered it all by now. His plan? To steal a boat and make his way across the line into more friendly territory. *McCann surely knows by now*, he thought. *Josiah and Maddie must be having a good laugh, leaving me to handle McCann by myself.*

Their day of reckoning will come he thought. *I just need to stay on my toes.* He checked his carbine for ammo and started cleaning his weapons, laying the gun in the sun to dry out after it landed in the creek during the fight.

Every now and then, he stopped and look out across the landscape, keeping an eye out for Arnett. He knew it would be Arnett coming for him. His ego would not allow anyone else. Over the next few days, the hair on his neck stood on end as he got the feeling of being watched. *Maybe it's Arnett,* he wondered.

Not Arnett's way, though. Arnett's like a bull, full frontal confrontation is his forte. That is what the judge had told him, warning him that McCann was smart and fast with a gun. Akins knew this day was coming... if not McCann, someone else.

Harrison's son always made a point of going to the creek and spying on the strange man in the cave. The first time he saw him he thought it was a ghost, so he stayed hidden until the day the ghost's rifle glinted in the sunlight.

Arnett arrived at the narrow passage Harrison told him about. *He was right,* Arnett thought. *No way anyone on top of those rocks could see the bottom of this trail enough to ambush him.*

He made sure to ease Babe along the trail, keeping her sure-footed and calm. McCann stopped and listened to the sounds of the forest, and the babbling of the nearby creek.

Babe whinnied. "You smell that water, don't you Babe? I hear it up ahead. I'm going to have to leave you a bit, though, but I'll take you for water in a bit."

He tied her rein straps to a small sapling jutting out of the narrow passage, and tiptoed across the ground peppered with dead brown leaves. He considered removing his boots, but thought twice, not wanting to be that vulnerable. After all, pointed toes were good for kicking ribs.

Thirty yards down the path, it was time to plan his point of attack. He knew Akins was as good a shot as he, so a direct confrontation was out. He was going to have to implement an old Shawnee tactic. *May work, may not,* he thought.

Across from the cave, a downed black oak lay cross the bank supported by a smaller forked oak. Gnarl vines had worked their way underneath the log, thick enough to hide his legs from the angle of the cave. He took his hat off and laid it on the ground. A bullet whizzed past, barely missing him.

"That you, Arnett," Akins called out. "Kind of out of your jurisdiction, ain't ya, Marshal?"

"Yea, it's me, Thomas. What the hell happened to you, Deputy?" It's over, Maddie's been arrested for treason. Probably already on the train to Alton."

He took a shot at Akins, causing Akins to lose his balance for a moment.

"You're lying, Marshal. Not even you would put an animal in that hell hole. Otherwise, you wouldn't be gunning for me." Akins shot, again; this one hitting the log directly in front of Arnett.

"How's that, Akins?"

"She's not here."

"Let me guess, she hung you out to take the fall."

"Probably already in Tennessee, Arnett; you lose."

"How do you know about Alton?"

"Everyone knows about that hellhole," Akins shouted, firing another shot.

"What was the plan, the cave?" Arnett asked, shooting and missing on purpose to keep Akins distracted.

"You're a smart one, figure it out. But duping you, was the easiest, McCann." Akins yelled, firing yet another shot as Arnett scrambled on the ground along the side of the log.

McCann noticed the slope, the one that days earlier Akins used to get to the rim. *Just might work,* he thought. He needed a decoy and fast. He grabbed his hat and placed it as straight as he could on the vine, hoping Akins could see it.

"You're awful quiet, McCann; you hit?"

"Reloading, besides I'm healthier than you; time to end this. I don't want to have to kill you."

"Not happening, McCann; this ain't gonna end with a rope around my neck."

The two traded several shots, not gaining much ground. *I need to get above him without being seen, doubt he is leaving his perch with an injury,* he thought. His rifle had just enough clearance for Akins to see the tip of the barrel.

Arnett crawled back to where he could get to the slope. With luck, the slope's blind spot would get him to the rim's top above the cave, and all he had to do was get across the stream without being seen.

"Why so quiet, McCann; what you up to? You out of ammo, wounded, or better yet, dying?" Akins chuckled, pacing across the ridge's rocky platform. He stopped, suddenly when he thought he saw McCann's rifle tip, so he fired a shot off. The bullet zinged McCann's hat and it toppled to the ground.

"Oh, you're a smooth one, McCann." A twig snap behind Akins and he turned, but the rim was covered with too much vegetation. Then he saw him.

"You old sly dog," Akins said, with an ornery smile on his face.

He cocked his rifle, but his rifle was empty, so he reached for his pistol. McCann leaped from his hiding place in the vegetation, his fist connecting with Akins' jaw squarely as the two tumbled, almost sliding off the rim.

They took turns delivering blows, rolling around on the Rim's floor. Arnett managed to stand and give Akins a decisive blow. Recovering, Akins saw an opening and charged, knocking them both off the cliff. They both tumbled down the incline, sliding next to each other at the bottom, both coughing in the stirred up dust.

McCann's natural instincts kicked into place, his pointy-toed boots kicking Akins' midsection, and flipping him over. Arnett's vision blurred, then blackened, his lungs desperate to regain the air knocked from them when he fell on his back.

He expected Akins to attack. It never came. Arnett tried raising up using his elbows.

"Ahhhh," he screamed, pain shooting from his kidneys. His head, shoulders, and back burned with a sharp pain. Assuming Akins was unconscious, he lay still for a moment, trying to refocus and steady his breathing. The pain subsided and he stood, then stumbled over to Akins.

"Thomas? Thomas!" he yelled, the pain surging with every shout. "Dangit!"

Dropping to his knees, he plunged his face into the cool water. When his mind refocused, he looked up at Akins, then cupped a handful of water, sprinkling some on Akins' face. Akins came to, with a cough.

"Damn you, son of a bitch!" Akins whispered. Arnett put his ear closer.

"I, I'm not Akins."

Arnett grabbed him by the collar.

"What?" he hollered.

Akins looked directly into Arnett's eyes and laughed, coughing up blood, repeating what he said. With one last gasp, his head fell back and his eyes closed.

Arnett stumbled back to his horse, his lungs hurting with every breath. He knew he had to get back to Harrison's village before he passed out. He also knew, from the pain, that he had more than one rib broken from the fall.

Getting on his horse and riding presented another problem, not knowing whether his broken ribs would allow him to ride. He had no time to think about Akins's last words.

"Easy there, Babe," Arnett said, reaching behind the horses right front leg and pressing her upper leg with his fingers. She bowed down on her front knees. He eased his leg up into the saddle, wincing as pain shot through his lungs and back, squinting and gritting his teeth as Babe stayed calm.

"Mommy, look, it's the Marshal!"

Lurinda hollered in excitement as she and the other women looked up from their clothes washing basins.

"Harrison!" Lurinda screamed as she motioned to one of the ladies to come help her. She grabbed Babe's reins, as one of the others grabbed hold of Arnett's legs to steady him on his horse till a couple of the menfolk could help him off.

Three days later, Arnett woke up on a cot.

"Oh, good, you're finally awake."

"Where am I?" thinking he was still back in Washington D.C.'s hospital.

Lurinda appeared in front Arnett's face. "Ahh," he winced, trying to set up.

"Just you lay there, Marshal. You drank enough Elderberry wine last night to kill that pretty horse of yours. Head throbbing?"

"Oh, is that what hurts?"

"What happen to you? Run into a bear or something?"

"No, ran into your boy's gun owner."

"You want coffee?"

"Yes, please."

"Who is he?"

"Doesn't matter, he's dead."

"Sure about that? You did quite a lot of talking in your drunken stupor over the last three days."

"Three days! Good Lord, I need to be moving. I have to get back to Marion!"

"Marion will keep, you need to get well."

"I can get well riding."

Chapter 4

**September 1861
Camp Dunlap
Jacksonville, Illinois**

"Come on in, Colonel Logan. Nice to see you again."

"Likewise, General."

"Would you care for a drink?"

"Thank you for asking, but I shall humbly decline the offer sir."

"Always the lawyer, or should I say politician, sir."

"My father down in Murphysboro used to tell me before I went off to Vandalia as a state legislature for the first time, that politics never leaves a man once he enters the profession."

"I would say, Colonel, that I would have to agree with you on that. Please, sit," the General said, toasting Logan with a shot. "So how are the men taking to training? Do you think the regiment is ready for battle?"

Logan pondered the question before answering, stroking his mustache before answering.

"As ready as anyone ever is going into war, I suppose. The ones that were already with the militia will be more than ready at a moment's notice. I suspect the new raw recruits will fall in line like all good soldiers."

"A nice summation Colonel, however, this is no courtroom."

"Battle is always somewhat of a court fight, is it not?" Logan replied.

The General nodded. "Have you picked which officer is going to give the mustering-in speech yet?"

"Yes, I have; Captain Pitcher is more than capable, General."

"What about that other one? That friend of yours?"

"You mean McCann?"

"Yes, that's the one."

"He was a loan from the U.S. Marshal's office."

"Hmmm, interesting; well, it's not important. I will be on the parade stage and hand Captain Pitcher the mustering orders straight from General Grant. Tomorrow too early, Colonel?"

"No, not at all."

"Excellent; then, ten a.m.?"

"Ten is fine."

Logan watched the General rise from his desk, then looked out the window, waiting to be dismissed, and wondering about the General's inquiry of McCann. Finally, the General turned and looked at Logan with a questioning look. *He reminds me too much of Grant, like brothers,* Logan thought.

"You were with Army in Mexico were you not?" the General asked.

"Yes, sir, a very young Lieutenant, I might add."

"Hmm,... right. You are dismissed," the General said, saluting.

"Thank you, sir." Logan saluted back and turned in a perfect about-face.

This damn war has everyone on edge, Logan thought. *Wonder if he knows McCann's real job? He sure as hell, is not going to hear it from me.*

Camp Dunlap
Parade Ground
September 18, 1861
10:00 A.M.

The marching rolls of the fifers began as the regiment marched toward the parade grounds with their sabers drawn. The men waited patiently at attention next to their tents as the line formed, then each fell in, forming rows in front of the podium, each soldier standing at attention in the warm Autumn sun.

"At ease," Captain Pitcher ordered, standing on the side of the stage alongside Colonel Logan.

"It is a great pleasure to introduce Brigadier General John Alexander McClernand," Logan announced.

Thank you, Colonel Logan. Please, excuse my appearance. I have just come from fighting on the front lines to prepare you for what lies ahead. I want to welcome you to the United States Army. You men came from all walks of life to serve your country and to preserve the Union, that is, these United States. I know this regiment will be a major force under Colonel Logan's expert guidance. With that, I will turn it back over to your commanding officer."

Logan stepped forward and cleared his voice. "The ones that know me well know my abilities on giving speeches, but also know that I am a stern and fair commander. Therefore, in regards to speech-making, I hereby shall refrain from giving one." The men cheered loudly. "All I will say is this. Today is your day and you make our esteemed President Abraham Lincoln proud as you stand with him and for these United States of America. Captain Pitcher, please, read the mustering order from President Lincoln. Captain Pitcher, if you will?"

Captain Pitcher adjusted his hat and approached the podium as Colonel Logan handed him the decree.

"Attention!" he shouted; unrolling the decree, he read:

"On this day, September 18, 1861, by the order of Abraham Lincoln, President of these United States of America, I do thee declare and name this newly formed regiment at Ft. Defiance, Cairo, Illinois in the Western Theater of the Union Army, under the command of General McClernand's Brigadier Company, Commander of the Western Theater, to be commanded by Colonel John A. Logan, U.S. Army, duly signed by President Abraham Lincoln and Secretary of War Cameron."

Captain Pitcher did an about-face, handed the decree back to Logan, saluted and returned to attention at his place on the stage.

"At ease, men." Colonel Logan addressed the men, once more. "By God, give yourselves a cheer, men; training is over!"

Hats flew in the air as the regiment was now official, everyone congratulated each other and patting each other on the back.

"Captain Pitcher, if you will proceed once again," after the men had settled back at ease.

"Company, about face! Parade, march forward on fifer's roll."

The fifer's snare drummed, and they marched forward, leaving enough space so first line could pass in front of the regiment's officers.

Logan smiled at each man that passed by... and yet, in the back of his mind, he wondered how many of them would not see next spring.

November 4th
1861

"When we going to quit this drilling every day and get into action, Sarge?"

"Quit you're yapping in formation, soldier. I wouldn't be in no damn fire hurry to reach the battle, if I were you. But, if you are itching for a fight that bad, I can make sure to put you out front. Understood?"

"Yes, sir!"

"Colonel, I know your men are itching to get in this fight. I can't for the life of me, understand why General McClernand has your regiment sitting on their hands. I just cannot fathom a reason."

General Grant reached for a lighting stick in the fireplace and relit his cigar. After a couple of puffs and several coughs, he turned his attention back to Logan.

"Unroll that map Colonel." Grant leaned over the map, along with Logan, pointing to different key points. "We have gunboats on the Mississippi here, and in St. Louis. Johnny Reb has a small encampment at Belmont, here. If we can take Belmont in Kentucky, we can back door Tennessee, take Ft. Henry, the rest of Tennessee and surprise Lee in Virginia. This damn war will be over, without too much damage. But McClernand says you're not ready. What do you say, John?"

"I say, Abe didn't give me orders to organize this regiment if he didn't intend for us to use it. A good part of this regiment knows me well, sir; I suspect they will follow me into hell if I ask them, within reason, of course."

"I knew I could count on you."

"What's the plan, General?"

"In two days, Fremont will bring USS Tyler and Lexington down from St. Louis along with five steamers to transport your troop. Once the banks are cleared by the gun boats, we can enter Kentucky and bring the fight to the South. Do not expect a pretty picture, Colonel. It's not going to be like the Mexican War."

"May I speak, sir?"

"Of course, John."

"Every year this war rages the more this country is going to disintegrate. I think we need this to be over quickly. It's a good plan, sir."

"Colonel, in forty-eight hours, be ready."

"Yes, sir."

After two days in the saddle, and in need of a bath, Arnett arrived in the south side of Williamson County, still harboring resentment, pain, and grief after the last week he just endured. Approaching a small pond, he rolled off his horse and plunged his head in the water.

His shin throbbed as he lay on the bank and he decided he needed to get Marion as quickly as possible. He dipped his hat in the water, pouring the water over his head, and waited for his horse to drink her fill. He reached in his saddle bag and pulled out an apple, took a bite, and gave the rest to her.

"There you go, girl. Like that, don't ya? Wish we could lay here awhile, but we got business to attend to."

He grabbed the saddle horn and pulled himself up in the saddle. "Let's go, girl; sooner we get to Marion, the sooner you can have a rest."

Arnett had no idea what to expect when he rode into Marion. He trotted up to the Sheriff's office and tied Babe to the railing, then went inside. Hendrickson sat in his chair with his boots up on his desk.

"How many marks you going to leave on that desk, Sheriff, before you decide you need to take those spurs off?"

"Well, my God, Arnett, we all assumed you were either halfway to Atlanta or dead."

"Dead? Not likely."

"Where's your deputy, uh, Akins?"

"Dead."

"What happened?

Arnett reached for his tin dangling on a hook filling it with coffee. "I figured you already knew, Sheriff."

"Hey, just what the hell you accusing me of, Marshal? You talking about letting your federal prisoner escape? While you are throwing accusations around you seem to have things a bit mixed up, Arnett. My job is protecting this county and taking care of prisoners."

"There, what you just said... taking care of prisoners." Pointing his finger at Hendrickson's chest.

"County prisoners, not Federal Prisoners," he said, pushing Arnett's hand; the tin bouncing on the floor and spilling the coffee.

Arnett glared at him.

"Look, Arnett, I know your tired; you've obviously have had a bad week, so, I'm going to let that slide while we're still friends."

"Akins, the girl, and your deputy... yes, *your* deputy, were all in this together. Who knows, how many more. We may wake up tomorrow to Confederate cannon waylaying us. I just wanted to see your reaction when I told you."

"You've known all this time?"

"Yea, Pinkerton told me, Allen."

"You're working with Pinkerton?"

"Not officially; he figured the train to Cairo was quicker, so he took a gamble and let me in on some things. Where's my cables?"

"There's not any, since you left."

"Back to square one with a couple agents still on the loose. Just lovely."

Arnett stormed out the door as angry as ever, only satisfied that the sheriff was not a player. He rounded the corner, almost colliding with two ladies walking past the office's wooden sidewalk. Usually, he would have stopped, tipped his hat and at least said "ladies" and apologized.

Arnett cleared his throat and hollered at the ladies, realizing what he just did. "Ladies I apologize for almost running you down." He flashed a smile and tipped his hat.

"Are you alright, Marshal?" one of them asked. "You look positively worn out."

"Sorry for the way I look, ladies. Too much time in the saddle."

"No, need to apologize, Marshal, we understand. Oh, by the way, I heard there's a letter waiting for you at the hotel."

"Good day, ladies."

Arnett hurried to the hotel, chuckling. *Good to see Marion's gossipers are still functioning.*

Laura stepped off the train onto the platform.

"Just what we need," a passenger, a man getting ready to board the train, commented to his wife. They both glanced at her rouged cheeks and red dress.

"No concern of yours, Alf; we're not coming back, remember? You're mine now."

"Yes, dear, how could I forget such a thing.

"Beyond me," she replied as Alf gave one more look at the tall slim brunette.

Arnett lay on his back on his bed, snoring and still wearing the same clothes he wore on the trail. One foot still on the floor, and an empty bottle toppled over below his dangling hand. He stirred as the door handle twisted, a woman's voice lilting into his ear.

"Thank you, and see that the Marshal's bath is drawn."

"Yes mam, right away," the maid said with a curtsy.

"Arnett," she whispered, pulling back the drapes. "Arnett, wake up," she demanded. "Arnett!" she hollered.

"Uh, what; who's here? Where am I?"

"Your hotel room, darling."

"What the hell are you doing here?"

"Well, Arnett, it's like this. I've been looking for a lizzie of a gentleman for a long time and you seem to foot the bill." Her voice oozed with sultry enticement. "You're being quite the tricky one, aren't you? Thinking you can get away from me. The maid is drawing a bath for you. You look like hell."

"You're the third damn woman to tell me that today."

"Oh really? The maid says you been up here three days, drunk on your backside. What happened, did she leave?"

"Yea, well... sort of. She left straight to Atlanta, or one of them dang cities south of the Mason Dixon. Help me with my boots?"

"Dammit, Arnett, I came because I was told you weren't doing your job; we aren't at the damn whorehouse."

"Okay, I'm sorry. Please... help me with my boots."

Chapter 5

Mississippi River
November 7, 1861

The steamboats arrived three days later in the early morning fog from St. Louis just as General Grant ordered. The Illinois thirty-first boarded the steamboat Columbia at Cairo's port.

Colonel John A. Logan stood on the gangway watching three-thousand men board seven steamers bound a short distance down the Mississippi to Belmont, following the Grant/McClernand plan, making their way into Tennessee. Grant and Logan watched them through field glasses from the captain's roost.

"Your men are well trained, Colonel. You're to be commended for your prompt training."

"Thank you, General."

"You have a match, Colonel?"

"Yes, General," he replied, producing a match and lighting the General's cigar.

"Have we received the reports of the Tyler and Lexington's excursion's yet, Colonel?"

"Yes, Freemont says Polk has dug into trenches, same reports as the recon scouts that swam across the Ohio last night. Freemont says it should be a cake walk."

"Hhmph," Grant scoffed. "In my many years of battle, Colonel, I've never found anything to be a cake walk."

"My exact words to the naval commander, sir."

"If we can get your troop into Tennessee while the

Pennsylvania army advances into Virginia, we can cut their supplies off of these two rivers and put a hurt on them they will not soon not forget."

One of Grant's officers arrived with the captain of the steamship. "Tyler reports the Rebels have stopped return fire."

"Captain shall we proceed?"

"Secure the gangplanks, let's get underway." The steamboat's Captain ordered the crew's Lieutenant.

The steamboats steamed toward Belmont, the boats at full speed arriving before dusk. Intent was to capture the Confederate's well-equipped Columbus, Kentucky 's garrison.

The garrison sat on the highest bluff overlooking the Mississippi, built by Polk to control river traffic North and South, making it the most strategic advantage for both sides.

The Union was in dire need of a victory and Grant saw this as an opportunity to move up. Grant considered himself to be more qualified than present leadership after the bungling of Bull Run which threatened Washington. And he was the man for the job.

Private Bettinger, guarding the Confederate stronghold at Columbus, Kentucky, whistled "Dixie" while gazing though his spyglass across the Mississippi river on the morning of November 7th, 1861. His eyes burned after he had pulled duty two nights in a row.

No damn sleep again, Betti thought. *You can do this; no need for sleep at all,* he whispered to himself.

Sergeant Dunlop approached from the bunker overlooking the river. "How's it going Betti.?"

"Quiet as a church on a Saturday night in Memphis, Sarge."

"Well, Betti, you know us Tennessee boys aren't just going to roll over and die, now, are we?" he said with a grin, peering through his field glasses.

"At least the fog's lifting early, sir."

'So, it is. Don't worry son "Lady Polk" will keep at bay any Yankees brave enough to tread these waters."

Bettinger rested his elbows on the wall and gazed over at "Lady Polk" through the fog, a one hundred-twenty-pound howitzer, one of the largest guns in the Confederacy, compliments of former Vice-President Breckenridge.

"James will be relieving you shortly after he's had his breakfast."

The bugler blew revelry. Dunlop retrieved his pocket watch. "Right on time. Carry on, Private Bettinger."

Life at Columbus, Kentucky and the rest of the state had made a push to remain neutral until Sept 3rd, 1861, when General Leonidas Polk's occupation of Columbus put an end to Kentucky's bid to remain neutral.

Under Polk's command, they set up five ten-pounders on either side of "Lady Polk". and several ten-pounders looking out over the Mississippi River. He also set up a smaller outpost on a high bluff across the river in Belmont, Missouri. The Confederacy now controlled the Mississippi shipping lines from the Illinois border to New Orleans.

"General Grant," a young steamboat sailor addressed him.

"Yes, son, what is it?" he asked, looking up from his coffee at a table he shared with his officers, after discussing what he hoped was to be a much-needed Union victory.

"We're just about to bank at Hunter's Farm per your orders, sir."

"Thanks, you're dismissed. Well, gentlemen, I suggest you inform your regiments. The day is about to commence."

"Good luck, General," the men said as each of them shook hands.

The sergeant major addressed the men of one of the regiments of the Illinois thirty-first. "Men I know you're concerned about being in battle for the first time. Listen to your corporals and sergeants, keep your head down, and remember your training. One more most importance thing. I will have no cowards in my regiment. You run, I will shoot you myself; understand?"

"Yes, sir!"

"Okay, saddle up."

With only two and a half months of training at Fort Defiance, the soldiers of the 31st were about to get their first taste of battle.

Indian summer came late to Belmont, sizzling across the battlefield with unbearable heat and humidity. The dry cornfields shielded any cool breeze coming off the river as the Calvary's animals disembarked, and waiting for the last of the regiment stole precious time.

General Grant unrolled his map of Hunter's Farm. "Captain Stewart, I need a reconnaissance sent over to the farm through these woods here. Three companies should be enough. If it's clear, send back word so we can get this day started."

"Yes, sir."

"Lieutenant Pouffe bring your men up with another company, we're headed to the woods with orders to engage anyone that is at the farm."

The ride through the woods was slow going. Briers snagged on britches legs and across exposed flesh, and the air was sticky hot.

"I can see why they never cleared these woods," Lieutenant Pouffe stated, riding a narrow path below the oak trees, dusting burrs off his pant leg.

Captain Stewart stopped and took a drink out of his canteen and looked back at the long line of cavalry. "We need to pick up the pace. I damn sure don't want to get caught in these dang blasted trees."

Hunter's Farm

"Did you see old Hunter's face when we told him we were going to hang him?"

"Yea, his eyes bugged out like a coon at midnight."

The two soldiers were part of the Missouri State Guard dispatched to Hunters Farm by the Missouri legislature with orders to investigate an allegation that the farmer harbored runaway slaves.

They fought alongside Confederate troops commanded by Confederate officers. Hunter was arrested and escorted back to the capitol while the Guard stayed a few days to make sure no slaves tried to seek comfort at Hunter's farm. They ransacked the farmhouse, looting and tearing up the interior, while part of the company escorted the family along with the prisoner.

"That deer stew is going to be damn good," a soldier exclaimed.

The remaining Missouri Guard sat around a black kettle hanging from a tripod.

"Yea, sure is. I hear tell their eating rats in Richmond and the war has just started," a second guardsmen said.

"All the meat is going to the army. You can't even get a pint of milk in Nashville." The guardsmen sat around eating and talking of the war. Most were not even wearing the Guard's uniform having been called up so quick after reports that Ft. Defiance's recruits were ready for action after just six weeks. Most of the regulars were in or around Richmond and Atlanta.

"You see what I see, Captain?"

Captain Stewart, who could have been Colonel Logan's brother with his striking similar mustache and coal black hair, looked through the woods. He motioned for the others to stop in silence when they had finally reached the edge of the woods.

"Those guys aren't regulars; no uniforms."

"See if you can get a bead on the inside of the house," Stewart ordered as he scanned the farm's yard.

"One, two, three, four cook fires. Must just be a company," Stewart said.

"Langland follow the edge to the other side, slow and easy. Catch these bastards sitting on their ass with a full stomach. Walk the horses, and try not to be heard. Use your mirror as a signal when you're in place."

"House looks looted, Captain."

"Yea, they've been having a grand time. I saw a couple jugs being passed around," Lieutenant said, "Pass the word, line the edge, ready to fight."

"Yes, sir." By then Sergeant Davis had pulled up along the officers and was given the order as he scrambled back along the ranks.

"Adams, stick with me; you're about to give your first licking."

Sergeant Davis and Private Adams stood side by side, muskets ready. Adams hands tremble as he attempted to load his gun. "You're going to have to load faster than that, boy, or you won't last the day. Come on now, I taught you better."

"Nervous, I guess."

"Any man, including officers, that say he's not nervous before battle, is either lying or he's a damn fool." Davis said, biting off from a square of chewing tobacco and offering Adams a bite.

Adams paid no mind, for his eyes fixed on the soldiers with no clue about the horror about to unfold.

"There it is, Captain; the signal."

"Acknowledged, Lieutenant." Lieutenant Pouffe took a small mirror out and sent the acknowledgment.

"Follow up with 'now'," he said.

Lieutenant Pouffe flashed out the order as Sergeant Davis watched, ordering 'bayonets' with his signal back, and for the foot soldiers to open fire.

All hell broke loose as the cavalry detachment ascended upon the farm with a roar. Gunpowder smoke filled the area as men on both sides dropped, one after another. Private Adams looked over at Sergeant Davis just as Davis took a ball directly in his neck, falling to the ground.

An enraged Adams charged into the thicket of smoke, knocking a soldier with the butt of his gun and using his bayonet on as many as he could handle. With pistols discharging, horse soldiers wielding sabers slashed through the enemy. Cries echoed through the trees from the men caught off guard while they enjoyed their last meal.

The Union soldiers slit the throats of the border guards, and cut down the officers bolting from the farmhouse door. What lasted for only a half an hour, passed by in slow motion to those in the midst of the chaos. The battle, itself, was short as small skirmishes go. An officer approached a wounded horse and placed a merciful ball into the animal's head.

Lieutenant Plouffe came out of the house's back entrance with four prisoners with their hands held behind their heads and ordered to kneel on ground.

One of the sergeants ordered a couple of privates to dig graves while the prisoners were interrogated.

"Don't worry about individual graves, boys, just dig a hole big enough for ten bodies."

"One more in the farmhouse, Corporal."

"Don't leave him behind."

"Yes, sir, Lieutenant."

As the detachment command sat around, they discussed their next move and how many needed to stay to guard the farm.

"Lieutenant Plouffe, I want your men to secure the area and you can use the gravediggers for guard duty." Captain Stewart glanced at his pocket watch looking up at the sun, shielding his eyes. "Four already; we need to be getting back to command. Meeting dismissed, gather your men, be ready to move out."

Stewart rose and shook Langland's hand. "Lieutenant Langland, I wish you luck. I am sure, the general will not keep you out here hanging. This is the best approach to Belmont."

"Not concerned, Captain. The Missouri/Kansas border will keep Johnny Reb busy enough, and the river, of course."

Both men saluted as the troop's cavalry led the way back through the cornfield, making an easy path for Grant's army to make an advance.

By the time they arrived back to the river, it was five p.m. Grant stood at the rail of one of the steamboats watching them arrive. The wounded Union soldiers were placed in buckboards commandeered from Hunter's Farm.

At the lead of Stewart's column were four members of the Missouri State Guard, the ones sitting around the fire eating stew.

"Looks like intelligence was right, General."

"Make sure your men eat well tonight, Captain We march to Hunter's Farm after mess and assault Belmont at first light."

At six p.m., the army continued the process of readying the troops for their march to Hunter's Farm, arriving in time for a good night sleep. The field of corn directly behind the back yard had been trampled down, so the march was not a burden after six weeks of training at Cairo. At three a.m., they arose to cold hard tack and coffee, then the men started their four-mile trek from Hunter's Farm.

"No bugle, no fifes," one of the lieutenants ordered, "double line forward!"

The line headed double time down to Belmont on a narrow dusty road. Captain Stewart sat on his horse alongside Colonel Logan watching the troop move out.

"You sure no one escaped detection yesterday, Captain?"

"Always a possibility, Colonel. Looks like they cut all the tall trees out across river to make room for their guns, but we're out of reach of them."

"In theory, Captain; best hope the theory is right."

When the scouts arrived at Bird's Point Road, one of the scouts informed the rest of the troop of the Confederate's location, so they hunkered down in the thicket. As soon as the sun rose, the troop overran the Confederates, pushing them to the riverbank.

The ruckus alerted General Polk, who had been watching the Union's activities on the Illinois side of Paducah, which Grant used as a decoy to overtake Belmont. After engaging the enemy, three thousand troops descended upon the Belmont camp, looting, and burning buildings while disabling the cannons. Before long, the retreating Confederates ran out of ammo.

Polk, sensing Paducah was a diversionary tactic, sent twenty-five hundred men back across the river under the hail of Columbus cannon fire as the Union retreated into the timber.

"What shall we do?" one of the officers asked Grant.

"We got ourselves into this mess, only one thing to do is fight our way back to the boats."

The seventh Iowa were surrounded by the Confederate reinforcements who had been watching Grant's diversion at Paducah.

The Illinois thirty-first broke through the lines as the remaining troop escaped. Finally, around two p.m. they reached the boats.

Around five hundred men were wounded as the rag-tag group escorted four prisoners of war. By five-thirty, the boats got under way when Confederate reinforcements arrived on shore, and fighting broke out again as the Union troops fired from their position onboard the steamers. Boats from both sides caught fire from Columbus batteries.

Chapter 6

February 1862
Ft. Donelson
Kentucky

On a snow-covered frozen ground, the Illinois Thirty-first under the command of Colonel Logan, embarked once again up the Ohio River toward the same Tennessee River that carried Maddie and Josiah back to safety behind Confederate lines, months earlier.

"I just can't leave my father like this in that dreadful Yankee forest."

"I can see how much this troubles you, dear. However, it does not take away the fact that had we waited on your father at the cave, it would have put us in grave danger. We all could have ended up in a Yankee prison or worse hanged."

"Sometimes, Josiah, you can be so callous."

"How long have we been working together now, Maddie? There's no time for love loss, especially family."

Maddie gave Josiah a "go to hell" look.

"Cap'n, fort is just up ahead."

Grant made several attempts to capture Vicksburg, but was turned back as winter set in. Plans to attack again were being laid as citizens of Vicksburg dug themselves into the hills around the city. Confederate troops dug in, as well, forming a wall around the city facing the Mississippi River.

Secretary of War Cameron had a difficult decision to make. In the Eastern Theater, both sides were amassing at Gettysburg, Pennsylvania at the same time Grant made plans for another assault on Vicksburg and total control of the Mississippi River.

A difficult decision was finally made to move forward. McClernand would join Grant's Army, which now included the Illinois Thirty-first. Logan's men were more than ready for a fight after pulling guard duty of Union Supply lines at Jackson for the past year. After the eighty-mile three-week march along the west Bank of the Mississippi, the Army engaged the enemy in five battles, taking thousands of prisoners.

In February 1862, after retreating to Camp Johnson, Grant set his sights on Ft. Henry and paved the way to Nashville, cutting the Western rivers off from the Confederates. Ft. Henry in the lowlands of the Tennessee River was an outpost leftover from the War of 1812, armed with an antique battery near the city of Dover, Tennessee.

After heavy winter rains, the fort flooded, making it a nightmare to defend. The fort was taken easily, and Logan's men were ordered to stay put, rest, and guard the rail lines, while the rest of McClernand's Army marched to take Ft. Donelson in Western Tennessee.

At two a.m., Logan received word from McClernand. They would reinforce Grant at Ft. Donelson's right flank. Logan was expecting his troop to return home on leave and then return to Ft. Henry. By three a.m., Logan's troop started the twelve-mile trek to Donelson's fort marching in double-time through the cover of early morning darkness.

The hardest part of the march was the Dover marsh, recently fortified by the heavy rains. By nine a.m., the fighting resumed on both sides, advancing and falling back repeatedly. After a short breather, the fighting increased when the Confederacy tried pushing through Grant's right flank.

During the mayhem, Colonel Logan could be seen riding from one side of the flank to the other, shouting orders to hold the line, while firing upon the enemy. He saved several men's lives. General McClernand looked over at Grant from the sidelines.

"General, are you seeing what I am?"

Grant stopped long enough to take his cigar out of his mouth before speaking. "If you're talking about Colonel Logan, yes, I am."

A group of Confederate's reached the area near the Colonel, shooting Logan in the shoulder, and another in the thigh as the Colonel's horse raised his front legs high in the air, toppling Logan to the ground. As he fell to the left, he landed on his side, on his own pistol, which fired into his side, knocking him unconscious. Needless to say, the wounds bled profusely.

"You, two, grab a stretcher; get my officer the hell out of there." Grant's two aides look dumb founded. "Are you going to move or wait till he dies?" a disgusted Grant asked, gritting his teeth.

The two aides gathered Logan up on a stretcher, hauling him to the field hospital as blood dripped to the ground from his shoulder and side. A volunteer held her hand to her mouth as she saw the amount of blood on the stretcher.

"Surely, this one is not alive?" she wondered loudly.

A doctor looked up, seeing the man was an officer and walked over to feel his pulse.

"No pulse," he said. "This one is gone. Over there with the others."

The battle ended, as more wounded from both sides arrived on stretchers, some on their own power, struggling with bloody makeshift bandages unfurling, and some brought in dead.

For days, Logan lay with the dead as he drifted in and out, oblivious to his surroundings; indeed, thinking himself to be dead. He imagined himself writing his last letter to Mary: "My dearest Mary, I have such bad news. I was so looking forward to seeing you in the coming days. Alas, our liberty has been rescinded as we will march in early morning's dawn to Ft. Donelson. I long to hear your voice, gaze into your eyes, and feel your warmth next to me. I know not when I will see you again or if I shall. Lovingly, John."

The bad dream continued, the vague, clouded images of his family, friends, and his dear Mary. A weary General McClernand dismounted and walked inside the hospital as men and women scurried about like mice.

"General," a doctor saluted. "Can I help you?"

"One of my officers was brought in. Did he survive?"

"Only officer is over there, and the rest, are all gone; sorry, sir."

"Thank you." A dejected McClernand left the area in grief. Outside he was hounded by journalists watching the battle from the sideline. He rushed up and asked the general a question. "I haven't seen the report yet, sir," he snapped.

"We lost a brave man today, and a friend."

"Who's that sir?"

"Colonel John A. Logan, Illinois Thirty-first."

The reporter wasted no time, not even stopping long enough to respond as he ran over to the telegraph tent.

This was not the first time Colonel Logan had a brush with death. During the fight back to the boats at Camp Johnson, his horse was killed from underneath him. The fighting in the wooded area was intense as men fought hand to hand trying to make it back to the steamboats. Logan walked the rest of the distance alongside his men. General Grant, watching him from the boat looked at one his aides.

"They love him," the aide said.

Grant responded by saying: "He's going to make a fine General, one day."

February 1862
Marion, Illinois

"Please sit, Mrs. Logan. Have you seen today's paper yet?"

"What's the matter with you, Sheriff? I thought we addressed each other by our first name. You and my husband have a disagreement over that traitorous female?"

"No, Mary we have not," he said, clearing his throat while sitting back at his desk.

"Well?" she asked, getting impatient.

Sheriff Hendrickson hated this part of his job terribly. He just never could find the right words. John and Mary had helped him get elected years before.

"Maybe you should just read this," he said, shoving the newspaper across the desk. Mary slowly opened the paper, not fully understanding what to expect.

"Noooo!" she cried, looking at the sheriff who held out his handkerchief. He predicted this was going to be bad, awfully bad. The headliner was in bold large print. Colonel John A. Logan killed at Ft. Donelson, February 14, 1862. Mary, at once, lost all control, sobbing profusely and wrapping her arms the sheriff as if clinging to her long lost husband. Sheriff's Hendrickson's eyes welled up, for he too lost a dear trusted friend.

After the crying subsided some, the sheriff had retrieved a bottle and glass, pouring Mary a drink.

"Here this will help."

Mary just looked at the glass, not being a drinking woman. She took the glass in all at once, her usual steady hands trembling.

"I assume you will accept my offer to help you in this time of grief."

"Huh?" Mary asked confused.

"I can go claim your husband's body for you Mary. The least I could do."

Mary paused a moment before saying anything. "No, no Sheriff, your job here is too important. I will go myself. I want to see where John died."

The two sat in silence, each immersing themselves in memories of the Colonel. Finally, Mary asked. "Do you have any idea where Marshal Arnett is?"

"No, but I can get a message to him through the Judge."

Mary rose from the chair and picked up the paper, holding the page to her breast... like her last attachment to her husband.

When they stepped outside the door, a small crowd gathered outside, waiting to give Mary their condolences.

Mary spoke briefly to the crowd. "My John was a good and decent man, and I know you all will miss him terribly. So, now, I shall go make arrangements to bring my husband home. If any should see Marshal McCann, please tell him I need to see him as soon as possible. Goodbye and God bless." The crowd watched her carriage until it disappeared down the street.

Ft. Donelson

"You want me to do what?"

"Inspect the dead bodies in the morgue. I'm looking for Colonel Logan."

The doctor wrinkled his brow. "I have not the time to go through a bunch of dead soldiers to find one Colonel. Jonesy and I are trying to keep from joining the ones already in the dead room. If they are not moved, they will be stacked four high on top of each other, and then it will not matter. You won't be able to find him anyway."

"You will do as you're ordered, doctor, or you will be in the stockade with the rebels for the rest of the war; am I clear?"

"Yea, yea," the old physician said, shaking his head muttering as he turned to leave. "Major, I could have saved two lives while we were going through whatever this is. You want to report me, by all means, report away."

"Doctor, his widow will be here in two days for his body, maybe as soon as tomorrow. He was a hero to many; do your duty as so ordered."

The doctor never heard the last words, for he was halfway to the Dead Room.

The battle for Donelson ended after two days. The Union had secured a strategic victory with a straight path to gain a foothold the Tennessee, Columbia, and Ohio rivers, cutting supply lines to the West. Within hours of the battle's end, the ground around the makeshift white canvas tents converted to a hospital and morgue.

A short-lived thunderstorm hung over the battlefield, as if seeking to cleanse the land from the bloodstains. Instead of a cleansing, the blood-soaked ground transformed into a hellish mudhole, trampled under by boots, cannon, wagon wheels, and cannonball craters.

The traffic of the walking wounded, and soldiers carrying wounded left a trail of horse manure, and puddles filled with blood and muddy rain. The doctor tried tiptoeing through the murk, not wanting to track mud into the hospital, but it was futile at best.

A sign hung over the tent flap opening to the morgue, reading: "The Dead Room". The doctor waited on two soldiers to exit. Even though the rain had stopped, a chilling wind swept in, adding to the morose atmosphere. He stood shivering as the soldiers saluted him.

"Either of you two know this Colonel Logan that was killed?"

"No sir, Captain, we're from a different unit."

"OK... carry on."

Bivouac morgues were always pitch black, even with a bright sun. Ice stored in large wooden crates placed strategically in the tent's corners kept the dead in chilled conditions. He shivered walking inside. Lighting a lantern, the flame's shadows danced across the walls like ghosts, the old man could feel his arm hair rising.

"Damn morgues. I hate them," he whispered. Raising the lantern around the tent, the light shone across the dead laying on top of each other in haphazard stacks. He held a handkerchief over his mouth and nose, he stench bringing back memory of Jackson where they just dug a moat, set the bodies on fire, and cover them up.

The white crossed belts with gold braided buttons glinted in the candlelight. Eyes staring their last blank expressions of surprise hardened as the days passed.

"Here I am, seventy years old, looking for someone I have never seen in a stinking tent full of dead bodies," he growled. "Goddamn, Army. You think after the last one we would have learned. I should be back at the ranch, sitting on the porch and look where the hell you are now... talking to dead men."

"You'll know him. He has Colonel oak leaves with jet coal black hair and a matching handlebar mustache. He should have a ball hit on his left shoulder in his side and a pistol shot in his leg he got falling from his horse from his own pistol," the Major said, walking up behind him.

"You're crazy, that's like looking for a needle in a haystack."

"He was one of last ones to go in the second tent. He might have been moved to the house's parlor. Either way, you have twenty-four hours to find him before his widow gets here. We need to make him presentable."

"All this for a Colonel?"

"He's a personal friend of Grant and the President's, and a former Congressman."

After searching the two tents and the house, the old captain could not for the life of him find the dead Colonel.

The Major will be pissy, he thought as headed back to headquarters. The rain finally stopped, leaving the well-traveled pathway of drying blood, mud, and guts with the foul stench of death.

He could not shake the image of blue and gray uniformed bodies, some piled on top of each other, as toppled pawns on a chess board, abandoned by the players.

"Major, I have found Colonel Logan," the doctor announced, standing at attention and quite pleased with himself.

The major stood over a table which served as his desk, while looking over the reports from the last two days of battle before ushering them on to General Grant.

"Well doctor, I'm waiting," he retorted without looking up.

"He's not dead."

"What do you mean. he's not dead? Here's his death certificate."

"The Colonel is alive and is in the infirmary, wounded badly."

"You're sure it is him?"

"Yes, sir. One of the nurses removed his jacket and, it seems, the Officer's jacket was placed over a soldier who later died."

"So, how did you find the Colonel?"

"His hat was under his cot out of view. I was just lucky enough to see it when I entered the hospital."

"Yes, indeed you were. Let us go see the good Colonel."

Dammit, there goes my chance to make Colonel anytime soon, thought the Major.

Chapter 7

Cairo Illinois
Ft./Defiance
Two days earlier

Marshal McCann stepped off the train station platform, wearing his best black suit he usually saved for court proceedings, traveling lightly with one carpetbag and his saddle bags. Unfortunately, he had no time to grieve for his closest friend. He still was having a hard time wrapping his head around Logan's death.

He looked around the small village of Cairo, which had not changed much from the last time he shook Grant's hand with his orders to return to Washington. Regardless of the fact, it had been a couple of years earlier, a few more businesses had cropped up and a couple of new saloons.

The gunsmith's shop was still in the same place, a cornerstone for the new recruits of the Union Army leaving civilian life for the last time.

Nothing changed much, Arnett thought as he watched several platoons in their new blue uniforms marching on the parade grounds. He wanted to have a drink before he embarked on a solemn, and possibly dangerous, trip, which he preferred not to think about.

He took a slow draw on a cigar, tossing the match, then headed to the camp's bivouac. He pulled his long coat tighter at the collar, the smoke dangling in the February winter's snowy wrath as a crisp chill breezed off the Ohio.

He gazed at the sea of white tents, recalling the nights of drunken laughter, while he, General Grant, and the Colonel, spent the evenings playing cards, smoking, and drinking.

He felt as if he was indeed privileged to be in the company of such men of greatness. McCann, himself, never thought of being great; he just did what he always did, obeying orders to the best of his ability. A light cold drizzle stopped and started, banking on the wind. He looked at his watch from his breast pocket... another fifteen minutes yet.

He sighed heavy, succumbing to his weakness and headed to the saloon for a quick shot. He recalled something Grant had once said.

"You know Marshal, you and I are a lot alike."

"How's that General?" he had answered.

"This," he said, holding up the bottle as they both broke out laughing.

He touched the heel of his boot on the wooden sidewalk and stopped abruptly.

"No," he thought. "Mary needs me." A twinge of loneliness crept into his gut as he backed away from the saloon and headed to the hotel, tipping his hat to several passersby. *I remember Cairo being such a lonely town during the winter, except for the saloon.*

"Arnett is that you?" one of the working girls passing by asked.

"Regina, nice to see you."

"Is it true?"

"If you're asking about the Colonel, yes, sadly, it is true."

"I'm so sorry, Arnett."

"Yea, thanks. Is his widow here yet?"

"Yes, in the hotel lobby talking with a newspaper man."

"Thanks, Regina, I need to get going. I don't want to keep Mary waiting."

"You look tired, Arnett."

"We all are... tired of this damn war."

Regina reached up and gave him a peck on the cheek. "Take care of yourself."

He walked into the hotel lobby and glanced in Mary's direction as she sat in a chair in a corner while the local newspaper reporter sat next to her with a notepad. Mary quickly rose and excused herself, walking towards McCann.

"Marshal," she said, extending her hand, to which he kissed.

"Mary, you're looking well, considering. The Rob Rory is down at the dock waiting to load troops for Ft. Henry. General Grant has been nice enough to secure a cabin for us to Camp Johnston and onward to Donelson. I have to warn you, Mary, the trip could be hazardous, and the view through some of the battle areas, hard to look at."

"I'm a soldier's wife, Arnett; remember? No reason to delay any longer, Arnett."

Later, sitting in their private cabin, alone, for the short trip to the Cumberland River, which was now in Union hands, Mary studied Arnett's face.

"How are you really, beneath those weathered dark eyes that never look at anyone directly?"

Arnett looked down at his muddy boots, pretending to snooze.

His thin graying eyebrows raised, and he caught his reflection in the cabin window. Dark eyes, was how Mary Logan described them. He stroked his slight handlebar mustache, a tribute to his friend, though his was salted with gray midst the blonde hair, and gazed directly into Mary Logan's eyes. For the first time, Mary noted the lack of fire and energy in Arnett's eyes, not like when she first met him. Then, before the war drained him, along with all the loss and grief, he was an unstoppable force, full of passion and resolve... as if he channeled all his grief over losing Martha into his job. Now, after so much loss... the flood drowned that passion in his eyes, and the emptiness there affected her in a profound way.

She reached across and placed her hand on his arm. "I know losing Kathleen was devastating. You know I understand, now, after losing John."

"You mean Kathleen, Maddie, whatever her name was... which one, Mary?" Arnett answered in a slow soft deep voice Mary had not heard before. "I don't miss that bitch. Kathleen was nothing but a spy. That traitorous Breckenridge's whore. I was playing her. It was my job... simple as that."

Mary just sat there, listening, feeling Arnett's need to tell someone. Arnett spit on the floor, knowing Mary would normally be appalled by such an action.

"There have always only been three loves in my life, Mary." He sighed. "Martha, Anne, and my job. If I had not been summoned by the Secretary, I would have been by John's side, knowing that you could not be. I should have been with him."

"You can't blame yourself, Arnett. My dear husband was as stubborn as the mules your father raised. He would have demanded you do your duty to the courts, without reservation."

"That he was, Mary. That he was. When we reach the Cumberland River, it is a short ride to Ft, Henry. The Judge informed me General Grant has requisitioned his carriage for us with a small detail for the short trip."

"Be sure to thank the General for his kindness."

"I believe you will be able to when you see him. My understanding is he is returning to Cairo aboard the Alek, while John's army guards the railways at Ft. Henry. We will transport John's body back to Cairo aboard the Alek, if there is room. Of course, military communication being what it is in war, who knows between now and then."

The ride to Ft. Henry was a cloud of memories for Mary Logan, until the day they arrived at Ft. Henry. The weather was colder than usual for Kentucky with an inch of fresh snow making the travel slippery and wet. When they arrived, the Major greeted them, grinning from ear to ear. Mary frowned, thinking the man quite rude to be so joyous as he took her and Arnett to the General's tent.

When the Major pulled back the tent flap, Mary's gaze went straight to Grant's face as he stood, not noticing the other soldier lying on the cot nearby. She set her hands on her hips, scowling at the same smile on the General's lips.

"I declare, what is everyone so happy for when I've come all this way to collect my dead husband?"

A voice whispered from the darkness, and both Arnett and Mary gasped.

"John?" Arnett asked.

Mary fell to her knees beside him, sobbing into her husband's chest. The reunion brought tears to the rest of these hardened soldiers... and Arnett collapsed in the chair beside his friend.

The Major told them the news of what happened. John had been hastily declared dead after being found alive by a Federal Reserve Officer, who brought him in to help with the wounded.

His injuries put him in a critical fight for his life - a left shoulder wound, a left thigh wound, and a pistol shot that broke a rib, lodging just outside the tissue lining of his left lung.

Grant, deciding he could not wait any longer, fearing he was going to lose two officers, decided it was time to move closer to friendlier territory, fearing the entire regiment would all succumb to pneumonia.

"We must move them to St. Louis," Grant had said.

March came in like a lion, with the worse ice storms and record cold along the Mississippi river from Memphis to Cairo.

A few days later, after Arnett and Mary's arrival, the Illinois Thirty-first stayed behind as General Grant's staff, and three medical personnel, along with a company of soldiers boarded the Alek as she tried cutting through the ice forming on the river, to no avail.

Barely making it past Belmont before dangerously getting the steamboat bogged down in ice, they shored the boat close to some abandoned houses along the river and set up a field hospital. While Mary nursed her ailing husband, Arnett, sent word to Marion and a group of Mary's friends, and all sent medical supplies stocked with morphine, bandages, alcohol, and other supplies. So much so, there was a surplus before they finally returned to Cairo, and then off to Marion.

One day after arriving back home, a messenger knocked on the door with an envelope and a telegram from Secretary of War Cameron. It read:

To Colonel John A. Logan. In your service of our country, you are recommended to return to Washington as soon as you are well enough to travel to receive your Commission, General Logan, as an aide to General Grant.

"Oh my God, John, you have been promoted to General."

John stood, looking out the window and leaning on a cane as Mary read the telegram.

"What does it say about my unit."

"It doesn't mention them."

In the weeks that followed, the Illinois Thirty-first, under General Grant, broke through General Donelson's right flank to take the city of Nashville. From there they joined General Sherman on his march to the sea, through Atlanta and into the Carolina's. General Logan was promoted to Major General Logan on General Grant's staff. Grant, in turn, was promoted to supreme commander of all Union Armies.

The Thirty-first became known as the dirty thirty-first after a two-hour march to Ft. Henry after engaging the enemy in a two-hour skirmish. They marched with full packs, double time. They arrived sweaty with muddy boots, and dusty blood-covered uniforms.

Chapter 8

September 27, 1864
Centralia, Missouri
Columbia Train RR Depot
Columbia, Missouri

"Going to be a hot day on the rails this morning when that sun comes up," the tail lamp man stated. Course you won't be in the hot sun today," he stated to the ticket master.

"I won't have the open window wind though," the old ticket master stated.

"You two have anything to do besides carry on like two hens in a chicken house?" the engineer of the North Missouri RR. interjected. "Let's go, we're picking up a platoon of soldier boys on leave and get back to St. Louis. I'm off the next week and I have some serious drinking to do."

At four a.m., the engine's engineer gave two blasts on the whistle as the firemen stoked wood into the steam boiler. They had no passengers on this trip, which was not that unusual for this time of day, and no guards.

"Get that boiler fired up, time to move."

Sergeant Goodman rubbed his scraggly hair and put his hat on. His platoon of twenty-four men stumbled over from the saloon, missing the last train the day before. They were on a two-week furlough home in a small town on the Missouri frontier.

Dawn arrived, promising another day of uncertainty. His men looked as if they had stayed on a two-week drinking binge. Goodman was anxious to get back to their unit, for he sensed the war was feverishly peaking, and he didn't to miss any of it. He opened his pocket watch, glancing back over his shoulder at the sunrise, the whistle of the North Missouri piercing the night air, once again on the move since late last night from St. Louis.

Some of the boys in the platoon were raw recruits, not yet trained but were being shipped to the Missouri-Kansas border, where so called militias, were terrorizing the citizens along the free state of Kansas, trying to coerce their votes for Kansas as a slave state and practicing guerrilla warfare.

In Boone County Missouri, the day before on the west side, a group of guerrillas left a couple of Federals hanging after being beaten to death with their rifle stocks.

Bloody Bill Anderson scalped them while still alive. The Federals were from a group that terrorized Frank and Jesse James' mother, Zerelda. There were around one hundred and fifty men split between the Quantrill Raiders and Bloody Bill.

They started drinking the day before, and their mentality was revenge. No one was going to stop the wrath they were about to thrust upon the Federals for running their slaves, for killing family members, and stealing their land.

Some rode with Colonel Logan before he became Unionized, as Jim Younger had called it. The James' brothers, Jesse and Frank, also rode with the group from along the border and Jim's brother, Cole Younger, who had come up with the idea of staging Akins's assault before the gang left Logan's militia along the Illinois border.

The Sergeant's assault came while the group played cards. They plotted leaving Logan in a lurch. Only Quantrill was privy to what Akins's plan was per the discussion at the roundtable back in Mexico.

Quantrill, however, was not privy to the fact that Akins was not Akins at all. Only the Knight's leaders, which included Vice-President Breckinridge under President Johnson, knew the Confederate actor who had fled Spain years earlier, hired to deceive the sheriff into thinking he was Akins.

Bloody Bill Anderson earned his nickname. He scalped, cut-off human parts, and sometimes beheaded his victims. Quantrill's had a disdain for such mutilations, and on this peculiar day, decided he had enough and discussed it with several men. Around one hundred-fifty men left the group with Quantrill towards Kansas City, leaving Anderson with around eighty men.

Anderson knew McCann would pursue them to the ends of the earth for such vile acts. He considered himself to be a soldier even though he never liked taking orders, only giving them. Anderson looked around his small group and decided he had enough of war and was going after all he could get.

Cole Younger, his brothers, Jim and Bob, the James boys, Frank and Jesse, traumatized from watching his stepfather's torture, all sided with Anderson. Anderson took a liking to Jesse and took him under his wing, of which sickened his brother, Frank.

Jesse became the hardened brother of the two, as did Cole of the Younger's. Quantrill tried to get Frank to follow him to Kansas, but Frank was not going to leave little brother under any circumstance, citing there was 'no fear worse than Mother Zerelda's wrath', of which Jesse could attest to.

"So, what's the plan Bill?" Frank asked as the two stood watching the others galloping away toward Kansas.

Bill Anderson was not much older than Frank, short-tempered, shaggy, and never cared much about how he looked or who he killed. He swallowed the last swig from his now empty bottle, tossed it in the air and let out a rebel yell as he blew it apart with a blast from his pistol. Young Jesse following suit.

"First things first. You know these parts, Cole Younger," Anderson said, hobbling drunk while talking. "Centralia, East."

Anderson glanced at Jesse and winked. As the rest of the eighty stood there waiting to see what was going to happen next, Anderson's eyes burned a hole into his soul.

"Well now, I guess, we'll be riding to Centralia; saddle up," Jesse replied.

Preparing their horses to ride, Frank watched Anderson attempting to mount his horse, laughing like a madman as he toppled over. "Stick close, little brother," he whispered to Jesse. "Hard telling what this fool is leading us into."

"You nary need to worry about me, brother, I can take care of myself, besides, I'm a better shot than you."

Cole rode up in between them and leaned over to Frank. "I've got his back Frank. Just watch Anderson."

"Quit y'alls yapping; let's ride," Anderson ordered. "You want to say something Preacher before we ride?"

"May God watch over whosoever's soul crosses our path the wrong way today."

Anderson never waited to hear the prayer.

Centralia was nestled in the pines of central Missouri, a small sleepy town that existed because of the railroad's need for wood. The guerrillas hit several small towns, killing a few while they burned and looted. By mid-morning, they had reached Centralia, their horses kicking up dust with guns blazing as citizens cowered into corners, watching the terror.

They pulled barrels of whiskey from the saloon, while throwing bottles in the air for target practice Two of the men were so drunk, they rolled in the dust with one of the barrels, laughing as they punched the cork trying to drink from the barrel while others drank from new boots stolen from the town's general store.

Anderson rode back and forth from one end of town to the other, firing his gun in the air. Someone threw a lighted torch into a window and the building alighted.

Citizens snuck out back doors, trying to escape the melee. The chaos stopped when one of Anderson's guards, the one who usually watched the entrance to a city, shot his pistol in the air and hollered "train" from the top of the water tower.

"Form a line!" One of the lower officers called out as they stood at attention along the tracks as the train pulled in. Anderson stood with his arms crossed, his hands just above his pistols.

"You two, off that engine," Anderson ordered the engineers.

One of the men shoved the two engineers over to the sidewalk.

"There's soldiers in that car." One of Anderson's men pointed out.

"I got eyes, you drunken fool!" Anderson retorted. "I don't care who it is, but one of *ya'll* needs to get out here right now before I burn this fucking train down with all the blue bellies inside," he shouted, emphasizing the word 'ya'll' in his southern drawl.

There was shuffling inside the car as the twenty-three raw recruits looked for their sergeant's response. The young men gathered next to each other, gazing out the windows to get a glance of what they were up against.

"Jesse, light a torch."

A fellow guerrilla handed Jesse a torch. Anderson took his thin cigar and gave it to Jesse.

Sergeant Goodman, heavyset, with a receding hairline and bushy goatee, nervously stepped onto the platform and stood in front of Anderson.

"Look at that, men. Yankees with no guns," Anderson chortled, then looked at Jesse with a wink and a broad smile on his face that quickly faded to a cold dark stare. Sergeant Goodman looked more like a schoolteacher than a veteran.

He eyes darted across the men standing before him, a lump in his throat and a feeling that the situation was about to become nasty. Anderson took one of his pistols in his right hand with the barrel resting on the Sergeant's forehead and smiled.

"In about two seconds, if the rest of you blue belly Yankees do not get out here, your school marm here will get a slug in his forehead."

Sergeant Goodwin stood at attention, glaring at the man in front of him, expecting any minute to be his last.

He thought of the raw recruits, not yet trained, most just fresh from puberty and did not expect any of them to come to his rescue. The men stared in disbelief at how their Sergeant, who was now sweating profusely, looked down the barrel of a forty-five with such a calm demeanor.

"What shall we do?" one of the men asked another.

"How the hell should I know? I'm not an officer."

"We can't just leave him out there to die at these thug's mercy," another one stated.

"I don't know about you all," another said, "but we swore an oath and I aim to honor it. You all not going to honor it, you might as well join those yahoos. I'm going out with Sarge," he said as he exited the car. Two more looked at each other, shrugged and scoffed as the brave recruit glared at the ones still glued to their seats.

"Git them dang Yankee hands up above your heads," Anderson ordered. Jesse, Anderson's favorite sidekick since the last foray, chuckled. Anderson had taken notice of how well Jesse handled his gun, and some of the older men took a liking to his wisecracks around the enemy.

"Alright, you boys," Anderson shouted, "shuck them uniforms."

The first man out of the car looked down the line to Sergeant Goodwin, nodded and started stripping, laying their uniforms on the ground before them stood, and stood at attention, sweating in the September sun.

"C'mon, off with the clothes," Frank ordered.

Anderson stood directly in front of the Sergeant, his pistol glued to Goodwin's forehead. Anxiety-fueled sweat poured profusely down the Sergeant's chest and forehead.

"No more blue bellies," Anderson scoffed as his eighty men burst into laughter at the sight of the few raw recruits standing in their skivvies. Anderson's eyes turned cold as any mean son of a bitch Goodwin ever had the misfortune to come across.

He was sure this was it for him. A slight breeze blew Anderson's straggly black shoulder length hair as Goodwin looked away. He could not bring himself to look further into those dark soulless eyes.

Anderson pulled the hammer back, turned and smiled with a wink directed at Jesse. In one fluid motion, he turned his gun on the man closest to the Sergeant and blew a hole through the man's forehead, his brains splattering against the train car. The signal was as clear as the details of the previous night's discussion.

Instead of shooting, Jesse grabbed his blade and thrust it into the man standing directly in front of him, piercing the jugular Blood gushed forth, the man dropping as Anderson's men's predatory instincts took over. A barrage of bullets tore into Goodwin's men. He stood there, horrified that he had no choice but to watch the slaughter. Severed heads rolled, sliced limbs thudded on the boardwalk, and Anderson's men stuffed detached genitals in the recruit's mouths to stop the cries of agony.

Just as it started without warning, it stopped just as quick. Twenty young men lay in pools of blood, guts, sweat and dust. Gun smoke filled the air as Goodwin could no longer hold his stomach and he puked in merciless spasms. The men had grown silent, some just staring at the melee while others drank from their canteens, their eyes in a hypnotic gaze.

Anderson looked at his men with the proud smile of a devil. He turned and poked Goodwin, who was still bent over.

"Git yourself cleaned up. We ain't through with you, just yet. Put your damn clothes on, your fat ass is making me sick. Rest of ya, git changed."

"You heard the man, move," Frank ordered. The men moved and rifled through the dead men's uniforms for ones that would fit them. Within an hour, the men had their usual clothes stowed. Frank stood, ready to mount and looked at Jesse. *He's aged... this damn war and all that he has seen has aged him fast*, Frank thought.

"He sure isn't Quantrill, is he, Jesse?"

"No, he sure ain't, brother; but everything's going as planned."

Frank was startled that Jesse was privy to Anderson's plan and felt he had been left out purposely.

"I think you like this killing a bit too much."

"Just like the Feds liked beating an old man in front of Ma. How do you think she felt about that?"

"Wouldn't know, Jesse, I wasn't there."

"That's right, Frank, you weren't."

"Burn the damn train! The whole blasted depot," Anderson hollered.

Torches were lit as the remaining townspeople watched in horror at the sidelines, keeping their distance, yet wondering what would happen next. After burning half the town, Anderson mounted up, with their one prisoner in tow.

Sergeant Goodman, with his hands bound in front of him, stumbled along behind the horse as they rode across the flat land of prairie grass. The men were boisterous as they headed across field, stopping in a wooded area near Centralia to rest the horses to eat and interrogate their new-found friend.

As usual, Jesse, Frank, Cole Younger and his brother Jim had their own fire going with lots of ribbing, drinking, and bragging. Frank tied his horse and walked over to Jesse, who was by himself, to confront him. Anderson interrogated Goodman as most of the men gathered around to watch the fun.

"What the hell you were talking about back there?"

"Back off, brother. You don't need to know, better if you don't."

"What have you gotten yourself into?"

"We're not just guerrillas, Frank. There's more to it."

"What the hell are talking about? You, buying into this Quantrill shit?'

"Everything okay, boys? Looked a little intense from over here."

"Big brother stuff, Cole, nothing more."

Cole studied the James' boy's faces, moving a blade of wheatstraw back and forth in his mouth.

"Okay boys, I'll bite."

"Let's see what's Anderson has in store for this Yankee," Jesse said, putting his arm around Cole and walking off. "You a 'coming, brother?"

"In a minute," Frank replied, amazed at how much Jesse had shot up the last three years. Skinny as a rail, his hair already to his shoulders. The war turned him into a senseless cold-hearted killer. Frank was glad his mother was not here to see it.

Major Johnston had just been handed one-hundred and forty-three raw recruits of the newly formed thirty-ninth infantry, sat tall on his horse waiting for his scout to go investigate the fires burning at the Centralia Depot.

"Looks like a guerrilla outfit attacked the town, sir. From what I could see, civilians are cleaning up the mess."

"You are probably correct, Avery. No report of regulars in this area. Load your weapons!" The order went down the column by twos. "Sergeant, keep the company tight."

The Sergeant trotted back though sixty sets of men, pushing powder down their muskets. He circled the last two and headed back to the front.

"Soldier, pack that powder tighter. You don't want that barrel exploding on you." *God help us,* he thought.

"They're ready, sir."

Major Johnston glanced back through the troop and gave the order: "Forward! No fifes."

Children stood in the streets, crying at the gruesome scene as they watched adults cleaning up body parts. Major Johnston's troop slowly entered the town. The Major at once recognized the scars of battle from earlier in the war. Johnston stood on his stirrups and looked up and down the street at the carnage. "You there, who did this? Anderson?"

The man nodded.

"Well Major, he doesn't carry the name Bloody Bill for nothing."

"I reckon not, obviously, Mr. Clay." Raising his voice so everyone could hear. "Lieutenant Macomb! Take thirty-five from the back of the column, set your guard post according to the book. The rest, help these Godforsaken people put these fires out, and a burial detail for these brave men. Now, lieutenant."

"Yes, sir!"

"You heard me; get going," he shouted to one of the sergeants.

The townspeople went back to the chore at hand, while commands were given at the end of the column.

"Shall we proceed, Captain?"

"Mount up."

"Which direction did they go, sir."

"Straight west through the prairie," a young bystander said.

"My guess is, they headed for the border. How many?"

"Not sure... sixty, maybe eighty."

"Mr. Clay," he hollered. "Head out and see if you can pick up their trail. We'll be along as soon as the Lieutenant has the detail in order."

"Were going after them?"

"What's your point, Mr. Clay?"

"Anderson is my point, sir. These are battle hardened guerrillas. You're asking a greenhorn troop to stop the worse bunch you will ever have to go up against."

"I am touched, Mr. Clay, of your concern for this troop; however, may I remind you, I make the decisions of what this troop does."

"I won't be a party to this stupidity."

"So noted, Mr. Clay. War dictates the actions of these vile men be stopped, and we are the only ones available. Do I make myself clear?"

"Yes, sir," Jacob answered, reluctantly. Jacob Clay had been hired because he knew the territory's worse outlaws that the Kansas and Missouri border had to offer, and he could pinpoint, most of the time, their hideouts. Bloody Bill Anderson was another story.

Besides holing up in Saint Louis before the war started, there were not many prospects for taking settlers out west. Being fifty didn't help matters either. "Whatever you say, Major," he replied, galloping off grudgingly. *Going get us all killed,* he thought.

Clay rode, for only God knew how long, across the parched prairie. He watched the ground for tracks, making direct angle searches along a direct path. That many horses should not be that hard, although the dirt was packed hard. The day was heating up and he stopped for a drink from his canteen, wiping his buckskin sleeve across his brow, and shaking the dust off his wide brim Stetson.

A breeze picked up, causing his sweaty hands to lose grip on his hat. He dismounted to pick it up, and there it was, hoof prints, clear as day. He walked a bit further. *Heading for the draws*, he thought. *Not more than an hour. Be difficult and time consuming through them draws.* He remounted and pulled his horse back in the direction where the Major headed.

"Halt," the Major ordered as a rider approached, kicking up dust.

"Looks like Mr. Clay," the captain reported looking through his glasses.

"So, it is," the Major answered.

Jacob pulled the reins, halting his horse, the dust clouding around them. The Major waved his hat to clear the air.

"And?"

"They're about an hour out down in the draws. I saw their camp smoke and lots of tracks," Jacob answered, catching his breath.

"How far does this prairie stretch?" the Major asked with a petulant tone.

"I just said, about an hour ahead."

The Major's habit of pulling his pocket watch out to check the time annoyed Clay.

"Two o'clock," said the Major, as if the time really mattered. "Let's move, Captain."

"Forward!" the captain ordered.

An hour later they could see the tree line where the draws of the land began.

"Halt!" the Major ordered. "Do you know exactly where they are?"

"No, I was not able to make it out. The land is full of draws and deep forest with boulders. Looks like they are holed up in the second line of draws in the trees. I saw their campfires; seems the effects of alcohol has slowed them down. But..."

"What is it? Spit it out, we don't have all day."

"I would not underestimate them. Their resolve for violence is clear after what we just witness."

"You made your point."

"Major, looks like you won't have to make the decision; riders approaching."

"You make one false move, and I will not hesitate to blow your spine apart," the Major stated.

"You don't need to concern yourself, I aim to live to see tomorrow."

Cole kept his hand as close to his holster as possible without arousing suspicion as they rode the last one-hundred yards towards the troop.

"Union uniforms, sir," the captain said.

"Quite the observant one, Captain," the Major said.

"Good afternoon, gentlemen. I am Major Johnston. What is your unit?" the Sergeant asked, clearing his throat.

"The twenty-first, sir."

"Is Captain uh, uh, what's his name?"

"No, he's no longer with us."

"And who are you?"

"The names James, sir," Jesse answered, diffusing the Major's attempt of trickery, to reveal who they were. Jesse pointed his gun directly at the Major as the front of the line froze, unaware of Jesse's intent.

"Tell your men to drop their weapons, leave their mounts, and walk away, or we will kill every single one of you."

"Such tall orders coming from one so young."

Major Johnston, not giving an inch, stared straight into Jesse's face. Jesse glanced at the unwavering Major and blew a hole in his head, then took out the captain, and shot the sergeant in the back as bolted back to the troop.

On the first shot, twenty men on the troop's left flank charged out of the woods with guns ablaze. dropping five troopers while they scrambled to pull their rifles from the opposite side of their saddles. In a hail of gun fire, a second wave of twenty men on the right flank returned fire, led by Jesse's brother, Frank.

In a matter of minutes, Johnston and his troop lay dead.

"Dang, boys, looks like we got left behind on this one," Anderson said, looking around at the men with him, awaiting their assault. Sergeant Goodman lay on his stomach, trying to slow his breathing as the two groups merged and trotted around, making sure no Yankees remained alive.

"Nice work, gentlemen. Grab the fresh horses; let' move. I wanna make the border by dark tomorrow."

Goodman lay for a long time, making sure the only sound he heard was the wind blowing before sitting up. He spotted one of the gang's worn-out horses still in the hedges, and made his way back to town.

Chapter 9

Kansas City District
Supreme Court Justice
Robert Cozier
October 1864

Judge Cozier's reaction to the Centralia Massacre, after reading it in the newspaper over his morning coffee, was one of appalling anger, which prompted a summons for U.S. Marshal Arnett McCann and Alan Pinkerton. He tossed the newspaper to Mr. Pinkerton.

"Have you read this? And in my own jurisdiction."

A man of stature with a disheveled receding hairline and mutton-chop whiskers to match, ran his hands across the little bit of hair he had left. "The army tells me they do not have the men to go after these murderous thugs that call themselves military."

Mr. Pinkerton glanced at the paper and passed it to Arnett.

Arnett read out loud. "Unarmed Massacre of Recently Formed Unit. One-hundred fifty in total... if you count the unarmed men from the train," Arnett added, receiving a perturbed look from Pinkerton.

Robert Cozier, an attorney, as well as manager of the First National Bank in Leavenworth Kansas, whose father had started the Leavenworth newspaper, scowled. "Don't give me specifics, Marshal; I want to know how we are going to stop them permanently."

Obviously, the Judge doesn't like the thought of criminals working freely in his district, Arnett thought.

"I understand, Judge. Sherman is on the march in the South, the war should be over in less than a year, and all these thugs will go back home," replied Pinkerton.

"That's your summation, Allan?" the judge replied, perturbed. "Care to join in, Arnett?"

"Not to disavow Allan's input, but being experienced in these types of criminals, I just don't believe this will stop when the war ends. I don't think you can assume these men will just stop and go home."

"I think the Marshal's office and the Pinkerton Agency can work together and restore law and order," the judge said.

"That's not realistic, Judge," answered Pinkerton. "The Agency is too busy protecting the Federals within the Administration, which of course, involves the President."

"Let me understand. The Feds won't be helping?"

"Judge, you're not being fair. The war is still a problem and there have been threats against the President. Good men are hard to find that are not already Officers tied to their duty." Judge Cozier stopped pacing and sat back at his desk, stroking his "lambchops".

The Judge rested his jaw on his hands and heaved a heavy sigh. "Marshal, you and I will be discussing this further; I expect you to be available this week. Mr. Pinkerton, there is no further need of you here. Go back and protect the President, even though there is a full regiment stationed in Washington."

Mr. Pinkerton offered his hand to Arnett, who accepted the handshake.

"Have a safe trip back, Allan."

"Thank you, Arnett, and good luck." Pinkerton tried to shake the Judge's hand, but ignored the gesture.

"Don't be surprised Mr. Pinkerton, if the Leavenworth Press renders a not so flattering view of your agency."

"I am fully aware of the Leavenworth Press in relation to you, Judge. Good day, Arnett." He tipped his hat and left.

Arnett stood up in the Judge's office and lit a cigar. *What a pompous ass*, he thought to himself. *Cannot figure Abe's fondness for this man.*

"Anything more, Judge?" asked Arnett.

"Tomorrow, four o'clock at the club."

"Tomorrow, then. Have a good day, Judge."

"Like wise, Marshal; go arrest somebody."

Arnett chuckled and headed out the glass door. Judge Cozier always dismissed his law officers with "go arrest somebody."

Allan turned when he heard the door open behind him as a water wagon rolled down the street, wetting the dust just enough so as not to produce mud.

"Thought you would be well on your way, Allan? Judge came down hard on you."

"Used to it Arnett. Justice Department thinks they should be protecting the President."

"And the courts expect one lone Marshal to handle a whole district," Arnett replied.

"It will never change, my friend. Good luck with that Anderson bunch. You know, you are right about one thing."

"What's that?"

"They won't stop after this war is finished."

"Walk with me to the hotel. I need to retrieve my bag before the train arrives."

"I was headed that way myself," Arnett replied, patting Pinkerton on the back.

4 p.m.

Marshal McCann stood at the mirror in his hotel trying to adjust a tie he hardly wore.

"Dang fool thing."

"Here, let me," replied Laura.

"Funny thing meeting you in Leavenworth last night. If I were a gambling man, I would say I am being set up here."

Laura, stretched across the bed with just the bedsheet wrapped around her, rose to help Arnett with his tie. "You are a gambling man, darling; every time you pin that badge on. So, the Judge is setting you up, for what?"

Arnett rested his forearms across Laura's shoulders and looked her in the eyes. "I try not to think on that."

"Oh you! You're going to be late."

"Give me a kiss," he said, laughing and patting her back side. He put on his hat and headed to the door.

"Be here when I get back?"

"Of course, if I have anything to say about it, I wouldn't let you out of my sight."0

Laura pulled the collar of his shirt with her fingers, urging him towards the bed. He chuckled, kissed her, and left.

God, I hate these clubs, Arnett thought, walking along the wooden sidewalk, tipping his hat to various pedestrians strolling the sidewalk as he crossed the street. His destination - a massive building with a row of columns at the portico, and a cherry-wood sign bordered with gold braids reading: "Masonic Gentleman's Club."

A doorman stood at the top of the steps, holding the door.

"Marshall McCann, I assume?"

"Yes, sir," Arnett replied as he stepped in.

"I'll take your hat, if you don't mind, and there is a "no guns allowed" policy in the social room. You can hang your holster on the peg over there on the wall."

"Feels like a damn courtroom," Arnett muttered under his breath.

"Pardon?" the doorman inquired.

"Just thanking aloud; sorry."

"Through those double doors on the right."

Arnett felt his knees knock as he entered through the double doors. Judge Cozier stood at a table with a drink in one hand and waving a cigar in the other, making a point to someone Arnett normally would not be associated with, under the circumstances.

Kansas Frontier

"We need to be going, Jesse."

"Not quite yet, brother, these charcoals need to cool."

"Why the secrets?" Frank asked.

"No secret. Anderson just wasn't sure if your heart was with us."

"I ought to bust you in the mouth for that comment."

"Just back off, Frank, and let me finish this."

Jesse stood near a huge boulder using a half-burnt limb to scrawl his initials toward the base. Jesse stood back and admired his work. "Now, they can find it."

He mounted his horse while Frank doused the fire. "Out with it, Jesse," Frank barked.

The two rode back toward the border, bypassing towns and outlaying farms along the hill and gully countryside of Kansas.

"Well, Quantrill and Anderson are not really just fighting for the Confederate Army."

"What fool notion is that?"

"We work under the financiers of this war. The Cause, known as the Knights of the Golden Circle."

"Who put that foolish notion in your head?"

"Well, one night after my first skirmish, I stumbled up on Anderson and Quantrill arguing about it. There's a whole network working for the Cause behind the scenes and enemy lines."

"And they trusted you and not me with this information?"

"They just weren't sure enough, Frank. After they saw how I handled myself under fire."

"They watched your reaction back at Centralia. I buried Morgans back at that cliff, while you were napping from the last train we heisted."

"Why did they send me with you, then?"

"They want you on board."

"Sure, I'm on board, Jesse, Zerelda would kill me if I let anything happen to you."

"Like wise, brother."

"Let's see what the girls look like in the next town."

"I'm game."

Arnett left the club, at a loss as to why the judge would waste his time displaying him around like a debutante or a prized horse. *He's planning something by using me, like I am a housemaid or something. This shit is sure enough going to stop,* he thought.

He went to his room to get ready to hit the trail in the morning after reading the judge's report of what criminal needed hauling in before the court.

A young lad selling the "Leavenworth" in the hotel lobby approached him. "Can I interest you in a paper, sir? Latest war news."

"Sure son."

He doubted that Laura would allow him time to read it. *What the hell, good to have something to read on the trail.* He read the headlines about the Centralia Massacre on the front page in large, bold print. He continued his reading while opening the door to their room.

"Laura, have you seen this; Laura?" He flung the newspaper on the bed. The small area for clothes where Laura kept her dresses was empty. Arnett wasn't surprised at all; women were always disappearing on him.

He sat on the edge of the bed, his elbows on his knees and his face buried in his hands. He looked at the bottle on the stand, grabbed it and threw it across the room. Pulling off his boots, he flopped on the bed and finished reading.

Think I know what has upset the judge so much, he thought.

A restless night passed for Arnett. Akins blank stare still haunted him, and his last words. "I'm not Akins," he had whispered, pulling Arnett closer, laughing till a cough took his last breath.

He awoke before dawn, stepping on a piece of glass from the bottle. "Ouch!" he shouted, grabbing his foot and hopping on the other one back to the bed.

He gently pulled a tiny shard of glass from his callused foot, put his socks and boots on to greet another day he was not ready for.

Shouldn't have drunk that damn bottle of whiskey, he thought. He tried to show his most recent boss that drinking was not a crutch, but *what the hell. What is the matter with women? No one ever says goodbye. Damn war,* he thought, *getting where you cannot trust anyone.*

He looked in the mirror at someone he no longer recognized, sloshed some water on his face, and slicked back what hair he had left, then put on his hat. Satisfied, he descended the stairs, bag in hand and tossed the key on the counter as the hotel clerk jerked awake from his slumber.

The lobby was empty as he stepped into the early morning light. He set his bag down, and thumbed the top edges of his vest, inhaling the sweet fresh air, a habit he got since his deadly encounter with Akins... or whoever he was.

The diner's breakfast smoke wafted down the street, filling his nostrils with the aroma of eggs and ham. He picked up his bag and headed down the street, hoping the old Chinese man would let him in early, as he usually did, so he could avoid the breakfast rush. He arrived at the half-glass door and there stood Ha Chi, unlocking the door for him.

"Morning, sheriff; Morning, sheriff," he said, bowing twice.

"Morning, Ha Chi. It's Marshal, not sheriff. We have been through this, many times."

"So sorry. Would you want the same, Sheriff?"

"Yes, thank you," Arnett replied, shaking his head as he headed to his usual seat where he could keep an eye on the door and the street.

"Good morning, Marshal." Ha Chi's very young wife bowed. McCann returned the bow, smiling as she tiptoed back to the kitchen.

I'm beginning to think the Sheriff has put Ha Chi up to calling me sheriff, he thought.

"Here you go," Ha Chi's wife said, setting the plate of victuals on the table.

"Looks good, Ma Chi."

"Thank you."

"You're welcome."

She bowed twice, the same routine every time McCann visited the diner.

McCann started on the ham and eggs, watching Ma Chi's delicate frame stroll to the door and flipped the open sign. *How she ever had that passel of kids is beyond me*, crossed his mine.

"How is breakfast, Marshal? More coffee?"

"Very good, Ma Chi. No more coffee."

"Morning McCann; the usual, Ma Chi," said the sheriff as he pointed at the chair across from Arnett. "Do you mind?"

"Free country still, as of last night anyway, Sheriff."

The sheriff pulled the chair out and sat across from him, then poured himself a cup of coffee from the tin pot.

"Did you get a chance to read yesterday's *Leavenworth*?"

"You mean the headlines?"

"Yes, wars are a bad business for soldier boys."

"That was downright murder. We don't even treat Indians this brutal."

"Yea, we have."

"What's your point, Sheriff?"

"Judge Cozier wants me to tag along with you and see if we can't stop some of these guerrillas."

"I saw Cozier last night at the club, parading me around like a prized horse. Lost my respect, which was already in short supply. I left before he had a chance to relay that news. Besides, who's supposed to keep law here if you come "tagging along", as you put it?"

"He suggested the army will keep order."

Arnett chuckled at the sheriff's response. "I don't need the judge or you to know when and if I need help."

He finished his plate, wiping the remaining yolk with his biscuit. Ma Chi arrived at the table, like she always does, with the Marshal's food supply in a white cotton bag.

"And you can relay that to the honorable judge," Arnett said. "Ma Chi, you outdid yourself as usual."

Bowing twice, he handed her a few bills.

"See you around, Sheriff."

Chapter 10

Mineral Springs, Texas
Winter 1864

"Who are you writing, Jesse?"

"If you must know, Frank, I'm writing mother. I would think you would."

"We had this conversation before, Jesse. Stop doing my thinking for me and come join the festivities. Bill seems to think you dislike weddings. Wasting your Sunday-Go-to-Church-Meeting duds sitting here writing Ma, when there's pretty girls sitting over there itching for a dance."

Frank sighed, studying Jesse's face, his writing pad propped on his knee, as they sat on the Mim's family farmhouse porch.

"Not sure how Quantrill is going to take kidnapping that old man and now off and marrying Miss Mims."

Jesse stopped writing and looked up. His older brother looked tired.

"Seems to me, Frank, you fared well around those young ladies at that old Yankee's farm."

"That I did, Jesse," he replied, smiling.

Jesse stood, folded his letter and stuck it in his suit breast pocket, stretched, and scanned the crowd.

"Dang blasted dry Texas winter; I'm parched. Think I'll stroll over and get a drink first."

Frank watched Jesse head to the drink table, adjusting his Colt's hanging at each side. He glanced at Jesse's pad and saw that newspaper man Newsome's name on it. *Why would he lie about writing to Ma?* Frank thought.

He never could figure Anderson's fondness for Jesse at such a young age. *I fear he is turning Jesse into someone I no longer recognize. Maybe it isn't Anderson at all.*

This damn war has changed us all, he thought, watching Jesse shake someone's hand he did not know. He turned, as a fiddle player picked up the beat, and approached a group of young ladies, offering his hand to the prettiest girl.

"Bill, or should I call you Mr. William Anderson since you gone and got yourself hitched," said Jesse, laughing and shaking Anderson's hand.

"Jesse, I want to introduce you to someone. This is Colonel Jackson of the Texas Stars."

"Glad to meet you, sir," he said, shaking the man's hand.

"Likewise, son. Bill has been telling me of your brave exploits in the field."

Anderson noticed his new bride beckoning him to the dance stage. "Gentlemen, I shall relinquish this conversation. My bride seeks my attention."

"Very well, Captain Anderson."

Jesse tipped his hat in the lady's direction, then dipped a cup into the punch bowl.

"I could use a good man such as you, Mr. James; someone that can handle themselves well under pressure. The Stars work with a group called the Knights. Are you familiar with them?"

"I have heard Quantrill mention them before. Look, I have no desire to remain in Texas. My home is in West Missouri and always will be."

"What if I told you there is no need to." Jesse scoffed as the man continued. "The Knights have been bankrolling the Confederacy since their infancy."

"I'm listening."

"There is no doubt in a Texan's mind, the Confederacy cannot win this fight. It was lost at Gettysburg."

"However true that may be, what does that have to do with me or my brother?"

"There's an entity within the Stars," he said, revealing a simple five-pointed star on the inside of his wrist. "We are Tin Stars and we're going to make sure the Cause continues, whether the Confederacy's bungling ends it or not. We will take the fight directly to the very people who run the country - the banks and the railroads - when this thing ends, which it will and not in our favor. We'll suck them dry for the Cause."

"You want me to rob banks and railroads for you, after the war? What do we get out of it?"

"A piece of the take, enough to live well. Look Jesse, the Knights will fight for the Cause for as long as it takes. Either at the voting booth, or with those six shooters you have strapped on."

"I already belong," Jesse said, showing him the same small tattoo. "Can I pick my own men?"

"Yes, of course. I would not have it any other way. Anderson thinks very highly of you, and now that Bill's married, you're the only logical choice."

"Lord knows, I've seen farms and families torn apart by the Federals. Talk with the boys, Colonel, is all I can do. I'll let you know of our decision. Right now, I see a pretty filly, beckoning for a dance."

The Colonel watched Jesse saunter toward a row of young ladies. *Handles himself well. I think we made a good choice,* he thought.

Not much happened the next few months as Anderson's men stayed drunk, played poker in the nearby saloons, and chased the ladies, and killed civilians who tried to get in their way. On one of these short trips was to the Shirley farm.

Mr. Shirley's son Bud was the scout for Anderson's band of guerrillas. John Shirley moved to Texas to escape being hassled by the Federals for harboring groups like Anderson and Quantrill. When it was too hot to be on the trail, fights broke out between the men over minor things. Supplies and liquor were in short supply, as well as money and ammunition.

"Alright, I'll talk to him," Frank said.

"Do it now! We can't sit on our heels while this war rages without us."

"That's right, we got families to take care of back home."

"The men are right, Frank, or would you rather Jesse handle this?" Cole asked with a smirk, the men chuckling.

"Now, now, boys, Frank has been here longer than I. He is the educated one. Go ahead Frank."

Cole sat on a straw bale, cleaning his Colt, and pushed the brim of his hat with the barrel. Taking his hat off with his other hand, he cocked his head toward Jesse who winked.

"How about it, Frank?" Cole asked.

"You all think I'm afraid to bitch at Anderson? Screw you?" He stormed out to confront Anderson.

Anderson was as clean as Frank had ever seen him in his wedding clothes, even though the wedding had been months ago. Anderson was whispering in his bride's ear, who was sitting on his lap, giggling.

He patted his wife's behind, sending her off into the house.

"What the fuck do you want bothering us, Frank?"

"The men are getting restless, Bill, and supplies are getting low."

"Honey, we're getting low on coffee," his wife called out from the kitchen.

"Okay, not now, Bush."

The two men waited till she closed the door.

Bill lowered his voice. "Take Cole and his brother over to the Shirley's place and see what they can spare. Leave Jesse here with me."

Frank turned to walk back to the men. "Oh, make sure the boys stay out of trouble."

"Yes, sir, Captain."

When he returned to the men, he relayed Bill's order. "Saddle the horses; you, Jim, and I are heading to the Shirley's. Captain wants to talk with Jesse, right away."

"Okay, brother; you heard him, saddle up. I'm sure the rest of you can find something that needs to be done while they are away."

They rode off to the Shirley farm, Bud Shirley riding point as usual.

"You're awful quiet, Frank."

"Concerned what Bill is turning us all into, especially Jesse."

"It's war Frank. It'll be over before you know it."

"This kind of killing just doesn't stop for a man like Anderson. What the hell we supposed to do when this, ends? Not like the Feds haven't already pushed or burned us out of our homes."

"Revenge is what awaits, Frank. You know Bill's not going to want to stop."

"Yes, I understand, Cole. Now Anderson's got Jesse hoodwinked into this. Ma's gonna be none too happy about all this."

Cole reached across and touched Frank's arm, pointing to Bud who had his hands raised. Two unidentified men had rifles pointed at Bud. Cole motioned towards the woods as his brother slipped into the woods to flank Bud's perpetrators on both sides. Cole was in listening distance, almost right where two men had been hiding.

"I don't believe you." The man questioning Bud looked like he had not bathed in a year. "We all know Bud's with Quantrill in Missouri."

"No, he isn't in Missouri, you damn idiot."

One of the men cocked his weapon and raised it. "Drop them guns, you're coming with us."

"Like hell he is. You all drop your weapons or I'll put a ball in the back of that skull of yours," Cole commanded, his pistol inches from the one doing most of the talking.

"Easy there, mister."

"That's Captain Younger to you. Drop your weapons," Frank commanded.

"Sorry mister, we just guarding house like Mr. Shirley ordered."

"That is Mr. James to you, boy. Lead the way," Cole ordered smiling at Frank.

"You heard them. I don't cotton to being shot by my own family."

"Pa, riders coming up the lane."

The grass was trimmed with a lane of white rock wide enough for a buggy and two horses, with a hitching post and a water trough in front, and a high porch of stained wood, and two white rockers. "Dang Bud, you never told us your daddy was rich."

"People a lot richer than us."

"I think that's Bud's daddy yonder."

"Go in the house Belle, you don't need to be out here. Now." Mr. Shirley, a hotel owner by trade, dressed so well every day most thought he was a preacher or a banker, or both. He stood and grabbed his rifle leaning against the railing.

"Wasn't sure it was you, Bud. Who's that with you?"

"This on my right is Captain Younger from the Quantrill Army and this is Frank James."

"You boys let them get the jump on you?"

"That would be my fault." Cole answered. "Snuck in behind them."

"Here boys, take your guns back. You can water your horses." Mr. Shirley said, pointing at the trough.

"Mighty obliged, sir," Frank said.

"Belle, I said git in the house. Tell your mom, Bud's home."

"Yes, sir, daddy." Belle stood in the doorway admiring Cole, while he took care of his horse.

"Get back to your post, try not to get shanghaied this time," he barked to the guards.

"Yes, sir, Mr. Shirley."

"Son, bring these boys up here and state your business. I'm sure this isn't a social call. Belle, bring out some tea iced."

"I'm going to go say hi to mom."

"Go ahead."

"Mr. Shirley, Cole and I have been sent by Mr. Anderson to inquire whether you have supplies you can spare. We can pay handsomely."

"Anderson planning on staying in Texas with Miss Mims?"

"No, sir," Cole replied. "We're planning to head back to Missouri, sometime this spring."

"As soon as the honeymoon is over," the men chuckled. "We hope."

Belle traded silent flirts with Cole, who considered himself a lady's man though he would not have been considered one by Southern Belle standards; but he never passed on an opportunity. Some found him to be quite attractive a man's man, if you will, blessed with a talent of one-liners. A young lass craved attention at such a coming out age.

Belle Shirley was nothing special, herself, but she did know how to manipulate a man when the occasion presented itself. Oftentimes she acted like some of the ruffians her father knew came to the house on occasion. He complained to his wife that Belle forgot she was supposed to be a girl. Truth be told, her brother Bud taught her to ride, shoot, curse, and fight dirty like a man when the need dictated the outcome.

Belle and Cole became a perfect fit for their short time together.

"Mr. Shirley, I hate to intrude upon your hospitality, but my horse was limping like he had pebbles in one of his shoes. Mind if I use your tools? I don't like using my knife on such a fine animal, sir."

"Sure, in the barn by the stalls."

John Shirley never refused a man who used fine manners when asking a favor, especially a Captain of the South. He was about to have Bud help him, till Belle spoke up.

"Papa, I'll show the captain," she replied, recognizing an opportunity.

John Shirley scratched the stubble on his cheek. "Okay Belle, you mind your manners, child." Accenting the word child for Cole's benefit. Frank remained aloof, knowing Cole's reputation.

"This way Captain." Cole's face was expressionless for Belle's father's benefit as he concentrated on her walk in front of him. No words were needed as they helped each other lift the gates beam that held the doors shut.

Once inside, however, was a different matter. Cole continued the farce, heading to the nearest stall, still pretending.

"What's your name?" Belle asked in a sultry tone.

"You were on the porch when your brother introduced us," he said, ignoring her.

"Oh, Cole Younger! Don't you like me?"

"I thought I made that clear, Belle." Cole checked his horse's shoe, glancing at the ground toward Belle, then looking at her figure from the ground up, half wanting her to notice, half not wanting her to notice. She was close enough to be in his arms. *Nothing special*, he thought, *but there was a war on, and a man cannot be too particular.*

He released the horse's leg and grabbed Belle by the waist fast enough she had no time to react.

"Well, Captain Younger, seems you have me totally flanked." Cole had both arms resting on her legs, massaging her thighs, and looking up into her eyes.

"Be ready, I'll be by some night. Give your Pa time to forget me. But I'll be here, after dark."

She reached down to plant a kiss, but Cole had other ideas and pushed her back, laughing as she fell in the water trough behind the stall's fence.

"God damn, you bastard, Cole Younger!"

Cole turned, laughing, as he led the horse back outside.

"That should cool you off."

Bud, Mr. Shirley, and Frank were going over the supply list and looked up at the ruckus coming from barn. Belle came out of the barn, soaking wet, still cursing as she headed to the back door.

There was no way she was give her Pa the satisfaction or a chance to scold.

"You seem to have your hands full with that one," Frank said politely."

"We're well aware of that," Bud chuckled.

Belle's father ignored the comments, not being one who would discipline a child in front of strangers or friends.

In the few weeks left, Belle and Cole met in the dark of night as lovers do. Belle, barely considered an adult, was just as wild with the many men, mostly outlaws, she would meet during her tumultuous life. She would hang with the outlaw type, and some considered her to be an outlaw, herself.

Out-riding and out-shooting the men, she eventually marrying the outlaw, Sam Starr. Belle Starr would later say "being married to Sam Starr and living with his Cherokee family, learning the outlaw ropes, were the happiest times of my life."

In August 1864, Anderson's guerrilla force, fully rested and restless, were itching to get back into the war. Anderson's wife, Bush, had become demanding and unsatisfied with Anderson's way of life.

Regularly supplied by John Shirley, who supported the Cause and a bit worrisome of the gang's influence on Belle, pushed for them to return to the war to drive the Yankees out of Missouri once and for all. The men headed back to the Little Dixie area, creating mayhem, looting, and destroying Unionist farms, and small communities, alike.

At November's end, they were the most hunted group after the Centralia Massacre, prompting the Federal District court in Kansas under Federal Judge Mark Daheley, a close friend and a President Lincoln appointee, to summon Marshal McCann to Kansas City. Daheley a surveyor by trade of British descent, had not been an attorney long and new little about the Western frontier.

He did, however, understand the war was winding down in the east and needed a lawman's perspective on how to deal with these guerrillas.

Not being from a military background, with little management knowledge of local outlaws and even less in his neighboring state of Missouri, of which he presided. *Times were changing*, Arnett thought, as he sat on the train staring out the window. *I never see Annie; I have not been home since I was thrust into West Point. My, how she must look*, he thought.

The many passengers on board were oblivious to McCann, as the train's whistle blew twice going around a curve. The constant clang of steel against steel lured him into a stupor as he stared at the Kansas countryside that was fast giving way from the flat wheat fields to the hilly approach toward Kansas City. He had just delivered a psychotic killer disguised in a military uniform to Leavenworth Prison, and needed sleep.

"Is this seat taken, sir?

"Huh?" McCann said, startled that someone had even noticed him sitting there. "Sorry, I was half asleep, the wheels you know. Let me move my bag so you can sit."

"I wouldn't have moved, but the gentleman I was sitting by smelled something awful and I saw that you were here by yourself."

"Uhm," Arnett said, shaking his head. Arnett tried not to stare and looked back out the window as the woman's perfume scented the air around him. In his stupor, he swore he was looking at Martha. *Am I dreaming?* he thought.

After much rustling with her belongings, she cleared her throat and thrust a gloved hand under McCann nose.

"You have a name? Mine is Abigale Charles, Mrs. Abigale Charles."

"Nice to meet you, Mrs. Charles," he said, barely touching her hand. "McCann."

Arnett turned back to the window, trying his best not to carry on a conversation. He pulled his hat tighter around his eyes, a tactic he had discovered that worked well in the past.

"My, such a conversationalist."

Arnett looked up. "I don't recall inviting you to impose upon my space, Mrs."

"How rude. Are you always this rude?"

"Not being rude, just honest. My mom taught me I should always be honest," he said, tipping his hat.

"Well, I'll be," was the only response she could think of, while looking for another seat. "Why aren't you in a uniform like most of the men these days?"

"My, you are a pushy one," showing his badge from inside his jacket.

"A sheriff?' she exclaimed.

"Can't read?" going along with the game.

Abigale scoffed. "A Fed?"

Arnett put his forefinger to his lips. "Shh." Arnett sat up. "Please, cease heading down this track, Abigale; may I call you Abigale?"

"What in this God forsaken territory should I call you?"

"How about Arnett?"

"Fine, now that we got that unpleasantness out of the way."

Arnett had the talent of scoping a woman's figure without the lady noticing.

"Interesting figure underneath all that wasted cloth," he whispered to himself.

"What did you say?"

"Nothing," Arnett replied, wondering if she was a psychic. *Am I that much of an open book?* Arnett thought.

The whistle blew twice as McCann realized he had missed the outskirts of Kansas City. The train slowed as it rolled into the station, pulling up to the Depot's platform. Both were engrossed in their conversation, they missed the conductor announcing Kansas City.

"Sorry," she said as they butt heads, reaching for their bags at the same time. 'Maybe we shall run into each other during our stay."

"Doubtful, Miss, I spend a lot of time in the field. Kansas City is my headquarters."

"How interesting."

"How's that?"

"So is mine."

Maneuvering through the passengers, she turned to say something, but her new-found friend had slipped out the other direction. She sighed and went on her way.

Arnett made his way through the streets of Kansas City, looking for a hired buggy to take him to the office.

"Need a lift, Arnett?"

"Hey, sheriff, thanks. Pretty sharp buggy for a sheriff, isn't it?"

"Won it playing cards last night over at that new establishment."

"You have time to play cards? I must be doing something wrong."

"You always were one to get right to the point Arnett."

"Pappy used to say, "a man that beats around the bush, misses the bird."

"You must take after your pappy," replied the sheriff.

"Didn't mean to be standoffish, sheriff. Dang female on the train tried to ruffle my feathers."

"One of them kind," the sheriff replied. "Anyone we know, Marshal?"

"No, never seen her before. Just as well, obviously not my type."

"You mean, her type?" They both chuckled.

The Sheriff pulled the buggy up alongside his office, after Arnett had hitched a ride from him.

"Looks like your sign's about to fall down, sheriff."

"Had some ruffians ride in Saturday night, shooting up the town. If Uniforms had not been in retreat, it could have gone real nasty. Come on inside, we can talk in private."

"I don't have much time. I'm supposed to meet the judge in an hour."

"You got time. Court's been moved up to two. Lester's waiting inside. Coffee ready?" he said to his aide.

"Yes, sir, Sheriff. Coming right up." Lester was a freed slave with graying hair and a barrel chest.

"Meet Marshal McCann, Lester."

"Howdy, sir, nice to know you," he said. Arnett extended his hand. At first, Lester wasn't sure what to do, not used to a white man offering his hand upon introduction.

The Sheriff nodded and Lester shook his hand.

"Tell him what happened the other night, Lester."

Lester stroked his chin, sadness filling his eyes.

"Well, sir, I had just come from the diner around closing, Mr. Sims won't let me eat till it's close to closing, and then I have to eat in the kitchen. Doesn't want the customers seein' me."

"Go on," Arnett said, raising his eyebrows in the sheriff's direction.

"These Yankee's came in hooting and hollering, shooting up the town. I ran down to git the sheriff. They said I was a runaway, and they were going to lynch me, Marshal. This young one with long hair like a woman with a cold stare in his eyes. They scared the town folk back into their homes. No one tried to stop them. That's when the sheriff saved me."

"Lucky for him I had the double and came around where the buggy is parked. I shot one of them they called Schmidt, from the General store. I came out and we ran them out."

"Thing is, Marshall, them wasn't Yankees."

"You sure they weren't Yankees, Lester?"

"Yes, sir. I've seen enough good ole Southern boys to recognize one, no matter what uniforms they'd be wearing."

"What your thoughts Arnett?"

"Surprised you ran them off that easy."

"It wasn't all that easy. They robbed the bank of sixty-grand. Figured the one sporting a beard and double pistols didn't want to waste time sticking around."

"Think you could point these men out?"

"Yes, sir. They be still in my dreams."

"Who are they, Marshal?"

"Sounds like Anderson's bunch that killed them boys over in Centralia. I best skip the judge and get on after them."

"You're not going alone, are you? That's the army's job."

"Not anymore, they robbed a bank."

"Did you see that old nigga? Thought his eyeballs coming right out of their sockets," Jim asked Cole as they rode along the trail. "Where did Jesse and Frank get off to?"

"You sure are full of questions," Anderson popped off. "Why don't you shut up and keep an eye out?"

"Think he's missing Miss Mims again."

Anderson pulled his horse around and pulled one of his 45's out, pointing it at Jim Younger. "You ever mention her again, I'll drop you standing."

"Come on, Bill, you know how Jim gets after a drunk night."

Anderson turned the gun toward Cole. "Don't even consider it," Cole challenged. The rest of the group sat still, waiting to see if this was a play for control.

"Can't a man have fun? Less talking, more riding."

"Stop this buggy!" the judge ordered his driver. "McCann, get over here."

"I was just heading to see you, Judge. I just left the sheriff's office."

"You were supposed to be in court. What have you got to say for yourself?"

"I was told the docket was moved up."

"Like hell you were."

"Well, I think I've got more important things to do at the moment, anyway. I'm going after a gang of bank robbers pretending to U.S. Army. Last I know that's a federal offense."

"Who do you think it is?"

"Anderson's bunch."

"Best take some help. I'll requisition a unit."

"You'll do no such thing, Judge; it will attract too much attention."

"Dammit, Arnett, your arrogance is beginning to play on me. Take two men out of uniform."

"I'll take one, my choice."

"Done, keep me posted. Don't go off and get yourself killed."

"If I didn't know any better, Judge, I think you actually care."

"Hmm." the judge scoffed.

"I ought to tell you, the man I went after wasn't Akins."

"What?"

"Told me right before he died, he wasn't Akins."

"Go on."

"He was a plant to get the lady out of jail, to keep her from a noose."

"Hmm," the judge responded, "report back in two weeks. If not, I'll assume you're dead."

Dang old cuss, Arnett thought. "Be more than two-weeks, Judge."

"Two-weeks, Marshal."

Arnett shook his head.

The horses in the corral scattered as Arnett opened the gate and headed to the barn.

"What you got for me this time, Sammy?"

"She's not Babe, but she's a fine gal," Sammy commented, as Arnett finished grooming the chestnut mare. "Have you named her yet?"

"Nah, seems like every time I start calling horses by their name, I lose them. You do good work, Sammy."

"Thank you, sir." The boy looked a bit perturbed.

"Something wrong?"

"No, just tired of people calling me Sammy."

"Have you said anything to your folk?"

"Yea, I mentioned it a couple of times. I am almost sixteen, Marshal. Sammy's for kids."

"I'll say something to your father, okay, Sam?"

"Thanks, Marshal."

"Don't let it fret you none, son. I was called Arnie for years."

"Be seeing you," Sam said, smiling.

"Likewise."

McCann headed to the Burgess farm on the outskirts of town. Burgess was a full-blooded Cherokee who, besides being a blacksmith, was one of the finest trackers that Arnett had ever worked with.

Burgess's many talents enabled him to stay in the white man's world while others were killed off or on the Oklahoma Reservation. The ride was pleasantly short, bringing him to Burgess' stable.

"Marshal, been awhile, what can I do you for? If the horse needs attention fine. If not, keep on moving."

"That's not a very friendly hello, Burgess."

"Not to friendly these days, Marshal," he said, pointing to three fresh dug graves.

"What happened?"

"Had some Confederate sympathizers last week. Didn't turn out so well for them."

"Were they wearing Yankee uniforms?"

"Yea, why you're here?"

"Well, I need you along on this one. If you're up to it."

"Let me gather my things."

"I'll saddle up for you."

"Thanks."

The two rode off a slow pace, picking up tracks. "Sure you going to be alright, Burge. Need to bring them in alive."

"Might as well understand, Arnett. This group not the type to come in alive."

"Yea, I get it. How's the young one?"

"They raped her, Marshal."

"So sorry; she inside?"

"No, she's at the boarding house so Doc can keep an eye on her."

"Sorry, Burge, really I am. We find them, I don't care what you do with them. I won't stop you."

"Judge won't cotton to that, Arnett."

"Yea I know, but the good Judge's opinion doesn't count out here."

They headed west, finding dozens of tracks showing a large party.

"Yea, but who? Arnett said. "Can't imagine Union troops this far into Kansas. Judge's military report showed most of them in Missouri."

"It has to be them. This shoe print was on my land."

"What business would they be having this far?" Burgess asked Arnett.

"I reckon we will find out soon enough."

They followed the shoe print through the flat land that turned into gulleys inside Nebraska. Huge rocks jutted from the slopes with trails cutting through the tall grass. It was clear that horses had recently tromped through, leaving narrow paths.

"Fill that mason jar."

"How much you want in this one, Jesse?"

"All the Morgan's you can fit in it. Paper money rots. Besides, Anderson took most of the cash. Hand me that burnt branch Jackson."

Jesse took the branch and carved his double J mark on the biggest rock, stuck the two mason jars in the hole and covered it, placing a smaller rock on top just below his mark.

"You tell no one about this, you hear me? Time to head to town and spend some of this money."

"Aren't we meeting at Orrick? Like Anderson said?"

"You ask too many damn questions," Jesse said, as the two rode off.

"Looks like they circled back toward Orrick to throw a posse off their track. Most likely, we're on the right track."

"Why Orrick?"

"Fort, more soldiers. Who knows? Burgess, I'm going to see if I can get a bead on where they're headed. You see if you can track the other two."

"These men are killers, Marshal. I don't cotton for you gettin' after these by yourself."

"I'll be fine."

"Just the same, Marshal, they like killing."

"I get your point, Burge."

"What do you want me to do with the other two."

"Whatever, I don't care to know. Make sure you collect that bounty on them. If you lose their trail, then head home. Keep yourself safe, Burgess."

"You too, Marshal."

Burgess looked back as he watched Arnett ride towards Orrick.

Arnett's mind cluttered with memories of home. He had not seen Martha's grave since the war started and nothing of Annie. *God how she must loathe me. Bank probably owns the place by now,* he thought. He stopped, taking a draw from his canteen. *Looks like they were not in much of a hurry.* Hours later, around midday, he stumbled upon a body. He almost missed it, except for the stench and the buzzards overhead.

A Union soldier, the maggots already feeding along with the buzzards. Arnett buried his face in his elbow. The smell made him gag, so he took a drink and spit it out. Then, he saw them. Thing was, they were all Yankees. He dismounted and walked past the corpse.

It was clear from the scene, must have been one hell of a fight with evidence of hand-to-hand combat and bayonets. *Trouble was, who had they fought?* Two more bodies lay nearby, one on top of the other... enemies in the same Union uniforms. Anderson's bunch.

He rolled the bodies over with his boot, trying to get a look at their bloated faces to see if he recognized them from their wanted posters. There was Anderson, laying on his back with a bloody chest and forehead, his horse dead a few feet away.

"So, they finally got you. You bloody stinking bastard. They gave you a hell of a fight." Arnett spit on him. "You are going to Orrick if I have to drag you behind my horse."

He walked through more carnage leading his mare past the scene. He untied a rope from the saddle, intent upon dragging Anderson all the way. Startled, the horse jerked to the side, eyes wide. *Something is up,* he thought.

A young man in uniform moaned. Arnett touched his palm to his chest to see if his heart was beating. Without warning, the kid opened his eyes and thrust a bowie in Arnett's side. Arnett grabbed the kid's wrist with all his strength, pinning his hand to the ground while a warm flow of blood oozed down his side. Once he had the boy neutralized, snatched the knife and sliced the kid's juggler.

Arnett rolled off, clutched his wound, and hollered. *Dammit all, lucky strike.* Arnett laid on his back, gasping for breath. He sat up, realizing he needed to move quickly; his shirt was already soaked with blood. The knife had barely missed the same wound from the bayonet at Bull Run.

He jerked the dead kid's shirt, ripping a strip and balling the rest up over his wound. He winced... *maybe not as bad as*

I thought. He lifted himself up with a nearby rifle as a crutch and stumbled to the mare.

The horse came to her knees... just like Babe. Arnett slid on top, screaming as the pain seared through his ribs.

"Home girl." The horse trotted off, McCann hanging on for dear life, fading in and out of conscience.

"Levi, make sure that pump is off."

"Yes, ma."

She watched her son pour the water into the horse trough inside the corral they had just finished, after a group of renegade soldiers tried to accost her, to no avail. She remembered her husband made a point, saying that anything can happen on the frontier.

The renegades stole the few head of wild horses they had wrangled to sell the Army, along with the chickens, and whatever else they could find. She and Levi hid under the floor in the closet next to the kitchen, their storm shelter, while the renegades ransacked the house.

"You keep that shotgun loaded by the bed within reach. Levi, you sleep with your mother, till I get back."

Her husband had said years ago. 'Getting back' never happened in the five years since. She was forty, no man except for a child to handle, and a five-acre ranch. Not much, but they had worked hard to make it work.

Together, they had wrangled that wild herd, but the war pretty much decimated that endeavor. She was tired... raising a child, keeping their heads under a roof... and all alone.

Many times, she had thought of giving up. She dismissed the thought, watching Levi sleeping comfortably beside her. She remembered her husband's remark when she offered the name Dugan when he was born.

"Are you nuts? Where on earth did you come up with that name? One of those books I find you reading, in the middle of the night?" He had stormed off upset she had chosen the name herself. She found him in the barn sulking. "You know, he will be made fun of when he starts school?"

"Since when can you read the future? Besides, I've already told the judge."

She snuggled up to him looking in his eyes. "Dang girl, you know I've never said no to you."

In the end she went to the judge and changed Dugan's name to Levi.

"Ma, rider approaching."

"Keep an eye out while I grab the shotgun."

"You won't be needing the shotgun ma. He's barely on the horse." The horse came to a stop twenty yards from the corral. Levi climbed the corral fence.

"Levi, wait."

"He's bleeding ma, bad!"

She dropped the shotgun running. "Wait, I'll help." By the time she reached the mare the horse had already dropped to her knees.

"Hurry, Levi, help me lift him off." She placed Arnett's arm over her shoulder as the two of them dragged him across the dusty area through the corral and into the house.

"Stoke the fire," she said, while tugging at Arnett's shirt.

She remembered his face as the man on the train. She stopped, her eyes glistening in the fireplace's flickering light.

"U.S. Marshal, Kansas." she said to herself.

"He's not wearing a uniform. You think he's one of them?" One of those bunch, which terrorized us."

"No, he's not. Now, keep his arm up while I tie off this bandage."

They had their supper while the sun went down the firelight bouncing off the walls. Arnett slept on the nearby bed.

The fire in the fireplace was the only light she would allow, so as not to attract unwanted attention at night.

"Time for your reading lesson, Levi."

"Aww, mom. What about him?"

She pinched his cheek. "I doubt we will hear from the gentleman tonight. He looks worn."

"Which book do you want me to work on, ma?"

"Any," she said from her rocking chair while she ripped clean bandages from a bedsheet. "Why not a big book, Levi, a bit of history reading."

He climbed the chair to a shelf her husband had built to hold all her 'teacher' books.

"What is that one by your hand?"

"The History of the Roman Empire," Levi read slowly. She stood, helping Levi from the chair.

"I remember this book, almost bigger than you. Sit there on the rug in front of the fire."

She returned to her task at hand as Levi read aloud. He asked his mom a question about a word, but before long, she was fast asleep in her chair. He stood up, walked over to the bed, watching McCann sleep.

Levi had always loved shiny objects, and a U.S. Marshal's badge was no different. He unpinned the badge, holding it up in the firelight, then he climbed the short stairs to his loft, and fell asleep, clutching the badge.

Two days went by after Levi went to town to town to fetch the doctor. When the doctor finally arrived, little had changed, except the frightful dreams Arnett experienced during his feverish days and nights.

"His fever indicates an infection," Doc said. "He's lucky to have come your way, Abigale."

"I met him on the train a few months back. I even sat by him. He seems disturbed, somehow. From the war, I assume."

"Fever seems to bring out men's worst memories," the doctor suggested. "He should come around, but then again..." The words trailed to nothing as the doctor shook his head and buttoned up his bag. "I'll be back in a couple of days unless the war catches up. Levi, you keep an eye over your ma."

"Yes, sir."

She sat by the bed, wiping Arnett's face as he mumbled several women's names. *Martha, Kathleen, Anne, Laura,* as well as a list of others, and she wondered what it all meant.

Suddenly, the night before the doctor was supposed to return, he woke screaming names, one after another.

"Easy there, easy there," she said. He started to sit up, until the pain drifted him back into a dreamless slumber. The fever went on for two more days.

His soft cry for water startled her from sleep.

"No," she called out as she rushed to the bed. "No, don't try and sit up. I'll fetch you water. Stay laying down or the doctor's stitches will come loose."

She poured water from the basin and put it to his lips, holding his head with her other hand. He struggled with a faint, "Thank you, Martha.

"You were stabbed, and I'm not Martha. I'm Abigale, remember? We met on the train awhile back. Do you remember?"

"What?' he managed.

She helped with another drink. "You're too weak. Levi, bring a small bowl of that broth."

"Yes, ma."

"Where am I?"

"At the Charles' farm, outside of Kansas City."

"Kansas City. I need to get there pronto."

"Not tonight. Tomorrow, maybe, when the doctor sees you."

"Hey, I know you. The lady from the train."

"And you're the Marshal." She looked over her shoulder, seeing Levi twirling the Marshall's badge in his fingers. "Levi, bring me the badge, please."

"Ahh, ma, I can never hide anything from you," handing her the bowl of broth and the badge.

She helped him eat, ladling the beef broth and dabbing his chin with a cloth. He managed half a bowl before the pain overtook him again, slumping him to the pillow.

"You rest now. Daylight will soon be upon us."

Arnett slipped back into slumber, not hearing her words.

Levi kept busy re-stocking firewood when the doc arrived short of breakfast the next morning. "I see you are following my orders, young man."

"Yes, sir."

"Good morning, doc," Abigale said, greeting him at the door.

"Morning, Abby. How's the patient?" He came to last night. Took in a half bowl of broth."

"You're a good nurse, Abby. If I wasn't such an old man..."

Abby chuckled and patted him on the arm. "Such a charmer."

Arnett was working on breakfast when the doctor entered the room.

"Let us have a looksee at that hole."

"Anytime a doc says 'hole' and not 'wound' has me worried, Doc."

"Henderson's the name," he said, removing the bandage. Now, raise up your arms."

Arnett raised his arms with a grimace.

"Tender, huh?"

"A bit."

"I see you have another injury, from the war?"

"Yes."

"Hole looks fine. No riding or work for a week. Pull that thread out and you'll have hell to pay. From the wound, and me. Abby, make sure he minds his manners."

"Shotgun is still loaded, Doc," she said with a wink and a smile.

"Thanks, Doc," Arnett replied.

"Don't thank me, yet. You haven't seen my bill, Marshal."

"That would go to the good Judge. He pays the bills."

"Wish mine got paid that easy."

"What's a bill?" Levi asked. They all laughed.

"Tomorrow morning, see if he can get out of bed to the table. I let the judge know yesterday that you are here recuperating."

"Thanks."

"Don't mention it. Judge wanted me to relay, that was Anderson's bunch that poked you."

"I know, I was getting ready to haul Anderson into town when I came across one of them alive. Did the James' boys get away?"

"Both; one of the Youngers was caught with a bad wound."

"Thanks again."

"Wow! You really are a Marshal," Levi exclaimed.

"Can one of you hand me my shirt? I need to get out of this bed." Rising from the bed, he stumbled, trying not to reveal pain that was shooting through his side.

"Let me help, Arnett," Abby said, putting her arm around his waist.

"Thank you, Abby," he replied, pulling her closer than she expected.

After the short stroll to the table, she realized how much she enjoyed the closeness.

Levi chowed down, oblivious to the chemistry in the air. Arnett glanced at Levi and turned his attention toward Abby as she served him breakfast. She had a lovely glow about her, more so than when he saw her on the train, and his heart flip-flopped. The three sat in silence, filling their mouths and stomachs.

"It's been a long time since I've sat down to a... breakfast," Arnett stammered.

"You mean, in a family setting, Marshal?" Abigale asked without looking up.

"Yes, in a family setting. It's been a long time."

"Are you married, Marshal?"

"Please, call me Arnett. I'm widowed. I have a daughter, who is probably a doctor by now."

"How did it happen?"

"She died giving birth to Annie."

"May I be excused mom?"

"Yes; chores first. He doesn't like adult discussions."

"Most boys don't."

"Where is your daughter now?"

"Back home in St. Joseph, Missouri, I suspect. Most likely doctoring by now, I suppose. Seeing there is a war on."

"The war. This damn war! I'm so sick of it."

"Hey, hey,", he said, holding her hands. "War is almost over."

"And how do you know that?"

"I know what I see and hear; I know people."

"You know people? Can you tell me my husband is coming home alive, maimed or dead?"

Arnett lifted himself from his chair, placing his hands on her shoulders.

"We're a fine pair. My love is forever lost, and you have no idea whether yours is or not. Look, my boss is a federal judge and a dear friend of mine is a General. Maybe, if we do some delving, we can find what happened."

"What if I don't want him found?" she said, her eyes watering.

Chapter 11

Western Missouri
1865

"Are you writing Ma, Jesse?"

"Nah, just setting this Newman fella straight."

"Who?"

"That newspaperman from Kansas," he said, tossing a paper at Frank.

He looked at the headline. Anderson, Leader of Cold-Blooded Killers, Dies. "I wouldn't put much stock in this Newsome fella, Jesse."

"Yea, you wouldn't, Frank. We're going to use him, to get people back on our side."

"Yeah, you were writing him when you said you were writing ma. Why lie to me?"

Jesse ignored the question, continuing with his own thinking.

"We need someone in the press on our side. He can help rekindle the Cause."

"The Cause is dead, Jesse. Confederacy nothing but a pipe dream. The boys have been grumbling about home now for weeks."

"Read the paragraph at the bottom of Newman's piece," Frank said, reading it out loud. "*Governor considering amnesty for guerrilla's that lay down their arms in peace.* That's what the boys are saying they want."

"You actually think they're going to let us just ride in there, lay down our guns after Centralia and Lawrence? What are we going to do Frank, farm?"

"They'll drop us before we make it to the courthouse," Cole added.

"Cole's right, Frank."

"Where you, all going?" Jesse asked, as several of the remaining members road up to the porch.

"Home," Jim Younger said. "Fellas, in town says Lee is surrendering today, and I haven't seen my family in five years."

History's Chase
Leavenworth, Kansas
June 1874

"Read all about it! Read all about it! The Seventh Calvary doomed at the hands of Sitting Bull in the Black Hills!"

"What do you think all the ruckus is about, Arnett?"

"Sounds like some fool has done got himself killed," Arnett said.

Arnett, now pushing beyond fifty, with receding hair, wore a "gallon" Stetson, which had become his trademark since the war ended. He ran his hand across his clean shaven face... except for the handlebar mustache which he chose to keep.

"J.D., mosey on over there and grab us a couple sheets so we can see for ourselves."

Deputy Marshal J.D. Kinley, Arnett's newest partner since burying his last partner, Akins. Or whoever he was... whose death still stuck in his craw.

"Sure thing, Arnie." Letting his front legs drop to the wooden sidewalk, J.D. stretched, and raised his arms while a horseless carriage rolled past, kicking dust up. J.D. chuckled at Arnett waiving the dust away.

He waited for some cock-eyed comment that never came, then sauntered the few yards to the newsboy.

"Paper, mister?"

Arnett watched him with a fondness he hardly had for young pups, as he liked to call them. J.D. Kinley was one of the few, he let get by with calling him Arnie. He thought of the last time his father had called him Arnie, the day he left for his first assignment to West Point.

What a greenhorn I was.

"What's that you say?"

"Muttering to myself. Wasn't nothing," Arnett said, reaching for his paper.

J.D. noticed a tear in Arnett's eye, thought better of mentioning it. *Probably just the dust and steam from earlier,* he thought. J.D. had come up from Texas as a Ranger, who took to the job of Marshall like a seasoned veteran.

"One hell of a shot," General Logan had said in a letter to Grant. Now a U.S. Senator, back in Washington, Logan had written a letter to the Judge recommending J.D. as a possible replacement for Arnett when he was ready to retire.

That was, if Arnett felt J.D. was ready. Nothing much was said while they read the story of Custer's Last Stand.

"Burgess should be coming in shortly. I have to finish up the paper-work, before the meeting with the judge. You mind?"

"Sure, Marshal, consider it done. Need anything?"

"No, coffee is still sitting on the stove, thanks."

J.D. wiped his brow with his sleeve, adjusted his hat and started for the train platform, a few blocks away. *They sure make Texans tall,* Arnett thought to himself, returning to his work. *Wish the hell I could figure what Pinkerton and the judge were cooking up,* his mind whispered as he looked through the wanted posters.

J.D. stood watching through the windows of the train, as the steam engineer closed the flu to let the fire slow as the breaks brought the train to a stop.

"How's Arnett taking it?" Burgess asked, coming up from behind.

"Thought you were with the passenger cars? I could have helped."

"Train people are unloading the casket now. Ticket porter wouldn't let me ride with the passengers," he replied.

"Makes sense, but I understand," J.D. said, holding up the paper. "Still, it ain't right."

"I heard it all in the guard's car."

"Get a bit testy in there?"

"At times. I pretend to sleep very well, remember? Ignored them mostly. We have time to eat?"

"Yea, Judge has called a meeting. Something's afoot."

"Hmm," Burgess replied, scratching his graying hair. "Come on, let's get to the diner."

"You arrest an Injun?" one of the patrons taunted as they sat down at their usual table. The Chinese waitress face broke into a huge smile.

"Verry wice to see you're back, Sheriff Burgess."

"Thank you, Hop Si. I will have my normal."

Burgess watched Hop Si walk off to the kitchen and turned his attention to the heckler.

"You know them?"

"No, saddle tramps, I suspect."

The patron stood, flopping his towel on the table and approached their table. "The big drunk fella," Burgess said under his breath, reaching for his sidearm under the table.

"I said, why's this Injun here? I'm not eating next to an Injun."

"There's the door." Burgess replied.

"Why you no good..." stopping when he heard Burgess's Colt hammer cock under the table. Burgess kept eating, ignoring the heckler. J.D. reached over to Burgess's vest, revealing the Sheriff's badge and laid his Deputy Marshal's badge on the table.

The heckler's eyes widened. One of his companions watching the encounter, rose and grabbed his friend by the arm. "Sorry; Jim here has had a bit too much to drink. Sorry he's being a bother," he said, pushing the big man to the door.

"Git your hands off me, Bickley."

Bickley shoved Jim Younger up against the side of the building outside. "I told you about that loose tongue," Bickley's hand shoved into Younger's chest. "You could have blown this whole thing."

"Let's go, we're attracting unneeded attention," Frank said, riding up next to them. "Jesse is waiting."

"You hear that name? Sounded like Bickley." Burgess asked.

"Who's he?" J.D. asked.

"One of the Confederate financiers. Come on, Arnett needs to know."

They tossed their bits on the table and tipped their hats toward Hop Si, leaving in a hurry. Burgess's focus was on one thing, which direction the men headed. When they returned to the office, the judge was already there, along with Arnett and General Logan.

"Get Thomas unloaded, Burgess?"

"Safe and sound, sir."

"Well," said the judge, "we have things matter of importance we need to discuss before we lay Thomas Akins to rest, the real Thomas Akins. Have a seat, gentlemen. First, we put Thomas in a bad situation, which cost him his life. He took great pains to get me this information. The James-Younger Gang must be stopped. They've netted over two-hundred thousand in bank and train robberies since the war."

"Didn't Jesse try to turn himself in during the amnesty period?" asked J.D.

"Yea, and he damn near got his head shot off for it, and under a white flag, I might add," Arnett added.

"People are still pretty jumpy, Arnett."

"If we shut down Newman from printing all that bull, maybe people would stop helping them."

"I understand, but shutting a newspaperman down will get us into a heap of trouble with Washington. Might rekindle animosity we can ill afford. Thomas' last telegraph alerted us to fact that the Knight's are still pushing an insurgence since Lincoln's assassination. I wanted to let you all know before I forget, Thomas achieved the brevet rank of Marshal for his work infiltrating the gang. This will allow his family whatever benefits Congress decides upon."

"I thank you from the Marshal's family Judge."

"Thank you, General Logan, it was his idea."

"How did they find out about Akins?" Burgess asked.

"Someone from Josiah's camp knew the double had been killed," Arnett answered.

"Whew!" J. D. exclaimed. "A double agent."

"No, just a double look-alike."

The next day, they lay U.S. Marshal Akins to rest. The judge asked Arnett to say something before the casket was lowered. Arnett politely declined.

In the months following the war, the James-Younger gang terrorized their favorite targets of banks and railroad lines. Their assaults were often printed, thanks to an editor named John Newman who glorified them as Robin Hood-like heroes. Dime store novels even glorified them.

Jesse and Frank James turned their life around, as upstanding citizens, when things became too hot. They married, raised children, and farmed like ordinary citizens, One robbery, ten miles South, near the James' homestead of Kearney in Liberty, netted the gang sixty-two thousand dollars in February 1866.

Chapter 12

**Late summer
1876**

"Why on earth Minnesota, Jesse? It doesn't make sense."

"Of course, it makes sense. First, no one knows us in Minnesota."

"Remember how that Yankee of a scum Ames made Quantrill look?"

"He has money in that bank," Cole retorted.

"Besides the women and gambling in St. Paul," replied Stiles. The group chuckled.

"So, out with the plan, or is there even a plan?" Frank asked. "For one, Minnesota's over five-hundred miles away. Two, how we gonna get there."

"Easy, if we take a train. We should know trains well enough by now," Jesse answered sarcastically.

"St. Paul has a lot of drovers coming in from out west," Stiles added. "Easy to hide and a quick ride."

"Where's the money coming from?" Bob Younger asked.

"The train."

All eyes turned to Clell Miller, who rarely presented any ideas of his own, preferring to be in the shadows.

"I thought you were asleep," Cole responded. cocking his head in Clell's direction. Clell sat back against the barn wall, perched on a pile of hay.

"Reason number three, there's a fact you all are ignoring. A seventy-five thousand fact in that bank." Cole added.

"I read it in the paper and most of it is Ames' money. That, split eight ways, is almost ten-thousand a piece; enough to retire on," Jesse added.

"We're in," Jim Younger added, with Frank being the last.

"What about our chances for amnesty?" Frank brought up.

"Pinkerton was quoted in the same paper. The only amnesty for the James Younger gang is a rope. It's right here, besides, I was shot up trying to get that so-called amnesty," Jesse retorted.

Kansas City

"You trying to make my job harder?" Pinkerton asked. "What the hell are you talking about McCann?"

"This," he said, slamming the paper on the bar.

"Inconsequential, McCann. If you even know what that means."

"I know what it means. This is a local issue. Missouri Governor promised them amnesty."

"Grant doesn't believe amnesty works, and for that matter, neither do I," Pinkerton answered. "Barkeep, give McCann a drink before he gives himself a heart attack."

"No," Arnett hollered at the barkeep.

The barkeep mumbled a curse word after pouring the drink. "You're paying for this Pinkerton."

Allan tossed a coin down the bar. It was mid-morning and a slow day in the saloon.

"Go back to Washington, Allan, we don't need you here."

"Oh, you are handling it very well. Five robberies in the last two weeks and two trains. Stay out of my way, McCann.

We have word they jumped a train in Iowa. Were on the trail. Using inside men is what got Akins killed."

"Akins made a fatal mistake."

"The only mistake he made was becoming a Pinkerton agent." McCann scoffed and stormed out the saloon.

He headed back to the sheriff's office.

"Here comes McCann," Kinley said from his chair in front of the office. McCann put one dirty boot on the wooden sidewalk and his raised elbow on the overhang's support pole. "You two grab your horses and follow Pinkerton. Keep your eye on him. I'm going to grab the first train north to Iowa and figure what the gangs next move is."

"Okay, boss, he still in the saloon?"

"Yes, stay in touch. I don't care if he knows you're following."

"He knows me too well," Burgess said. "I'll get the horses."

"Don't make it too obvious," Arnett finished.

"Sheriff we have any maps on Iowa?"

"Map file. Here," the sheriff said, handing Arnett a map from the file. "What's in Iowa?"

"James-Younger gang," Arnett answered. "According to Pinkerton."

Arnett looked over the Iowa map, looking for clues to where Pinkerton was headed. "Mind if I borrow this?"

"Keep it, out of my jurisdiction."

"You have forty-fives to spare?"

"There in the gun cabinet drawer."

"Thanks," he said, holding two boxes up and headed out the door.

"What destination did Pinkerton get tickets for?" Arnett asked the conductor.

"I can't answer that, he's a Fed."

"By God, you can. What the hell do you think I am?" reaching for his gun, "and you will."

"Okay, Marshal, okay." He said, nervously looking around, making sure none of Pinkerton's men were within hearing distance, he grabbed a small receipt and wrote down the name.

"When's the next train?"

The teller looked at his pocket watch. "In about twenty. You will be wanting a ticket, I assume?"

"What do you think? I'm standing here for my health."

Arnett sat in the waiting area and pulled a cleaning kit out of his vest pocket, breaking down his pistols and cleaning them thoroughly. By the time he was finished, the distant wailing of the train's whistle announced its arrival.

Arnett was seemingly involved with his task at hand and paid no mind to Kinley riding toward him. Kinley cleared his throat to get Arnett's attention.

"I know you're there. Question is, why?"

"We overhead Pinkerton's bunch in the livery."

"And?" he asked, without looking up he gave the chamber a whirl. "They were saying the gang was heading north through Iowa and into Minnesota. I didn't hear it, but Burgess said Mankato."

"Hmmm," Arnett replied. "Keep to the plan. Keep a close eye. Telegraph me when you arrive. If Mankato is where they are headed, then I'm heading on up to Northfield. Wire me there. Get on back to Burgess. I don't cotton to losing another."

"All aboard!" The conductor ordered. Arnett boarded, took a seat, and opened the map.

"Tickets."

Arnett took his ticket with his left hand still holding the map as the conductor walked by, pulling the ticket from his hand. Arnett gave the map one more look and deposited it in his breast pocket, careful not to expose his badge. *No use in advertising it,* he thought.

He made a quick scan of passengers, feeling lucky no one was seated beside him. Satisfied, he balled up his jacket as a pillow, leaned up against the window with his hat covering his face, and slept peacefully.

Arnett woke to the sound of the train's whistle as it passed many towns along its route, chugging along through the flat lands of Iowa. He had slept the whole day.

Through the window, endless cornfields stretched to the horizon and the September moon rose high above the trees, casting a glow through the frost gathering at the corners of the glass. The lanterns lighting up the inside of the cars offered only a shadowy hue, as if in a dream.

Maybe he was dreaming, he thought. He looked at his watch. Nine p.m. - a lot of passengers were calling it a night. He rose, stretching, deciding to see if the kitchen car still had coffee. He made his way through into the next car, stopping on the platform a bit to take in the fresh air. A gentleman in an expensive white suit and hat, clutching a leather satchel, was about to cross to the next platform when he saw Arnett.

"Anybody have coffee still?" he asked the man.

"Two cars back, near the caboose."

"Got a light," Arnett asked, realizing he was out of matches.

"Sure," the man said, holding up a light.

"Thanks," he said, with a puff of smoke as the cigar end glowed.

Arnett watched the man make his way through the second car. Then it hit him. He recognized the man's tattoo on the inside of his wrist. He had seen the same mark on another man's wrist many years ago before, at the beginning of the war. An assignment that never panned out because he was thrust into his friend's Logan's service, considering he probably owed him his life at Bull Run. Ironically, it had cost Akins his, eventually.

Josiah hurried back through the car, stepping over passenger's legs dangling in the aisle. Trying hard not to attract attention, and ignoring the conductor as he went by. Josiah realized the man with the cigar watched him. And he knew it was Marshall McCann. He scurried out to the next platform and up the handrails to the roof of the car. The foot rails were slick with early autumn evening moisture, and he lost his footing.

"Damn McCann, he's got to be everywhere," Josiah cursed. "How does he know me? Has to be Maddie." He shook his head, but the thought remained. His mind raced while he wobbled down the roof, the wind blowing his hat off as he sought traction. *Can ill afford detection now, not with thirty thousand on the line.* He clutched the bag of money to his chest as he balanced.

Arnett peered through the next car while Josiah alluding him. *Damn,* he thought, *must be on the roof.* Reluctantly, and with no gloves, Arnett stood on the platform railing and jumped across, catching the second step on the ladder going up to the roof. His hand tightened as his body slammed into the car; grunting, he caught his breath.

While the crisp air pelted his face, he took a risky gamble, laying his gun on the roof while praying that it didn't slide off into the darkness. "Getting to damn old for this shit, Arnett," he said to himself.

With all his strength he could muster, he pulled himself to the top of the car, his feet struggling to find the rungs to get a foot hold. Arnett's hat blew by the wayside as he felt the familiar zing of a bullet pass his ear.

At last, his foot found the rung and he pulled up to the top,

"Forget your gun, Marshal?" Josiah shouted through the wind, pointing a gun at him.

"You're not that good a shot," Arnett replied, with one arm twisted around the railing. He reached up, searching for the gun still on the roof. Josiah shot at the gun, the bullet sparking off the roof. The barrel was cold as Arnett's fingers wrapped around. Josiah fired again, wasting another bullet. McCann returned fire, missing him.

The wind howled along with the clanging of steel upon steel as a steamy cloud blew past from the locomotive's funnel stack.

"The eyes are the first to go, McCann," he said, firing off another shot. "How did you find me?"

"Tattoo was a dead giveaway."

"Maddie sends her love. My wife is quite a woman."

"You mean Kathleen, the woman of many personalities? Quite an actress, she should have chosen the theater for her profession, instead."

They continued trading shots as the train ascended into a pine forest with deep gullies as the cars swayed, the tracks winding through the rocky territory. Josiah barely missed Arnett as the train rounded a curve on a steep cliff, throwing Arnett off balance, enough to lose his grip. He grabbed the lower rung, his body banging against the platform with his legs dangling over the edge.

I hit him! Josiah thought. "Give it up Arnett! You're old and washed up."

Arnett pulled himself up onto the car behind an air vent. waiting for the right moment.

"Arnett, you still with us?" Josiah hollered with a laugh.

Arnett peered around the side of the car, noticing the river waters below and the trestle ahead. It was now, or never. He rose above the vent and aimed his gun.

"Throw the gun over the side."

"You must be joking? The only place I'm going is back inside... and without you."

"Drop the gun, it's over, Josiah." The wind whipped into a fury, the train going around another curve, the wheels caught a bump, just as Josiah wasted another shot.

"You're out of bullets," Arnett said, pointing his gun at Josiah, not wanting to have to kill him. He pulled himself up to the roof, and approached cautiously. Josiah pointed his weapon at Arnett.

"Be the last thing you do," Arnett hollered in the wind.

"I think not, Marshal."

Josiah took a last look at McCann and jumped as the train crossed the trestle over the river below. Arnett got down and crawled to the edge to see if he could see Josiah. Nothing.

"Anything else Mr. Ames?" the bank clerk asked. "No Mr. Heywood. Thanks for filling in for the teller."

Mr. Heywood closed the door behind him when a well-to-do gentleman walked in and headed over to Heywood.

"The President of the bank in?" Arnett asked, showing his badge.

"Your name? So, I can tell Mr. Ames."

"McCann. Hurry up, we're wasting valuable time here."

Heywood knocked lightly. "What now?" asked Ames, trying to read the newspaper.

"A gentleman says he's a U.S. Marshal McCann, here to see you, sir. Says it is urgent."

"Then send him in. We shouldn't keep the law waiting."

The snow billowed in sheets as Levi worked, piling the wood for the inside fireplace. The winter was proving to be a snowy one as the end of 1874 closed in. Abigale, Levi's mother, worked in the house, going through winter clothes.

"You're going to need a new coat; you're getting so big," she said.

Levi was more interested in getting his chore done so he could stay inside. Doing lessons was even better than the December wind.

He had to fight the wind to open the door when he noticed a shadowy figure moving through the white out. He rubbed his eyes and the outline of a horse and rider emerged.

"Mom, there's a rider approaching."

Abigale at once headed for the rifle. "

Mom, it's the Marshal!"

Abigale ran to the door as Arnett sat on his horse, smiling even wider when Abbie appeared at the door. Their eyes locked.

"Don't just sit there, Arnett, the wind will blow out the fire."

Arnett dismounted and handed Levi the reins. "Take care of her, Levi."

"Sure, Marshal," he said with a smile.

"Welcome home, Marshall," she said, as he leaned her back and kissed her... finally.

THE END

REFERENCES

U.S. Illinois General Web

The Gilder Lehrman Institute

Memoirs of a Soldier's Wife

by Mary Logan

Wikipedia

A & E History Channel archives

Shawnee National Forest DNR Official website

Pinterest

Civil War Trust

The American Experience Public Television

Civil War Documentaries YouTube

Civil War films YouTube

Library of Congress photograph archives

Library of Congress Civil War Battles

About the Author

David Spitz

Born and raised in rural Southeastern Illinois and has lived there, most of his sixty-six years. A published lyricist through Changemakers Publishing of Berkley California, debuts his first Civil War drama.

Lincoln's Agent highlights the heroes, the players and the outlaws, as well as the men of justice quest to stop them.

Southern Illinois, Missouri, and Kansas are chocked full of historical sites and events. There are thousands of stories born out of the Civil War, which makes it such an interesting writing and reader's experience. - **David Spitz**

Follow the Author

www.davidspitz54.com

HISTORIUM PRESS
2022

www.historiumpress.com